OPPRESSED
and
Empowered

THE VISCOUNT'S CAPABLE WIFE

BY
BREE WOLF

To Michelle Chenoweth
A wonderful friend and proofreader
Thank you for your keen eyes

Acknowledgments

My thank-you to all of you who've helped with feedback, typo detection, character and plot development, editing, formatting, cover creation, and the biggie...spreading the word...so that countless readers can now enjoy these stories of love's second chance.

To name only a few: Michelle Chenoweth, Monique Taken, Zan-Mari Kiousi, Tray-Ci Roberts, Kim Bougher, Vicki Goodwin, Denise Boutin, Elizabeth Greenwood, Corinne Lehmann, Lynn Herron, Karen Semones, Maria DB, Kim O'Shea, Tricia Toney, Deborah Montiero, Keti Vezzu, Patty Michinko, Lynn Smith, Vera Mallard, Isabella Nanni, Carol Bisig, Susan Czaja, Teri Donaldson, Anna Jimenez and Tammy Windsor.

Author's Note

This book was a bit of a challenge in a quite unfamiliar way. Certainly, outlining characters and bringing them to life is always an exciting and at times frustrating experience. However, the character of Richard Davenport, Viscount Ashwood, was one of the most challenging ones I've ever written.

Although the disorder as such was not yet known during the Regency era, I've always wanted to write a character who has a so called high-functioning form of autism spectrum disorder, also referred to as Asperger's syndrome.

People with this condition have great trouble with their social skills as they cannot read facial expressions or interpret another's tone of voice. Neither can they show emotions and often sound robotic in their speech. Since they can neither sense "intuitively" what goes on around them and why nor determine how this affects them, they dislike change and especially have trouble coping with sudden and unexpected changes, which do not follow a logic they can understand.

That being said, people with Asperger's syndrome feel the same emotions as others. They are generally no more or less intelligent than those who do not have this syndrome. However, they experience the world in a different way.

Part of being a writer is looking at the world through another's eyes, and the experience of seeing everything through Richard Davenport's eyes was quite enlightening. It expanded my horizon, and I'll be forever grateful to him for allowing me to see the world in a different light. After all, there is no greater gift than understanding.

OPPRESSED
and
Empowered

Prologue

London, June 1808 (or a variation thereof)

"Richard!"

At the sound of his mother's voice, Richard Davenport, Viscount Ashwood, looked up from the letter he had been writing to his steward, his gaze fixing on the sturdy door to his study. Behind it, he heard his mother's hastened footsteps as she was no doubt hurrying down the corridor toward him at this very moment.

What on earth was going on? He wondered, rising to his feet. It was not like his mother to call out to him. In fact, never had she acted so irrationally and against proper decorum. In fact, now that he thought about it, Richard found her behaviour quite odd.

And alarming.

Opening the door, he found her all but running toward him, a sheet of paper clutched in her hand and her face flushed in such a way that his own unease grew. Although Richard knew that ladies tended to get agitated for all sorts of insignificant reasons, he also knew his mother to be a composed and level-headed woman. Never had he seen her like this.

Not since the death of his father at least.

"Richard, the most awful thing has happened," she exclaimed, her grey eyes—so much like his own—finding his. "She's done it! Now, she's done it! All is lost!"

Stepping aside, Richard escorted his mother to one of the upholstered armchairs and urged her to sit down. Then he fetched her a drink to settle her nerves, his gaze drifting to the sheet of paper she still held clutched in her left hand as though her life depended on it. "What happened?"

Downing her drink, his mother coughed, the red of her cheeks darkening. "She's gone!"

"Do you speak of Claudia?" Richard enquired, unable to think of anyone else who would put his mother into such an agitated state. As far as he knew, only his younger sister possessed that talent. Still, he had to admit that his mother's current state of distress surpassed any other reaction he had ever observed.

"She has run off!" Nodding her head vigorously, his mother stared up at him. "With William Montgomery."

Inhaling a sharp breath, Richard felt his jaw tense and his teeth grit together. "Are you certain?" he asked as a rather unfamiliar emotion claimed his heart, tensing the muscles in his body and curling his fingers into clenched fists.

His mother nodded, holding out the crumpled sheet of paper to him.

Uncurling the fingers of his right hand, Richard took it, smoothing out the paper as his eyes glided over his sister's rather child-like handwriting.

I'm away to Gretna Green to marry my dearest William. Please be happy for me as I cannot help but follow my heart. I shall see you soon.

"Headstrong fool," Richard forced out through clenched teeth, feeling a mild headache begin to form behind his left temple as it always did whenever his sister threw all caution to the wind and acted against society's rules. However, so far her indiscretions had been of minor consequence. Clearly, that was no longer the case. "Are you certain she is referring to William Montgomery?"

His mother nodded, her face suddenly pale as she leaned back in her chair. "She's been speaking of him for the past fortnight."

Richard closed his eyes.

"I've tried to counsel her," his mother continued, her voice feeble, "reminded her that he is betrothed and to a duke's daughter no less. But she would not hear of it." Closing her eyes, his mother sighed, "Still, even I would not have thought that she would do something so irresponsible." Jerking to her feet, his mother came to stand before him and placed her trembling hands on his crossed arms. "Oh, Richard, what are we to do?"

Stepping away, he turned to the door. "I shall go after her in the hopes of preventing what would be a major scandal, one she would never live down." Hastening down the corridor, he called for his butler, his mother's hastened footsteps echoing behind him. "When did she leave?"

"I do not know. I only discovered the note a moment ago. I shall go speak to her maid."

"Don't bother, Mother," Richard said before turning to his butler and instructing him to have his fastest horse readied without delay. Then he spun on his heel and faced his mother once more. "Whether she left only an hour ago or ten does not signify. There is only one reasonable course of action. Pray that I'll catch up to them before she ruins her life for good. Speak of this to no one and act as though nothing is amiss."

"Godspeed," Richard heard his mother whisper before he rushed out the door, wondering what he would do if he would be unable to prevent his sister from marrying William Montgomery, the Earl of Mowbrey's second son, a man betrothed to another, a young lady of impeccable standing, daughter to one of the most influential men in all of England.

It would indeed be a dark day.

A day that would plunge all those that followed into darkness as well.

Why could his sister not be more reasonable?

Chapter One
CONSEQUENCES

Farnworth Manor, November 1808

Five Months Later

"Richard!"

At the sound of his sister's harsh voice, Richard's hand jerked, and the quill scratched across the parchment, leaving a long, black line in its wake. Gritting his teeth, he set it aside and rose to his feet, preparing himself for yet another one of his sister's emotional outbursts.

"I need to speak to you!" Claudia announced, her voice rather shrill, as she all but threw open the door and rushed inside without bothering to knock.

On her heels, a young footman by the name of Maxwell Adams mumbled an apology as he tried to persuade her to turn back even now.

Claudia, however, completely ignored him, and Richard would not be the least bit surprised if she had not even noticed his presence. When in such an emotional state, his sister was far from observant.

"It's all right, Maxwell," Richard told the young man. "You may leave us." When the door closed behind the footman, he turned to look at his sister, her face flushed, her eyes wide and her hands resting on her sides. All signs that she was agitated...about something. "What can I do for you, my dear?" Richard asked, trying to remain calm. After all, a shouting match between the two of them would not benefit anyone, and from experience, he knew that his sister had very little self-control.

"How dare you!" she hissed, and her eyes narrowed in what Richard presumed to be accusation. "How dare you post a guard at my door? Am I a prisoner now? Not allowed to come and go as I please? Why would you–?"

"If you were to cease talking," Richard interrupted, taking a sudden step toward her, "I could actually reply to your accusation."

Pressing her lips into a thin line, his sister glared at him, her nose scrunched up in open displeasure.

"I am your brother," Richard began, hoping to discuss this like two reasonable adults. However, the way his sister rolled her eyes, he found himself losing all hope. "It is my duty to look after you. I've already failed you when you ran off to Gretna Green five months ago, and I refuse to do so again."

"You did not fail me," Claudia objected, her voice no less harsh than before. "It was my decision!"

"You cannot in all honesty claim that you have no regrets?" Richard demanded, unable to make sense of his sister. On normal days, she confused him. However, ever since he had brought her back from Gretna Green, her behaviour as well as her words baffled him.

Again, her lips thinned, and for a short moment, she was uncharac-teristically silent. "Regrets or not, I do not deserve to be imprisoned in my own home. I–"

"Yes, you do," Richard objected. "You brought this on yourself, running off with a man betrothed to another. If you had indeed married, it would have been a major scandal, and if anyone were to find out," his voice dropped to a whisper, "that you're with child, you would be ruined beyond redemption. Do you not see that? Do you not understand what that means?" Shaking his head, Richard stared at his sister, wondering why she refused to see reason. After all, he only wanted what was best for her...as much as that was still possible at this point.

"I understand very well," Claudia retorted, her face twisted into a grotesque mask, making Richard wonder if she was angry or rather in pain. "I understand that you always think you know better–"

"I thought that was obvious," Richard interrupted his sister's hurried speech, his hand gesturing toward the small, as-of-yet well-concealed bump under her dress. "If you had listened to me, none of this would have happened, and you would not be under house arrest right now."

Although her jaw looked painfully clenched, Claudia ran a gentle hand absentmindedly over her midsection. "You ought not have interfered. It was not your place."

"I did not make it to Gretna Green in time if you recall," Richard reminded her, remembering his own shock at encountering young William Montgomery in the company of his elder brother on their way back to England. However, when he had discovered that his sister was not with them but had insisted on staying behind in Scotland, Richard had almost toppled over with outrage. He could not recall ever having experienced similarly strong emotions than in that moment! "It was William's brother, Lord Crowemore, who interfered and prevented his brother from marrying you." Staring at Claudia, Richard shook his head, still at a loss. "I cannot fathom what possessed you to remain in Gretna Green on your own, without a chaperone, without any kind of protection."

Crossing her arms over her chest, Claudia stared at him through narrowed eyes. "I was too disappointed in William," she replied, her voice suddenly heavy with an emotion Richard could not quite determine. "He bowed his head to his brother and abandoned me." Gritting her teeth, she shook her head defiantly. "No, nothing in the world could have persuaded me to return with them, to sit across the seat from him on the long journey back. I'd rather have died."

Rolling his eyes at his sister's foolishness as well as her tendency to be overly dramatic, Richard snapped, "And this is your reward." Again, he gestured at the small bump under her hand. "This is what your irresponsible behaviour brought you, a child in your belly from a man you cannot even name." He took a step toward her, his gaze fixed on hers, wondering if he would ever be able to understand her motivations. Richard doubted it very much! "You acted like a stubborn child, not like a well-brought up, young lady. At least, William Montgomery had the sense to recognise his mistake. You, however, allowed yourself to be inebriated and bedded by a man you did not even remember the next morning. Now, you have a price to pay, and you cannot blame anyone but yourself. Countless times I warned you, counselled you to amend your behaviour, but you would not listen. Now, your circumstances are direr than I ever would have thought possible, and if you are to have any chance at making a suitable match, then no one can know that you are with child. Do you understand me?"

Lost in his own anger, Richard had not noticed the change in his sister. Only now did he see her quivering lower lip and the way her hands clenched around her upper arms as though she feared she would break apart if she were not to hold tightly to herself. "I do understand," she mumbled, a tear sliding down her cheek. "I do understand that all you see are my mistakes."

Swallowing, Richard refused to allow the hint of guilt that rose in his heart to influence his actions. After all, he had done nothing wrong, and there was no reason for him to feel as he did. Quite on the contrary, it was his sister who ought to learn how to suppress her wayward emotions and allow reason to govern her actions. "Can you truly fault me for it?" Richard demanded. "All I am trying to do is guide your feet back onto the path set out for you, but you fight me at every step. I do not understand you; nor do I believe that I ever shall." Ignoring the paleness of his sister's cheeks, he continued, "You will stay far away from society until your child is born. Then you may return to London, and I pray that you will be able to procure a suitable husband as fast as humanly possible. I tell you honestly, that I will not mourn the day when I will no longer be responsible for your actions."

Swallowing, Claudia nodded, her pale eyes barely looking into his. "That is all I am to you," she whispered, "a responsibility that you wish you could rid yourself of. Tell me, dear brother, am I so unlovable?"

Confused by her question, Richard chose to ignore it. "Indeed, since father's passing, I am responsible for you," he stated, wondering why she would ask such a thing. "And you cannot fault me for wishing it were otherwise considering the immense effort it takes on my part to ensure that you do not ruin yourself for good." He shook his head, eyes narrowing as he watched her face, wondering if she truly did not see her actions as unreasonable. How was this possible?

For a moment, Claudia's gaze remained fixed on his, her eyes unblinking. Then, however, her lids closed once, only to open for the barest of moments before her eyes rolled up and all tension left her body. Within the blink of an eye, her body sank toward the floor, and Richard had to lunge forward to catch her before she hit the ground hard.

"Claudia," he whispered as her limp body hung in his arms, her head hanging backwards, her eyes closed. Swallowing, Richard felt his heart beat quicken as a hint of fear swept through his body. He did not care for it, not in the least, and so he pushed it aside and focused on what needed to be done.

"Maxwell!" he called, knowing that the young footman would not be far. Although he had only been in their employ a little over a year, he showed great dedication to any task given to him, which had been precisely the reason Richard had sent him to guard his sister's movements.

"Yes, my lo–" Maxwell's voice broke off as he stepped over the threshold, his eyes going wide as he watched Richard lift his unconscious sister into his arms.

"Take the carriage and fetch Dr. Procten from the village immediately," Richard instructed, settling his sister securely in his arms before striding out the door. "Tell him that it's urgent and that I ask him to attend to my sister immediately."

Without a moment's hesitation, Maxwell darted away.

Carrying his sister upstairs, Richard could not prevent his thoughts from drifting to Dr. Procten's headstrong daughter and the last time they had spoken. After his father's death, his mother had been inconsolable, taking to her bed, her cheeks white as a sheet and her eyes red-rimmed for weeks on end. It had been Evelyn Procten who had sat with his mother hour after hour, and after Lady Ashwood had finally recovered, she had voiced her delight at having had such a capable, young woman tend to her in her time of need.

Naturally, Richard had to admit that Miss Procten's presence had helped his mother. However, that was a far cry from possessing medical expertise. Nonetheless, it had been Miss Procten who–quite unnervingly–had instructed *him* to call on *her* instead of her father in case of another medical situation. Ever since her father had begun to involve her in his work, allowing her to tend to patients alongside him, she seemed to be thinking of herself as a doctor as well.

What nonsense! As though women had the necessary calm and faculty of reason to hold another's life in their hands. Looking down at his sister, Richard sighed. If that were the case, he would not be in this predicament.

Still, despite his justifiable reasons for calling on the doctor himself instead of the man's daughter, Richard could not shake the small tremble that gripped him as he thought of her deep brown eyes and the way they looked into his.

Always had she upended his rational thoughts.

And he could not allow that to happen. Not now. Not when his family needed him to make the right decisions for all of them.

No, it would be better for everyone if Miss Procten were not to return to Farnworth Manor...

...as much as his traitorous heart longed to see her.

Chapter Two

A WOMAN'S PLIGHT

Tamworth Village, 2 miles from Farnworth Manor

Surveying the trembling young man before her, Evelyn Procten inhaled a slow breath. Sweat stood on his forehead and his jaw was clenched in pain, his right hand wrapped protectively around his left arm. "Your shoulder is dislocated," she said, her voice gentle but steady, her eyes holding his without flinching. "It needs to be pushed back into its socket."

Young Tom Harvey, barely eighteen years of age, shifted on the small stool he sat on, instantly gritting his teeth and sucking in a sharp breath when the movement caused another stab of pain to shoot through his shoulder. "When will Dr. Procten be here?" he asked through clenched teeth.

Evelyn sighed, well aware that most people did not think a woman capable of such work. Certainly, women knew how to take care of other women as well as children when it came to childbirth or little scrapes and bruises. However, resetting a bone or relocating a shoulder was a man's work. Hating that her gender kept her from being the doctor she knew herself to be, the doctor her father had passed on his knowledge to, Evelyn tried to remain calm. After all, an emotional outburst would only discourage the man sitting at her feet from bestowing his trust in her.

After all, the fact that he would not meet her eyes, suggested that he disliked insulting her by asking for her father instead of allowing her to help. It was not much, but Evelyn was determined to seize this opportunity.

Leaning forward, she met the young man's reluctant gaze. "Soon," she said, her voice gentle as before, but with the same strength of conviction she had heard in her father's tone all her life. "However, the longer we wait, the greater the pain. I advise you to allow me to reset it now without delay."

His hand tightened on his injured arm, and he pressed his lips together tightly as his green eyes searched hers. "Have you done this before?"

Evelyn nodded. "I have." Only once though, for lack of another opportunity. "May I take a closer look?" she asked, hoping to gain his permission to treat him step by step.

Inhaling a slow breath, Mr. Harvey nodded.

"I need you to remove your shirt," Evelyn said, her face trained to show no emotion, simply professional determination.

Mr. Harvey swallowed, and she could see a hint of doubt in his eyes.

"Here, I'll help you." Before he could change his mind, Evelyn urged him to relinquish his claw-like hold on his injured arm. Then she unbuttoned his shirt, aware that the young man's face turned a darker shade of red. Pulling his good arm out of the sleeve, she stepped behind him and moved the shirt around to his injured shoulder, gently easing it down the arm. Then she ran her fingers over his skin, feeling for the bones underneath.

At her touch, he flinched, then groaned in pain.

"As I said," Evelyn remarked, ignoring his reaction to her proximity, "it's dislocated." Her gaze found his once more, and her brows rose in question.

A moment of silence stretched between them that had Evelyn's nerves wound tight. Still, she forced herself to wait calmly and not pressure the young man into making his decision. After all, a doctor needed to treat not only the body but the mind as well.

Finally, Mr. Harvey sighed, his gaze darting to her, before he nodded his head.

Pride swelled in Evelyn's chest, and she could have hugged the young man for putting his trust in her, for allowing her another opportunity to feel like a doctor. However, that would have been far from professional, and so she merely cast him an appreciative smile and set to work.

Pulling up another stool, Evelyn placed it right next to Mr. Harvey's injured shoulder. "This will hurt," she warned, noting the way his muscles tightened even more. "However, it will be nothing compared to the pain you've endured so bravely thus far."

Mr. Harvey exhaled a slow breath, and she could see a touch of pride in the way he lifted his head. "I'm ready."

"Good." Setting her foot on the stool, thus bringing her knee level with Mr. Harvey's left shoulder, Evelyn gently put her hands on his arm. "Try and relax your muscles. It will be much easier and faster this way."

Swallowing, Mr. Harvey did as he was asked, or at least tried to for his jaw was still as clenched as before.

When she lifted the man's arm and placed it over her knee, Evelyn saw beads of sweat pearl up on his forehead. His jaw was locked tight, and yet, a small groan escaped his lips. "It's almost over," she whispered, positioning one hand on the man's shoulder and the other on his upper arm.

The moment she was about to apply pressure in order to encourage the bone to slide back into the socket, the door to her father's examining room flew open, revealing Mr. Bragg in its frame.

As her father's official apprentice, Mr. Bragg had been living in Tamworth Village for about a year, training to take over as her father's health was beginning to fail. Unfortunately, the man felt no calling for the profession of a healer. Still, that did not prevent him from walking about the village with an enormous ego and the ill-conceived idea that he knew all there was to know.

His eyes widened as he found her beside a half-clad patient, the man's arm laid across her knee, a fact which instantly turned the bewildered expression on his face into one of scandalised outrage. "What do you think you're doing?" he demanded as he stepped into the room, closing the door with an unnecessary loud thud that made Mr. Harvey flinch, causing him needless pain.

Meeting Mr. Bragg's accusing gaze with a determined one of her own, Evelyn replied with a calm voice, "Treating my patient." Then, before her father's apprentice could interfere, she simultaneously pushed down onto Mr. Harvey's shoulder and upper arm, feeling the pressure of the man's taut muscles against her hands. Still, a moment later, the bone relented, sliding back into place with a soft *pop*.

Instantly, Mr. Harvey slumped forward, a groan escaping his lips, as his muscles relaxed. His right hand came up to curl around his left shoulder, a small smile of relief on his red face. "It feels better," he mumbled as though to himself. Then his gaze met hers. "Thank you."

"You're welcome," Evelyn replied with a smile, determined not to look at Mr. Bragg and allow him to ruin this glorious moment for her. "I'll put your arm in a sling to promote healing. You mustn't move it for at least a week."

Mr. Harvey's face darkened, and she knew that idleness was nothing he was accustomed to nor ever would be. Life was far from easy, and most men needed two good arms, legs and a strong back to provide for themselves as well as their families.

After tending to Mr. Harvey, Evelyn sent him on his way, aware of the dark presence behind her. Still, she refused to look at Mr. Bragg, instead busying her hands by tidying up the small room.

"Have you lost your mind, *Woman*?" Mr. Bragg's voice was low and almost menacing as though she had wilfully insulted him. Slow steps carried him closer, and Evelyn could feel the hairs on the back of her neck rise in resistance to his words and their meaning. When had the term *woman* ever been used as an insult? Still, with each day, Evelyn felt that it was one. The worst one. The one that kept her from her rightful place.

Straightening her shoulders, Evelyn turned to meet the man's hateful glare. "Not at all," she replied evenly. "I merely tended to a patient. He had a dislocated shoulder, and I–"

"I saw what you did!" Mr. Bragg spat, taking a threatening step closer. "What you did was indecent. He was half-clad, and you had your hands on his naked skin."

"I'm his doctor," Evelyn objected, doing her best to hold back the anger that boiled within her. "Would you not have asked him to remove his shirt? Would you not have touched him?"

"You're a woman," he sneered.

Evelyn shook her head, annoyed that every discussion always reverted back to the same argument. "That does not signify," she insisted, hands on her sides as she leaned forward, meeting Mr. Bragg's stare with an unflinching one of her own. "My father trusts my skills. He—"

"I do not!"

"Well, that is your problem then, not mine."

With steam coming out of his ears, Mr. Bragg stepped forward, his breath brushing over her face. "You might think you're a doctor, but you're wrong," he hissed. "No one would allow you to treat them if it weren't for your father's reputation. You're nothing without him."

Evelyn swallowed, knowing Mr. Bragg's words to be true, and yet, she could not surrender. Would not. Not ever. "Simply because people do not trust in my abilities does not mean I do not possess them," she told him. "People can be wrong in their assumptions...as you must know." Although Evelyn rarely succumbed to hidden insults, she could not help herself in that moment. Mr. Bragg's overbearing attitude riled her, and she could not in good conscience bow her head to him.

A hint of shock came to his eyes when her meaning sank in, causing his face to turn dark red. "You harlot!" he hissed, and his hands curled painfully around her upper arms. "Your father ought to have taught you how to behave as a woman."

Ignoring the touch of fear that crawled up her spine, Evelyn glared back at him. "He taught me how to be a doctor."

A growl escaped Mr. Bragg, and he yanked her against him. "Once you're my wife, you will learn how to—"

"I will never!" Evelyn objected, fear finally urging her to shove against him. Unfortunately, he was right about one thing: her strength was no match for his.

A satisfied smile curled up the corners of his lips when she struggled against him unsuccessfully. "You will," he sneered. "Once your father is gone, I will be your only chance to get anywhere near a patient." Suddenly, his gaze dropped from hers, lower, and she understood his intention the moment he crushed her against him, his mouth seeking hers.

Averting her head in disgust, she felt his lips brush over her cheek. Her leg pulled up of its own volition, like a reflex triggered by his attack, and her knee connected with his groin.

A howl escaped his lips, his hands falling from her as he bent in pain, cursing her under his breath.

Swallowing the panic that still coursed through her, Evelyn stepped back and brushed her trembling hands down her dress. "Someone ought to teach you how to behave like a gentleman," she said as she stepped around him, eager to leave this room.

Closing the door behind her, she inhaled a deep breath and then crossed through the kitchen, hoping that her father had returned from his walk. She needed to speak to him about Mr. Bragg. There was no way around it. Unfortunately, her father had been wrong in his assessment of the man. Not only did he not possess the skills or dedication needed in order to heal others, he also had a backward way of looking at women. Even if she married him—as had been her father's suggestion—he would never allow her to work as a doctor as he had made unmistakably clear only a moment ago. They would have to think of another solution.

"Ah, my dear, there you are," her father greeted her warmly as she stepped into the small parlour. Sitting in his favourite chair, Whiskers curled up on his lap, purring contentedly, he smiled at her, his white hair almost blinding in the sun streaming in through the window.

"Hello, Father." Approaching, Evelyn did her best to forget about her encounter with Mr. Bragg and focus on the more important occurrence that morning. "Mr. Harvey allowed me to relocate his shoulder."

A smile came to her father's face. "That is wonderful. The young are not as stern in their ideas as those that have seen more winters." He chuckled, patting the armrest of the chair next to him.

Sinking onto the seat, Evelyn exhaled a shuddering breath, noting the way her hands still trembled.

"Is something wrong?" her father asked, his watchful eyes gliding over her. Decades of treating patients had given him a keen insight into human behaviour. "You seem out of sorts."

Evelyn sighed, "Mr. Bragg objected to me treating Mr. Harvey on my own. He was quite adamant."

Sadness came to her father's gaze as he nodded, and she knew that he felt guilty for bringing that man into their lives. As skilled as he was at reading people, her father had allowed himself to be deceived by Mr. Bragg due to his own desire to find a young man eager to be trained. A man who would secure his daughter's future and see to the health of the people of Tamworth Village.

"Father, we need to talk about–"

A horse's whinny interrupted her thoughts, and Evelyn turned to the window as the sound of wheels churning on gravel reached her ears. "Someone is coming," she said, rising to her feet. The moment her gaze fell on the Ashwood crest on the carriage's door, her heart beat faster.

"Who is it?" her father asked from his seat by the fireplace.

"A carriage from Farnworth Manor," Evelyn called over her shoulder as she stepped up to the front door and pulled it open. A young man exited the carriage, his long strides carrying him closer. He had a friendly smile on his face, and stopping in front of her, he inclined his head to her. "Miss Procten, I presume."

Evelyn nodded. "You'd presume right. How can I help you?" Although she had never met this man before, Evelyn knew him to be a footman at the Ashwood estate as he was dressed in the same black and gold livery.

"I'm Mr. Adams," he introduced himself. "Lord Ashwood sent me here to call on Dr. Procten. His sister, Miss Davenport, has fainted, and he bade me to return with your father as soon as possible."

Evelyn's smile faltered. Had she not asked Lord Ashwood to call on her instead? Why would he ignore her request?

Sighing, Evelyn forced her hands to unclench, very well aware why Lord Ashwood would insist her father treat his sister. It was for the same reason Mr. Bragg had all but forbidden her to treat patients and Mr. Harvey had hesitated to allow her to relocate his shoulder.

Apparently, Lord Ashwood was yet another man who did not trust in her abilities.

Frustration surged through Evelyn as she recalled the man's haughty gaze. However, the moment his silver-grey eyes appeared before her inner eye, she felt her heartbeat quicken and the breath catch in her throat.

Curse that man for the effect he had on her!

Where Mr. Bragg's arrogant glare had always repulsed her, Lord Ashwood's sharp, almost hawk-like gaze did something to her insides that she did not dare admit even to herself.

"Please come inside," Evelyn mumbled, belatedly recalling her manners. Escorting the young man to the parlour, she introduced him to her father, who immediately sat up, his gaze narrowed with concern. "The young miss has fainted?" he asked, already pushing himself to his feet and ignoring Whiskers' mewling protests. "We should leave immediately."

"Father, you're in no condition to travel," Evelyn objected, trying to urge him to sit back down. However, as expected, he would not hear of it.

"Did you not hear what he said? We need to leave immediately."

"I can go, Father," Evelyn suggested, holding her father's gaze. Although she still felt miffed by Lord Ashwood's slight, she did not want her father to overexert himself.

Mr. Adams took a step forward, a hint of unease on his face. "I'm sorry but Lord Ashwood specifically asked for Dr. Procten."

"I will go."

At the sound of Mr. Bragg's voice, Evelyn exhaled an annoyed breath. This was truly one of those days that ought to be stricken from the calendar.

Turning around, she met Mr. Bragg's challenging gaze as he walked into the parlour, a touch of discomfort on his face as he set one foot in front of the other. "I'm Dr. Procten's apprentice," he told Mr. Adams. "I'm more than qualified to see to Miss Davenport."

At a loss, Mr. Adams looked from Mr. Bragg to Evelyn's father, at odds about how to decide.

"I will not stay here," her father objected. "The late Lord Ashwood was one of my closest friends, and if his daughter is ailing, I will see to her." His gentle eyes were hard, and Evelyn knew that there was no use in arguing with him.

"Fine," she said, looking at Mr. Adams. "I suppose then we shall all go." She turned to Mr. Bragg. "Unless you wish to stay behind?"

Staring at her, he slowly shook his head, the glare in his eyes all but promising retribution.

Offering her father her arm to lean on, Evelyn cursed her bad luck. Why did she have to be born a woman? Everything would be so much simpler if she were a man. After all, her father would not live forever. What was she to do once he passed? The thought brought tears to her eyes, and she quickly blinked them away.

Still, the day he would breathe his last, she would not only lose the only parent left to her, the one man who had supported and encouraged her throughout her life, but also the one thing she needed to be herself. Being a doctor was not what she did, but who she was.

Who would she be if she no longer was allowed to treat patients?

Chapter Three
A DELICATE SITUATION

P acing the length of his sister's bedchamber, Richard watched as his mother gently placed a wet cloth on her daughter's forehead. Stretched out on the bed, Claudia lay with her eyes closed, her chest rising and falling evenly.

It was a strange sight for Richard, and he could not deny the lump of apprehension that settled in his stomach. Never had he seen his sister so still. She was always so vibrant, never remaining seated for long, always rushing from one place to another, her mouth rarely ceasing to speak her mind. When she entered a room, people noticed, people turned to her, sought her presence and welcomed her into their midst. With a smile and a few kind words, Claudia found friends wherever she went, and Richard could not help but envy her for the ease with which she found and claimed her place in this world. Despite her dire circumstances at present, Richard doubted that he was the happier of the two.

Still, her happiness might be snatched away by the threat of society's censure, and so it was up to him to protect her and ensure that her future remained the carefree place she wanted it to be. Even if he had to force her hand. Perhaps one day she would come to see the wisdom of his decision and thank him for his tenacity.

He could only hope so.

"How is she?" he asked, glancing out the window for what seemed like the thousandth time. "Where is Dr. Procten? He ought to be here by now."

"There is no need to worry, my son," his mother counselled as she rose from the chair beside her daughter's bed and walked over to where he continued to pace. "She merely fainted. That is not unusual in her condition. Was she agitated?"

Richard shrugged, staring at his mother. "Isn't she always?"

A knowing smile came to his mother's face. "She certainly is forceful in her demands and her idea of what is her due. Still, great sadness can hide behind a smiling face." Sighing, his mother placed a gentle hand on his cheek. "Remember that she is more than yours to protect, my son, but she is also simply your sister."

Looking into his mother's eyes, Richard found himself at a loss as his mother's words did not seem to make sense. Was Claudia not his to protect *because* she was his sister? What did his mother mean? Was she criticising the way he looked after his family?

Not knowing how to reply, Richard kept silent, cursing his own inability to connect with others. Why was it that his sister seemed to possess that skill in abundance while he himself was more often than not completely at a loss when it came to understanding others?

When a soft sigh echoed over from the bed, his mother turned and hastened over to her daughter's side, feeling her forehead, her watchful eyes intent on her child's face. "Claudia, my dear, can you hear me?"

No answer came, and Richard's heart clenched painfully. Still, a moment later, confusion drew down his brows when he saw a gentle smile curl up the corners of his mother's mouth.

"She's fine," Lady Ashwood said, lifting her eyes to his. "She'll come to shortly."

Richard exhaled, momentarily closing his eyes. Stepping closer, he wondered how his mother could tell. For all intents and purposes, Claudia looked as pale as he had ever seen her. Her eyes were still closed, and all the movement he was aware of was the rhythmic rise and fall of her chest. What was he missing?

"Don't worry," his mother told him, her kind eyes suddenly fixed on his face instead of on his sister's. "Before long she'll be arguing with you again." A soft chuckle escaped her.

Frowning, Richard tried to understand how his mother could be so cheerful. "I hardly think that is reason for joy, Mother," Richard objected, unable to keep quiet. "With her headstrong attitude, she threatens to undo everything I am working so carefully to put into place." He glanced at the door. "While I hope that the servants are not yet aware of her condition, it will not be long before she won't be able to hide it. What will we do then? I was thinking it might be a mistake to have her here at Farnworth Manor for much longer. Perhaps we ought to remove her to a more remote estate, sending along only two or three trusted servants to care for her until the child is born." As he spoke, Richard noted that his mother's eyes had dimmed, and her lips seemed to be pressed together. However, he could not say if she simply disagreed with him or was more worried about her daughter than she had led him to believe. There could be a number of reasons, and one was as likely as any other.

At least for him.

Gently, his mother took her daughter's hand into hers, her thumb brushing back and forth over the back of her hand. Then she looked up and met Richard's gaze. "If you send her away, it'll be the death of her."

Annoyance washed over Richard, and the air rushed from his lungs. "I would ask you not to exaggerate, Mother. Perhaps a little peace and quiet will do her good."

"It would do you good, my son," his mother said, her voice determined. However, her gaze was gentle as she looked at him. "Your sister, however, needs company like the flowers need the sun. Alone, she will wither. You cannot send her away."

"What if her condition is discovered?" Richard asked under his breath, his gaze once more darting to the door. He could only hope that no one had their ear pressed to the other side. "What if one of the servants talks? What if someone outside Farnworth Manor learns of this?" He swallowed. "She'd be ruined. For good. You cannot want this, Mother."

"Of course not." Closing her eyes, his mother inhaled a slow breath. "I admit I do not know what the right course of action is here. For it seems that every choice comes with a significant sacrifice."

Richard frowned. "I would think that a few weeks of solitude is a small price to pay in order to avoid societal suicide."

For a moment, his mother's gaze swept over his face, searching, studying, as though she had never truly seen him before. "For you it might be a small price, but not for her."

Before Richard could reply, a knock sounded on the door and Wilton, their butler, announced himself. Calling for him to enter, Richard strode toward the entrance, relieved to see Dr. Procten follow Wilton into the room. His hair seemed whiter than Richard remembered, and his breath seemed to rattle in his chest. Still, there was the usual air of authority about him, and Richard could not deny that he felt better knowing that his father's oldest friend was here.

"Good day, my lord," Dr. Procten greeted him before his gaze shifted to the still figure on the bed. "What seems to be the matter? Mr. Adams said she fainted."

Richard nodded, trying to find the right words to inform the doctor of his sister's condition. However, the moment he was about to open his mouth to reply, the air was sucked from his lungs when his gaze fell on the dark-haired, young woman standing in the doorway.

Richard barely took note of the doctor's apprentice beside her. All he could see were her dark brown eyes, so wide and yet focused as they took in the room and then came to rest on his sister. Without even acknowledging his presence, she stepped forward and went to his mother's side, whispering something he could not understand.

Richard knew of his mother's fondness for Miss Procten as she had spent many days here at Farnworth Manor after his father's passing. Upon losing the man she had loved almost all her life, his mother had succumbed to despair, refusing to see anyone, to leave her chamber, even to eat. It had been Miss Procten who had found a way to reach her, to bring her back from that black abyss of despair and return her to her children. It had taken weeks, but ever since then, Lady Ashwood had a soft spot for the doctor's kind daughter in her heart as was evident by their almost familial greeting.

Back then, when Miss Procten had spent weeks in this house,

Richard had found himself torn between the desire to seek her company and the fear that she would reject him. After all, Miss Procten seemed to have an uncanny ability to see into people's souls, always knowing exactly what they needed. It was an ability that baffled but also fascinated him like nothing had ever before, for he could not for the life of him understand how she knew what she did. It was almost as if she could read her patient's minds, responding to their needs before they had even had a chance to voice them.

It had been that thought, the thought that she might look into his mind, that had been–and still was–greatly unsettling for Richard. What would she see if she chose to look at him? Would she see what everyone else saw?

Despite his tendency to keep to himself, Richard was well-aware of his reputation as the cold-hearted viscount. He knew very well that people disliked his company and thought of him as strict and unfeeling. And a part of him did not even fault them for it because he feared that they might be right. After all, he could not even relate to his own sister. What did that say about him?

True or not, Richard knew with absolute certainty that he would not be able to bear having Miss Procten look at him that way, and so he kept his distance from her. When his mother's health had improved, and Miss Procten had returned to the village, Richard had been relieved...and saddened at the same time.

And now she was back.

Right here.

Only a few steps away.

"My lord?"

All but flinching at the sound of the doctor's voice, Richard forced his eyes from the man's daughter and turned his attention to his father's oldest friend. "I'm afraid this is a fairly delicate situation, Dr. Procten," he said, glancing from his sister to the man's apprentice now stepping into the chamber. "As it is, my sister finds herself in...dire circumstances." Holding the older man's gaze, Richard wondered if he would need to speak more plainly when he saw the doctor's eyes widen slightly before his head bobbed up and down in acknowlededgement.

In the back of his mind, Richard wondered if he would have understood such a mere hint of a suggestion. He doubted it very much.

"Therefore," Richard continued, "I'd appreciate it if you could tend to my sister alone."

"I understand your concerns," Dr. Procten said, his voice kind as he spoke. "However, I'm afraid that my own health is not what it once was, which has led to the conclusion that it is time to train a successor." He gestured to Mr. Bragg, a young man with a rather unpleasant expression on his face.

"Good day, my lord," Mr. Bragg greeted him as he came to stand beside the old doctor. "I assure you I am highly qualified and will tend to your sister with the utmost dedication."

Richard nodded. However, he could not help but dislike the man as his words clearly indicated that he had been listening to the quiet conversation between Richard and Dr. Procten. If he dared invade others' privacy without deeper thought, would he treat his sister's condition with the necessary confidentiality? Richard could only hope so.

"I'm glad to hear it," Richard said, wishing he possessed Miss Procten's ability to read others and see into this man's mind. Involuntarily, his gaze drifted back to his sister's bed and the young woman currently speaking to his mother.

"I find that my daughter has a very calming effect on female patients," the doctor said, quite obviously in possession of that same unnerving ability as his daughter. "Women generally are more comfortable speaking to her about what ails them. If you do not object, I would suggest that she be the one to speak to your sister."

Richard drew in a slow breath. Here was his chance to rid himself of Miss Procten, to send her home and reclaim his peace of mind. However, as much as he knew he ought to—for all the right reasons—he knew he could not. For deep down, his desire to have her near overruled every rational thought. Somehow over the past few months of her absence, his need for her had grown...and he had not even noticed.

Gritting his teeth, Richard cursed silently. *Oh, why did she have to disregard his request? Why could she not simply have stayed behind? Why did she have to come?*

Giving his approval, Richard stepped outside into the corridor, hoping that he had not just made a severe mistake in allowing Miss Procten to stay. Still, she would only be here for an hour or two. His sister would not require the same care as his mother had then, would she? The thought of Miss Procten once more staying under the same roof sent his heart into an uproar, and he clenched his teeth together painfully to keep from cursing out loud.

As he hastened down the corridor, he barely noticed Maxwell standing guard outside Claudia's room, his eyes straight ahead and his arms linked behind his back, giving him the expression of a true guard rather than a footman. Still, Richard had no thought for the young man as he all but rushed to the sanctuary of his study. Only when the door was firmly closed behind him did he dare exhale the breath he had been holding.

What if he were wrong? What if Miss Procten would stay with them once more? Claudia and his mother would certainly be thrilled.

Great sadness can hide behind a smiling face.

As his mother's words echoed in his mind, Richard realised that he was no closer to a solution with regard to his sister than he had been that morning. If his mother was right, then sending Claudia into isolation would pain her—in what way Richard could not fathom. However, if she stayed, he had no doubt that she would cause trouble due to lack of entertainment. Perhaps he ought to invite a few trusted friends for the holidays in order to pacify his sister and divert the servants' attention at the same time.

Naturally, it would have to be someone he could trust with his life. The only one who came to mind was his childhood friend, Sebastian Campbell, Earl of Weston, a man who—despite his numerous, but good-hearted complaints about Richard's own rather cold heart—had never strayed far from his side. Sebastian might not understand him, but he was loyal...to a fault.

In any case, if Richard were to allow his sister to stay, then it might be good to have someone keep her company, in which case he could only hope that Miss Procten would be willing to return to Farnworth Manor once again. Certainly, her presence would be torture for him, but he had to think of his sister's future. If Miss Procten was the solution to keeping his sister's tantrums to a minimum, then that was a price he would have to pay.

Richard could only hope that he would not lose his mind over the constant struggle that assaulted him whenever he laid eyes on her. What would happen if he was to see her every day?

Richard swallowed, very much afraid to know the answer.

Then he headed back upstairs to hear from Dr. Procten—and hopefully not his daughter—how his sister was doing.

Chapter Four

FARNWORTH MANOR

"Good day, Lady Ashwood," Evelyn greeted the late viscount's widow as she approached the bed. "It is good to see you again. I hope you are well."

"I am." A gentle smile came to the older woman's face before she squeezed her daughter's hand with tense fingers. "It is my daughter I'm concerned about." Her gaze shifted about the room before she stepped closer to Evelyn. "You see, she finds herself with child."

Evelyn's eyes widened as she looked at the viscountess, not having expected that. Then her gaze travelled to Miss Davenport, taking note of her pale skin and fast pulse, the way her eyelids would twitch upon occasion and the rhythm with which her chest rose and fell. "I suspect she merely fainted," Evelyn concluded, not seeing any reason for alarm. "What was she doing when it happened?"

The viscountess dropped her gaze as an indulgent smile came to her face. "She was arguing with her brother, I'm afraid."

"I see." Careful not to appear to be looking, Evelyn glanced at the young viscount out of the corner of her eye. Concern rested in his pale eyes, and yet, she thought that the tension that held his shoulders rather rigid spoke to yet another matter that plagued him. Surely, he did not believe his sister in medical distress. Surely, he had to know that it was a mere faint as well. What then was it that currently occupied his thoughts?

Cursing her own curiosity, Evelyn inhaled a slow breath, noting the way her heart sped up whenever she dared glance in his direction. What was it about him that drew her near? After all, he was the kind of man who ought not appeal to her, was he not? The way he seemed to look down at others with those sharp, grey eyes of his, like those of a hawk hunting for prey, seizing up those around him, spoke of a man who felt superior to others. There was a calm and often calculating hint in his eyes as though he constantly measured those in his presence for their worth. Certainly, most peers possessed that quality as it had been drilled into them from birth. However, his parents had always been kind-hearted people. People Evelyn had always respected and even come to care for. What made him so different from them? From his own sister?

And yet, every once in a while, Evelyn thought to see something in the way he almost hung his head, in the way his shoulders would slump the barest fraction, the way his eyes dimmed on occasion, that spoke of a deep vulnerability as though this cold demeanour of his was nothing but a mask to hide who he truly was. And as was the case with every mask, here and there, it slipped.

Or was she fooling herself? Was she conjuring a far-fetched reason to paint him in a better light because she could not reconcile herself to the fact that she found herself wanting to be noticed by a snobbish sort of man?

Always had Evelyn thought of herself as independent. As much as she knew that becoming a doctor in her own right was nigh on impossible, she had vowed early on to not leave any chance unexploited to see her dreams realised. Always had she known that marrying would limit her freedom, making her a wife, someone's accessory, and she had never thought herself the kind of woman who would only feel complete if married. Certainly, society thought differently. However, Evelyn knew that it was wise to allow her mind to take precedence over her heart. Deep down, she knew she needed to remain her own person, not someone's wife to be ordered about.

And yet, ever since she had tended to Lady Ashwood the previous year, she had realised that day by day her whole being had slowly become more and more aware of the lady's son. She could almost feel him when he was near and longed to be closer, to unravel the secret that she saw behind his eyes. And yet, he barely took note of her the same way he barely took note of anyone. Did he never long for anything or anyone?

"Are you all right, dear?" Lady Ashwood asked, jarring Evelyn from her thoughts. "You seem lost in thought."

Clearing her throat, Evelyn forced her gaze away from the son and back to the mother, noting with some surprise the amused crinkles around Lady Ashwood's eyes. "I apologise."

"There is no need," the viscountess assured her, smiling, and Evelyn wondered what went on in the lady's head. Had she noticed Evelyn gazing at her son like a love-sick dolt?

When Lord Ashwood stepped outside, her father and Mr. Bragg approached the bed, saving Evelyn from having to conjure a reasonable reply. Relieved, she turned to her father. "Considering that Miss Davenport is expecting, her breathing and pulse appear to be normal."

Mr. Bragg nodded, stepping forward and in-between Lady Ashwood and Evelyn's father as though he wished to display his own perceived importance. Annoyed, Evelyn glowered at him, remembering that she had not yet had a chance to speak to her father about Mr. Bragg's apprenticeship. "It obviously was only a faint," he stated as though he was the first one to do so. "All she needs is rest."

Fighting down her annoyance with Mr. Bragg, Evelyn inhaled a deep breath, focusing her mind on what was important. "I suggest we elevate her legs and encourage blood flow to the brain."

From the corner of her eye, Evelyn noted Mr. Bragg's brows drawing down in disapproval. His mouth opened, and she expected him to lash out at her for being presumptuous. However, before a word escaped his lips, his gaze came to rest on Lady Ashwood, whose presence seemed to change his mind for he remained silent. Apparently, there was at least a little sense in Mr. Bragg's mind after all. On the other hand, that seemed to make him more devious for he adapted his behaviour according to those in his company.

Evelyn could not wait to be rid of him. She could only hope her father would agree and terminate Mr. Bragg's apprenticeship. However, finding out whether or not he did agree would have to wait. At least, it was quite obvious that her father agreed with her on the present matter, for he nodded his head in approval.

Without hesitation—let alone addressing Mr. Bragg—Evelyn turned toward the door. Opening it, she stepped outside, relieved to find a footman waiting patiently. Out of the corner of her eye, she could see Mr. Bragg step toward her father and whisper something under his breath. Oh, how she wished she knew what he had said! Something hateful, no doubt! Why was it that that man only saw her as a threat? Was there something antagonising about her of which she was not aware?

"Is there anything I can help you with, Miss?"

At the footman's question, Evelyn's head snapped around, and belatedly, she forced a smile onto her face when she saw the honest concern in his eyes as he glanced toward Miss Davenport's chamber. "Yes, indeed. I require a few pillows. Four or five would be good."

"Certainly." Inclining his head, the young footman strode off.

Watching him disappear around a bend in the corridor, Evelyn inhaled a deep breath to settle her nerves. Anger was not a good emotion when one was tending to a patient. After a few more deep breaths, her heartbeat slowed down, and her hands stopped trembling. Slowly, her body calmed, and she felt the strain ease off her mind as well.

However, the moment she was about to return to the room, Evelyn almost tripped over her own feet when Lord Ashwood appeared as though out of nowhere at the other end of the corridor. For a second, their eyes locked, and Evelyn felt her heart jump into her throat, her fingernails digging painfully into her palms as she fought to maintain control.

Curse that man for the effect he had on her!

Unfortunately, he seemed completely unaffected. His silver-grey eyes remained cold and calculating as he slightly lifted his head in that snobbish sort of way of his and broke their eye contact—as though she was not worth his attention. Then he strode toward her with measured steps, his gaze fixed on the half-open door behind her.

Fresh anger grabbed Evelyn's heart, and for a brief moment, she felt the almost uncontrollable need to slap him. Fortunately, it passed quickly, leaving behind a sense of disappointment and embarrassment. After all, she ought to have more control over herself, ought she not? This was truly mortifying!

"Is my sister all right?"

Swallowing, Evelyn blinked, momentarily stunned to find Lord Ashwood standing in front of her. His grey eyes met hers—if only briefly—and she was surprised to see honest concern in them. More often than not, he appeared as cold as a block of ice. However, perhaps she was wrong in her assessment.

"She is," Evelyn mumbled, clearing her throat to dislodge the uncomfortable lump that had settled there. "Or she will be. It was merely a faint, and I trust she shall recover quickly."

Lord Ashwood's eyes closed and remained so for a second or two as though he were savouring the moment. Evelyn watched him curiously. Had he truly feared for his sister's life? He did not seem like a man prone to entertain irrational fears. However, as someone with an untrained eye for the sick, perhaps he had simply not been able to assess his sister's situation with the same ease Evelyn took for granted. Perhaps she had judged him too harshly.

However, where Lord Ashwood was concerned, she seemed to be going from one extreme into another. Either she found herself swept away by his mere presence or riled into anger by his cold dismissal.

"I'm glad to hear it." Nodding his head to her, Lord Ashwood glanced past her shoulder. "When will she awaken?"

"I expect within the hour," Evelyn replied, trying her best to focus her thoughts on her patient. "I should get back," she whispered as though more to convince herself to move than for any other reason. Reluctantly, her feet turned, and she forced her gaze toward the chamber and away from the unsettling man before her. Her eyes fell on her beloved father, and the sight of his gentle face gave her the strength to step way.

Unfortunately, the moment her eyes focused on him, she detected the slight strain on his face that had often preceded another episode.

Without another thought, she rushed toward him as he began to sway on his feet. "Father!"

At the sound of her voice, everyone turned toward the old doctor.

"I'm fine," her father insisted in the very moment his hand reached out and grabbed the first thing he could find. In this case, Mr. Bragg's arm.

Evelyn was relieved to see him steady himself. Still, her trained eyes recognised the small signs of exhaustion. "You need to rest," she told him, mimicking the same authoritative tone he sometimes took with his patients. "Mr. Bragg would you please take my father downstairs and ensure that he rests."

For a second, her father's apprentice seemed to scowl at the way she was ordering him about. However, he could not have refused her without betraying a very unbecoming side of him, and so he nodded, took her father by the elbow and escorted him out the door.

"Don't you worry, my lord," Evelyn heard her father say to Lord Ashwood as they slowly made their way down the corridor. "My daughter will look after your sister."

"I admit I should feel immensely better if she had a doctor by her side," the young viscount replied to Evelyn's great dismay, and for a moment, she closed her eyes to keep herself from challenging his words.

"I assure you my daughter is very capable," her beloved father said, his voice gentle but insistent. "She's the best I've ever trained."

Evelyn's eyes snapped open. Oh, if she could only see Mr. Bragg's face! The man's head had to be as red as a tomato!

"Do not mind my son," Lady Ashwood said, and Evelyn slowly turned to look at her. "He knows very little of women, which I have come to realise is not as unusual as it ought to be." A hint of sadness and regret hung about the widow's eyes, and yet, there was a slight curl to her lips and a spark in her eyes as though she viewed this unfairness as a challenge only. Something that was to be changed over time. Something that presented an opportunity for women everywhere to overcome the prejudices associated with their gender. "Believe me. The world still has a lot to learn about the strength of women."

For a moment, the two women looked at one another, and Evelyn felt as though something passed between them. An understanding. An insight. An agreement.

Then a knock sounded on the door, breaking the spell, and Evelyn strode forward, thanking the young footman for the pillows he handed to her. With Lady Ashwood's help, she moved Miss Davenport's legs, positioned the pillows in a small stack and then draped the young woman's legs gently about them. Then the two women sat with her, alternately cooling her face and checking her pulse.

After a small while, Miss Davenport's eyelids began to flutter before she finally opened them. Her gaze was unfocused, and her forehead crinkled in confusion. "Where am I? What happened? Mother?"

"Everything's all right, my dear." Brushing a gentle hand over her daughter's head, Lady Ashwood bent over her, her gaze meeting Miss Davenport's as she spoke in hushed tones, ensuring that her daughter remain calm.

When Miss Davenport's breathing had evened, Evelyn stepped forward, once more examining the young woman's vital signs. "Are you feeling any pain? Are you experiencing any dizziness?"

"No," Miss Davenport whispered, glancing a little fearfully at her mother. "I only feel a little weak as though my limbs are too heavy to be lifted."

"That's all right," Evelyn assured her. "Give yourself some time. I suggest you remain with your feet elevated for a little while longer. As far as I can tell there is nothing wrong with you." Her voice dropped lower. "Considering your condition, there is nothing too unusual about a fainting spell. However, you ought to try and avoid agitating situations at present."

Miss Davenport scoffed, her blue eyes once more flashing with the strength of character Evelyn had seen in her before. "Then I suggest you speak to my brother. After all, it was he who *agitated* me." There was a hint of bitterness in her voice. However, the look in her eyes spoke of disappointment, of pain and regret. What had happened between the two siblings?

"Indeed, we should inform my son that Claudia has awakened," Lady Ashwood said, her gaze travelling to Evelyn. "Would you mind? I'd rather stay here with my daughter."

"Certainly."

Although Evelyn would have rather avoided seeing the young lord again, she could not very well deny Lady Ashwood, and so she took her leave, stepping out of the room and granting mother and daughter a moment of privacy.

"May I ask," the young footman addressed her, a cautious look on his face, "is Miss Davenport all right?"

Smiling at him, Evelyn nodded. "It would appear so." Remembering that no one was to know about Miss Davenport's condition, she did not dare say more. "Thank you for your assistance, Mr. ...?"

"Adams," the young footman supplied. "Maxwell Adams."

"I'm Evelyn Procten. Nice to meet you."

"You as well." Holding her gaze for a moment, Mr. Adams then turned to gesture down the corridor. "I believe, his lordship as well as your father and his apprentice headed to his lordship's study. Would you like me to escort you there?"

"Thank you, Mr. Adams. I'd appreciate that."

A small chuckle escaped the young man. "I would not consider it remiss in my duties as I assume Miss Davenport is in no condition to get herself in trouble at present."

Taken slightly aback by the man's forthright manner, Evelyn glanced at him. "His lordship has you watch over her?"

The smile vanished from his face as though he had just now realised that he had crossed a line. "Only to ensure her well-being, I assure you."

"I see," Evelyn mumbled as he guided her down the stairs and through an arched doorway into a small corridor. All the while, she wondered what to make of all the many things she had learnt about Lord Ashwood that day.

When they reached the study, Mr. Adams excused himself to return to his post. Knocking on the heavy door, Evelyn waited to be invited in before opening the door and stepping over the threshold, willing her gaze to see only her father.

And possibly Mr. Bragg.

But not Lord Ashwood. Could she simply pretend he was not in the room? Or was that too childish?

At her entrance, the three men rose to their feet, which caused her father to sway on his, prompting Evelyn to rush forward and pull his left arm through hers to steady him. "Father, you should have remained seated," she chastised him, urging him to sit back down.

"Oh, I will not portray bad manners in front of his lordship," her father chuckled, remaining stubbornly standing, "or my daughter. What kind of man do you think I am?"

Disarmed by his sweet manner, Evelyn smiled. "The best kind, I assure you." Then she inhaled a deep breath and turned to Lord Ashwood, finding his watchful eyes on hers the moment she lifted her head. "My lord, your sister has awakened. She feels a little weak, which is to be expected, but otherwise does not complain about any discomfort. I trust she shall be fine."

"Thank you," Lord Ashwood replied, his shoulders once tenser as though he had not just received good news. Instead, his gaze remained almost painfully focused, his arms linked behind his back as he held her gaze. "I appreciate all you've done."

Evelyn frowned. Did he truly mean what he said? After all, he had not wanted her to tend to his sister in the first place.

Before Evelyn could dwell on this question further, her father's hand brushed over her arm in a fleeting, seemingly unintentional gesture before he toppled backwards and almost crashed into the armchair he had vacated only moments before. "Father!" Evelyn exclaimed, lunging herself forward and reaching for his arms to keep him from dropping to the floor.

Chapter Five

CAREFUL THOUGHT

lthough Richard could not deny that he felt relieved to hear that his sister had awakened, he could barely concentrate on anything appropriate to say as Miss Procten's deep brown eyes seemed to tie up his tongue in the most inconvenient way. Dimly, he could hear himself stammer a thank-you as well as something else—probably unintelligible—which he could not recall the moment the words left his lips.

This was hell! Utter and devastating—

Her eyes narrowed, and Richard froze, wondering what that meant. Was she confused? Displeased? Angry? Had he offended her somehow? If only he could recall what he had just said!

Then her gaze shifted from his, and he drew in a deep breath, feeling the tension leave his muscles as though her eyes had kept him trapped in the moment...and he was now free again. Himself again.

"Father!" the word tore from her lips with such a cutting edge that Richard's head jerked around, his gaze landing on the pale-faced doctor. In the next instant, the old man seemed to disappear from view as though he was being sucked down into quicksand.

Miss Procten reached for his arms lightning-quick—quite obviously, her thoughts had not been clouded by that strange haze that had befallen him—and pulled her father toward her, sliding one arm under his head and then easing him to the floor. Her face was flushed, and a strand of her hair had come undone by the time she sank to her knees, her quick hands flying over her father, lifting his eyelids and pressing down on the side of his neck. Then she momentarily closed her eyes and exhaled a deep breath.

Everything happened so fast that both he as well as Mr. Bragg had failed to react. The latter was only now joining his master's daughter by his side on the floor. "He merely fainted."

Miss Procten's lips tightened at the man's words; her eyes narrowed. Still, she did not utter a word. Instead, she continued to gaze down at her father before rising to her feet. "Lift his legs," she then told Mr. Bragg as she reached for the armchair her father had sat in only moments before. "We need to elevate his legs."

Mr. Bragg scoffed, "That seems to be your answer to everything." He shook his head at her and did not move.

Miss Procten's gaze narrowed once more before she chose to ignore the man by her side. Pulling up the chair, she then positioned her father's legs a bit awkwardly on the seat while moving the chair into the optimal position. Then she knelt back down, brushing a gentle hand over her father's forehead.

Within moments, he came to, blinking his eyes.

"Are you all right, Father?"

"I believe so," the old doctor replied. "What happened? Why am I staring up at the ceiling?"

"You fainted," his daughter told him, a sharp edge to her voice that Richard could not understand. Was she angry with him? After all, he could not have made himself faint intentionally, could he?

Dr. Procten chuckled. "I do apologise for being such an inconvenience." Then he tried to sit up, but his daughter pushed him back down.

"You will not rise until I tell you to; is that understood?"

Mr. Bragg scoffed, "Who are you to tell your father what to do? He knows very well—"

"He does not!" Miss Procten's brown eyes seemed to have darkened as she rose and turned to glare at Mr. Bragg. "As is evidenced by his position on the floor. Now, if you wish to be of any assistance at all, you will ensure that he does not get up. Have I made myself clear?"

Mr. Bragg seemed to be equally taken aback by her harsh words, for he merely stared at her without objecting to her orders—for that is what they were, orders! Unbelievable! Never had Richard seen men ordered about like this!

To Richard's great surprise and utter consternation, Miss Procten then directed her gaze at him. Swallowing the lump in his throat, he watched her step around Mr. Bragg and approach him, her brown eyes softening a fraction—if he dared believe his eyes!

"My lord, may I have a moment?"

Richard cleared his throat, wondering what she would do if he were to refuse her. "Certainly."

Walking over to the window, she waited for him to follow her, her shoulders tense and her hands almost balled into fists. Clearly, she was agitated about something. Was it her father's fainting spell? Her argument with Mr. Bragg? Or – God forbid! – him, Richard?

"My lord, as I have mentioned before," she began, her brown eyes settling on his in a rather frank way, "my father's health is not what it once was. Any form of agitation—be it good or bad—can cause his blood pressure to drop."

She inhaled a shuddering breath, and for a second, Richard feared she might join her father on the floor. He almost reached out a hand to steady her, but then thought better of it. What would it feel like to touch her? Would it rob him of his faculties altogether?

"My father ought never have come here," she continued, her voice sharp as though all of this had been his fault.

But then again it had, had it not? *He* had been the one to call on her father. *He* had been the one who had insisted her father tend to his sister. His gaze narrowed as he watched her and tried to understand the hidden meaning of her words. Did she blame him for this? Was she indeed angry with *him*?

"However, he cares very deeply for your family and would not be persuaded to remain behind."

Apparently, she had tried and failed, Richard surmised, absentmindedly watching the small curl of her cinnamon brown hair that had come loose and now danced up and down beside her left cheek as she made her point.

Richard blinked. What *was* her point? He cursed himself, gritting his teeth as he fought to listen.

"My father needs rest," Miss Procten said, her eyes wide as she looked up at him. "I do not wish for his health to decline further."

"Nor I." Clearing his throat, Richard held her gaze, amazed by the softness he found there. "Of course, he is welcome to stay at Farnworth Manor until he has sufficiently recovered to return home." There. A coherent sentence. Was that so difficult?

A smile came to Miss Procten's face that seemed to light up the whole room. "Thank you, my lord."

"I trust Mr. Bragg will then tend to my sister?"

In an instant, the light vanished, and Richard found himself facing the same woman who had snapped at Mr. Bragg only minutes ago. How had this happened?

With narrowed eyes, she glared at him, hands on her hips. "I'm perfectly capable of tending to your sister, my lord. Mr. Bragg, however, ought to return to the village in case medical assistance is required there."

Disappointed by the sharp tone in her voice, Richard nodded.

Naturally, he could insist Mr. Bragg stay and order *her* to leave instead; however, the words would not leave his lips. As much as he abhorred the effect she had on him, there was something deep inside him that sought to keep her near at all cost. And now she would stay, would she not? As long as her father and his sister were recuperating, she would stay at Farnworth Manor. After all, he had invited her to do so, had he not?

As she returned to her father's side, Richard frowned, trying to recall their conversation. Indeed, he had offered, but had it truly been his idea? Had it not in fact been *she* who had guided him to that conclusion? Had she manipulated him into agreeing to what she wanted?

Richard inhaled a deep breath, cursing his inability to read her intentions. It had always been thus. Only people of long acquaintance, like his family and childhood friend, was Richard able to understand on a deeper level. Their underlying intentions and meanings he could detect here and there. Not always, but comparatively more often. However, when it came to those he barely knew, he mostly found himself at a loss. If they were not forthright in their speech, which people generally were not, he mostly found himself at their mercy. If they did not want him to know, there was no way for him to tell.

It was utterly frustrating!

Unfortunately, the only way to become aware of Miss Procten's hidden agendas was for him to get to know her better. But did he dare? What would she be able to learn of him in return?

He would have to give this careful thought.

Very careful thought.

Chapter Six

AN UNWISE DECISION

After a quick breakfast with her father, Evelyn walked down the corridor toward Miss Davenport's bedchamber. Even from afar, she could determine what door it was for Mr. Adams stood guard beside it, his head swinging to look at her as she rounded the corner. "Good morning, Miss Procten," he offered when she had approached. "I trust you're well."

"I am. Thank you." Relieved to see a friendly face, Evelyn smiled at him. "And a good morning to you as well. How is our patient?" she asked when Miss Davenport's rather agitated voice came echoing through the door.

"Oh, I wouldn't presume to know." Despite the calm in his voice, Evelyn thought to detect a hint of humour in the soft crinkles around his eyes.

Knocking on the door, Evelyn entered and found the late viscount's daughter propped up in bed, a tray with tea, bread and jam beside her. "Good morning, Miss Davenport. How are you this morning?" Closing the door, Evelyn approached the bed, taking note of the slight flush on the young woman's cheeks.

"Miss Procten, I'm so glad you're here," Miss Davenport exclaimed, eagerly pushing herself farther upright. Once again, the words flew from her mouth as though the young woman had no need to breathe or had found an alternative way to do so that did not require her to cease talking. "My mother insists I not eat bacon and eggs," she complained, gesturing at the tray beside her with a hint of disgust, "for she says I ought to start out with something simple to test my stomach. Is that true?"

"Well, I–"

"It cannot possibly be so," Miss Davenport interrupted, completely unaware that Evelyn had begun to reply to her question. "I feel perfectly fine and see no need to be deprived of my breakfast. After all, I merely fainted. There was nothing wrong with my stomach. Do you think Mother is right? Or would it be all right if I had some eggs?"

"As long as you–"

"Oh, curse my brother!" the young woman exclaimed abruptly, waving a clenched fist as though she wished to plant it in his face. "I am certain he had a hand in the matter. You see, he never grants me anything. He is an absolute bore, and he cannot fathom that there are others who would feel trapped by the life he leads."

Unable to deny her own curiosity, Evelyn asked–before Miss Davenport could cut her off once more, "What do you mean? I noticed Mr. Adams outside your door."

The young woman frowned. "Mr. Adams? Oh, you mean the footman." Her face darkened, and yet, her hands gestured wildly as though fresh energy coursed through her body. She seemed indeed perfectly fine. Merely upset. "Yes, that is precisely what I mean. He has me locked up! Do you believe that?" Staring at Evelyn with wide eyes, Miss Davenport for once seemed to be waiting for an answer.

Pulling up a chair, Evelyn sat down. "I cannot imagine why he would do so."

"Neither can I," Miss Davenport exclaimed, exhaling audibly as she sank back into her pillows. "I shall die of boredom I tell you. Locked up in this house all day, with no one to talk to and a guard following my every step. I expect I shall become raving mad any day now."

"I'm sorry to hear that you are so unhappy," Evelyn said carefully.

Clearly, the young woman was in almost desperate need to share her story, and Evelyn could not deny that she longed to hear it. "I'm certain it was not your brother's intention to see you thus."

Miss Davenport scoffed. "I do not believe he even noticed." Turning to Evelyn, the viscount's sister leaned forward conspiratorially. "You see, my brother is not like other men or even other people. He does not share my need for companionship and, therefore, does not see the misery I'm in. He thinks I'm merely spoilt, a head-strong child he needs to admonish. It has always been thus. He's always been like a third parent rather than my brother." A touch of sadness clung to her voice as she spoke those last words, and Evelyn got the distinct feeling that above all Miss Davenport dearly missed her brother.

"Not that I agree with his methods," Evelyn began, thinking it a bit harsh of Lord Ashwood to lock his sister up, "however, I cannot help but think that he merely does so out of concern for you and a deep desire to keep you safe."

Miss Davenport sighed, "All my life, I've been chastised for who I am. No one ever understood my need for...living life, for adventure, for...something more than this." The young woman's blue eyes settled on Evelyn's face, all but pleading with her to understand. "I cannot help who I am."

"Neither can your brother." Before Evelyn knew what she was saying, the words had left her lips.

"Certainly, that is true," Miss Davenport agreed, sounding unexpectedly reasonable, quite unlike the effervescing young woman Evelyn knew. "However, he is the one who intrudes on my life, not the other way around, while I'm the one who suffers because of what he thinks is right, is proper, is expected." Shaking her head, she once more leaned back as though all strength had left her. "I cannot live like this."

Evelyn swallowed, wondering if enquiring further would cross a line. Still, she was no match for her own curiosity. "Is that how you came to find yourself with child?"

Miss Davenport's eyes rose to meet Evelyn's, and she placed a gentle hand on the slight bump under her night gown. "I suppose it is," she whispered, momentarily closing her eyes. "Still, I do not blame my brother," she suddenly exclaimed, once more sounding rather agitated. "This is *my* life, and it was *my* choice. It might not have been the wisest choice I've ever made, but it was mine nonetheless." Her features calmed, and for a long moment, she held Evelyn's gaze, clearly torn between confiding in another and the risks that came with revealing a secret. "I never loved him," she finally whispered, a calm determination coming to her eyes.

"Who?" Evelyn asked gently.

"William Montgomery." Sighing, Miss Davenport sank further back into her pillows. "We danced. We chatted. We drank champagne. We laughed." A soft smile flitted over her face at the memory of one of the rare, carefree moments in her life. "He saw me. He listened when I talked. He was sweet, and he cared about me. At least a little. The idea to elope...I can't even remember whose it was...but it seemed the answer to my prayers. Before I knew it, I found myself in a carriage to Scotland."

Evelyn inhaled a deep breath. The viscount's sister had run off to Gretna Green? Admittedly, now she understood at least partly why Lord Ashwood had her watched. Still, it did not explain how the young woman suddenly found herself with child, but still unmarried. What had happened?

"His brother discovered us before we could...," she scoffed, "tie the knot and demanded that William return with him to England at once." A long, drawn-out sigh followed, one that spoke louder than any words, allowing Evelyn a deeper glimpse at the disappointment this young woman had faced. "And he did. He abandoned me."

Shocked, Evelyn gawked at her patient. "He left you behind?"

Shaking her head, Miss Davenport met Evelyn's gaze. "His brother said I ought to return with them, but...I simply couldn't. When William turned from me, it was as though I lost every last hope of ever finding even a shred of happiness." Blinking rapidly, she tried to will back the tears that threatened, and her lips pressed into a determined line. "I became so angry. I've never felt anything like it. I barely remember how I got back to the inn where he had secured a room for us. For our wedding night. Everything was lost. I knew I'd be ruined no matter what I did, and so...," a soft smile played on her features as she shook her head, "...I threw caution to the wind. I wanted one adventure. Only one."

A disturbing sense of foreboding encroached on Evelyn as her gaze shifted down to Miss Davenport's midsection. "So, Mr. Montgomery is not the father of your child?"

The young woman shook her head, quick fingers brushing away the lone tear that had spilled over. "I suppose not. At least, he denies that we've ever been together."

Once again, Evelyn found herself gawking at Miss Davenport. "What on earth do you mean?" she demanded, belatedly realising that she was not talking to a friend, but a patient instead.

Miss Davenport, however, did not seem to object as her gaze remained distant, her mind conjuring the few memories she still possessed. "Never in my life have I indulged beyond a glass of champagne or two. After all, my brother would not allow me. But that night, I suppose I took it too far, for I cannot remember anything between returning to the inn and awaking in our room the next morning."

Staring at her patient, Evelyn felt goose bumps crawl up and down her arms. "You do not know who your child's father is? You don't remember him? Being...with him?"

Closing her eyes, Miss Davenport shook her head. "Does that make me an awful sort of person? I never thought anything like that would ever happen to me. I always thought that despite everything, I was a good person." Once more, her blue eyes found Evelyn's. "I never meant for this to happen, and I know that I made a mistake, but...does that mean I deserve to be locked away?" Another tear spilled over and ran down her cheek. Only this time she did not bother to brush it away.

Understanding Miss Davenport's desperate need, Evelyn rose from her chair and sat down beside her on the bed, gently drawing the young woman's trembling hands into her own. "You are a good person," Evelyn said gently but insistently. "Don't ever doubt that. Certainly, it was not a wise decision, but that does not change who you are deep down. You made a mistake. That's all it was. And I do not believe that your brother has you watched because he wants to punish you. I think it may be his way of trying to protect you."

A sob rose from Miss Davenport's throat, and she clenched her jaw to prevent another from escaping. Her hands curled tightly around Evelyn's as she fought the urge to fall apart.

"Have you spoken to your mother?"

Miss Davenport shook her head. "I do not dare. When father died, it broke her heart, and for weeks, we feared that she would join him. You remember how she was."

Evelyn nodded, able to recall only too clearly the utter despair in the viscountess's eyes. Not unlike the one Evelyn now saw in her daughter's.

"I do not wish to burden her," Miss Davenport continued. "And my brother does not understand. He is not one to dwell on emotions. All he sees he merely judges to be right or wrong. There is nothing beyond that."

Evelyn swallowed, her heart aching for the young woman. Still, she could not stop herself from wondering if the young woman's assessment of her brother was correct. "What will you do then?"

Miss Davenport drew in a slow breath. "My brother has determined that I am to have this...child...in secret." Again, one hand went to cup the small bump. "Then it will be given to a good family, so that I will be able to re-enter society and hopefully make a good match so that he can be rid of me." Her blue eyes held Evelyn's, almost begging her to contradict her.

But Evelyn could not.

From what she had observed since she had arrived the day before, Miss Davenport's estimation of her situation was correct. Clearly, Lord Ashwood wanted to keep his sister's condition a secret. Although a part of her could understand why, the thought that he would force his sister to give up her child riled Evelyn in a way she would not have expected. "Is that what you want?" Evelyn asked, knowing that Miss Davenport's wishes could not change the rules society lived by.

The young woman shrugged. "Do I have a choice?" she asked, her gaze clouded. "I've never thought of myself as the mothering type. Still, without a husband, I know very well that neither I nor my child have a chance if our situation becomes known." She scoffed. "I cannot even fault my brother for his decision because in truth it is to my benefit, is it not?"

Evelyn could not deny that.

Releasing Evelyn's hands, Miss Davenport lay back, her face pale and her eyes restless. "I wanted an adventure," she said as though speaking to no one in particular. "One moment that was mine to choose. One moment that would make up for a life of rules and restrictions." Again, she scoffed, "And whatever that moment was, I now cannot remember it. Does that qualify as an adventure?" She shook her head, fresh tears misting her eyes. "I do not mean to sound heartless, but if I keep this child, then my life will be over. I know that no matter what my brother would always take care of me—out of duty if nothing else—but once ruined, I could never re-enter society, never marry, never find love." Tears rolled freely down her cheeks as she turned to look at Evelyn. "I cannot imagine that. What would it feel like to have no hope?"

Not knowing what to say, Evelyn gently placed a hand on the young woman's shoulder, her gaze holding hers, trying to show that she understood. That she felt for her.

After a while, Miss Davenport's lids began to close before she then drifted off into sleep. Evelyn sat at her bed a while longer, wondering if Miss Davenport could truly fathom what it would mean for her to give up her own child. Would that not also break her heart and thus ruin her life? Was there not a way to avoid either?

Rising to her feet, Evelyn doubted it. After all, society was not known for valuing people's happiness above all else. Quite on the contrary, most rules appeared to have been made to ensure that unhappiness would develop one way or another. Would that ever change?

Stepping out of the chamber, Evelyn flinched when Mr. Adams addressed her, having all but forgotten his existence. "His lordship wishes to see you in his study." An apologetic smile came to his face. "I'm sorry I startled you."

Catching her breath, Evelyn shook her head. "There is no need. I... I was merely lost in thought I suppose." Then she mumbled a quick goodbye and headed downstairs, wondering what Lord Ashwood wished to talk to her about. In all likelihood, he wanted to ask her about his sister's well-being or to urge her to leave after all. Did he truly not believe that she was competent enough to take care of a woman in the family way? After all, this was far from complicated. The family situation at Farnworth Manor, however, had great potential of giving one the worst of headaches.

After knocking, Evelyn entered the room where her father had collapsed the previous day, and for a moment, she was relieved that her mind was distracted as she found herself facing the one man who seemed to be able to muddle her thoughts with his mere presence.

"How is my sister?" he asked as expected, his sharp grey eyes once more watching her carefully as though he hoped to spy a reason to distrust her. "I trust she is well."

Evelyn gritted her teeth at the insult. Did he truly think she would not have informed him if his sister had taken a turn for the worse? Had she not done everything in her power to ensure that Miss Davenport recovered swiftly? And had it not in fact been his cold demeanour that had put his sister in the sick bed to begin with?

"She is fine," Evelyn replied, unable to keep her annoyance from showing in her voice. "However, she needs to rest and avoid all unnecessary stress." For a second she hesitated, but then the words simply flew from her lips. "Therefore, I advise you to refrain from agitating her again."

Although Lord Ashwood's eyes narrowed, a touch of confusion in them, he did not rebuke her. Instead, the barest hint of a smile curled up his lips. "I assure you, Miss Procten, my sister does not mind agitation as much as she minds boredom. I have no doubt that her fainting spell resulted mainly from her confinement to Farnworth Manor rather than anything I might have said. After all, she's known me all her life."

Frowning at this unexpected reaction, Evelyn had to admit that she was surprised by Lord Ashwood's deeper knowledge of his sister's character. He clearly *did* see his sister. Was it simply that he disliked who she was and sought to change her? Did he not see that that would make her even unhappier than she already was? Had he even asked her if she was willing to give up her own child? Or had he simply ordered her to do so?

Blinking, Evelyn realised that silence had hung about the room for a short while. In consequence, Lord Ashwood's gaze was directed at her, his eyes slightly narrowed as they swept her face. "I might be mistaken," he began rather tentatively, "but it is you who seems agitated at present. Or am I wrong?" Stepping around his desk, he came toward her, his chest rising as he inhaled a deep breath. "Is there a problem, Miss Procten?"

Chapter Seven

A RARE MOMENT

Richard felt the muscles in his shoulders tense as he waited for her to reply. Her eyes held his, and yet, her face was almost blank—at least to him—and he found it very unsettling not to know what she was thinking. In that moment as he all but held his breath waiting, Richard realised how highly he valued her opinion, how much it mattered what she thought of him.

Was she truly angry with him? What could he have done? Did she still blame him for her father collapsing the day before?

"I spent the past hour with your sister," Miss Procten finally said. For all intents and purposes, it was a fairly neutral statement. A mere fact. Free of emotions or censure. Nothing that would explain the anger he sensed in her. Still, her voice held nothing friendly. In fact, she seemed to force out the words slowly to keep herself from throwing them at his feet.

Richard wondered what his sister could have said that would have upset Miss Procten thus. "I see," he mumbled, completely at a loss. His gaze remained on hers, and yet, the way she looked back at him made him feel as though he was missing the point. Had he not been listening? Had she said more than he had heard? "What is it that you wish to say?" Giving up from trying to decipher the expression on her face,

Richard took a step forward, determined not to allow himself to be seen as indecisive or even unsettled.

Crossing her arms in front of her chest, Miss Procten inhaled a deep breath. "She spoke to me of her...situation."

Richard held his breath. Certainly, Miss Procten already knew that his sister was with child. However, he had never intended to share more with her—or the good doctor—than that. Had Claudia told her the whole, unfortunate story?

Gritting his teeth, Richard mumbled a silent curse.

"You disapprove," Miss Procten commented, her dark brown eyes seemingly reading him without trouble. "Do you not think me trustworthy?"

Her lips had thinned, and Richard knew from his sister's antics that that was not a good sign. "I do not know you well enough to determine whether or not you are indeed trustworthy," he finally said. "Would you hold that against me?"

For a moment, the tension in her face seemed to weaken as though she realised that he was indeed correct. However, whatever had caused her initial disapproval of him quickly had her features hardening once more. "I am her doctor, and as such I need to be aware of my patient's circumstances, anything that might promote or hinder her recovery."

Richard frowned, taken aback at her bold-faced lie. "But you're not her doctor. In fact, you're no doctor at all."

Seeing her face turn red, Richard felt oddly reminded of the description of a volcano eruption he had read some time ago. Her muscles seemed to tense almost to their breaking point, her hands clenching at her sides as she stared at him through narrowed eyes not unlike those of a hunter on the prowl. Any moment now, Richard was certain she would lash out at him.

But for what? Had he not merely stated the truth? Would she honestly hold this against him?

However, instead of erupting, Miss Procten seemed to manage to calm herself by taking a few slow but deep breaths, her eyes never leaving his as though he was the one to give her the strength to do so.

Once again, Richard was completely at a loss. Would he ever understand this woman?

"I did not come here," Miss Procten finally said, her tone surprisingly even, "to talk about me. I came to speak to you about your sister. As her doctor," she paused as though daring him to contradict her, "I felt compelled to inform you that your sister is quite affected by the decision you have forced upon her."

Richard frowned at her accusation. Still, he was relieved that she was finally willing to explain herself. Although the underlying meaning of words often eluded him, at least on the surface words gave him more to work with than facial expressions did. "Pray tell what decision I forced upon her?"

Scoffing, she shook her head. "To give up her child," she said, clearly disappointed that he even had to ask.

Shaking his head, Richard approached her. In reaction, her dark eyes widened ever so slightly, and Richard momentarily wondered why. "You are mistaken," he said as calmly as he could as being near this woman *and* have her accuse him of a moral wrongdoing was slowly stirring his blood. "It was not my decision. After all, any young lady who finds herself in such a...predicament is offered this one option to return into society's good graces. It is an unwritten rule. Ruined or not, as long as she can keep it quiet, hidden, she receives another chance."

Again, Miss Procten's eyes narrowed. However, Richard failed to detect the previous signs of anger he had seen on her face. Was she confused then? Still, how could what he had just said have confused her? Had she not been aware of society's unwritten rule? As a doctor's daughter, perhaps she had indeed not been.

"Quite frankly, my lord, I care very little for society's rules," she said, her arms once more rising to cross in front of her chest. "What I am concerned with is my patient's well-being. Therefore, I feel it is my duty to inform you that forcing your sister to give up her child might have severe consequences."

Not having expected that, Richard stared at her. "Quite on the contrary, Miss Procten, not giving up the child will have severe consequences," he corrected her, wondering if he had misjudged her intellect. Was she a bit slow in the head?

As though to prove him right, Miss Procten's eyes grew almost as round as plates and her jaw dropped a fraction. "Are you trying to play me for a fool, my lord?"

Never had anyone dared speak to him thus, and Richard could not decide what to make of it. Clearly, they were not communicating—at least not well—and he was not quite certain what the problem was. Still, in the back of his head, a very familiar voice whispered that usually under these circumstances it was him who was the problem. Or it had been him before...countless times. What was it that he did not see? What was it that he had misunderstood?

A deep frown drew down her brows as she absentmindedly took a step closer, her eyes studying his face. "You truly don't understand, do you?" she whispered, a strange tone in her voice that Richard could not decipher.

However, what he did understand was that Miss Procten seemed to have realised his deficiency. Or at least was beginning to suspect it. In answer, his heart clenched, and he swallowed hard, humiliation at having his weakness revealed tensing his muscles. "I understand that you feel the need to meddle in other people's affairs," he snapped, saying the first thing that came to mind in order to throw her off his trail, "and I must say I do not care for it. I'll ask you kindly to see merely to my sister's recovery and nothing beyond that."

"I am," Miss Procten hissed, anger once more darkening her face, and yet, her eyes still roamed his face, unwilling to give up their post. "Healing the body alone does not make a patient well if the mind and heart are grieving. If you force your sister to give up her child, she may never get well."

Taken aback, Richard stopped. "You cannot be serious," he mumbled, squinting his eyes in the hopes of detecting any sign of duplicity. Was it now *her* who was trying to play *him* for a fool?

Miss Procten heaved a deep sigh. "The loss of a child," she began, "can cripple a woman. Perhaps not her body, but everything else she is." She opened her mouth, but then paused, clearly choosing her words with care. "Do you not remember how your mother broke down after your father's death?"

Richard swallowed.

"It broke her heart," Miss Procten continued, her brown eyes suddenly soft as they held his. Still, there was a sadness in them that stole his breath. "It nearly killed her, and yet, her body was fine. Unharmed." She lifted her hands, and for a moment, Richard feared– hoped! –that she would touch him.

However, she did not.

Her hands danced through the air as she sought to explain something he assumed she had expected him to be aware of, something that was common knowledge, something that usually needed no explanation. "Your sister might befall the same fate," she all but whispered, "if you force her to give up her child. I beg you to reconsider."

Pain radiated through his jaw, and Richard realised that he was clenching his teeth together to keep at bay the sudden anger that had gripped him. Did she truly think he did not care for his sister's well-being? That he did not mind causing her pain? Did Miss Procten not realise that he did what he did to spare his sister pain?

"You speak of things you do not understand," he snarled, annoyed with himself for allowing his emotions to show. "My sister is not the kind of woman who would find happiness in motherhood. Her happiness requires something else, something I seek to provide her with." He took another step closer, noting the way her mouth opened and closed as she thought about how to reply. "And that is all I will say about this matter. Now, if you please..." He trailed off, merely gesturing at the door.

The moment Richard was about to turn away and head back to his desk, she spoke out. "No!" Her voice was determined, and the eyes that held his remained unflinching. "I will not. I demand that you hear me out. It's the least you can do."

Although Richard could not deny that her stubbornness annoyed him, neither could he help but applaud her courage to defy him so openly. Few people ever dared. After all, he was the cold-hearted viscount. The man with no heart. The man as cold as ice. Was that not what people said?

Lowering his head, he stared her down with a glower that had most people quake in their shoes. "This," he snarled, "does not concern you." There, he had done it. Surely, she would run from him now.

But she did not.

Instead, Miss Procten pushed back her shoulders, lifted her chin and then even had the audacity to take a step forward, a clear challenge lighting up her eyes as she invaded his privacy. "You are mistaken," she said quietly. "It does concern me."

Grinding his teeth together, Richard felt torn between pushing her away and yanking her into his arms. His hands pulsed with the need to reach for her, and he wondered if there was anything he could do that would make her back down. Still, the question remained how far was he willing to go? After all, he was a man of honour, and yet, her close proximity made it awfully hard to remember why.

"I'm certain there is another way," Miss Procten began, her warm breath tickling his chin, "that would allow your sister to keep her child and–"

"No!" Richard growled, feeling his faculties slip away. "This is none of your concern, and by not acknowledging that, you're overstepping a line."

Her lips pressed into an angry line, and her nose crinkled in disgust at the words he had hurled at her. Still, she did not retreat, and Richard realised that no matter what he said he would not be able to dissuade her. Perhaps if he...

The moment the thought entered his mind, his body acted on it without waiting for approval.

Sweeping her into his arms, Richard kissed her...the way he had wanted to for over a year now.

A gasp escaped her lips before his mouth closed over hers, and he could feel her muscles tense as his hands pressed her body against his. Aware of her lack of compliance, he almost broke the kiss then and there, a new sense of humiliation washing over him.

But then she kissed him back.

Her hands snaked up and around his neck, and her lips moved over his with the same urgency he felt in his own heart.

Utterly astounded by her response as well as his own, Richard wondered at his own lack of control. Never did he allow his emotions to override his faculties. Never did he do anything without giving it careful thought. Never had he felt so daring than in that very moment. After all, he had no business kissing her, and yet, ...

...he could not stop.

In the end, it was she who pulled back, her hands gently pushing against his chest.

Reluctantly, Richard stepped back, his breath ragged like hers as they stared at one another. Belatedly, he realised that his hands were still firmly wrapped around her waist, and yet, he did not move.

Neither did she. Instead, she said, "I had thought you an honourable man. Was I wrong?"

Richard swallowed, and his hands dropped from her sides. "I beg your pardon?"

Seemingly unaffected, Miss Procten watched him. "How do you feel about the man who took advantage of your sister?" she asked rather unexpectedly. "The man who fathered her child?"

Frozen to the spot, Richard had trouble organising his thoughts. "He is a disgrace," he ground out, teetering between renewed anger and utter confusion. "My sister deserved better. She deserved to be treated with respect."

At his response, a strange sort of a smile came to Miss Procten's lips. "And do I not deserve the same?" she dared him.

Finally, the full force of his deed sank in, and Richard could have kicked himself for acting so rashly. He ought to have known better. He ought to have been in control. He ought not to have forced himself on her.

And yet, she had kissed him back, had she not?

"If I had a brother," Miss Procten continued, "how do you suppose he would feel about *you* then?"

Richard swallowed. "Are you saying you're expecting a proposal now?"

Miss Procten's face seemed to derail at his words as her mouth dropped open in utter shock. Strangely enough, she did not seem to be among those women who sought to make a match beyond their station. Still, her reaction felt like a rejection, and Richard could barely keep himself from demanding to know why she would not accept him.

After all, objectively speaking, he was a good match. He was a peer of the realm. His reputation was impeccable if a bit cold. He possessed a sizable fortune as he was not prone to gambling like so many others of his peers. All in all, many women considered him a catch, willingly accepting his lack of emotion.

"Not at all," Miss Procten assured him. "All I sought to do was to point out that what your sister did was to give in to a moment of weakness, a moment of passion," a slight flush came to her cheeks, and for a second, she dropped her gaze, "a rare moment." She inhaled a deep breath, and her gaze found his once more. "Does she truly deserve to be punished for it? After all, we've all been weak at some point in our lives and can call ourselves fortunate if no severe consequences resulted from it."

Watching her, Richard heard what she said, and yet, he wished he could be certain of her meaning. Had she just admitted that their kiss had been a rare moment for her? Had he not been the only one to feel the need to have her close? Or was she simply trying to win this argument by whatever means necessary?

"Regrettably, your sister cannot count herself among those lucky enough to walk away unscathed. Please, do not punish her more. She already finds herself in a severe predicament."

Richard sighed. Clearly, Miss Procten only had one thing on her mind. "I'm afraid we are of two minds on this matter, and therefore—"

"Why will you not at least consider another solution?" she interrupted him, her soft brown eyes once more hardening as she looked at him. "Why must you be so stubborn?"

Decorum dictated he rebuke her for her insolent way of addressing him. However, deep down, Richard could not deny that he enjoyed her frankness. It was utterly confusing. "You're quite impertinent, Miss Procten," he finally said, unable to keep a hint of amusement from showing in his voice. "What then do you propose?" Had he truly just asked her that? Was he mad? This discussion could lead nowhere good, and yet, he could not bear the thought of displeasing her.

At his concession, her eyes lit up and she inhaled a deep breath as though readying herself for battle. "While I'm aware that your sister cannot openly raise the child as her own," she began, and Richard was relieved to see that she seemed to possess at least some sense, "nothing would speak against her taking in...say...the orphaned child of a relative. This way her reputation would remain intact, and she would not have to be parted from her own flesh and blood. Would that not be a better solution?"

Richard sighed, hating to disappoint her. He ought to never have let her speak. "At first glance, yes."

A dazzling smile came to her lips, and she clasped her hands together in joy.

"But," Richard hastened to say, lifting a finger in warning, "that would not be the end of the story." Her face fell, and Richard felt his heart tighten in his chest. "There are aspects you did not consider."

"What do you mean?"

"Well," Richard began, "you failed to consider the damage rumours and gossip can inflict. People do notice when something occurs out of the ordinary, and they love nothing more but to exploit it to their advantage."

Her gaze narrowed, but she seemed to be willing to listen.

"I doubt that my sister's departure for Gretna Green remained completely unnoticed. It could not have escaped everyone's attention how taken she was with William Montgomery, and even if they managed to depart London without being seen, I have no doubt that rumours followed their sudden absence. In addition, I did not return her to London after her transgression, but instead brought her to Farnworth Manor." He sighed, "At that point, I had no knowledge of the depth of her misfortune."

"I see," Miss Procten mumbled.

"Now, if I keep her concealed until the child is born as I must for there is no way around it," he continued, "she will miss the beginning of the next season as well, which is fairly out of the ordinary as far as my sister is concerned. In addition, she was forced to decline any invitation to house parties and the like between the end of last season and the beginning of the new." Richard shrugged. "All this will not fail to bring forth rumours of the kind that would only die down eventually once she re-enters society as though nothing has happened...and there is no child to speak of."

Never in his life had Richard spoken to another person in such an intimate way as he now did with her. Why he felt the need to make her understand instead of simply informing her of his decision, Richard could not fathom. It was quite unlike him. "You see, if I were to keep the child at Farnworth Manor, claiming I had taken in a relative's orphan, people would still suspect, would still whisper and my sister would still be ruined. No gentleman would ever dare ask for her hand. She would have no future."

Miss Procten sighed, and even Richard could see in the way she hung her head that she felt utterly defeated. After all, he had felt the same way upon discovering his sister's predicament. For days he had raked his mind, trying to find a solution, but had come up empty-handed.

"What if she were to marry?" Miss Procten suggested. Still, the look on her face lacked the vigour it had shown before. "It would legit-imise the child and protect them both."

"And who do you propose she marry?" Richard asked, knowing exactly why he had dismissed that thought. "Who do we dare approach with such a proposition?"

Miss Procten shrugged, "Surely, you could think of someone who could be persuaded to..." Her voice trailed off, and it was clear even to him that she was grasping at straws.

"My sister seeks love," Richard whispered, noting the way she lifted her head and her eyes travelled over his face. "If she marries for conve-nience, she will never have that." He sighed, feeling suddenly drained. "It is a true dilemma, one I cannot find a satisfying solution to. No matter what, she will need to part with something very dear to her. There is no way around that."

Miss Procten closed her eyes. "But her child?" She sighed, shaking her head. "It seems utterly wrong."

Richard nodded. "Unfortunately, I did not make the rules. I merely attempt to live by them. That is all."

Holding his gaze, Miss Procten once more stepped toward him and to his utter surprise placed her hands on his chest, her dark brown eyes looking up into his. "I've misjudged you," she whispered. "I'm sorry. I shouldn't have jumped to conclusions. It was wrong of me." She swal-lowed, and her tongue darted out, wetting her lips. "Will you forgive me?"

As his heart hammered in his chest, Richard felt certain that she felt it the same way he felt her fingers against his chest despite the layers of fabric that separated them. The breath caught in his throat, and he once more felt the sudden urge to pull her into his arms. Only now, it was not passion that fuelled him, but a softer, more intimate emotion.

Oddly enough, Richard felt as though she could look into his soul and see him for who he truly was with all his faults and weaknesses, and for once, he did not mind. Instead, he felt at ease in her presence, not subject to censure and judgement, but free to be who he was.

"There's nothing to forgive," he finally said, wishing he could see into her soul with the same ease, "for I believe I've made the same mistake myself."

A soft smile curled up the corners of her lips, and she dropped her hands. However, despite the lack of contact, Richard could still feel her.

What on earth had he gotten himself into?

Chapter Eight

A DEATH SENTENCE

A week passed, and Evelyn could not deny that she was enjoying her stay at Farnworth Manor. Although there was nothing much wrong with Miss Davenport besides the occasional, rather normal pregnancy symptom, Evelyn stayed on as her father was still too weak to be moved...despite his objections. However, from experience, she knew that he would often downplay his discomfort in order to not be a burden to others.

Feeling helpless was torture for him.

Still, Evelyn insisted he rest and regain his strength, allowing her to stay at Farnworth Manor to see to Miss Davenport. For although the young woman was in perfect health–physically speaking–her mood swings were rather alarming. Sometimes she was almost cheerful as though she had forgotten about her dire circumstances as well as the moment that had brought them forth. Then again, she would lament for hours about how uncaring her brother was, cursing him for locking her up. And at other times, she would be calm and collected, staring into the distance, a look of resignation in her blue eyes.

It broke Evelyn's heart to see her like this. After all, an expecting mother ought to feel delight at the new life growing inside of her, ought she not? Was that not one of the very fundamentals of life?

"There is nothing to be done," Evelyn replied to Lady Ashwood's question. "Your daughter's body is not ill. It is her mind, her heart, that suffer. I'm afraid they are much more difficult to cure." Allowing her gaze to travel from the viscountess to her daughter sitting on the settee, a piece of embroidery all but forgotten in her lap, Evelyn sighed, wishing she knew how to help. However, as long as Lord Ashwood refused to consider an alternative solution, there was nothing she could do.

At the same time, Evelyn had to admit that she had no idea what that solution could be. Begrudgingly, she had allowed herself to realise that Lord Ashwood had been right. There was no perfect solution to this problem for each one came with a sacrifice. A sacrifice that would undoubtedly ruin Miss Davenport's life one way or another.

At present, her happiness seemed to be an impossibility.

It was truly disheartening.

Lady Ashwood sighed, "It pains me to see her like this," she whispered in a hushed tone, concerned eyes resting on her daughter. "It is as though something extinguished the light in her. She's no longer who she used to be."

Evelyn nodded. "Perhaps you ought to speak to your son," she suggested carefully. "Perhaps together you might be able to find a solution that would put some joy back in your daughter's life."

Taking a step back, Lady Ashwood looked at Evelyn, a hint of resignation in the widow's eyes. "I doubt that my son would be willing to discuss this matter as he has already made up his mind." She swallowed. "There is no speaking to him when his reasoning is sound, and unfortunately, I have to admit that he is not wrong."

"And yet, he is not right, either," Evelyn replied quietly, hoping her direct words would not offend the lady. However, Miss Davenport's mother merely nodded, her gaze travelling back to her daughter before she walked over and sat down next to her.

Sighing, Evelyn stepped up to the window, her gaze sweeping over the bare fruit trees in the orchard. Winter was fast approaching, bringing with it a strong northern wind. The world seemed asleep, determined to wait out the cold that lay ahead, in order to bloom again once the sun returned bringing with it a much, needed warmth.

Would Miss Davenport ever regain her smile? Or would she continue on in a world devoid of warmth?

Remembering Lord Ashwood's demand that she drop the matter, Evelyn gritted her teeth, chastising herself for not being more insistent. After all, ignoring the problem would not make it go away.

Only too well did Evelyn remember that afternoon in Lord Ashwood's study when she had lashed out at him for not being more considerate of his sister. Equally well did she remember the moment he had pulled her into his arms and kissed her.

Kissed her!

Shaking her head, Evelyn felt her cheeks warm at the memory. Still, a part of her could not believe that it had truly happened. Had it only been a dream? Was it possible that her mind had merely conjured the moment? After all, Lord Ashwood had never shown any kind of interest in her. Never would she have thought that he desired her. Or had it merely been a way for him to end their argument?

A week had passed, and she had not laid eyes on Lord Ashwood since. Was he avoiding her? Did he now regret his thoughtless action? Did he not wish to be reminded of it?

All these questions and more kept Evelyn's thoughts well-occupied whenever her mind allowed her a moment of reprieve from the pressing matter of Miss Davenport's well-being. Still, the two were interconnected, and so no matter what Evelyn did, her mind always seemed to lead her back to that one afternoon about a week ago and the sensation of Lord Ashwood's lips on her own.

And she had kissed him back, had she not?

No matter what she had said to him afterwards, she had not minded his kiss. Certainly, she had been surprised. Stunned even. However, she could not deny that she longed for a repetition.

Curse her wayward heart! After all, there were more important matters to deal with at the moment. It was highly inconvenient for her to be distracted by such thoughts. And she was a doctor. She ought to possess more self-control.

Inhaling a deep breath, Evelyn forced her thoughts away from Lord Ashwood and back to the matter at hand. Fortunately, her heartbeat calmed, and she felt the strain ease from her muscles. With a new determination, Evelyn turned back to mother and daughter in the very moment when the door to the drawing room opened and none other strode in but Lord Ashwood.

Curse him!

At the mere sight of him, Evelyn felt her resolve waver, her heartbeat quicken and her insides melt. If this was not a sickness, Evelyn did not know what was. And a most inconvenient one indeed!

Enquiring after his sister's well-being, Lord Ashwood kept his gaze firmly fixed on the two women seated on the settee. Still, his shoulders seemed taut and his jaw clenched as though he was experiencing great distress. Did her mere presence annoy him so? Evelyn wondered. Or did the memory of their kiss have the same effect on him as it did on her? If only she knew!

"I've come to inform you," he told his sister, his voice even as though he did not have a concern in the world, "that preparations have been made for you to travel to Crestwood House in the new year." Miss Davenport's eyes grew round with shock. "A few trusted servants will accompany you and ensure that you won't be lacking any comfort."

"Comfort?" Miss Davenport all but shrieked, shaking off the calming hand her mother placed on her shoulder. "You know nothing of the comforts I need!"

Lord Ashwood's gaze narrowed, and his jaw clenched as he took an almost menacing step towards his sister. "You will keep your voice down!" he hissed, glancing at the closed door behind him. "You will not make a scene. You will not act like a spoilt child. Have I made myself clear?"

Sobbing, Miss Davenport slumped down. "You'll be the death of me!" she cried, sinking into her mother's embrace.

"Hush, my dear," Lady Ashwood hummed as though she were holding a child. "Do not worry. I shall accompany you. You'll not be alone. Hush, hush, my dear. All shall be well."

The soft lilt in the lady's voice momentarily reminded Evelyn of her own mother. Although she had died in childbirth when Evelyn was but five, she still possessed faint memories that would rise to the surface of her mind every once in a while. Usually when she least expected them.

"Miss Procten."

Blinking, Evelyn shook off the dim memory of her mother's kind smile, belatedly realising that Lord Ashwood was addressing her. His sharp, grey eyes caught hers, and she had to fight the urge to drop her gaze. "Yes, my lord," she mumbled, fighting off the confusion that clouded her mind.

"I would appreciate it," he began, his face tense, blank, almost unreadable, "if you were to stay and see to my sister until her departure. As you are aware, it is imperative that her condition does not become known. Therefore, I think it would be beneficial if you could assist her maid for the time being."

"My lord," Evelyn began, trying to sort through the maze in her head, "I would suggest that—"

"No!" Lord Ashwood interrupted, his voice harsher than she had ever heard it. "There is nothing to say. I've made my decision, and it is not open for discussion." For a moment, his gaze remained on hers, and Evelyn thought to see a hint of hesitation before he once more opened his mouth. "If you have no desire to stay on at Farnworth Manor, I will find a replacement for you." His brows rose as though in question. However, before Evelyn had the chance to answer, he spun on his heel and stormed from the room, closing the door a bit too loudly for comfort.

Evelyn fumed. Not only did she feel riled by his lack of sensitivity in informing his sister of his decision, but...*replace her*? Had she heard him correctly? Evelyn gritted her teeth, forcing the ache in her heart back down. Why did she care if he threatened to replace her? Certainly, there were others who could look after Miss Davenport as well as she could. Why then did it bother her?

For your own sake, a distant voice whispered, once more conjuring the moment in Lord Ashwood's study, the moment she had lain in his arms, the moment she had responded to his kiss.

"Blasted man!" Evelyn hissed, only becoming aware that she had spoken out loud when Lady Ashwood's head turned, and the woman's eyes found hers. However, instead of disapproval, Evelyn saw humour in the lady's grey gaze.

"My son can be rather stubborn at times," Lady Ashwood commented, her eyes watchful as they held Evelyn's, "however, he is

66

not unfeeling. He merely has a different way of seeing the world. Still," the left corner of her mouth crinkled in amusement, "it would do him good to be reminded that there are opinions out there differing from his own."

Surprised, Evelyn held the widow's gaze, trying to understand what the woman wanted her to do. In fact, if she were not mistaken, Lady Ashwood was all but urging Evelyn to argue with her son. If his mother believed him to be wrong, why would she not speak to him herself?

"You are a very compassionate, young woman," Lady Ashwood whispered to Evelyn, her hand gently brushing over her daughter's hair as the young woman's head rested on her shoulder, her eyes closed. "You have a way of seeing into another's heart." A memory of Lady Ashwood's own suffering following her beloved husband's death flitted across the woman's face. "Speak to him, and perhaps he will listen."

Evelyn swallowed, and for a moment she could do nothing but stare at the viscountess. Certainly, it was not her place to speak to Lord Ashwood, to lecture him, to argue with him, to persuade him. Still, whether or not it was proper, Evelyn could not deny that she longed to do as advised.

More than anything, she wanted to speak to him, to hear his reasons, to understand why he acted the way he did. For deep down, Evelyn was certain that there was more to Lord Ashwood than met the eye. As infuriating as he could be, she could not deny that there was a quality in him—well-hidden—that hinted of a caring man. Why on earth was he so insistent on hiding that side of himself?

"If you'll excuse me," Evelyn mumbled as she stepped toward the door, seeing Lady Ashwood's approval in the soft smile that came to her lips.

Slowly, Evelyn walked down the corridor toward Lord Ashwood's study, willing the trembling in her hands to cease and her thoughts to stop spinning so wildly. However, most of all, she wished her heart would slow its hammering and allow her a moment to catch her breath. Perhaps she was not the best person to speak to his lordship after all, for it seemed that her wits had finally abandoned her. In that moment, Evelyn felt like a bundle of fluttering nerves.

Nothing more.

Nonetheless, upon reaching the heavy door, she knocked, afraid she might change her mind if she dared hesitate. Lord Ashwood's strong voice called for her to enter, and she pushed open the door with trembling hands...only to stop short when her gaze fell on Mr. Bragg. "What are you doing here?" she blurted out, taken aback by this rather unexpected development. "Has something happened?"

"Not at all," he replied, his gaze narrowing as he took in her undoubtedly pale expression. "Are you well?"

As Evelyn nodded, Lord Ashwood rose from behind his desk and stepped around it. "I've asked Mr. Bragg here to fill in for your father. Since he is still unable to tend to my sister, I felt the need to have another doctor's opinion."

His words felt like a slap in the face, and Evelyn almost staggered backwards. Had he not heard a word she had said the other day? Or did he simply choose to ignore them? "As I've told you," she forced out through gritted teeth, fighting down the urge to strangle him, "I'm perfectly capable of tending to your sister myself. There was absolutely no need to call for Mr. Bragg."

For a moment, Lord Ashwood held her gaze, his own narrowed in confusion. Was it truly possible that he did not know why she was burning with anger in this very moment? How was that possible?

"Mr. Bragg," Lord Ashwood addressed the other man, "would you please see to my sister? I need a word with Miss Procten."

Although there was a satisfied spark in Mr. Bragg's eyes at Lord Ashwood's decision, he hesitated at the door and turned back to look at Evelyn. "Are you certain you're all right? You look a little pale. Perhaps you ought to lie down."

Annoyed, Evelyn snapped, "I'm fine. Perfectly fine." Anger boiled in her veins, and in that moment she could not even say at whom she was most angry.

"All right," Mr. Bragg said, nodding. However, before he stepped through the door, he turned back to look at Lord Ashwood. "I trust you will ensure my fiancée's well-being, my lord. Please do not hesitate to call me if she faints."

And then he was gone.

As the shock and outrage over Mr. Bragg's words reverberated through Evelyn's body, she slowly became aware that Lord Ashwood, too, seemed to have had the air knocked from his lungs for he stared at her as though he had just been issued a death sentence.

Chapter Nine

BETROTHED OR NOT

Actual, physical pain radiated through Richard's body as though someone had just now delivered a severe blow to his abdomen...or his heart. He felt an almost incontrollable reflex to sink to his knees and curl into a ball on the floor in order to alleviate the excruciating sensation, and his muscles tensed painfully as he fought to keep upright.

Dimly, he realised that he was staring at her, his eyes unblinking; and yet, he could not bring himself to avert his gaze. "Y-you're betrothed," he stammered, a lump forming in his throat that made it difficult to speak. "Y-you're betrothed to Mr. Bragg."

Somewhere in the back of his mind, Richard heard a faint echo of his voice of reason. Never had it been so faint. Always had it been right there at the forefront of his mind. Not now though. Only quietly, it whispered that he was overstepping a line. After all, who Miss Procten was or was not betrothed to was none of his concern...or was it?

His hands balled into fists at his sides as he fought the sudden urge to strangle the cursed doctor. How dare he!

How dare he what? His voice of reason piped up, daring him to answer.

Instead, Richard chose to ignore it, belatedly becoming aware of

Miss Procten's gaze as it once more seemed to study his expression. Without him noticing, she had even taken a step closer, and now peered at him like a scientist studying a rare specimen.

Squaring his shoulders, Richard raised his chin, groping for something to say that would distract her from her current observations. Before he could though, she suddenly shook her head as though shaking off a thought and her features relaxed. "I apologise," she began much to his surprise. "I did not mean to stare. I came here in order to speak to you about your sister." Despite the casualness in her tone, her gaze narrowed, and her eyes darted to the door through which Mr. Bragg had left.

Was she worried about being left alone with him? Richard wondered, his insides tightening once more. Did she fear he would force himself on her again? Did she wish for Mr. Bragg's protection?

That thought seemed to turn Richard's world upside down as he suddenly found himself the villain in this scenario. How had this happened? Always had he thought of himself as an honourable man. However, recently, his sister as well as Miss Procten seemed to be of a different opinion.

"Why did you call for Mr. Bragg?" Miss Procten asked as she turned her attention back to him.

Richard blinked, reminding himself to try and follow their conversation. "Because my sister is in need of a doctor," he replied, thinking that ought to be obvious. What indeed did Miss Procten hope to achieve by asking nonetheless?

Her lips thinned. "I've told you more than once that I'm perfectly able to see to your sister."

"But you aren't a doctor," Richard replied, "as I have told you before." Despite his growing concern about the direction of their conversation, Richard could not keep himself from staring at her, unable to forget the earth-shattering news he had just received.

What is it to you? His voice of reason once more objected.

And once again, Richard ignored it.

"Neither is Mr. Bragg." Hands on her hips, Miss Procten leaned forward like a soldier readying himself for battle. "He's been training with my father for only a year; whereas, I have been learning from him all my life." Her brown eyes held his as she took a step closer as though proximity would grant her a better understanding of him. "Why is it that you discount my abilities? Is it because I'm a woman?" Her jaw tightened, and she drew back her shoulders another fraction. "I will have you know that women are a lot more capable than you give us credit for." She sighed. "And that includes your sister."

Unable to concentrate, Richard blurted out the first thing on his mind. "You ought to have informed me that you are betrothed." Unfortunately, it was a statement rather irrelevant to their current conversation.

Miss Procten's gaze narrowed once more, and for a moment, she seemed at a loss.

Richard knew that feeling only too well.

"Why?" she demanded, her brown eyes once more sweeping over his features. "What is it to you?"

Richard cleared his throat, doing his best to appear nonchalant. "It's common courtesy."

"It is?" She inhaled a slow breath, and for a second, Richard thought she looked disappointed. However, then the expression on her face cleared, and he could not be certain. Not that he had been before. "It does not matter. It—"

"Of course, it does." Cringing at the sound of his own voice, Richard could not keep himself from advancing on her. "Do you make it a habit of kissing other men besides your own betrothed?" Unfortunately, that question only brought back the memory of their kiss, and he could all but feel her lips against his.

Miss Procten's mouth dropped open while her eyes seemed to narrow into slits. "How dare you?" she demanded. "Was it not you who kissed me?"

Richard swallowed. "That might have been so. However, I would never have done so if I had known you were betrothed to another. Did you not think he would object to another man kissing his betrothed? If it were me," he took a step toward her, "I would mind very much."

For a moment, Miss Procten remained rather still, her eyes widening ever so slightly, and her chest rose slowly as she inhaled a deep breath. "Is that so?"

"It is indeed." Feeling his pulse hammer in his veins, Richard watched her as she stood before him, the expression in her eyes changing in subtle nuances.

If only he knew what they meant!

"If you must know," Miss Procten finally said, her voice softening as her hands slid from her hips, "you are the only one who has ever dared to take such liberties with me." For a second, her gaze dropped to the floor before she forced it back up.

Stunned, Richard stared at her. "He didn't…? I mean, why would he not…?" His voice trailed off as he realised how highly improper his question was. Not that it mattered much. After all, whenever they spoke to one another, decorum seemed to evaporate into thin air.

A soft smile came to her lips as she looked up at him, and Richard could not help but think that she was pleased. The only question was, why? Certainly, learning that Mr. Bragg had not lain a hand on her—so far, at least—was greatly pleasing for him—for a reason he did not dare examine further. However, why would his rather inappropriate question please her?

"If you must know," she began once more, her deep brown eyes holding his with such intensity that Richard thought she did not wish to miss his reaction to her next words, "Mr. Bragg is *not* my betrothed."

In one whoosh, the air flew from Richard's lungs, and he could not stop his utter relief from revealing itself in a deep smile that drew up the corners of his mouth. "He's not?" he demanded, fearing he might have misunderstood her.

Miss Procten shook her head, a large smile on her face. "He is not."

"Then why would he say so?"

Her lips hardened, and her nose crinkled in a way that made Richard think she was getting angry once more. "Because he does not listen to me any more than you do, my lord." Exhaling loudly, she shook her head. "My father sought someone to train, to follow in his footsteps. He hoped that if he found the right man, he would eventually allow me to continue to work beside him…if we married." Her jaw clenched. "Unfortunately, all the world seems to believe women to be far less capable than men."

Richard frowned, wondering why she felt so passionately about this. "Do you truly believe yourself to be of equal capability as your father and Mr. Bragg?"

Miss Procten's eyes lit up dangerously, and for a second, Richard thought she would lunge herself at him. However, then she took a deep breath, her hands balling into fists before she unclenched them once more. "I admit," she began slowly, her jaw still slightly tense, "that I may still lack some experience compared to my father. However, that is only natural, given that he has been treating patients for decades. However, I truly believe– no! – I know that I'm more qualified than Mr. Bragg for two very simple reasons. One, I have been training for a lot longer than he, and two, his rather high opinion of himself often prevents him from acquiring further knowledge as he believes to already know everything worth knowing." Her hands trembled as she held his gaze. "Should the need arise, you'd do well to call on me, and not him." For a moment, she simply stood there as though to emphasise her words, to ensure that they would be heard, noticed.

Then, however, she simply turned on her heel and without another word left his study.

Remaining behind, Richard stared at the closed door, wondering if he would ever be able to make sense of Miss Procten.

Still, the only thing that echoed through Richard's body then and there was pure and utter joy at finding her still unattached. No one had claimed her as his own yet.

Not that *he* ever could. Or wished to.

After all, they would not suit each other...for more reasons than he could name.

Nevertheless, he could not deny that he was relieved.

More than he had thought possible.

Chapter Ten

A PERSONAL QUESTION

S tomping down the hallway, Evelyn felt her own footsteps echo in her ears like a stampede of thundering hooves. Anger boiled in her veins, and yet, she could still feel her heart jump and dance at the utter joy that had come to Lord Ashwood's face upon finding her a free woman still. Why had it pleased him so?

Shaking her head, Evelyn pushed those thoughts aside. After all, they served no purpose. Her silly infatuation with him needed to end. She would do well to remember that they came from different worlds, and so she clung to her anger rather than the soft tingles that swept through her body.

How dare he question her capabilities after everything she had done for his mother and sister? Why was it that people generally only saw her pretty face? Her skilled hands? Her gentle temper? Never had she been praised for her mind and its accomplishments. At least, not by anyone other than her father.

Turning down the corridor toward her father's chamber, Evelyn tried to calm her nerves when she found Mr. Adams walking toward her. As Miss Davenport was currently with her mother, apparently, there was no need for the young footman to watch her.

"Good day, Miss Procten," he greeted her kindly before his brows drew down and a hint of concern came to his eyes. "Are you all right? You seem upset. Is something amiss with Miss Davenport?"

Evelyn shook her head. "No, nothing at all," she assured him, aware of the hint of hostility that still clung to her voice. "I'm quite all right as well." Gritting her teeth, she cursed Lord Ashwood under her breath.

Mr. Adams' brows flew up, and a short laugh spilled from his mouth.

"I apologise," Evelyn mumbled, ashamed of her lack of control.

"There is no need," Mr. Adams assured her, a kind smile on his face. "As much as I appreciate my position here, I am well aware that those born to privilege have never known the need to prove themselves. It is rather easy for them to look down upon the rest of the world and believe it their right that they do so." He shrugged good-naturedly. "It may not be solely his fault though. After all, he was brought up like this."

Although Evelyn was surprised by Mr. Adams' forthrightness, she could not deny that being able to speak honestly was rather refreshing. "Indeed, there is merit to your words, Mr. Adams, however, would you say that that also means that none of them can ever be expected to rise above what they were brought up to be? For that can simply not be right. Should we not all strive for a world where men and women find themselves equals? Where we all have the same choices? Where we all can decide our own fate no matter what class or gender we belong to?"

A wistful smile came to the young footman's face, and yet, a hint of sadness rested in his eyes. "I pray for such a world, Miss Procten, and I can only hope that one day it will be no longer the dream it is now."

Evelyn nodded, seeing the longing in his gaze as it left her face and fixed on something in the distance. Clearing her throat, Evelyn quickly bid him farewell, knowing that it was not right of her to distract Mr. Adams from his tasks. After all, his livelihood depended on him fulfilling them to the family's satisfaction.

Hurrying on to her father's chamber, Evelyn knocked and then slid inside. To her satisfaction, she found her father still abed. However, the look on his face spoke volumes of his displeasure with the situation he currently found himself in. "There you are," he exclaimed, irritation strong in his voice, not quite unlike her own. "I've spent this past week in bed. Surely, even you must admit that I've done my duty and ought to once more be allowed to venture around freely."

Evelyn did not miss the teasing challenge in his tone, and an easy smile came to her face. "Certainly, Father. If you promise to go about slowly."

"Don't I always?" he asked, a childish gleam in his eyes as he sat up straighter. "Have you ever known me to act irresponsibly?"

Evelyn frowned. "Not where another's welfare is concerned, no. However, your own is a different matter." Inhaling a deep breath, Evelyn closed her eyes, willing her anger to subside and not transfer into other areas of her life. She would be dammed if she granted Lord Ashwood that power over her!

"Is something wrong, my dear?" her father asked, all humour gone from his voice. "You seem upset?"

Evelyn inhaled a slow breath. Ought she to confide in her father? Still, whether or not it was wise to do so ceased to matter in the next moment when Evelyn realised she would certainly explode if she did not allow her anger and irritation with Lord Ashwood to spill forth.

"He's insufferable!" The words flew from her lips like lava erupting from a long-dormant volcano. "He does not listen. He does not see what is right in front of him. He has the audacity to–" Evelyn stopped, noting the rather amused look on her father's face as he leaned back leisurely, his sharp eyes watching her carefully. "I'm glad you find this amusing, Father," Evelyn huffed, and her arms rose to cross in front of her chest.

Her father chuckled, "I assume you're speaking of Lord Ashwood."

Evelyn scoffed, knowing that if she were to open her mouth, she would say more than she ought to. Better to remain quiet...as hard as it was.

When it became clear that he would not receive a direct answer, her father shook his head at her, a rather indulgent smile on his face as though she were still five years old. "I've never seen you speak so passionately, my dear," he observed. "At least not when it did not concern a patient of yours."

"But it does," Evelyn objected, afraid that her father could somehow see the underlying reason for her anger towards Lord Ashwood. "It concerns Miss Davenport."

Her father shrugged. "Are you certain? For I cannot remember you mentioning her name once." His watchful eyes swept over her face. "Why does he infuriate you so...if not for the very simple reason that you have come to care for him?"

Evelyn's jaw dropped, and her eyes strained to fall from their sockets.

Again, her father chuckled, "Don't look so shocked, my dear. I admit you hide your feelings well. However, I've had the privilege of knowing you since the day you were born, and you cannot deny that that has granted me a deeper inside into your heart."

Evelyn swallowed. "You're mistaken."

"Am I?" His gaze narrowed. "The look in your eyes suggests otherwise, my dear. Why do you deny it? Are you so afraid to relinquish control?"

Staring at her father, Evelyn did not know what to say, confused about what was true and what she was only trying to convince herself of. Did she truly care for Lord Ashwood? Beyond a momentary infatuation? Or was that what her father was referring to? However, then why did he look so pleased?

Sighing, her father patted a spot beside him, and reluctantly, Evelyn sat down on the side of his bed. Gently, he pulled her hands into his, his eyes kind as they met hers. "Listen, child, I know that you're determined to follow the path you've chosen for yourself so long ago. However, you cannot ignore your heart's wishes. It will only lead to your unhappiness."

Frowning, Evelyn held her father's gaze. "What on earth do you mean, Father?"

He sighed rather exasperatedly. "I'm saying that your heart chooses on its own–and not always wisely, I grant you that. Still, if you ignore it, it will punish you for it." Gently, he squeezed her hands. "If you care for him, then allow yourself to see him for who he is."

"But I–"

"No, you do not," her father cut her off. "You see what everybody sees or at least you are determined to see only that. However, judging from the slight flush on your cheeks, I cannot help but think that you are very well aware that there is more to Lord Ashwood than meets the eye."

Evelyn averted her gaze. Were her cheeks truly flushed? For everyone to see? Had *he* seen it?

"If you hadn't noticed," her father continued, "I doubt your heart would be leading you down this path." Leaning forward, he looked into her eyes. "As much as you want him to see past his own prejudices, is it not right that you grant him the same favour?"

Evelyn sighed, reluctantly lifting her head and meeting her father's challenging gaze. "Why would you encourage me thus, Father?"

"Because he is a good man." A soft smile came to his face as he leaned back against the pillows, a distant look coming to his eyes. "I knew his father for a long time and knew him well despite our different positions in life. I have no doubt that he raised his boy right. Therefore, I am convinced that the harshness of Lord Ashwood's character is not something that speaks to who he is at heart."

"Still, I don't understand why you would—"

A knock sounded on the door, startling them both.

Rising from her father's bedside, Evelyn went to open the door and was rather surprised to see Lady Ashwood standing there. "Is everything all right with Miss Davenport?" she asked, suddenly alarmed that the young woman might have taken a turn for the worse after her brother's rather unfeeling declaration of her imminent departure.

"Oh, no, my dear, don't worry," Lady Ashwood exclaimed, quickly waving Evelyn's concerns away. "She is as well as she can be under the circumstances." Her gaze drifted from Evelyn's face to the bed behind her. "May I come in?"

"Of course," Evelyn exclaimed, quickly stepping aside to allow the dowager viscountess inside. If this was not about Miss Davenport, what had brought the lady of the house up here to the guests' quarters?

Closing the door, Evelyn noticed the way Lady Ashwood stepped forward, her gaze meeting her father's in a rather intimate way. Like old friends. Confidantes even. What could be the meaning of this?

Before Evelyn could try to voice a careful inquiry, Lady Ashwood turned back to face her. "May I ask you a rather personal question, my dear?"

Evelyn swallowed, wondering at the strangeness of that day. "Certainly, my lady," she all but whispered, praying that Lady Ashwood was not as observant and direct as her father had been only moments before.

"Are you betrothed to Mr. Bragg?"

Evelyn's gaze widened. Indeed, that she had not expected. Why on earth would Lord Ashwood have told his mother that–? She stopped, remembering that Lord Ashwood would have had no reason to inform his mother of her betrothal. After all, when she had left him, he had been very much aware of the fact that she was indeed *not* betrothed to Mr. Bragg. The only one who believed so was Mr. Bragg himself. Why was the man suddenly walking around spreading such lies?

"Did Mr. Bragg tell you that?" Evelyn asked, noting a slight frown coming to her father's face as he observed their conversation.

Lady Ashwood nodded.

Evelyn drew in a slow breath, annoyance once more rising to the surface. She would need to speak with Mr. Bragg as soon as possible. "I do not know why Mr. Bragg told you thus," she finally said to Lady Ashwood. "However, I can tell you that it is not true."

The hint of a relieved smile curved up Lady Ashwood's lips. "I am glad to hear it."

Reminded of Lord Ashwood's reaction, Evelyn frowned, wondering why the fact that she was not betrothed to Mr. Bragg was met with such relief. However, before she could ask, Lady Ashwood addressed her once more. "May I ask you to step outside, my dear? I would like a private word with your father."

Taken aback, Evelyn stared at Lady Ashwood for a moment too long before her gaze travelled to her father. There was something in the way his gaze met hers and then shifted to his old friend's widow that spoke of a deeper connection or a shared secret, which made Evelyn all the more aware of the fact that there was something in their past that she did not know about.

"Certainly," she mumbled and then stepped from the room, her mind whirling with what these two had to discuss that she was not allowed to hear. After all, if it concerned Miss Davenport's health, there was no reason to ask her to leave the room, was there? Then what could they have to discuss that she was not allowed to know?

Indeed, it was a most strange day, and Evelyn felt the beginning of a mild headache thudding beneath her left temple. Perhaps a little fresh air would do her good and help her make sense of the chaos in her head. Never in her life had she felt so at odds with the world around her. Always had she been certain of what she wanted, of the path that was meant for her. Always had she been able to judge people for who they were, aware of their true character.

But now, everything was different, and Evelyn wondered if she would ever feel at peace again.

Balanced.

She could only hope so.

Chapter Eleven

A FATHER'S DECISION

L ooking up from the letter he had been penning, Richard noticed the soft flakes of snow being blown about outside his window. They seemed to dance in the air, wildly and randomly, mirroring his own feeling of being tossed about without a sense of direction. As much as he had always been in control of his life and those in it—perhaps with the exception of his sister— now his world seemed to have turned upside down within a matter of days.

Nothing seemed certain.

Nothing made sense.

It was maddening…and terrifying.

Rising from his chair, Richard approached the window, his gaze fixed on the tiny flakes as they succumbed to the strong wind blowing them about. Others, however, had made it to the ground, settling on the cold earth or the evergreen trees growing in the gardens below.

Then movement caught his gaze, and he squinted his eyes, trying to see through the swirl of snowflakes. A midnight blue cloak appeared in his view, its hem lined with white fur.

Miss Procten!

Recognising the exquisite cloak his mother had given to the doctor's daughter for her dedicated care during her illness the previous year, Richard drew in a shuddering breath, his hands reaching out until he felt cold glass beneath his fingertips. As though bewitched, he stared at her, his gaze following the hooded figure down the small path and out into the gardens. Snow swirled around her, landing on her cloak like stars in the night sky.

Still, she seemed unhindered by the chaos that thrived around her, her feet sure on the ground as she proceeded onward.

A sudden knock made him flinch, and Richard gritted his teeth, loathing the effect Miss Procten seemed to have on him these days. "Enter," he called, his voice laced with anger as he forced his feet to turn from the window.

"Are you all right?" his mother asked as she swept into the room, her footsteps quicker than usual. "You seem upset?"

"It is nothing." Annoyed, Richard waved her concern away, belatedly taking note of the letter in her hands. "Is something wrong?"

Glancing down at the letter, his mother took a deep breath, the look on her face speaking of...

Oh, if he could only know! If he could only be certain!

While she seemed rather calm—not agitated enough for some kind of tragedy to have happened—her muscles were tense, and Richard was almost certain that whatever she had come to tell him was of a serious nature. Beyond that, he could not be certain of her reasons for seeking him out.

"I need to speak to you." Stepping forward, she glanced down at the letter in her hands, turning it back and forth as though she did not know how to begin.

"Is it Claudia?" Richard asked, feeling his skin crawl with concern for her. It had been obvious that she had been alarmed by his decision to send her away. Still, he had hoped that his mother and Miss Procten had managed to calm her, make her see reason. After all, he was only doing what was best for her. And if she could not see that right now, then he had no choice but to force her hand in order to spare her the ruination that was surely to follow if her condition became known.

He did not want that for her.

Anything, but not that. She deserved better.

"Don't worry," his mother replied, her gaze softening as she studied his face. "She'll be fine."

Nodding, Richard inhaled a relieved breath. "Then what have you come to speak to me about?"

Mimicking him, his mother inhaled a deep breath as though bracing herself for what was to come.

Richard felt his skin crawl.

"Your father," she finally began, "and Josiah Procten met in school. As unlikely as it was for them to cross paths, Josiah Procten had been able to find a benefactor who had early on seen his talent for healing and insisted he needed a comprehensive education. Thus, he found himself among peers, ignored by most of them for his simple origin."

Frowning, Richard watched his mother. "I'm aware of how they met. Why are you telling me this?"

His mother sighed, and her soft eyes held his as she reached out and took one of his hands. "Before your father met Josiah Procten, he was quite pretentious, thinking very highly of himself for the mere fact that he was a viscount's son." A soft chuckle escaped her as her eyes became distant, filled with memories. "In the beginning, he was one of those who ignored Josiah, tormented him because of his upbringing. Until one day something happened that changed his life."

Frowning, Richard shook his head. "Why do I not know of this?"

"I cannot be certain as your father–not unlike yourself–tended to keep his thoughts to himself," his mother said gently. "However, I do believe he felt ashamed for the way he treated Josiah and did not wish to be reminded of it, to have his children know the man he once had been. Beyond anything, he wished to be a good example to you, to guide you and ensure that you would become a good man."

Richard nodded, wondering what his father had thought of him before he had died. Had he, Richard, become a good man in his father's eyes? Or had his father found him lacking? "What was it that changed him?"

"One day, your father was attacked by a wild dog," his mother said, her fingers clenching around the letter in her hand as though she still feared for his life. "While his *friends* abandoned him, only looking to their own hides, it was Josiah who risked his life to save another;

84

someone who had treated him without respect until that day." A soft smile came to her lips. "Your father called it true heroism, and it changed him, changed how he saw Josiah and himself. It was that friendship that turned your father into the man you knew. It made him realise that a person's character is not defined by the station they were born to. It made him rethink everything he thought he knew." Sighing, his mother drew him toward the armchairs by the windows, urging him to sit beside her. "If it hadn't been for Josiah's influence, your father would probably never have married me as I was a commoner's daughter myself if you recall. We would probably never even have met."

With his eyes fixed on his mother, Richard tried to process all he had just learnt, considering the conclusions he could draw from such knowledge. Rationally, he had to admit that not much had changed. He was still his father's son. His mother was still a commoner's daughter. His father and Dr. Procten had still been friends since their youth.

Nevertheless, Richard knew that not everything was rational. As much as he tried to see facts—something tangible, unmistakable, clear—his heart urged him in a different direction, and although he usually tended to resist it, afraid of where it might lead him, the past fortnight had somehow weakened his resolve.

Unable to shut out the flood of emotions, Richard sank into his chair, a sigh escaping his lips. His father had been a different man once, and although his mother had not said it outright, Richard understood from her words that he himself had more in common with the man his father had been once than with the man Richard had known all his life. However, what did this mean?

Always had Richard felt like the one who did not belong. Although his sister was exuberant in her ways, pushing the limits no matter what she did, she was undeniably her parents' daughter. Only he had never quite fit in with his family. All of them possessed a way of relating to one another in an emotional way. How often had he seen them exchange glances and smiles as though they were words containing a deeper meaning? How often had he himself been at a loss when faced with such a silent conversation? How often had he felt as though they did not speak the same language?

Richard frowned. Had his father been like him once? Had his friendship with Dr. Procten truly changed him? Turned him into a different man?

Swallowing, Richard met his mother's gaze. "You find me lacking," he whispered when realisation dawned. "You disapprove of who I am since I am now as Father once was. Is that not so?"

His mother's eyes widened, and her mouth opened in a way that looked alarming. "Oh, no, Richard, you misunderstood." Placing the letter in her lap, his mother reached out both hands. They settled on his arm as it rested on the side of his chair, applying a gentle pressure that he found soothing. "Everything your father and I have always been concerned with is your happiness, whichever way you might find it." Her eyes softened, and she cast him a gentle smile before the expression on her face grew serious once more. "Still, from where I sit, I cannot deny that you look far from happy." Her gaze held his. "Or am I wrong?"

Richard inhaled a slow breath, honestly at a loss as to how to reply. "I am content," he finally said, finding his own words lacking, and yet, he could not find any that would be more fitting.

His mother inhaled a deep breath, her head nodding up and down. "I see," she mumbled, and for a second, her eyes darted to the side.

Richard had learnt over the years that it was a sign for her thoughts turning inward, remembering, contemplating, seeking to find the right words.

"You've always been so serious," she finally said, her eyes meeting his once more, a wistful smile dancing across her features. "Even as a little boy, you seemed...mature beyond your age. Claudia was different. Quite the opposite, in fact. She is the eternal child, carefree and thoughtless." His mother sighed, and Richard thought to see a hint of regret on her face. "For years, your Father and I had hoped that the two of you would find a way to...balance each other's temperaments. But I suppose you were too different in order to develop the kind of bond that often exists between siblings."

Richard sighed, wondering if his mother believed him to be at fault for this. If he had been more compassionate, would he have been able to have a closer relationship with his sister? Would he have been able to influence her in a way to prevent her current predicament?

"Although from what I was told your father was never as serious as a boy as you were," his mother continued, "he often saw similarities between the two of you. He recognised the way you sometimes looked at the world, judging it in such a rational way, seeing it only in black and white, right or wrong, that he...worried about your happiness."

Richard's jaw clenched painfully as disappointment swept through him. "He did not like who I was," he hissed, unable to better conceal his anger. "He hid it well though." Richard scoffed. "Or perhaps he did not. Not from those able to relate to others, but merely from me because I have a heart of ice, unfeeling and cold. Is that not what they say?" Bitterness clawed at his insides, and he jerked to his feet, starting to pace the length of the room. "I never would have thought my own father saw me the same way they do. I am such a fool!"

"Nonsense!" Shooting to her feet, his mother crossed over to him, effectively blocking his path, as she seized his hands, refusing to release them when he tried to tug them away. "Look at me," she demanded, her gaze wide open and compelling.

Sighing, Richard lifted his eyes to his mother's, afraid to see further disappointment there.

"You are not a fool," she told him, her voice steady and determined as though she spoke of a fact, something she knew to be true. "Nor are you cold-hearted. Yes, you have a weakness, but so do we all. Your sister could do well to think before acting upon her heart's desires. Your father disliked confrontations and often rather took a step back than forward. And I...I allowed him to be my whole world," she swallowed, her voice slightly choked, "and when he passed, I could not hold myself upright."

Staring at his mother, Richard felt some of the strain leave his body. Was it truly not only him? Did others have weaknesses similar to the one he saw in himself?

Her hands squeezed his. "You see, we all have our faults. Faults that threaten our happiness. Faults that make us vulnerable. Faults that require another's support. It's nothing to be ashamed of, my son. Believe me, I do not dislike the man you are. I only wish you were happier." Brushing a hand over his cheek, she smiled up at him. "Is that not my right as your mother to do what I can to see my son happy? Was that not your father's right also?"

A frown drew down Richard's brows as his mother's words echoed in his mind. Although he was rarely able to read between the lines, there had been something in the way her voice had hitched when she had said, *to do what I can.* "What have you done?" Richard whispered, a chill crawling down his spine as he saw his mother avert her gaze. "What else don't I know?"

For a moment, his mother closed her eyes before she sought his gaze once more. "About a decade ago, your father and Dr. Procten came to an agreement."

"An agreement? What agreement?" How was it that he did not know? After his father had died, Richard had taken over the estate and all of his father's assets. He had spent hours familiarising himself with his new duties, determined to make his father proud and continue his legacy as best as he could. Never had he found anything referring to an agreement between his father and Dr. Procten.

Richard was about to ask, voice his doubts, when he took note of his mother's gaze as it swept back to the chairs they had vacated moments before. There on the cushion lay the crumpled letter she had held upon entering his study.

"What is this?" Richard demanded, his voice hard as a cold chill spread through his body at the realisation that he had been kept in the dark.

His mother sighed as she walked back and retrieved the letter. "Your father wrote this years ago," she told him, her voice suddenly weak as though all strength had left her. "He could never find the right words and so he re-wrote this letter again and again until I took it from him. I told him you would understand even if he worded it poorly." A faint smile curved up her lips. "After all, you're his son." Then she extended her arm, holding the letter out to him.

Gritting his teeth, Richard swallowed, his eyes fixed on the envelope. His heart thudded in his chest, and for a moment, he was uncertain if he even wanted to read it. These were his father's last words to him. As long as he did not read them, there was still something left of him. Something that did not solely live in the past but could be carried into the future. Deep down, a small part of Richard wanted to lock the letter away as it was, unread and untouched, in order to keep his father's memory close. As though he were still here.

At least, a part of him.

Still, Richard could not for his father had wanted him to know whatever it was that he had written in this letter, and despite his own resentment toward the situation he suddenly found himself in, Richard could not bring himself to disappoint his father. Not even now.

Inhaling a deep breath, he slowly extended his arm and took the envelope from his mother. Then he stepped around his desk, needing a bit of distance, and sat down in his leather armchair. With a last sigh, he broke the seal, took out the parchment and unfolded it, his hands trembling as they never had before.

My dearest son,

I beg your forgiveness for this letter as I have no doubt that it falls far short of the explanation you deserve. I can only hope that you are able to make sense of the words I chose to convey this message.

Every day I watch as you become a young man I am proud to call my son. I see kindness and strength in you, and it gives me joy to see you come into your own. I have no doubt that you will do right by your family and ensure their well-being even before your own.

Still, every day I see traces of the man I used to be in the way your eyes look out at the world. I'm glad to say that you're by far more observant and honest than I used to be, but I cannot deny that I see something in your eyes that gives me reason for concern. Please, do not ever think that I am disappointed in the man you are becoming, for it could not be further from the truth. You possess all the qualities of a gentleman, and your conduct is beyond reproach.

What concerns me is the absence of happiness I see on your face. You only see duty and obligation, commitment and devotion, and I fear that you will never know the truest joys the world has to offer. I have tried but failed to open your eyes to them, and so I did the only thing I am still hoping might make a difference.

For me, it was Josiah Procten who made that difference. His selflessness and compassion have brought great joy to my life and turned me into a man worthy of your mother. Without his counsel, I might never have understood how fortunate I was to have met her and how dark my life would have been without her. He helped me see past superficial attributes and to the core of what is important in life. To this day, I value his friendship and loathe to think of the man I would be today if it had not been for him.

A few weeks ago, Josiah visited Farnworth Manor with his young daughter Evelyn. She is a delightful child, and I could not help but notice the way she looked out at the world with utter joy and an open heart. Being raised by a man like Josiah, I have no doubt that she will grow up to be an impressive, young woman.

A woman who might be able to do for you what Josiah did for me.

My old friend and I have come to an agreement as he, too, is concerned for his child's happiness. Even as young as she is, Miss Procten shows the same talent for healing that her father always possessed, and I have no doubt that she will follow in her father's footsteps. Understandably, Josiah worries about her future for the world might not yet be ready to accept a female doctor into its midst and pay her the respect she deserves.

In discussing our fears for our children's future, we came to realise that you and young Miss Procten might benefit from a union. You are two halves of a whole. Whereas you, my son, are the rational and strategic side, she is guided by compassion and empathy. Together, you might help each other grow beyond your own limits. We pray it will be thus.

Therefore, Josiah and I have agreed that the two of you are to marry upon Miss Procten's coming of age. While you might disagree with my decision, I can only urge you to honour it. Believe me, my son, there are more important triumphs in life than title and reputation, fortune and standing. In the end, happiness is based on love and family for those are the things that will make a man far happier than anything else the world has to offer. Put aside your objections for I know them only too well as they once were mine as well. Still, I never regretted opening my mind, and I urge you to do the same. Heed this agreement, Richard, and be good to Evelyn.

I have no doubt she will be good to you as well.

. . .

Your loving father

When Richard first put down the letter, his mind was reeling so fast he could not have told up from down. Staring at his father's handwriting, Richard momentarily believed himself to have strayed into a dream for this could not possibly be true.

None of it.

While his father's assurances that he had never found his son to be lacking had eased the ache in Richard's heart, he found the words on the page begin to dance before his eyes when he continued on to read about his father's agreement with Dr. Procten.

Evelyn.

Her name echoed in his mind, bringing back the memory of the day he had kissed her. It had been impulsive, irrational and so very wrong, and yet, he could not stop thinking about it.

About her.

Only too well did Richard recall his utter shock when he had thought her betrothed to Mr. Bragg. Oh, how he had loathed the man…and envied him if he were honest with himself. Also, he recalled the relief that had flooded him upon learning that it wasn't true.

Still, it had made no sense. After all, they were not suitable for one another, and therefore, a union between them would be impossible. Or so Richard had told himself again and again.

And now, he saw his father's words before him in black and white, telling him the opposite. Was his father right? Ought Richard to heed his father's advice and disregard all objections to the contrary?

Leaning back, Richard drew in a long breath, unable to think a clear thought. Certainly, it would be wrong of him to decide now in this moment when his faculties were impaired by the shock of this discovery. Yes, he ought to give himself some time and consider this proposition from all angles lest he make a mistake that could not be undone.

"Are you all right?"

Blinking, Richard lifted his gaze to his mother, who stood on the other side of his desk, her hands clutched together as she looked at him with tension marking her features. "You look pale," she observed, her eyes studying his face as though she feared he might faint.

Richard scoffed, "This came as quite a shock to me," he said, gesturing toward the letter on his desk. "And that in turn cannot be a shock to you, dear Mother?"

"Of course not." For a moment, she fell silent before her lips moved, her mouth opening and then closing, the words stuck in her throat. "Will you...? What will you do?" she finally asked, her gaze darting back and forth between him and his father's letter.

Sighing, Richard shook his head. "I honestly don't know." His gaze fell to his father's handwriting once more before he looked up and met his mother's eyes. "Why did I not know about this? Why are you informing me of this now? Today?" He frowned. "If I'm not mistaken," he swallowed before speaking her name, "Miss Procten is already of age."

His mother nodded, wringing her hands. "We meant to tell you. That was why your father wrote these letters to help him find the right words. Still, the right moment wouldn't come, and in the end, we decided to wait until Miss Procten was of age. But then..."

Richard swallowed. "Father died."

His mother nodded, tears misting her eyes. "He fell ill, and all our thoughts were for him," she whispered, her voice breaking. "And then when he died, my heart and mind were elsewhere. I'm sorry, my son, for not speaking to you of this sooner."

Richard nodded. "I quite understand, Mother." His gaze drifted to the window. "Does she know?"

His mother shook her head. "I spoke to her father before I came to you because Mr. Bragg told us that—" She flinched when Richard abruptly shot to his feet, the legs of his chair scraping over the floor as it was pushed back.

Growling a curse under his breath, Richard felt his hands ball into fists, and he pictured them raining down on the loathsome man. How dare he spread such lies? How dare he think he had any claim on Evelyn?

She's mine, Richard's traitorous heart whispered as his legs carried him over to the window. The snow still swirled through the air, and yet, within seconds his gaze locked on the hooded figure standing down below.

As she stood on the small slope near the pond, her cloak billowed in the wind, and he could see that her hands held on tightly to the soft fabric. Strands of her warm, brown tresses fluttered in the strong breeze and she held her head slightly bowed to shield her face.

For a long time, Richard simply stood by the window, gazing out at the woman whom his father had chosen as his wife. Still, his heart and mind warred over what was to be done, what decision was to be made when suddenly a strong gust of wind ripped off her hood.

Startled, she spun around, her hands eagerly seeking to pull the hood back over her head. For a long moment, Richard was able to gaze at her beautiful face, her cheeks rosy from the cold and her dark curls dancing around her head.

She's mine, his heart screamed at him, and for a small eternity, Richard was deaf to the objections his rational mind put forth. His father's words echoed in his mind though, reminding him why she had been chosen.

Had it not been for the simple reason that his father had hoped that she would change him, that she would teach him how to balance his heart and mind, that she would help him feel rather than think?

Richard frowned. Had she not already begun to do so?

Again, he became aware of his heart thudding in his chest...as though it had awakened after a long slumber.

Well then, the only question was: would he allow her to continue? Or would he send her away, retreating into a world made safe and clear because of guidelines and rules? Because of facts and rational thought?

Or was he daring enough to leave the safe haven his life had been and plunge ahead into the unknown?

Chapter Twelve

THE LONG REACH OF THE PAST

Inhaling a deep breath of the chilled air, Evelyn glanced at the silent woman beside her.

Like Evelyn, Miss Davenport was bundled up warmly, her hands protected from the piercing wind by a muff as she slowly walked down the garden path, her feet leaving soft prints in the fresh snow. It was a beautiful day, for despite the cold, the sun shone brilliantly, reflecting in the pure, white snow.

Yet, unlike Evelyn, Miss Davenport seemed to be blind to the beauty around her. Mostly she kept her eyes downcast, and even when they would occasionally sweep over the world around her, it seemed that they saw nothing at all.

Over the past week, Evelyn had all but dragged her charge outside, hoping that the fresh air and exercise would do her some good. However, while her body seemed to relish the gifts offered to it, her mind and heart remained subdued. Sadness clung to her so acutely that Evelyn began to fear Miss Davenport's melancholy would never surrender.

On her own, with only her mother and Evelyn to keep her company, Miss Davenport seemed like a mere shadow of the vivacious, young woman she had once been. Would she ever be able to reclaim her smile? Evelyn wondered, contemplating what exactly it was that had put the young woman into such a subdued state. Was it merely the lack of diversion she had complained about so vehemently before? Or was it the thought of giving away her child as her pregnancy advanced? Or was the burden of not knowing what had happened to her in Scotland too much for her to bear?

Evelyn sighed. It could be any of them, or even all of them together.

After a long time of silence, with nothing but the sound of snow crunching beneath their feet, Evelyn placed a gentle hand on Miss Davenport's arm, stilling her progress. "I wish you would speak to me," she said gently, her eyes watching the young woman's face carefully. "What is it that haunts you? For it is clear that something does." She nodded encouragingly when Miss Davenport cautiously lifted her gaze. "Please. I promise I will not breathe a word to anyone if that is what you wish."

Miss Davenport heaved a long, sorrow-filled sigh, and the eerie stillness left her face as she looked at Evelyn. "I keep trying to remember," she finally said, a sudden need to speak in her eyes as though she had remained silent for too long, "but there is nothing there." Gritting her teeth in angry disappointment, she drew in a long breath. "At least nothing tangible."

For a long moment, Miss Davenport's gaze remained on Evelyn's, and yet, her thoughts seemed to be miles away. Then she turned and continued farther down the path. "I dream of it sometimes," she whispered as though to herself, and Evelyn hastened to catch up with her. "Or at least I think I do, for when I wake up, my dreams retreat so quickly that I cannot hold on to them. I cannot grasp them. They're gone before I'm fully awake, and yet, I cannot help but feel that I dreamed of...that which I cannot remember." Her feet stilled, and she turned to look at Evelyn, a tentative smile in the gentle curl of her lips. "Sometimes I hear him whisper to me."

"Him?" Evelyn enquired, hopeful that perhaps Miss Davenport's memories could be recovered after all.

Sighing, the young woman shrugged. "I don't know who he is, or if he is even real. Believe me, I've contemplated the possibility that he is a mere figment of my imagination, drawn upon to fill the void that seems to rob me of everything I am." Scoffing, she shook her head, a tiny spark flashing in her eyes. "I know that I'm not myself. I know that you all are worried about me, and I'm sorry to cause you all such trouble."

"Do not concern yours—"

"A part of me wishes to remember," Miss Davenport continued, quite unaware that Evelyn had spoken, which Evelyn took to mean that her old self was re-emerging. It was a start. "Not knowing is torture. Still, I cannot help but wonder if it is for the best." Her eyes met Evelyn's and held them with an almost painful intensity. "What if what I don't remember is so awful that once I do remember, I wish I could forget? What if this...dream is simply a way to keep me from digging deeper? Something to shield me from the truth?" She sighed, and her gaze dropped from Evelyn's. "Perhaps he is merely a figment of my imagination. Perhaps I ought to be grateful for that. Perhaps I should not try to remember."

Seeing the misery on the young woman's face, Evelyn reached out and grasped her hands through the thick muff. "You said you hear him whisper to you," she said, holding Miss Davenport's gaze. "What does he say?"

"I don't know," the young woman whispered, utter disappointment darkening her eyes. "I can't make out the words. All I can tell is that they have a strange lilt to them and that they feel as though they're..." She swallowed, hesitating.

"They're what?" Evelyn urged, wondering if the strange lilt came from a Scottish accent. After all, whatever had happened to Miss Davenport had happened in Gretna Green. Scotland.

A slight blush came to Miss Davenport's cheeks, and she could not quite suppress the enchanted smile that forced its way up to the surface. "Endearments. As though they're endearments."

Gently squeezing Miss Davenport's hands, Evelyn returned her smile. "Do you think he was someone you cared about?"

The young woman shrugged; her eyes going wide as her mouth opened, groping for words. "I cannot say. How could he be though? If he is indeed real, then I must have met him there that night after

William had returned home with his brother. And then the next morning, my own brother discovered me in the room William had procured for us before we had been discovered." Staring at Evelyn, she shook her head. "It was one night. One night. How can he be someone I care about?" She sighed, and all strength left her body. "And if he is real, where is he? If he truly cared about me, why would he have left me alone?"

"I don't know," Evelyn whispered, her hand tightening on Miss Davenport's once more, urging her to look at her. "But I do believe that not knowing is worse than anything else for it will haunt you for the rest of your life. You will always be left wondering, trying to remember, asking questions there are no answers to. You will never be at peace."

Miss Davenport nodded. "I do believe you're right," she whispered, her voice weak, "but I cannot help but fear what I don't know."

"In your dreams, do you feel safe, at peace?"

Miss Davenport hesitated, her gaze turning inward as she recalled the moments of her waking when her dreams had slipped from her grasp. Then she nodded. "I do, yes. I feel safe. I feel...loved."

Evelyn smiled. "That's good. For even if what you see in your dreams is not exactly what happened, I do believe that the feelings associated with it are not a figment of your imagination. They're real. They're a clue to how you felt in that moment...even if your conscious mind cannot recall what happened."

A relieved glow came to Miss Davenport's gaze. "Do you truly believe that?"

Evelyn nodded, herself relieved to see her charge's spirits lifted. "With all my heart. Our mind might forget, but deep down, nothing is ever lost."

Miss Davenport heaved a deep sigh. "So, you think I should try to remember?"

Evelyn nodded. "Do not pressure yourself. Do what you can and try to hold on to as much of your dreams as possible. Perhaps over time, you'll receive some answers."

"I will," Miss Davenport mumbled almost breathlessly. "Thank you."

Evelyn could only hope that one day Miss Davenport would find out what had happened and that the answer might lead her to a happy life, perhaps even to a man who cared about her. Perhaps she ought to urge Lord Ashwood to have someone look into what happened in Gretna Green. Perhaps a Bow Street runner could find out more details. Certainly, it would be a risk; however, it might be worth it. After all, Miss Davenport's peace of mind depended on it.

Before Evelyn could open her mouth to suggest such a course of action though, she caught sight of Lady Ashwood striding toward them. The woman's pale eyes swept over them, only to narrow when they fell on her daughter's smiling face. For a moment, Lady Ashwood seemed stunned, shocked almost witless, before her mouth curved up into an equally relieved smile. "Here, you are," she beamed, rushing toward her daughter. "I'm glad to see you so well." Gently, she brushed a hand over Miss Davenport's cheek, her eyes shining as she looked at her child.

Touched by the way mother and daughter gazed at one another, Evelyn took a step back. "If you'll excuse me," she mumbled, wanting to give them a moment alone.

"Wait," Lady Ashwood said, turning to look at Evelyn. "My son wishes to speak to you. You'll find him in his study."

Evelyn nodded, confused about this sudden development. Ever since he had called on Mr. Bragg to see to his sister, Lord Ashwood had avoided her as though on principle. Not unlike he had after the day he had kissed her. What could he want now?

After changing out of her heavy cloak and sodden boots, Evelyn once more approached the heavy oak door behind which Lord Ashwood sat awaiting her. Upon her knock, he bid her to enter.

Once again, Evelyn's heart thudded loudly in her chest as she stepped over the threshold. Every step that carried her closer to him seemed to unhinge her more, and she cursed herself for allowing him to affect her thus. After all, he was only a man. A most insufferable man at that. There was nothing special about him. He had ordinary looks. An ordinary smile. Ordinary–

The moment his dark grey eyes met hers, a shiver went down Evelyn's back and all the way down to her toes, and she knew her words to be lies. While he may be insufferable, and he certainly had a talent for upsetting her, there was nothing ordinary about him.

His presence took in the entire room, and she could feel it like a caress on her skin. He stood tall, his head held high and his eyes watchful. Always watchful, as though he feared to miss something that was right in front of him. Although he rarely smiled, there was kindness in his eyes, as well as honesty. Never had he seemed conceited as though he held something back, as though he had an alternate agenda he tried to hide. Although Evelyn often disliked what he said, he never seemed to weigh his words, always speaking his mind.

And there was something deeply intimate about the way he sometimes looked at her as though their bond was far deeper than what the circumstances of their situation dictated.

"Miss Procten," he greeted her as she closed the door, his voice even, polite, and yet, his gaze swept over her as though he could not bring himself to look away. "Thank you for coming."

"Certainly," Evelyn croaked, then cleared her throat, trying to appear unaffected. Lifting her gaze, she forced herself to look at him, wondering what he wished to talk to her about.

Lord Ashwood, however, merely stood behind his desk as the silence between them stretched on. His gaze held hers, and although he said not a word, his mind seemed to be overflowing with unexpressed thoughts. Now and then, his jaw would tense, and his lips press together as though something had angered him. Then he began pacing up and down the floor, occasionally casting a glance in her direction that had Evelyn's senses reeling. What was going on?

"Is something wrong, my lord?" she finally asked, unable to bear the suspension any longer. Judging from the look on his face, something was horribly wrong. Never before had she seen him so at odds about what to say or do. He seemed completely at a loss, torn, as though his world had been turned upside down.

It frightened her to see him lose control thus.

Finally, he stopped beside his desk and picked up a parchment. For a long moment, his eyes seemed to trace the words written there before he looked up and strode toward her. "Here," he said, holding out the letter to her. "Read this."

Confused, Evelyn stared up at him, then slowly extended her hand and took the offered letter. For a short moment, they both held on to one side of the parchment, their eyes locked, before Lord Ashwood stepped back, releasing his hold, and returned to his seat behind the large desk.

With trembling hands, Evelyn dropped her gaze, unable to shake the feeling of foreboding that had come over her upon seeing Lord Ashwood's odd behaviour. Her eyes sought the words written on the page, and her heart skipped a beat when she realised it was a letter from his father, the late Lord Ashwood. Lifting her head, Evelyn looked at the young lord and found him looking back at her, his eyes watchful as always. "Are you certain you wish for me to read this?" she asked, wondering what reason there could be for him to want her to read such a private missive. "It seems rather personal."

"Read," was all he said, his gaze not wavering from hers.

Nodding, Evelyn once more dropped her eyes to the page, a sense of unease encroaching upon her as she began to read.

My dearest son,

I beg your forgiveness for this letter as I have no doubt that it falls far short...

...I see kindness and strength in you, and it gives me joy to see you come into your own...

Evelyn could not help but smile as she read his father's words. Although it felt intrusive for her to read them, she could not deny that they were true. Had she not thought the very same thing a moment ago? Or rather *admitted* it to herself a moment ago?

...I see something in your eyes that gives me reason for concern. Please, do not ever think that I am disappointed in the man you are becoming...

...What concerns me is the absence of happiness I see on your face. You only

see duty and obligation, commitment and devotion, and I fear that you will never know the truest joys the world has to offer...

...For me, it was Josiah Procten who made that difference. His selflessness and compassion have brought great joy to my life...

Evelyn's heart rejoiced at seeing her father's friendship thus appreciated. Always had he spoken with deep affection about his old friend, and she herself had fond memories of the late viscount. He had been a good man, and his death had grieved her.

Still, she wondered why Lord Ashwood would want her to read this letter.

...A few weeks ago, Josiah visited Farnworth Manor with his young daughter Evelyn...

...Being raised by a man like Josiah, I have no doubt that she will grow up to be an impressive, young woman...

Although the late viscount had always been kind to her, Evelyn would never have thought that he had held her in such high regard.

...A woman who might be able to do for you what Josiah did for me...

Here, Evelyn stopped, a frown creasing her forehead, before she chanced a glance at the man behind the desk.

With his hands folded and resting on the top of his desk, Lord Ashwood watched her. His gaze was still as was the rest of him. Almost painfully still, as though every muscle in his body was taut with anticipation of her reaction.

With a hammering heart, Evelyn turned her gaze back to the words on the parchment.

. . .

My old friend and I have come to an agreement...

...Josiah worries about her future...

...we came to realise that you and young Miss Procten might benefit from a union–

Shock froze Evelyn's features as a gasp escaped her lips. Her head snapped up, and she stared at the man behind the desk. How could he remain so calm when she felt like succumbing to panic?

But he was not calm, was he? He merely seemed calm. However, underneath that cold and controlled exterior of his, his emotions surely boiled...like her own.

Swallowing, Evelyn stumbled backwards, her left hand reaching for the armchair she knew was positioned somewhere behind her. Still, she could not bring herself to drop her gaze, to look away from those silver-grey eyes as they held hers, allowing her to breathe, holding insanity at bay.

Only when she sank into the steadying softness of the chair did Evelyn avert her gaze, returning it to the words on the page, hoping – praying! – that she had misunderstood.

You are two halves of a whole. Whereas you, my son, are the rational and strategic side, she is guided by compassion and empathy. Together, you might help each other grow beyond your own limits. We pray it will be thus.

Bright spots began to dance before Evelyn's eyes. This could not possibly be true?

"My father never told me," she mumbled, her mind reeling with the implications of this letter. "He never told me. He never said a word."

Therefore, Josiah and I have agreed that the two of you are to marry upon Miss Procten's coming of age. While you might disagree with my decision, I can only urge you to honour it...

. . .

What? Evelyn frowned. But she was already of age? Then why–?

Realisation dawned, and her gaze lifted off the page, once more seeking the other who no doubt felt as unhinged as she did in that moment. "Your father died when…"

Holding her gaze, he nodded while the rest of him remained unchanged.

Still.

Unmoving.

…Heed this agreement, Richard, and be good to Evelyn.
I have no doubt she will be good to you as well.

Your loving father

Staring at the words before her, Evelyn was at a loss. They wanted them to marry, did they not? She had not misunderstood, had she? But how could they agree to something like this? How could they…? And without saying a word.

"You didn't know." As a mere observation, Lord Ashwood's words hung in the air, and yet, they drew Evelyn from the stupor that had engulfed her.

Lifting her head, she met his eyes. "I did not," she whispered, shaking her head. Then all of a sudden, she surged to her feet. "Did you?"

Scoffing, Lord Ashwood rose from his chair as well. "Not until a few days ago," he admitted, crossing the room to stand in front of her. "Not until my mother brought me this letter."

Trying her best to ignore his close proximity, Evelyn could barely think. "Why now? Why not before? Why…?"

Lord Ashwood's features seemed to harden as though a sudden anger had seized him. "Because Mr. Bragg was kind enough to inform her of his betrothal with you."

"He…?" Slowly, Evelyn closed her eyes, unable to believe that such an egotistical exaggeration could have brought forth such a life-changing decision. What ought they to do? They could not possibly marry, could they?

Opening her eyes, Evelyn could not deny that as she looked into Lord Ashwood's eyes, her first thoughts were of his lips on her own and his arms holding her tightly.

As though he had read her mind, his gaze grew heated and he took a step toward her. "What do you wish to do?" he asked simply, and for a short moment, it seemed *he* knew exactly what he wanted.

The realisation made Evelyn shrink back, overwhelmed and completely torn between a sudden desire to comply with their fathers' wishes and the knowledge that it would be wrong to do so. After all, they did not suit. They were like fire and water, day and night. Was that not what his father had said also? Was that not why he wanted them to marry so they could...change each other? Bring each other...happiness?

Evelyn swallowed. Was that even possible? Would they not rather claw each other's eyes out? Live in misery as neither one of them could truly understand the other?

And what of social as well as professional repercussions?

Shaking her head, Evelyn hardened her heart. No, nothing good could come of this. It was paramount that she put a stop to this.

Immediately.

Before she could be tempted to–

"Do you truly care for what I want, my lord?" she said in as harsh a tone as she could conjure.

Her cruel abrasiveness did not miss its mark, and she watched with a heavy heart as Lord Ashwood's face grew hard. All tenderness and care she had glimpsed there before vanished, replaced by a cold and indignant mask. His jaw clenched, and his lips pressed into a thin line as though he fought to hold back the myriad of curses he wished to hurl at her head.

Despite a strong sense of guilt, Evelyn marvelled at the thought that he might have truly wished to marry her. Could he have? But why on earth would he want to? After all, a union between them was far from reasonable, no matter the argument his father had brought forth.

Before either of them could say more, a knock sounded on the door, jarring them both out of the paralysis that seemed to have come over them.

"Enter!" Lord Ashwood growled, his eyes never veering from hers.

Unaware of the tension in the room, Mr. Bragg stepped inside, a frown coming to his face as he took note of them standing almost head to head, glaring at one another. "Is something wrong?"

Inhaling loudly, Lord Ashwood finally broke their contact, his gaze lifting to meet Mr. Bragg's, an angry snarl still planted firmly on his face. "Nothing that concerns you," he snapped, then seemed to realise his rudeness and briefly closed his eyes in order to compose himself. "What can I do for you?" he then asked with forced politeness, stepping closer to his desk.

Clearing his throat, Mr. Bragg failed at hiding his curiosity as his gaze continued to study them. Nevertheless, he managed to speak with a certain fluidity. "I am here to inform you that Dr. Procten has sufficiently recovered and wishes to return home." His gaze, hard and somewhat challenging, met Evelyn's. "I agree with his desire to depart as soon as possible as the peace and quiet of his own home will do him good."

Evelyn could have slapped him for his overbearing attitude as though he knew best how to take care of her father. Not that he truly cared. This was nothing less than a struggle for dominance, for power over her. He wanted her to know that he was the one in charge.

Even if she had not been certain before, this proved to Evelyn once and for all that she could never marry Mr. Bragg...no matter what the consequences.

What of Lord Ashwood? A traitorous voice whispered.

"I assure you, my lord," Mr. Bragg continued, his face now bearing a polite expression as he spoke to Lord Ashwood, "that I shall return as needed to see to your sister and assure her well-being and swift recovery."

Lord Ashwood nodded in acknowledgement to Mr. Bragg's words. His gaze, however, never left Evelyn's face, and she felt the full weight of his stare all the way to her toes.

In answer, her heartbeat quickened once more, and she could

barely keep herself from averting her eyes, afraid he would see it as a sign of weakness, but equally fearing he might read her feelings for him on her face.

Never had Evelyn felt so insecure about who she was and what she wanted. Always had she stood tall, demanding to be heard. What had happened to her? Was this what love did to people? Robbed them of everything that made them who they were?

Love? That traitorous voice whispered once more.

Evelyn froze, and her eyes widened as she realised the implications of her thoughts. No, this could not be! This was impossible! After all, she was far too rational to allow herself to lose her heart to...

Her gaze lifted on its own, and she found Lord Ashwood's eyes still fixed on her, a slight frown on his features as he watched her. Could he tell the direction of her thoughts? Did he now know that...?

"Are you all right?" he asked, his voice gentler than it had been before. There was barely a touch of latent anger in it. Mostly, it held concern.

Lord Ashwood's gaze roamed her face as he stepped toward her, completely ignoring Mr. Bragg. "Are you well? You seem pale. Perhaps you should sit—"

Evelyn shrank back as he approached, his hand held out to her in offer of assistance, nothing more—she told herself. Still, his nearness once more threatened to overwhelm her good sense, and she could not allow that to happen. "I'm fine," she finally managed to articulate, her voice sounding harsh even to her own ears.

Stepping toward Mr. Bragg—the far safer option at the moment—Evelyn hesitated when she realised she was still holding Lord Ashwood's letter in her hand. Reluctantly, she turned back, forcing her gaze to remain steady as it met his. Then her arm extended, holding out the letter. "I believe this is yours."

Lord Ashwood inhaled a torturously slow breath, his nostrils flaring as he fixed her with a hard stare. "Not only the letter is mine," he said, his voice quiet, and yet, almost threatening...at least to Evelyn's resolve for she very well understood the meaning behind those seemingly unremarkable words.

She needed to leave.

Now.

After a hastily mumbled goodbye, Evelyn fled down the corridor, determined to lose Mr. Bragg before he could attempt to catch up with her. Her feet moved, and yet, her mind never saw the floor below them or the way ahead. All it saw were those dark grey eyes looking into hers.

Tempting her.

Her heart.

Her resolve.

Gritting her teeth, Evelyn surged onward as though outrunning Mr. Bragg would somehow put everything to rights. Of course, it wouldn't. That was nonsense! Evelyn knew that, and yet, her feet wouldn't slow down.

"Is something wrong?"

Jarring to a halt at her father's voice, Evelyn stared at his face. Her breath came in pants, and her heart hammered in her chest as her eyes swept over her father's good-natured and at present slightly concerned face.

"Why are you running?" he enquired as he closed the door to the chamber he had occupied during his recovery at Farnworth Manor. "Is something wrong?" he repeated, the tone in his voice becoming more urgent. "Is it Miss Davenport?"

Evelyn swallowed. "No, she's fine." Still staring at her father, she still could not believe that this man, the man who had been there for her all her life, had agreed to give her hand in marriage without ever even mentioning it to her. "I..." Her voice broke off, and she shook her head. "A part of me cannot believe it's true."

For a brief moment, her father's eyes narrowed before a note of understanding came to his face. "You know," he whispered as though he couldn't find the right words, either. "I suspected as much when Lady Dashwood came to speak to me."

A puzzle piece fell into place, and Evelyn nodded. "That's what she came to speak to you about," Evelyn mumbled, slowly feeling the numbness leave her mind. Her gaze cleared, and her eyes turned to her father. "How could you? You never said a thing. Never. Not a word. How could you?"

The left corner of her father's mouth curved upward. "Are you angry because of the agreement? Or because I never mentioned it to you?"

Evelyn glared at him. "Don't you dare jest at a time like this?" She heaved a deep sigh. "Both."

"I see," her father mumbled. "What do you intend to do?"

Evelyn threw up her hands. "Do? Nothing." Her eyes narrowed. "You do not intend to insist upon it, do you? You do not truly want us to marry?" For a moment, Evelyn felt her heart stop, and she wondered if she truly wanted him to say 'no'.

Stepping toward her, her father drew her trembling hands into his. "What I want does not matter," he said, his eyes gentle as they looked into hers. "What matters is what you want. Have you asked yourself that?"

Dropping her gaze, Evelyn inhaled a slow breath as a hint of panic stole up her spine. "It's not that simple, Father."

"But it should be."

Her gaze flew up. "But it isn't!" she snapped, annoyed with way her father sometimes looked at the world as though one only need to know what one wanted in order to succeed. If only life were that easy!

An indulged smile came to her father's face. "Tell yourself what you wish. However, the truth is that this is your decision. Yours and his, and no one else's." He sighed, his hands squeezing hers. "And so you must ask yourself, what do you want?"

Evelyn closed her eyes, a shuddering sigh leaving her lips. She could feel her father's hands holding hers tightly, grounding her, before they slowly fell away and she heard the sound of his receding steps.

A moment later, when she opened her eyes, he was gone.

And she was alone.

This was indeed her decision, and she would have to make it on her own.

Chapter Thirteen

ON HER TERMS

T he moment the door closed behind her–behind them! – Richard almost growled in frustration. Not until this very moment when she had all but refused him had Richard realised that he *did* want her.

Naturally, a part of him still argued against her. After all, she was far from a suitable match for a man in his position. He ought to choose a lady of noble birth, from a high-standing family. A woman who knew her place and would fulfil her role as lady of the house to his satisfaction.

Richard doubted very much that Miss Procten–Evelyn! –would ever submit to him...at least not without a fight.

Still, he could not deny that his father's words, his plea for his son to heed this agreement, meant something to him. Could he ignore such an honest and well-intended request and still call himself an honourable man?

However, it was not truly a request, was it?

No, indeed his father and Dr. Procten had agreed on it already. Which meant that if he were to refuse to marry Miss Procten, he would be going back on his father's word. He would dishonour him. Shame him and his family.

That was not the kind of man he was.

Therefore, he did not have a choice. Somehow, he needed to convince her that it would be in her best interest to agree to marry him.

Richard frowned, wondering what had made her refuse him. Indeed, if he was not mistaken—and it was not unlikely that he was—she had seemed almost frightened at the thought of tying herself to him.

Never would Richard have expected such a reaction. Certainly, he would never have thought her overjoyed at the prospect. However, this agreement was more to her benefit than to his.

After all, what girl from a simple household would ever refuse to marry a viscount? A peer of the realm?

Such a thing was unheard of, was it not? After all, what reason could she possibly have?

Frustration gave his limbs strength, and his legs carried him up and down the floor like a caged animal, restless and trapped. Richard did not know how long he paced, only that the chaos in his head riled him like never before. What was he to do? What was the right course of action?

Again, a knock sounded on his door, and his heart skipped a beat as an image of Miss Procten drifted before his inner eye. Within a few steps, he was at the door, all but yanking it open.

Disappointment engulfed him.

"Are you all right, my son?" his mother asked, her brows drawn down deeply as her gaze slid over him. "What on earth has happened? We heard Miss Procten is leaving."

As he glanced behind her, Richard took note of Dr. Procten standing off to the side, his watchful eyes taking in the scene. Why was the man here? Was he not returning home with his daughter? Was he not the reason she was leaving? Or had Mr. Bragg once more *stretched* the truth in order to remove Miss Procten from Farnworth Manor? After all, the man seemed determined to claim her for himself.

Suppressing a growl, Richard turned away and walked back into his study, unable to answer even such a simple question as the one his mother had asked. How was he to explain any of this to his mother?

He heard her and Dr. Procten step inside as well and the door closing behind them.

For a moment, silence hung about the room as he stood by the window, gazing out at the wintry landscape below.

"Will you simply allow her to go?" his mother enquired after a while.

Richard sighed. After all, there was nothing simple about this. "She does not wish to marry me," he forced out through gritted teeth, taken aback at how much it pained him to admit this.

"Did you ask her?"

Turning to face his mother, Richard inhaled a slow breath, forcing himself to remain calm as he saw her brows rise in challenge. Did she truly believe he acted wrongly? That he ought to have applied himself more? After all, this had never been his idea. It had been theirs, and now they simply stood there and berated him for not following their plan.

It was maddening!

Striding past them, Richard made to leave. "I mean no offence," he said as he pulled open the door, "but I do not wish to discuss this with you."

The door was already halfway open, his foot ready to stride forward when his mother called his name. "Please, I urge you not to run from this."

Stilling his retreat, Richard sighed, hanging his head. Decorum prevented him from simply ignoring his mother and striding out the door, no matter how much he wished he could do so.

"You need to make a choice, my son," his mother pleaded, her hand coming to grasp his arm, urging him to turn and look at her. "Ask yourself what you want, not what you *think* would be *right*. I do believe that is what your father has been trying to tell you."

Reluctantly, Richard met his mother's gaze, unwilling to relinquish his anger, and yet, unable to ignore the hint of desperation in her voice.

"Follow your heart." Holding his gaze, his mother nodded at him encouragingly. "I've never seen you simply act upon your own wishes, not if they were not also reasonable conclusions." Her hands clasped his. "This once, please, do as you want."

But she does not want me!

Gritting his teeth, Richard forced the words back down. "I know I am far from observant," he hissed, terrified by his imminent loss of control, "and I'm aware that others do not suffer from this affliction." He inhaled a laboured breath, unwilling to lash out at his mother. "Can you not see that I'm furious?" Dimly, Richard was aware of Dr. Procten's presence somewhere in the room. However, in that moment, he could not bring himself to care.

At his words, his mother's face softened as though she had hoped to hear him say thus. It made no sense. "And have you asked yourself why that is?" she demanded, her gaze watchful as it held his.

Because she refused me! Because she does not want me!

"I ask you not to patronise me, Mother," he growled, unable to keep his anger from showing in his voice. "By agreeing to this plan," he glanced at Dr. Procten, "Father tied my hands, and he did not even have the courtesy to inform me thusly. Now, I am honour-bound to marry Miss Procten, a woman who is most unsuitable and who has the audacity to act as though the advantage of this arranged union is all mine. Yes, Mother, I know quite well why I'm angry."

The hint of a smile curled up his mother's mouth, and the unexpectedness of seeing it robbed Richard of his composure. What was he missing? Was she laughing about him?

"I apologise for my shocked reaction."

Richard all but flinched at the sound of Miss Procten's voice, hard and indignant, as she stepped through the open door and into the room behind him.

"However, I assure you, my lord, I never had any intention of holding you to your father's word."

Slowly, Richard turned around to face her, seeing the way her lips pressed into a thin line and her eyes glared at him as though he was the source of all her troubles. "I apologise," he said, horrified that she had heard him speak of her thus. "I had no intention of offending you."

Miss Procten scoffed, "You did not? Well, even without intending to do so, you managed quite admirably."

Behind him, Dr. Procten cleared his throat. "Perhaps we should give them a moment to talk this through."

"Quite right," Richard's mother agreed, and within a moment, he and Miss Procten were alone, her brown eyes still as fiery as they had been before.

"This was not my doing if you recall," she snapped, her arms rising and crossing in front of her chest. "You act as though I intentionally trapped you into marriage and then refused you. Is that what you think of me?" At her question, her voice seemed to lose momentum, softening as though a different emotion had overridden her anger. "Do you believe me to be so conceited? So devious?"

Richard sighed, feeling his own anger subside. "I do not." His voice was surprisingly calm as he spoke. "I assure you I do not think ill of you."

Nodding, Miss Procten inhaled a slow breath as her features lost some of their tension. "Thank you," she mumbled, and the look on her face suggested that his opinion truly mattered to her.

Still, he could not fathom why? If it did, then why would she refuse him?

Clearing her throat, Miss Procten released the tight grip her hands had had on her arms and her posture softened. "Well, then I suppose there is nothing left to say." She made to leave.

"Quite on the contrary," Richard heard himself object as his legs carried him toward her. "There is still the matter of the agreement."

Her brows drew down and her eyes narrowed as she searched his face. "I assumed you agreed that a marriage between us would surely end in disaster. Did you not yourself state that we do not suit? Why then should we uphold this ludicrous agreement?"

"Because it was agreed upon," Richard stated simply, unable to understand her objections. "Our fathers—whether we like it or not—thought it the right course of action for us. They gave their word, making it a binding contract that cannot be broken without loss of respectability."

Shaking her head, Miss Procten stared at him. "But no one even knows. Not even we did until now."

"That does not signify," Richard objected. "We know now, and I, for one, cannot in good conscience break my father's word and dishonour him thus."

Miss Procten sighed, her eyes still narrowed as though his explanations were not enough for her. "What about what we want?" she asked in a small voice, and for a split second, she dropped her gaze before it held his once more, unwavering.

Almost.

Richard frowned, at a loss once again. "I admit I do not understand your objections. One would assume that a woman like yourself would be grateful for such an offer of marriage. After all, it is by far above anything you surely ever expected to receive. Or am I mistaken?"

For a long moment, Miss Procten simply stared at him, her jaw dropping ever so slowly. Then she jerked it back up, her teeth clenching together as her hands balled into fists.

Richard sighed. Apparently, he had upset her again. If only he knew how! Had he not simply stated facts? Common knowledge?

"Indeed, you are mistaken, my lord." A snarl on her face, she stomped toward him. "Never have I wanted to be anyone's *wife*." She spat the word as though it were poison. "I am my own person, not someone's accessory. I am a doctor—whether you admit it or not—and even without a husband, I will find a way to continue my work."

Taken with the way her eyes flashed as she all but yelled at him, defending herself, Richard barely heard a word she said. Only slowly did her reasons find their way to his mind, and he remembered how she had told him that her father had intended her to be Mr. Bragg's wife to ensure that she would be able to continue her work.

It seemed being a doctor was essential to her life. Something she cherished above all else. It was odd. Especially for a woman. However, it also presented an opportunity.

"If that is so," he said, his gaze seeking hers, wishing he could be certain of what she thought, "then name your terms."

Confused, she blinked. "My terms?"

Richard nodded. "Surely, even you must see that marrying me would have numerous advantages. Quite obviously, you are not interested in those that young women usually seek. However, I assure you that there are few limitations to what a union between us could do for you." He took a step closer, noting the way her eyes moved as she considered his words. "What is it that you require in order to agree to this union? Name your terms."

Chapter Fourteen

A LADY'S PREFERENCE

And there it was.

The one reason that Evelyn had held in front of her like a shield slowly began to slip away. Was he serious? Would he truly allow her to continue her work? Would he support her instead of stand in her way?

Ever since Evelyn had read his father's letter and understood its meaning–had that only been an hour ago? – her heart and mind had been at war. Although she knew that she would never be happy without the opportunity to tend to those who needed her help, Evelyn could not deny that she *wanted* to agree to this union.

She *wanted* to marry Lord Ashwood.

She wanted *him*.

Certainly, he could be utterly insufferable. The way he often misunderstood her riled her to no ends, and he had a way of seeing only... facts, of thinking in black and white as though he had never noticed the colour grey.

Still, most of the time, it seemed that his words were a simple truth–the way he saw it–and not meant to insult her ability or her notions of what to do, how to act, what to say. Sometimes, she swore he truly did not know why he was giving offence. It was utterly baffling!

Yes, he could be insufferable, and yet, there was something infinitely gentle and caring about him. Despite his cold exterior, it was obvious how devoted he was to his family—even though he expressed this devotion in a questionable way. He undoubtedly loved them and strove to protect them however possible.

That side of him appealed to her greatly, and Evelyn wished he would reveal more of his true self to her. Perhaps if she were his wife, she would find a way to see behind his mask.

Her heart hammered at the sudden realisation that if he meant what he offered, she had no reason to refuse him. The only thing holding her back was the fear to have her heart broken, for she could not be certain how he felt or even if he felt anything at all for her. Perhaps they could indeed come to care for each other.

Or perhaps not.

It was a risk. Was she willing to take it?

"Your terms," he pressed when she remained silent, staring at him like a fool. Then all of a sudden, his features tensed. "Or would you prefer to marry Mr. Bragg?"

As though slapped, Evelyn blinked.

"He certainly could ensure that you have every opportunity to practise your skill," Lord Ashwood continued, his voice growing tauter with each word to leave his lips. "If that is all you care about, then it would seem the only question is," inhaling a slow breath, he took a step closer, "which man do you prefer? For he clearly would not refuse you." His gaze settled more deeply on hers. "Neither would I."

Overwhelmed at having her options presented to her so rationally, Evelyn could not keep her heart from overruling her mind. For once she chose to ignore the facts Lord Ashwood had laid out before her. Instead, she looked at the expectant and slightly fearful expression on his face. She took note of the way his chest rose and fell with each laboured breath. And she noticed the way he leaned toward her ever so slightly as though he wished to be closer.

As though he wanted her to agree not because he wanted to uphold his father's word, but because he wanted *her*.

Evelyn swallowed. "You," she finally whispered, delighting in the slight widening of his eyes. "I want...prefer you." Inwardly, she cursed herself for hedging behind those words. However, fear held her back. Laying her feelings bare was a risk she was not quite willing to take yet.

Lord Ashwood swallowed, astonishment marking his features before the hint of a smile danced across his face. "Good." He cleared his throat, clearly pretending to be unaffected.

It was that glimpse of vulnerability that endeared him to Evelyn.

"Does this mean you give your consent?" he asked, a measure of apprehension still on his features as though he did not dare believe his ears.

Evelyn inhaled a slow breath, willing her mind to reawaken from its temporary slumber. After all, blind trust never led anywhere good. "I do give my consent," she replied, "if you promise not to interfere in my work." She swallowed. "I will be your wife and as such," for a second, her gaze dropped to the floor, "will fulfil all my duties. However, I am also a doctor, and you must promise you will allow me to fulfil my duties in that regard as well." She inhaled a deep breath, never having been so aware of standing at a crossroad. "Well, then, what is your answer?"

A hint of disapproval hung on his features, and Evelyn knew that allowing her to be a doctor went against everything he thought right. Still, he answered without hesitation. "You have my word."

Relieved, and yet, terrified, Evelyn nodded, realising that there was not a single doubt in her mind that he would keep his word. As he had said, he was an honourable man. For once, this was to her benefit.

"Since there is no reason to delay this," Lord Ashwood continued, "I suggest having the banns read within the week. This way my sister might be able to attend before her departure to Crestwood House."

There, Evelyn thought, another subtle sign of his devotion to his family. "I have no objection," she heard herself say, her hands trembling at the thought of becoming Lord Ashwood's wife within the month. "One month," she whispered, her throat dry and her voice sounding hoarse.

His gaze met hers, deep and meaningful, and for the first time, Evelyn felt as though they were thinking the same thing, understanding each other perfectly. "One month," he echoed her words, his chest rising slowly with a deep breath.

Inevitably, the afternoon he had kissed her right here in this very room came rushing back, and Evelyn inhaled a shuddering breath. Still, she also remembered her doubts about his motivations for kissing her. Had he truly wanted to? Or had it merely been a way for him to end their argument?

Now that her own heart was invested, Evelyn could not be certain. As easy as others were to read, she failed now when it mattered most. Doubt remained, and it would torture her if she did not stomp it into the ground.

Gathering all her courage, she stepped towards him, willing herself not to drop her gaze but instead observe the way he watched her approach. His eyes trailed over her face, and his brows drew down slightly in confusion. Clearly, he could not see what was on her mind, and for once, Evelyn was grateful for it.

"There's one thing I need to...know," she whispered, "before..." Her voice trailing off, Evelyn closed the remaining distance between them. One hand reached up to cup the side of his face, and before he could react, she pushed herself up onto her toes and pulled him into a kiss.

For a moment, Lord Ashwood seemed frozen in place. Only his heart beat wildly. She could feel it hammering beneath her other hand as it rested gently on his chest.

Not unlike her own.

Then he gently returned her kiss, his lips moving against hers, as he drew her into his arms. At first, he seemed hesitant, careful not to overstep a line. However, when she did not pull back, he grew more daring. His hand traced the line of her jaw and then slipped into her hair, holding her to him.

For weeks, Evelyn had dreamed of a repetition of their first kiss, and now, as she lay in his arms, she never wanted it to stop. It felt heavenly.

Utterly right.

Even if doubts remained with regard to their compatibility, she could no longer deny that there was something between them.

Something strong.

And powerful.

And overwhelmingly sweet.

The way he cradled her in his arms said more than a thousand words ever could.

When he finally lifted his head, his eyes gazed down at her in amazement.

Delighted, Evelyn could not prevent the smile that came to her lips. "One month," she whispered rather breathlessly.

"One month," he repeated, returning her smile with one of his own.

Never before had she seen him smile.

Not like this.

Not at her.

Chapter Fifteen
UTTERLY AFFECTED

ne month.

O The words echoed in Evelyn's mind as the days began to pass. One by one.

While her father and Mr. Bragg returned to the village, Evelyn remained in order to see to Miss Davenport. As expected, her father's apprentice had been furious upon learning that she had agreed to marry Lord Ashwood. Indeed, he had been quite expressive in his anger and disappointment, and sometimes when Evelyn lay awake at night, she could still see his dark eyes shooting daggers at her as he had snarled, *You will come to regret this. A man like him would never allow his wife to do such work. You are a fool!*

Fortunately, neither Lady Ashwood nor Miss Davenport shared Mr. Bragg's sentiments on the matter and welcomed Evelyn joyfully into their family.

"I had hoped my son would come to his senses and not allow you to leave," Lady Ashwood beamed as they sat together one afternoon, discussing wedding preparations. After all, mid-December was now *less* than a month away. "Sometimes it is difficult to glimpse his true intentions as well as his motivations."

Miss Davenport laughed, "That is rather an understatement, Mother." She turned her gaze to Evelyn. "Most of the time, it seems as though he does not feel at all. He merely contemplates all options and then chooses the one that makes the most sense." She shook her head in incomprehension. "Honestly, I've often wondered if he truly does not feel or if he simply denies himself the experience."

"Claudia!" Lady Ashwood chastised her daughter. "I do not belie—"

"Whichever it is," Miss Davenport went on unperturbed. "I cannot help but feel that it is a lonely existence, would you not agree?"

Although Miss Davenport often seemed rather unfeeling in her complaints about her brother, only seeing her own misery, Evelyn saw gentle concern in the way the young woman looked at her now. It seemed whether or not she agreed with her brother, she did feel for him nonetheless.

Evelyn nodded. "It certainly would appear so. However,..." She sighed, uncertain how to put her thoughts into words. After all, Lord Ashwood and his *odd* behaviour were the foremost things on her mind at the moment, and she had thought about him a great deal. "However, I cannot help but wonder if he would agree. After all, we are not all the same. While some people find joy in music, others detest it. I wonder if he truly suppresses his own wishes, or if he simply does not possess them." As the words left her mouth, Evelyn could not help but doubt her own reasoning. More than once, she had seen deep emotions in Lord Ashwood's eyes, in the way he had looked at her. Sometimes, his face seemed contorted with the desperate attempt to hold at bay whatever it was that currently threatened to overwhelm him.

No, he was not unfeeling, not a man without wayward emotions. Rather, it seemed that his control over them was highly developed. Still, even the most restrained person would eventually lose the battle between heart and mind.

Evelyn sighed, wondering what kind of a man Lord Ashwood would be if he allowed himself to act as he wished.

"You might be right," Miss Davenport mused, her gaze distant as she clearly remembered previous disagreements with her brother. "He rarely seems affected. I often wondered why that was." Then she shook her head. "Still, I cannot believe that he feels nothing. Why then does he sometimes get upset? Do you remember how he snapped at me when I dared object to being sent to Crestwood House?" She wrinkled her upper lip in disgust. "No, someone who doesn't feel would never have acted thus and lost his temper as he did. Perhaps he is simply better at hiding how he truly feels." She shrugged. "Why ever he feels the need to do so is beyond me though."

"Perhaps now that he is getting married," Lady Ashwood began, casting a gentle smile at Evelyn, "he will see that the risk of lowering his guard is well worth it."

Evelyn momentarily averted her gaze, aware of the two sets of eyes watching her curiously, and she wondered what they truly thought of her marrying Lord Ashwood. After all, his mother was very much aware of the reason for their union. Still, the way she spoke of their wedding suggested that she believed them to be attached to one another.

Evelyn's heart skipped a beat.

Did his mother believe that her son cared for her? Could she be right? Or was it simply wishful thinking? Certainly, there was some kind of magnetism between them, but did it truly go beyond physical attraction? More than anything, Evelyn wished she knew if Lord Ashwood harboured any kind of affection for her in his heart.

For a moment, silence fell over the room as even Miss Davenport lowered her head, absentmindedly holding her tea cup in her hands, her gaze directed at the swirling liquid. Then she swallowed, and her gaze hardened as though she had come to a conclusion. "Miss Procten," she said, a hint of tension on her face, "I was wondering if you would mind accompanying me to Crestwood House when my brother decides it is time for me to leave." A hint of bitterness showed in her voice.

Evelyn's mouth fell slightly open, not having expected that. And although she cared about Miss Davenport and wished to see her well, she could not deny that the thought of being separated from her future husband for weeks at a time was not appealing at all.

"Now, don't be selfish, my dear," Lady Ashwood interfered, gently patting her daughter's knee. "I can understand your apprehension. However, I doubt Miss Procten wishes to be parted from her new husband so soon after the wedding." Casting an understanding smile at

Evelyn, Lady Ashwood turned back to her daughter. "Don't fret, my dear. I promised to accompany you, and I certainly shall. You'll see everything shall be fine."

Returning her future mother-in-law's smile gratefully, Evelyn sighed, her thoughts returning to the big event only a fortnight away. Still, the term *big event* might be a bit of an overstatement as Lord Ashwood—in order to conceal his sister's condition—had announced that he would only invite his closest childhood friend and his family. And while Evelyn was well-liked in Tamworth Village, her rather unorthodox aspirations of becoming a doctor had not brought her many true friends among the villagers. In fact, many seemed to share Mr. Bragg's opinion that such was not appropriate work for a woman, hence her difficulty in finding patients willing to allow her to treat them. Therefore, only her father would be in attendance as her only remaining family.

Answering questions about flowers and food, Evelyn still experienced a certain sense of detachedness when it came to her impending nuptials. In fact, she could almost pretend that nothing had changed whatsoever, and she was simply still at Farnworth Manor to see to Lord Ashwood's sister. Only in moments when she and her betrothed would stumble upon one another did Evelyn *feel* that she was on a path quite unlike the one she had seen in her future.

Whenever they would find themselves in the same room—be it at mealtimes or rather by coincidence—Evelyn felt his gaze on her. And although he kept his face almost expressionless, she could still see the way he seemed to breathe in more deeply when he looked at her. His eyes, though always guarded, would follow her, tracing the line of her neck or the movement of her hand as she brought the fork to her mouth.

The intensity in her future husband's gaze sent delightful tingles into every fibre of Evelyn's body, which could only be surpassed by the feel of his touch.

Strangely enough, ever since they had become betrothed, Lord Ashwood appeared to find countless, seemingly accidental opportunities to touch her. His hand in the small of her back when he escorted her to supper. Offering her his arm when strolling through the snow-covered garden alongside his mother and sister—something she had never seen him do before. His arm brushing hers as he stepped past her as though nothing had happened.

In the beginning, Evelyn had thought these occurrences accidental indeed.

However, then she began to wonder about the frequency with which they occurred. And so, she started to keep an eye out for them, acutely aware when Lord Ashwood was near, and before long, she could spot something in his eyes that spoke of intention. He drew purposefully near—at least to her eyes—his face though remained an expressionless mask as though nothing in the world could ever touch him.

Only Evelyn knew how wrong that assumption was.

One morning, she headed downstairs toward the breakfast parlour without Lady Ashwood and Miss Davenport, her eyes sweeping over the lower floor as she descended the stairs, expecting to see Lord Ashwood appear as though by coincidence. Her heart beat wildly in her chest, and she could not help but wonder at herself, at her own reaction to his mere presence. In consequence, when he failed to appear, Evelyn's spirits sank, and a wave of disappointment swept through her.

Shaking her head at her girlish infatuation, Evelyn was about to take the last step down onto the ground floor when she registered movement out of the corner of her eye. Jerking her head around as though her life depended on catching at least one glimpse of him, Evelyn promptly lost her balance. Her foot slid off the last step, and her right arm reached back, blindly grasping for the banister.

Unfortunately, it merely grasped air.

Nothing tangible.

Nothing to hold her upright.

Nothing to keep her from falling.

The air rushed from her lungs, and her stomach did a flip at the disconcerting sensation of not having steady ground under one's feet. Pinching her eyes shut and gritting her teeth in anticipation of an undoubtedly painful landing—not to mention the bruise to her pride at having it witnessed by her betrothed—Evelyn held her breath.

A sound of alarm reached her ears, and Evelyn's eyes flew open in time to see Lord Ashwood appear before her as though out of thin air. His face held concern as well as urgency as his arms reached for her, closing around her middle a moment before she would have contacted the hard wood of the stairs.

Whatever air remained now rushed from Evelyn's lungs as she sank into his arms, her gaze meeting his, unguarded and vulnerable. It was a rare moment as he pulled her back up onto her feet, his eyes never leaving hers, his arms pressing her to him as though she were still in danger of falling. "Are you all right?" he whispered, his breath touching her lips as his eyes roamed her face. They were a dark grey, warm and welcoming, and Evelyn felt her heart open to him. "Are you hurt?"

"I'm fine," she said breathlessly, remembering the last time they had stood so close, and her tongue snaked out to wet her lips.

Mesmerised, Lord Ashwood's gaze followed the movement, and his hands tightened on her back, pulling her closer into his arms. Slowly, he lowered his head to hers, his eyes returning to meet her gaze, a question in them that needed no words. And yet, he asked, "Do you object?"

Evelyn sighed, a smile coming to her lips as she saw the seriousness in his eyes. "Not at all," she whispered, her voice teasing. "After all, it is only fair."

"Fair?" Frowning, he lifted his head.

Regretting her words, Evelyn stepped closer into his embrace, willing him not to misunderstand her. Perhaps he could truly not attribute the tone in her voice to the right intention. "It is indeed. After all, it was you who initiated our first kiss, whereas, I must take responsibility for the second," she teased, the smile on her lips urging him to understand her.

He blinked, and a soft crinkle came to the corners of his lips. "That is undoubtedly true," he replied, his gaze sweeping over her face, working to make sense of the subtle nuances of her expression.

"Therefore, it is now your turn once more," Evelyn concluded, thinking that she might enjoy teaching him the fine art of teasing. Always had she taken the required knowledge to do so for granted. Perhaps she was wrong.

Still, a lack of knowledge should never be seen as a deficiency, but always as an opportunity to learn. A most enjoyable opportunity indeed.

Returning her smile with a hesitant one of his own, Lord Ashwood gently placed his mouth on hers as though he was still not certain whether she objected or not. Only when Evelyn returned his kiss did he allow some restraint to fall from him.

As he kissed her, his hands tenderly brushed over her back, then slipped up to her shoulders before his fingers trailed up the column of her neck and vanished in her hair. Never before had he touched her so intimately, so thoroughly, and a rather bold part of Evelyn regretted that their wedding night was still more than a week away.

As voices drifted down from upstairs, Evelyn felt him tense before a moment later, he broke their kiss. Blinking once or twice, he straightened, his arms around her loosening, as the tender emotions she had seen there before slowly retreated as though they had never been. Then he took a step back and politely offered her his arm to escort her to the breakfast parlour.

Smiling, Evelyn slipped her arm through his. Although she could not deny that she felt a tinge of disappointment, she revelled at the thought that she had persuaded him to drop his mask.

If only for a moment.

Chapter Sixteen
TREACHEROUS WEATHER

O nce again, days passed, and the weather grew ever colder. Christmas was on the horizon, and so the inside of Farnworth Manor received a festive decoration.

Decorated evergreen boughs hung in archways and above windows, their fresh pine smell adding to the warmth that hung about the place as the fires in the hearths in the commonly used rooms downstairs seemed to be burning continually. Freshly baked pastries lent their own aroma, creating a wonderful contrast to the white landscape outside.

"It's so beautiful," Miss Davenport exclaimed as she and Evelyn walked through the gardens arm in arm. "Have you ever seen so much snow at once?" Smiling brightly, she laughed, then stuck out her tongue like a child to catch one of the elusive flakes.

As the day of Evelyn's wedding approached and with it the arrival of their guests, Miss Davenport's spirits began to improve. Clearly, the woman was starved for company, dissatisfied with only having her mother and future sister-in-law to talk to.

"I cannot wait to see her again," Miss Davenport suddenly exclaimed as though she could not imagine that Evelyn was at a loss as to whom she was referring to. "It has been quite a while. Not since

Lord Weston whisked her off to Gretna Green, robbing me of my companion." She huffed as though she still held this deed against him.

"Oh, you mean Miss Ferris," Evelyn exclaimed, remembering the young woman who had been found in the road not far from Farnworth Manor last year. She had been mildly injured and could not recall who she was. Lord Ashwood had taken her in and asked Evelyn's father to see to her when he had been at Farnworth Manor to tend to his old friend's widow after her husband's death. Evelyn, too, had met her once or twice, remembering the somewhat timid-looking, young woman.

As far as she remembered, Miss Ferris had become Miss Davenport's companion as she had nowhere to go, and Miss Davenport had been starved for company—something that seemed to occur on a regular basis. Then, not long after, an old friend of Lord Ashwood's—apparently the same friend now invited to her wedding—had stopped by for a visit and taken a liking to the young woman. Not long after, they had gone off to Gretna Green.

Frowning, Evelyn glanced at Miss Davenport. "May I ask? Might their story have been somewhat of an inspiration to you?"

Looking a bit bashful, Miss Davenport sighed, "I know it was foolish to run off with William. Still, I could not help thinking about her and how she'd found love so unexpectedly. I thought if I were only to take a risk, I might be equally rewarded."

Hugging Miss Davenport a bit tighter to her side, Evelyn smiled at her, thinking of her own risk and the fervent hope that it would lead her to happiness instead of misery. "I quite understand," she assured her friend. "Sometimes it is not easy to determine what the right course of action would be."

Miss Davenport scoffed, turning slightly widened eyes to her. "You sound like my brother," she observed. "Now, that's rather alarming."

Evelyn laughed, "As much as you dislike his attitude toward this… matter," she replied, wondering when she had come to agree with him, "you cannot deny that he is not wrong. That sometimes it is wise to think things through before acting."

Miss Davenport sighed rather theatrically, "I never said otherwise.

However, I believe it is equally important to simply follow one's heart every once in a while."

"That is certainly true," Evelyn agreed, hopeful that the young woman was slowly coming to see reason. "Then perhaps the two of you ought to meet in the middle. Perhaps you could learn from each other."

Miss Davenport laughed, "For that to work, I believe we are both lacking something rather significant."

"What is that?"

"The willingness to change." Shaking her head, Miss Davenport sighed, "Honestly, I want to live in a world where I can make mistakes because deep down I don't want to be careful all the time. I want to do as my heart urges me to do, and if it goes horribly wrong," she inhaled a shuddering breath, her right hand slowly skimming over the slight bump under her dress, "then so be it." Her blue eyes turned to Evelyn. "I don't want to live my life always wondering what it would have felt like if I had followed my heart."

Evelyn could not deny that there was merit in her words. "I never meant to suggest that you forsake your desires altogether," she counselled. "But I suppose finding a way to balance both would be advisable."

"And how would I know when to act rationally and when to act impulsively?" Dropping her gaze, Miss Davenport stared at the snow-covered ground before her gaze met Evelyn's once more. "After I found out that...," she glanced at her belly, "I had regrets. How could I not? I cursed myself for being so foolish." She swallowed hard. "But then after a while, I realised that it was selfish of me to regret what had happened. If I hadn't acted against all sense, my...child would never have been." Tears came to her eyes, and she quickly blinked them away. "So, in the end, I cannot bring myself to regret my actions. Even if I do not get to keep him...or her, at least he'll live." Her jaw clenched, and tears streamed down her face. "At least, he'll live."

Seeing the misery and utter sadness on her friend's face, Evelyn pulled her into her arms, her own heart heavy with the young woman's sorrow. Miss Davenport's arms came around her, holding on tightly as though she had no strength to hold herself upright any longer. Sobbing, she buried her face in Evelyn's shoulder, and Evelyn felt the little bump pressed against her own belly, knowing how precious the little life inside was to Miss Davenport.

Although to those who did not know her well, she might seem capricious and irresponsible and reckless and only interested in her own amusement; however, it had never been so clear that she loved her child.

With all her heart.

And it surely would break when the moment came to bid him or her farewell.

"Claudia?"

Still holding on to her friend, Evelyn took a step back and lifted her head, her gaze falling on Lady Ashwood as she stepped out onto the terrace. Her pale eyes were fixed on her daughter, concern creasing her forehead as she walked towards them. "My sweet child, what h–?"

In one moment, Lady Ashwood was still upright, and in the next, her left foot slid out from under her. With a cry of alarm, she went down.

"Mother!" Miss Davenport exclaimed, her voice strained with fear.

Darting forward, Evelyn rushed towards Lady Ashwood, only slowing her steps when she reached the terrace, her eyes gliding over the patches of ice here and there. "Miss Davenport, stay back!" she called over her shoulder. "It's too slippery here. Go around back and call for help."

Out of the corner of her eye, Evelyn saw the young woman disappear around the house. "Lady Ashwood?" she called to her future mother-in-law lying stretched out on the ice-covered terrace as she picked her way closer. "Lady Ashwood?"

A soft groan escaped the woman's lips as she began to move, a hand rising to touch her forehead. "What...what happened?" Her lids fluttered, and she swallowed hard.

Finally reaching Lady Ashwood's side, Evelyn sank down. "Look at me, please. Does anything hurt?"

Again, Lady Ashwood blinked, needing a moment to make sense of

Evelyn's words. "My head," she whispered, her breath laboured as she began to move her limbs. Then she flinched, another groan tearing from her lips. "And my ankle."

Feeling the woman's neck first, Evelyn then moved her hands up to her head, carefully probing for injuries. When she reached the back, Lady Ashwood gasped in pain. Still, Evelyn was relieved to find no blood on her fingers. "You have a nasty bump on the back of your head."

"I suppose that was to be expected," Lady Ashwood commented dryly. Still, there was a hint of humour in her voice, and she looked up at Evelyn with an apologetic look in her eyes. "I wasn't looking. I saw Claudia's face, and..."

"I know," Evelyn replied, then continued her examination, moving her hands downward over Lady Ashwood's body and checking for broken bones. When she reached the indicated ankle, her future mother-in-law gasped, cringing at the pain. "I think it's only sprained, not broken."

A shuddering breath left Lady Ashwood's lips when Evelyn removed her hands. "That's good," she whispered. "Can you help me up?"

Evelyn shook her head. "No, you must not—"

In that moment, the terrace door flew open and Lord Ashwood appeared in its frame, his eyes wide as his gaze swept over them, finally settling on his mother. "Mother!" Concern hardening his features, he stepped out onto the terrace.

"Stop!" Evelyn called, and he froze, his gaze shifting to her. "Pick your way carefully," she warned, pointing at the ground. "There's ice everywhere. You're no help if you fall as well."

Sighing, Lord Ashwood nodded, moving slowly and with caution as he picked his way to his mother's side. Behind him, Mr. Adams followed suit. After a long moment, they finally reached them.

Sinking onto his knees, Lord Ashwood grasped his mother's hand. "Are you all right? Are you hurt?"

Smiling, she patted her son's hand. "Don't worry, my dear. I shall be fine. It's merely a bump and a sprain. However, I'd appreciate it if you could help me inside. I'm getting rather cold."

Rising to her feet, Evelyn instructed Lord Ashwood and Mr. Adams on how to lift the viscountess and then carefully directed them around the treacherous patches of ice barring their way to the door. Fortunately, everything went without a hitch, and before long, Lady Ashwood was laid down on the settee in the drawing room.

Casting aside her warm coat, Evelyn quickly set to work, ordering tea for the shivering Lady Ashwood and asking Mr. Adams to bring down her doctor's bag from her room. Then she asked Lord Ashwood to escort his sister upstairs as Miss Davenport had gone rather pale and was slightly swaying on her feet.

"Don't worry about me," Lady Ashwood said with a smile, urging her daughter to listen to Evelyn. "Remember that you need to take care of yourself."

Miss Davenport nodded, her right-hand brushing over the small bump under her dress, before she allowed her brother to assist her upstairs.

Evelyn looked at brother and sister as they headed toward the hall, meeting her future husband's eyes as he glanced over his shoulder. Deep concern rested in his eyes, and Evelyn marvelled at the love he clearly had for his mother. Why would he not show it more openly?

When the servants returned with all she had asked for, Evelyn poured Lady Ashwood some tea before examining the lady's head further. There was a small swelling on the back of her head, and Evelyn turned to Mr. Adams, asking him to bring her a bucket of ice water.

Considering the freezing temperatures, that ought not to be a problem.

Upon his return, Evelyn soaked a piece of cloth in the water, feeling her fingers prickle as they reddened. Then she wrung it out and asked the maid who had brought the linen to hold it to the back of Lady Ashwood's head. "When it warms, soak it again, wring it out, and continue as before," she instructed, noting the way the maid nodded dutifully. "Thank you."

Then Evelyn asked Mr. Adams to step outside before she turned to remove Lady Ashwood's boot in order to take a closer look at her ankle. Fortunately, her first assessment had been correct; the ankle was not broken, merely sprained. "Still, you'll need to keep off your feet for a while," she instructed, gathering a few pillows to elevate the leg before draping a cooling cloth over it as well. Then she opened her little bag and drew out a small vial. "This is peppermint oil," she told her patient, who watched her curiously. "It'll help with the swelling."

Lady Ashwood sighed, sipping her tea. "My dear, I must say it is quite convenient to have you around. I already feel better."

A deep smile came to Evelyn's face at the lady's praise, and she realised how much her ability to help meant to her. Without it, she would feel incomplete. Evelyn could only hope that her future husband would come to understand that side of her. As much as she had come to care for him, she was nonetheless aware of the fact that on a deeper level they were still strangers. How much did she truly know about him? And he about her?

There was still much to say.

To learn.

To understand.

Once Lady Ashwood was comfortably settled in her room, Evelyn went to see to Miss Davenport, assuring the young woman that her mother would be fine and that she, too, needed to rest.

For the sake of her child.

That did the trick and assured Miss Davenport's compliance.

Exhausted, Evelyn headed back downstairs, considering where best to look for Lord Ashwood when she heard Mr. Bragg's voice echo over from the front hall. Changing direction, she hastened over, wondering what had brought him to Farnworth Manor.

The moment he saw her, he stopped in his tracks, his gaze narrowing as he glared at her with resentment. "My lady," he said, his voice mocking.

"Good day to you as well," Evelyn said as politely as she could. "What brings you here?"

For a moment, he looked at her, his gaze uncomprehending. Then, however, his eyes widened slightly, and a devious smile curled up his lips. "Lord Ashwood sent for me," he said, delight as well as the hint of a challenge ringing in his voice, "to see to his mother."

Evelyn's body tensed as she forced herself to inhale a slow breath.

"Apparently, she took a nasty fall," Mr. Bragg went on undeterred, clearly enjoying this moment of perceived superiority, "and requires a doctor." He inclined his head to her. "If you'll excuse me, I have a patient to tend to." Then he turned and headed up the stairs, that self-satisfied smile still on his face.

Evelyn fumed.

In that moment, nothing would have pleased her more than to claw Mr. Bragg's eyes out. Nonetheless, even in her anger, she was well aware that he was not at the core of the problem. Lord Ashwood was. After all, he was the one to have called on him.

Spinning on her heel, Evelyn headed straight for her betrothed's study, having concluded that he was in all likelihood to be found there even when the estate did not demand his attention for it seemed to be his retreat.

Without knocking, she burst into the room, enjoying the shocked look on his face as he shot to his feet, alarm coming to his eyes. "Is something wrong?" he demanded, rounding his desk. "Is my mother all right?"

Unwilling to torture him thus, Evelyn nodded. "She's fine." Closing the door loudly, she fixed him with an angry stare. "She is not the reason I'm here though. You are."

His eyes narrowed as he watched her, and she could see that he was confused. Did he truly not know? Still, in her anger, Evelyn was far from willing to excuse his behaviour. "Why did you call for Mr. Bragg?"

Lord Ashwood's frown deepened as though the answer to her question ought to be obvious. "This is my mother's health," he said, his words chosen with care, "and so I thought it right to have a doctor ensure that all had been done to see her well."

Nonetheless, his words were like a slap in the face. "I am a doctor!" Evelyn snapped, lifting a hand when it seemed he wanted to object. "Whether or not people grant me the right to call me thus is irrelevant." She swallowed, sadness chasing away her anger. "My knowledge is extensive. I've been training for years. I know what I'm doing. I would never endanger anyone, especially not your mother. She's a wonderful woman, who's always encouraged me, supported me, and I care for her deeply." Holding his gaze, she stepped forward, finally asking the one question that had been on her mind for a while now. "Why can you not trust me? Even though your family does, you still doubt me. Why?"

Chapter Seventeen

AN ENIGMA

R ichard stared at her.

Although a part of him could understand her anger, he was certain he had done nothing wrong, nothing to justify such a reaction. After all, facts were facts. There was no changing that. "You cannot truly want me to risk my mother's well-being," he said, at a loss. Did she truly value her pride more highly than his mother's health? "I know you did what you could, but where is the harm in asking another's opinion?"

Briefly, she closed her eyes, a deep sigh leaving her lips. "You did not hear a word I said, did you?" she asked, her dark brown eyes sweeping over his face as though she were a scientist examining a new specimen.

Gritting his teeth, Richard felt at a loss—as always. Although he often found himself misunderstanding the people around him, he had never made his peace with it. It still riled him that others knew with a single glance what he could not puzzle out in hours. "I will not apologise for my decision," he replied, his tone harsher than he wanted it to be. "However, all my life, I've watched my sister get into scrapes because she does not think, because she does not contemplate the consequences of her actions and only follows her heart as she calls it."

Huffing, he shook his head. "The latest consequence is a true and utterly alarming testament to her misguided way of making decisions. While it seems rather obvious that I cannot change her, I refuse to participate in her downward spiral. I always have and always will base my decisions on facts, on reason, and I will not apologise for it."

Towering over her, Richard felt his limbs tremble with the agitation that coursed through his body. Never before had he explained himself to anyone. Not like this. Not while his pulse hammered in his veins.

Suddenly free of accusation, her eyes held his. "Believe me, I understand what you're saying, and I do not fault you for basing your decisions on reason."

Richard blinked, wondering if he had heard her right. "You do not?"

Miss Procten shook her head. "I do not. I've even spoken to your sister about this, encouraging her to act with more caution."

Surprised and still at a loss, Richard stared down at her. "Then why are you...upset?"

Slowly, she inhaled a deep breath, her eyes darting from side to side as though she was trying to find the right words. "You say, you base your decisions on facts. Then let me ask you, what is a fact? What makes a fact a fact? Yes, my father is a doctor, and I am not. But it is also a fact that neither is Mr. Bragg. He is merely an apprentice."

Richard nodded, glad to have her speak in such reasonable terms. "That is true," he admitted. "However, it is also true that you are neither."

For a moment, her lips thinned. "I suppose that depends on your perspective."

Unease sneaked up his spine as he shook his head. "This is where you're wrong. A fact is a fact no matter what perspective."

Miss Procten swallowed, the muscles in her jaw working. "Fine. Then tell me, what makes a doctor a doctor?"

Richard frowned, wondering how this line of thinking would help her make her point. "All right. A doctor is one who receives said title from an educational facility specialising in that area. Like your father."

"And under what circumstances would such a title be awarded?"

Richard shrugged. "When the person in question has proved that he is qualified enough to be deserving of said title." Surprised, he noted the ghost of a smile that tickled the corners of her mouth and wondered how what he had just said could aid her in proving her point.

"So, what you're saying is that that title ought to be awarded to those who have sufficient knowledge in the field of medicine, is that correct?"

"It is," Richard said carefully, somehow sensing that she was close to turning his words against him.

"Well, in that case," Miss Procten said, her eyes never leaving his, "I deserve to be awarded that title. I may not have trained in a recognised medical facility. However, you yourself stated that my father is a man of expertise, and it was he who taught me everything he knows the same way he has been teaching Mr. Bragg. The only difference is that Mr. Bragg has been learning for a year, whereas, I have been learning ever since I can remember." She took a step closer, a challenge lighting up her eyes. "Now, tell me for what reason I am not qualified enough to see to your mother?"

Stunned to hear her state her qualification so simply, Richard wondered about the life she had led. "I was not aware of that," he began, intrigued to learn more about her. "Did your father truly teach you the same way he taught Mr. Bragg? Are you certain he never kept anything from you? Shielded you from...injuries that were too severe?"

"You may speak to him if you do not believe me," Miss Procten said, the tension in her shoulders lessening. "However, he will tell you the same. I've not only birthed children, but also set broken bones, healed infections, treated burns and once even amputated a foot. Would you consider that sufficient qualification, my lord?"

Richard felt his jaw drop at the last item on her list. "I had no idea," he mumbled, realising his own foolishness. "I apologise for drawing the wrong conclusion. I assumed that you merely assisted your father in...certain matters as is commonly done. I didn't think that he would include you in every aspect of his professional life. I've never heard of a father doing so." Clearing his throat, Richard nodded. "I admit I was wrong."

"Thank you." Inhaling deeply, Miss Procten shifted from one foot onto the other, her shoulders relaxing. Still, her gaze remained firmly locked on his face. "I suppose you did not know any of this because you never speak to me, you never ask me anything." She sighed. "We are about to be husband and wife, and in truth, we know very little about each other. Does that not frighten you?"

"Frighten me?" Richard echoed, surprised by the change in conversation. Quite honestly, he had never once thought about it. "Does it frighten you?" He swallowed, wondering what she was trying to tell him. "Do I...?"

Shaking her head, she sighed. "You misunderstand, my lord. I am not frightened of you, but of...marrying a stranger. Someone I don't know. Should husband and wife not trust each other? But how can they if they know nothing of one another? I'm saying I want to feel safe in my home, in my family. Don't you?"

Safe? He wondered. Did she feel threatened here? Did she not think he would protect her?

Staring at him in wonderment, she stepped closer. "I can see that you're misunderstanding me once more. You have that look in your eyes that speaks of utter puzzlement as though..." At a loss for words, she shook her head. Then her eyes sought his once more. "Look at me and tell me what you think I'm feeling right now." As though to throw him off, her lips quirked up into a smile.

Taken aback, Richard stared down at her, increasingly aware of the fact that she seemed to know about his deficiency in reading other people's facial expressions. Was she trying to play him for a fool? Although he had no idea what on earth she could be thinking, let alone feeling in that moment, he had a strong sense that the smile right now curling up her lips was not a genuine smile. Still, anything beyond that was a mere guessing game.

His teeth clenched together almost painfully, and Richard had to fight the urge to lash out at her as shame rose to heat his face. "This is ridiculous," he pressed out, stepping around her and toward the door.

"Wait!" Her hand settled on his arm, light and yet determined, and kept him where he was. "I can see that I've upset you." Once more she stepped in front of him, her wide brown eyes gentle as they swept over his face, no doubt reading him like an open book. "I assure you it was not my intention."

For a long moment, she simply looked at him, and Richard felt his insides settle. Then he nodded in acknowledgement.

"You're an enigma," she suddenly said, an amused curl to her lips.

Richard's eyes widened. "Excuse me?"

Miss Procten nodded. "You are. I've never met anyone like you. You're difficult to read." A laugh escaped her. "And I usually don't have any trouble understanding another's motivations. It is part of being a doctor, seeing how others feel even if they cannot put it into words or even try to hide it."

Intrigued, Richard asked, "What do you see when...you look at me?"

The moment the words left his lips, he cursed himself for offering himself up for her censure. No doubt, she had little good to say about him, and hearing her criticise him would undoubtedly increase the chasm between them that seemed to grow wider every day. Had she not a moment ago told him that they were nothing more than strangers?

"I see a kind and caring man," Miss Procten answered his question, her gentle voice feeling like a balm to his tense soul as he listened to words he never thought he would hear. "You see it as your responsibility to provide for those in your care, but more than that, you have a desire to see them happy. You know those you care for well, even if you don't understand them, and while you sometimes wish you could change them, you never force their hand...unless it's for their own good. And even then, it makes you feel guilty for using your position to go against their will." Her brown eyes held his, and there was a gentleness to her face that he had never seen before. "You feel misunderstood because you allow reason to guide your hand, which others often perceive as the acts of someone unfeeling. At the same time, you are often frustrated because...understanding them in turn does not come easy to you, does it?"

Richard swallowed. "It does not," he admitted, feeling utterly vulnerable, his weakness bared for all the world to see. Perhaps not all the world, but her. Would she think less of him now?

"What do you see when you look at me?" Miss Procten returned his earlier question, her gaze briefly dropping from his as though she, too, feared his censure.

Richard shrugged. "I cannot say with certainty," he admitted, feeling utterly liberated to have someone know what lived in his heart. "As you've deduced so accurately, I generally fail at reading others."

"Tell me," she insisted, her gaze once again steady, urging him to speak his mind. "Tell me what you see when you look at me, for I do not believe that you see nothing."

Richard swallowed, praying that his words would not miss their mark by far, that she would not hold them against him, that he would not come to regret them for the rest of his life. "You...you care deeply for others," he began, uncertainty clear in his voice. "You do not hesitate to help if need be, and sometimes even forget to think about yourself in your desire to assist others." Seeing the soft curl to her lips, Richard felt his voice grow stronger. "You are determined and headstrong. You're not afraid to fight for what you want, for what you deem right. You see the world in many facets, and you try to find a balance between heart and mind."

Holding his gaze, Miss Procten exhaled slowly. "I guess I was wrong," she whispered. "We're not strangers, are we?"

Richard swallowed, inordinately pleased by her words. "Neither do we know each other well though," he could not help to point out.

She smiled. "You're utterly honest, too," she amended her judgement. "I appreciate that."

For a long moment, silence hung between them as each looked at the other, trying to assess where they could go from there. They were not strangers, no. Quite obviously, they had come to learn about the other. However, they were far from being confidants, from knowing each other in and out. Still, there was potential here, was there not? A chance for a deeper connection than Richard had ever dreamed possible, and from the way her eyes looked into his, he thought she had come to the same conclusion.

"Will you promise me something?" Miss Procten asked into the stillness of the room.

Richard nodded.

"Will you promise to speak to me? To listen to me?" She inhaled a slow breath. "I want to know the man you are. I want to understand you, and I want you to understand me. We don't have to agree on everything, but as long as we can understand each other's motivations and reasonings, I believe we can come to respect each other's opinion, each other's decisions. But in order to do so, we need to speak to each other, to get to know each other." She smiled up at him, and Richard felt the sudden impulse to agree to anything she asked. "Will you promise me to do so?"

Seeing the promise of a future in her eyes, Richard nodded. "I shall try."

"As shall I," she replied. "It's all anyone can do."

Richard sighed, wondering what she would think of him if she knew the man he was deep inside. After all, few people truly liked him, especially not once they got to know him better. They thought him cold and calculated, opinionated and arrogant.

Still, she would be his wife soon, and he could not refuse such a simple, and yet, heartfelt request. Perhaps sharing more of himself with another person would not inevitably lead to disaster. To disappointment. Perhaps she would come to understand why he was the man he was and not see anything wrong in his thinking, in the way he felt.

Perhaps she was the one person who would finally understand him.

Chapter Eighteen

A NEW FAMILY

Standing in front of the tall mirror in her chamber, Evelyn gazed at the young woman looking back at her. The sight was rather unusual as Evelyn never tended to dress in such finery. However, her soon-to-be mother-in-law had insisted on having a new dress made and had offered her own lady's maid to work on Evelyn's hair.

Now, Evelyn simply stood there, framed by Lady Ashwood and Miss Davenport, her eyes gliding upward over the pale blue gown, accenting her dark eyes. Small flower blossoms had been woven into her hair, and she had donned the simple pair of silver earrings her mother had left her.

"You look beautiful, my dear," Lady Ashwood beamed, her smile radiant, happiness filling her eyes as they met Evelyn's. "I could not have hoped for more on this day. I'm so glad my son has found you."

Considering the circumstances, Evelyn found her future mother-in-law's words a bit odd. After all, theirs was far from a love match. Still, Evelyn could not deny that she did harbour tender emotions for her betrothed, and if she was not thoroughly mistaken, he cared for her as well, did he not?

Naturally, doubt remained, and Evelyn accepted it as a part of life.

How could there not be doubt when two people joined their lives together under the present circumstances?

"Thank you, my lady," Evelyn said, nodding to Lady Ashwood, who affectionately brushed a curl from Evelyn's forehead.

"Oh, please call me Camilla," the older woman asked, tears misting her eyes. "After all, you will be my daughter after today."

Touched, Evelyn returned the woman's smile, feeling her own heart twist and turn, unable to settle on one feeling alone. For in this moment, Evelyn could not help but miss her own mother terribly. Although she barely remembered her, it was the idea of a woman holding her hand through sadness and joy, someone to guide her and watch over her, that she missed, that she had longed for all her life.

Looking at Lady A-Camilla, Evelyn wondered if this marriage would not only bring her a husband, but a mother as well. From the look on Camilla's face, it was apparent that Evelyn was not the only one strongly affected by today's events.

"And you must call me Claudia," Miss Davenport insisted, a beaming smile on her face. "And we shall call you Evelyn."

Laughing, they all agreed, and after a few quick hugs so as not to wrinkle Evelyn's dress or upend her coiffure, they all proceeded downstairs.

Wrapping thick cloaks over their exquisite dresses, the three women braced the harsh wind and stepped out into the cold to walk the few steps over to the small chapel. Fortunately, Camilla's ankle had healed quickly, and she could already walk with the help of a walking stick to help keep most of her weight off her injured foot.

The moment they stepped into the warmth of the small chapel, Evelyn's gaze sought her betrothed, who stood up front at the altar, his childhood friend, Lord Weston by his side.

Two days ago, Sebastian Campbell, Lord Weston, and his wife Charlotte Campbell, Lady Weston (who was indeed the young woman Evelyn had tended to about a year ago), had arrived at Farnworth Manor. They had been accompanied by the young lord's sister Victoria, her three-month-old son Philip as well as his mother, the dowager countess. From what Evelyn had learnt, Victoria's husband had died in a tragic accident before the birth of their son.

The moment Lord Ashwood turned, and his gaze met Evelyn's, she drew in a shuddering breath, her skin tingling with utterly new emotions. Would he ask her to call him by his given name as well? Or would he insist on her calling him *my lord*?

Realising that it was rather unlikely that he would, Evelyn wondered if she ought to do so instead. After all, he was a man who required the certainty rules brought into his life in order to guide him in his actions. Therefore, she doubted that he would ever willingly venture away from what he undoubtedly deemed his lifeline. It was as though rational thought was his north star, and without it, he was lost, unable to find his way, doomed to wander around aimlessly.

More than once, Evelyn had taken note of the fact that he seemed to have trouble reading other people's facial expressions, which in turn often led to severe misunderstandings. Only too well did she recall the puzzled look on his face when she had snapped at him for asking Mr. Bragg to see to his mother. For the life of him, he had not been able to understand what had made her so angry.

More often than not, he tried to hide this uncertainty under a cold demeanour, hoping that others would not see that he was at a loss. Clearly, he felt embarrassed and considered it a shortcoming.

Evelyn smiled, knowing an opportunity when she saw one. Determined to make the best of the situation they found themselves in, she vowed to gain his trust. Perhaps if she were to express herself more clearly and not rely on him deciphering the tone of her voice or the look in her eyes, he would come to trust her. After all, was it not the unknown that people generally feared the most? At the very least, it was a way to avoid future misunderstandings.

Still, it would require some adapting on her part as well, for people often held back, fearing to give voice to deeper sentiments that they felt made them vulnerable or caused them shame. Would she be able to do it? Voice her feelings in such a way?

As Evelyn came to stand beside her betrothed, she took note of the few people in attendance. Smiling at her father, she found him sitting with Lady Ashwood–Camilla! –as well as Claudia. Their faces held joy, giving her the strength, she needed to meet Lord Ashwood's gaze.

Gently, he held her hand in his as the priest rambled on, tying their lives together with a few simple words. His gaze was rather stern, and yet, she thought to see a slight quirk of his upper lip as though deeper emotions fought to the surface and were held back by sheer willpower alone. Could it be that he was glad to see her made his wife? Was it something deeper than the physical attraction that had overwhelmed them here and there? Could he...come to love her?

A myriad of thoughts tumbled through Evelyn's mind as they were declared husband and wife and then quickly drawn apart by the few well-wishers in attendance. Hugging her new sister, Evelyn saw Lord Weston slap her husband on the shoulder, whispering something she could not hear. In answer, Lord Ashwood rolled his eyes, shaking his head at his friend, who laughed freely, delight lighting up his eyes.

At the wedding breakfast, Evelyn barely exchanged a word with her new husband as their guests claimed their attention. Lord Weston seemed to have a lot to say to her husband–Evelyn could not help but wish she had an inkling what it was! –while Evelyn found herself in the company of her new sister as well as Lady Weston.

"Would you say he looks happy?" Lady Weston asked, her eyes sweeping over Evelyn's new husband.

Turning her own gaze away from where her father chatted rather animatedly with Camilla as well as Lord Weston's mother and sister, both cooing over three-month-old Philip, Evelyn looked to Claudia, realising that she would very much like to know the answer, having asked herself the very same thing.

Claudia, however, shrugged, her gaze narrowing as she looked at her brother. "It's hard to tell. As you might be aware, he hardly smiles. Sometimes I even wonder if he knows what it means."

Seeing her suspicions confirmed, Evelyn nodded, wondering if she would ever truly *know* how her husband felt.

"Well, I barely know him," Lady Weston admitted, "thus I cannot speak with anything close to certainty." She turned gentle eyes to Evelyn, a smile tugging on the corners of her mouth. "However, my husband said that while he was quite surprised by your match as he had expected his friend to enter into a *strictly* sensible union, he was equally surprised to see his face so...so expressive today." A twinkle came to the lady's eyes. "I thought you might like to know. After all, these two have known each other since childhood, and despite their differences, they are as close as brothers."

"Expressive?" Claudia echoed, incredulity in her voice, before Evelyn could thank Lady Weston for her kind words. "Was that truly the word he used?"

As Lady Weston confirmed her answer, Evelyn's gaze once more drifted toward her husband, and she had to admit that the thought of her affecting him thus brought joy to her heart. For years now, she had treasured the little moments she had spent in his company, knowing that he would never see her beyond being the doctor's daughter. Often had she told herself to forget about her girlish thoughts and turn toward more worthwhile endeavours. Still, her wayward heart had clung to him as though it knew it only needed to bide its time.

And now, all of a sudden, nothing was impossible any longer. After all, they were married now. Married! It still seemed surreal. Could he come to care for her? Beyond the kind of affection, one would harbour for someone who shows kindness toward them? Would he ever think about her the way she thought about him? Would she ever breach his shell and gaze upon the man he was at heart?

It was possible.

Utterly possible.

Chapter Nineteen

AN ULTERIOR MOTIVE

Out of the corner of his eye, Richard watched his wife as she spoke to Lady Weston, her eyes bright like the sun and her smile utterly disarming. When she had walked toward him in the chapel, he had nearly forgotten to breathe, not because she had looked breathtakingly beautiful–she had! – but because of the way her eyes had sought his as though she truly longed to be with him.

"You seem lost in thought, my friend," Sebastian observed, jarring Richard from his daydream. "I must say I quite like that new look on your face."

Clearing his throat, Richard shifted on his feet, briefly dropping his gaze before looking at his friend. "What look?" he asked, knowing the moment the words left his lips that he should not have. After all, Sebastian had always loved teasing him, and there was no doubt he would see this as anything else but an encouragement to do so.

As expected, a wide grin drew up the corners of his friend's mouth. "A look of utter fascination," he replied. "A look of disbelief that such a woman would accept you."

Inwardly, Richard cringed. Did his friend not think him worthy of Miss Procten? Of...Evelyn?

"I quite remember it," Sebastian continued, a sigh in his words. "I felt exactly the same way when I first saw Charlotte." He laughed, "And when she accepted my proposal, I believed my hearing to be impaired."

Richard relaxed. Once again, he had misunderstood his friend. Sebastian had not meant to criticise him but had rather tried to share an experience.

"Still, I admit it took some convincing," Sebastian mused, his gaze distant as he remembered the time he had first met his wife. "When I asked for her hand, she gawked at me. She told me I was a fool for asking her, that I was acting like a spoilt child, wanting what I couldn't have."

Richard felt the corners of his mouth lift up involuntarily. "Miss Procten looked at me in a similar fashion." Remembering the day, he had given her his father's letter, Richard shook his head. Never would he have thought for it to turn out like this.

"Miss Procten?" Sebastian questioned. "She is Miss Procten no longer, is she?"

Richard inhaled a deep breath. "No."

"She's your lady now and quite a fine one, I must say." He clapped Richard on the shoulder. "I'm glad to see you married to a good woman."

Richard frowned. "What does that mean?"

Grinning, Sebastian shook his head, a hint of incomprehension in his eyes. "I thought that was fairly obvious." He glanced at...Evelyn. "She is a kind and good-hearted girl, loyal and devoted. She's a wonderful match for you."

"How can you tell?" Richard asked, wondering how his friend knew after having made her acquaintance only two days ago.

Sebastian shrugged. "I can't say. I simply believe so."

Quite dissatisfied with his friend's answer, Richard shook his head.

"Well, as glad as I am, I'm also surprised," Sebastian went on unde-terred, "that you married a woman who does not fulfil society's unwritten requirements of birth, dowry and connections." His gaze sobered, and he nodded to Richard. "I'm glad I was wrong. I'm glad you chose a wife free from these restraints."

"Why?"

Sebastian sighed, and Richard could tell that his friend was getting impatient and possibly a touch annoyed to have to explain himself in such detail. "Because societal marriages are not of the kind that make those involved happy." Once more, his gaze drifted to Evelyn and the corners of his mouth quirked up before he returned his eyes to Richard. "She cares for you."

His friend's words almost sent Richard tumbling backwards, and his eyes widened in shock.

Sebastian laughed, "What? You didn't know?"

"How do *you* know?" Richard snapped, fighting to keep his composure. "She never once said…"

Sighing rather indulgently, Sebastian shook his head. "You truly didn't know," he said, and Richard found himself getting annoyed with his friend's enjoyment of this situation. "Well, all you need to do is look at her. It's in her eyes when she sees you. The way she smiles. The way she's always aware of where you are, of how you are. It's a million little things." Humour once more lit up Sebastian's eyes. "The same things that tell me that you care for her as well."

Gritting his teeth, Richard chose not to take the bait and ignore that last comment. Still, he could not help but remember how she had asked him to tell her how she felt. Always had he known that reading another's emotions was far from his strong suit; however, now, he felt utterly inadequate. Were these things so easy for everyone to see? Was he the only blind man? Could a deeply passionate woman like Evelyn ever truly come to care for a cold-hearted man like himself?

"I don't mean this disrespectfully in any way," Sebastian said, the look on his face not teasing for once. "I simply mean to advise you to consider yourself lucky that she agreed to marry you. Cherish her. Never take her for granted."

Richard scoffed, "While our match might not have been agreed upon for the usual *societal* reasons, it was nevertheless an arranged match. You are mistaken when you think she accepted me out of anything other than obligation."

Sebastian frowned, and Richard could not deny that a part of him rejoiced to see his friend taken aback. For once, he had been the one to misinterpret. The one who had drawn the wrong conclusions. "What do you mean?"

Leaning closer, Richard held his friend's gaze. "She only agreed to marry me because our fathers agreed upon it years ago. In addition, I had to promise to allow her to continue her work. Otherwise, she would have refused me."

Nodding, Sebastian said, "That is a reasonable request. Do you fault her for wanting to be her own person? From what Charlotte said she is quite a dedicated doctor. She has a way of putting her patients at ease as she seems genuinely interested in their well-being. That's a rare trait these days."

"Of course, I don't," Richard snapped, wondering why his friend's words upset him so. "I merely meant to point out that you have the wrong idea of what motivated her to accept me. You cannot compare our union to yours and Lady Weston's."

Annoyingly, Sebastian laughed, "I thought you knew that when Charlotte first accepted my proposal, she did not do so because she had suddenly fallen in love with me. Quite on the contrary, she only agreed because she had no other choice. She had nowhere to go, and I admit I...took advantage of her situation because I wanted her." His face darkened somewhat. "It was not my finest moment."

Surprised by this admission, Richard stared at his friend. "I remember that you had an ulterior motive to marry her as well. However, you did seem quite taken with her if I recall."

An approving smile lit up Sebastian's face. "I must say you're not as unobservant as I thought. Yes, I was taken with her, but her feelings took a little longer to develop. Still, my point is that even if there were other reasons than deep affection for you to agree to this marriage, there is every chance that it will turn into something deeper...if you let it." For a long moment, Sebastian held his gaze, his eyes imploring as though he feared Richard would do something unwise and ruin his chances for happiness.

Knowing his friend's words came from a good place, Richard nodded, refraining from voicing his doubts. After all, Sebastian was a kind-hearted and affectionate man, whereas he, Richard, was not.

Certainly, a man like Sebastian could win a woman's heart, but could he, Richard, do so as well?

Laughter echoed to his ears, and he turned to see his mother and sister chatting animatedly, their faces glowing as they enjoyed themselves. As far as Richard could tell, they seemed happy. A few weeks ago, they had seemed quite different. Had this been Evelyn's doing?

Deep down, he did not doubt it, for she had a way of taking care of those around her. She even took care of him. The only question was: did she do so out of the simple kindness of her heart or because she cared for him beyond that?

If only he knew.

Chapter Twenty

REVELATIONS IN THE BRIDAL CHAMBER

P acing her bedchamber, Evelyn played with the band of her robe which she wore over her night rail. Her limbs were far from tired, and she felt a nervous energy course through them that bade her abandon all thoughts of slipping into bed to patiently await her husband's visit. For although she cared for him, Evelyn wished they could get to know each other better before sharing that aspect of life together.

But how would he react if he found her out of bed and pacing up and down the rug?

Over the course of the past week or two, Evelyn had slowly come to realise that Lord Ashwood's cold demeanour often hid something else entirely: insecurity. In fact, his inability to understand those around him often led to confusion, to misunderstandings, and judging from the expression on his face, there seemed to be few things in life he hated more. Which, of course, was understandable. After all, who would cherish loss of control if it plunged one into utter chaos?

Life's rules gave him security, and so he clung to them like a drowning man.

One such rule was that a marriage was consummated on the

wedding night. How would he feel if she asked him to wait? Would he object? Not necessarily because he felt a deep desire to share her bed? But simply because breaking another rule would once again find him at a loss?

Inhaling what she hoped would be a fortifying breath, Evelyn resolved to be honest. If they ever were to have a deeper under-standing of one another, then they needed to speak their minds truth-fully. After all, she could hardly expect him to do so if she herself was unwilling!

As though he had known that her mind had finally settled on a decision, a knock sounded on the door a moment later, followed closely by Lord Ashwood stepping over the threshold. As expected, his gaze swung toward the bed, his eyes narrowing slightly as he found it empty. Stepping forward, he closed the door, and Evelyn could see a deeper tension coming to his shoulders.

Then he turned and saw her standing on the other side of the room, her fingers still toying with the band of her robe. "Is everything all right?" he asked, his feet slowly carrying him closer as he watched her face. Still, his features held a hint of frustration, and Evelyn knew that he was unable to deduce what was happening and why.

Shaking her head, Evelyn watched him, curious what he would do or say. Deep inside, a voice whispered that she was not being fair to him. Still, she herself felt far from level-headed in that moment as her own heart beat rapidly against her ribs. She felt her breath catch in her throat and her knees tremble as his grey eyes swept over her, seeking to understand.

His gaze studied her face, momentarily dropping to her hands still playing with the band of her robe. Then his jaw tensed, and he seemed to draw in a fortifying breath as well. "Do you wish for me to leave?" he asked, his voice rough, and Evelyn could see only too clearly that he hated groping in the dark. To him, this had to appear like a guessing game without even a single clue to point him in the right direction.

"No." Her voice sounded weak even to her own ears, and she could see a hint of doubt on his face. Reminding herself that he was the one at a disadvantage, Evelyn took a brave step forward, realising that although she wanted to postpone their wedding night, she would not object to another kiss. In fact, she silently vowed she would not allow him to leave her chamber without one.

A smile drew up the corners of her mouth at the thought, and she bit her lower lip to suppress it lest he think she was laughing about him.

Doubt remained on his face, and yet, his gaze dipped lower, tracing the line of her mouth as he inhaled an unsteady breath.

Encouraged by his reaction, Evelyn closed the distance between them, her hands sliding up the front of his shirt, over his shoulders and around his neck. "It's my turn again, isn't it?" she whispered, noting the slight widening of his eyes before she pushed herself deeper into his embrace, her mouth seeking his.

Without a moment's hesitation, Lord Ashwood's arms closed around her, drawing her closer as his lips responded to her kiss.

A tantalising heat shot through Evelyn, and for a moment, she wondered if she truly wished to postpone their wedding night as curiosity stole over her, quickening her pulse and weakening her knees. His hands on her back felt utterly wonderful, and when he deepened the kiss, she sank into him. Still, the moment he gently urged her towards the bed, Evelyn broke the kiss.

Confusion clouded his face as he looked at her, his arms still tightly wrapped around her middle, refusing to release her. "What is it?"

Evelyn swallowed, hoping he would not be angry with her for asking him to break a rule. "I...I was wondering if you'd mind," she licked her lips, hoping courage would not fail her, "waiting...until we know each other better." After briefly dropping her gaze, Evelyn boldly looked into his eyes, seeing the confusion on his face deepen.

However, when he spoke, it was she who found herself surprised. "I would mind," he replied, his voice determined but not unkind as his arms tightened their hold on her. He swallowed, and for a moment, it was as though he dropped his mask—the cold detachedness he always wore—and she could see deep longing in his eyes. "I've waited long enough."

Taken aback by his forthrightness, Evelyn stared up at him,

enjoying the honesty that rang in his words. "I've waited longer," she challenged him, delighting in the small quirk that came to his lips.

Then slowly he shook his head. "I doubt that."

A wide smile fought to break through, and suddenly feeling completely at ease, Evelyn let it. "Is that so? Would you care to elaborate?"

His brows quirked. "Would you?"

Evelyn laughed, her fingers trailing down the front of his shirt, feeling the warmth of his skin through the fabric. Noting the way his eyes closed briefly and he seemed to hold his breath, she whispered, "I've always–quite inexplicably–found myself drawn to you especially since last year when I spent more time here after your father's passing."

His gaze widened, and Evelyn could see as plain as day that he had not noticed, had not been aware of her partiality toward him.

"I always found my thoughts straying to you," she admitted, feeling the muscles in his arms that held her relax slowly, "and my heart skip a beat whenever you were near." Evelyn's insides quirked at such bold honesty, and yet, it felt unexpectedly liberating.

Lord Ashwood exhaled an audible breath and blinked rapidly a couple of times. "I didn't know."

"You didn't see me," Evelyn retorted, unable not to tease him. "You didn't look at me beyond the doctor's daughter. You didn't see–"

"No, I–" He swallowed, his narrowed gaze sweeping over her face. "I *did* see you. I simply...I didn't see how you felt." He nodded. "But I saw *you*."

Stunned, Evelyn stared at him.

A hint of discomfort flitted across his face before he sighed, his feet shifting a bit away from her. Still, his arms remained where they were, firmly holding her in place...as well as himself? "My thoughts were drawn to you as well," he finally admitted, his gaze watchful and a touch apprehensive. Could he truly not see her surprise? Could he truly misread it into something disapproving?

His brows drew down further. "You didn't notice?" he asked, surprise and a hint of pleasure warring in his voice.

Closing her eyes, Evelyn bit her lower lip, slowly shaking her head.

"I did not," she said, her gaze seeking his once more. "I thought you disliked me. I thought you disliked me being here."

"I did."

Evelyn felt her eyes widen as the shock of his words slowly stole over her limbs, weighing them down as though they were suddenly filled with lead. "You did?" she all but stammered, taken aback at the sudden pain that radiated through her heart.

"Whenever we would cross paths," he began, "all I could think about was...you." He swallowed, clearly uncomfortable with this level of honesty. "I...you..." Again, he swallowed, unable to express the over-whelming emotions that had seized him as much as her.

Evelyn smiled as she finally understood his objection to her presence. Never before had she received a more wonderful compliment. "It would seem you are not the only one misinterpreting situations," she said lightly, her heart thudding wildly at the delicate promise that hung on their words.

Nonetheless, at her observation, his eyes widened, and his arms finally dropped from her waist. "What?" he all but gasped, a hint of panic in his eyes.

Evelyn frowned, wondering what had shocked him thus. After all, had she not said something to that end to him before? Was he truly so terrified of sharing that secret with her?

"You don't wish for others to know," she observed, thinking out loud as she tried to make sense of him. "You'd rather they think you cold and uncaring than confused. Why is that?"

His jaw clenched, and he stepped away, putting a painful distance between them. "I'm not confused," he insisted, his voice rough and defensive.

"Yes, you are," Evelyn objected, closing the distance he had created between them, unwilling to allow him to hide from her. "Admit it."

His dark grey eyes met hers. However, below that look of exaspera-tion, she thought to see a flicker of desire to confide in her. Then, his face hardened once more, and it was gone. "Do I truly have to explain this to you?" He turned away from her. "What man would wish to be known by others as easily confused? Why should my family trust me to see to their well-being if I cannot even...?" His voice trailed off, and more than anything, Evelyn heard loneliness in his words. Never had he shared these thoughts with anyone, had he?

Stepping up to him, she placed a hand on his shoulder, feeling him stiffen as he held himself firmly away from her. "My words were not meant as insult or criticism. They were merely an observation."

"Of my greatest weakness!" he hissed, the muscles under her hand tensing. "Of my deficiency! Of—"

"No!" Her hand tightened on his shoulder, and she urged him to look at her, stepping around him when he held himself rigid. "Look at me!" she demanded, her voice hard as she sought his eyes. "You are the only one who thinks of it as a deficiency. Certainly, we all have strengths and weaknesses, but those do not make us worth more or less than anyone else."

His gaze hard, he finally met hers. "I've seen the way others look at me," he snarled. "They're appalled, or they pity me."

"You're wrong!"

He scoffed, "Of course, you would think so as I cannot read their thoughts the way you can."

Although not unaffected by the pain in his voice, Evelyn still felt her anger rise. Grabbing him by the arms, she stood tall in front of him, daring him to ignore her. "What pushes people away is not your struggle to understand their meaning," she told him, feeling his muscles twitch under her fingers, "but your insistence to hide how you feel, hoping to deny them what you feel you've been denied: the ability to interpret and thus understand." She inhaled a deep breath, noting the way his gaze held hers.

Listening intently, he had given up his attempt to free himself from her, a hint of curiosity in his silver-grey eyes.

"What pushes people away is that cold demeanour of yours," she whispered, praying that her words would not offend him anew, "as though you don't care, as though you don't feel." She stepped closer, and as her hands slowly slid up his chest, he once more drew in an unsteady breath. "But you do feel. You feel just like I do." She nodded to him, her gaze holding his, urging him to believe her. "Don't hide yourself, and I promise I shall do the same."

His forehead creased the slightest bit.

"Honesty," Evelyn stated. "Speak to me and listen to me as I shall, too." Her fingers curled into the front of his shirt, hoping that he would not try to run from her for she had already decided that she would not let him. "Ask me. Ask me anything, and I promise I shall tell you the truth."

Chapter Twenty-One

FEAR OF REJECTION

S taring at his wife, Richard had never felt so overwhelmed in his life.

Never before had he focused on his emotions as they were chaotic and unstructured. More often than not, he did not know what to make of them. Early on, he had learnt to ignore them, to force them back and treat them as insignificant. Only emotions supported by reason, responses he had learnt to be appropriate, he allowed to surface.

However, lately, whenever he found himself near Evelyn, random emotions broke through without permission. Richard had no idea what to do about that.

Holding his wife's gaze, he realised that she meant what she said. Her dark eyes were open and fixed on his as she patiently waited for him to ask his question. Swallowing, Richard wracked his brain as her closeness, the memory of her touch seemed to addle his mind.

Then he remembered her confession that she felt drawn to him. "How...?" Richard swallowed, realising that he had never before spoken so intimately to another. "How did it make you feel when I kissed you?" he finally asked, his gaze holding hers, unwilling to allow any little hint to her emotions slip by him.

At his question, her jaw dropped a fraction and her eyes widened slightly before a soft flush darkened her cheeks. Had he embarrassed her? Was she angry with him? Disappointed?

"Should I not have asked that?"

Shaking her head, she stepped forward. "No. No, it's fine. I—" She licked her lips, and for a moment, her gaze seemed unfocused as it slid around the room. Then the muscles in her jaw tensed, and she forced her gaze back to meet his. "You were not wrong to ask. It is an honest question, and it deserves an honest answer. However, I have to admit I was...taken aback." She exhaled a rapid breath, a tentative smile playing on her lips. "I tell you honestly, I'm not used to expressing such intimate thoughts and emotions to another, especially one I barely know."

Surprised by the depth of her honesty, Richard felt his own curiosity grow. And so, despite the unease she had just admitted to, he asked, "Why?"

Her fingers returned to the band of her robe. Her eyes, however, did not fall from his. "Because doing so makes one vulnerable. Like a warrior who dons his armour in order to protect himself, we all shield the most vulnerable parts of who we are. We're afraid to be wounded, to feel pain, to suffer."

Richard nodded, recognising the emotion she described. "What you say makes sense," he agreed, noting that his own unease seemed to be decreasing when he saw how affected she, too, was by revealing what lived deep inside.

"Deep down, emotions always make sense," Evelyn replied, the colour in her cheeks diminishing, "at least to the one concerned. There is always a reason. Always a connection. A cause. A consequence. Deep down, emotions are logical. However, to understand their logic is far from easy because we ourselves are not solely logical, either." Evelyn scoffed, her lips curling into a smile as she shook her head. "Did that make any sense at all?"

Enjoying the look of confusion on her features, Richard nodded.

"All I'm trying to say is that if we were honest with ourselves," she continued, "we would see the truth and understand why we feel what we feel. However, in order to protect ourselves, we often choose to look the other way, to not dig deeper in order to understand, even to lie to ourselves because we fear to know the truth."

Taking a step toward her, Richard held her gaze, his own curious as he searched her face. "What truth did you fear?"

Briefly, Evelyn closed her eyes. "That...that I care for you."

Richard felt the muscles in his body tense. "Why?"

She licked her lips. "Because I believed you could never care for me," she said, her gaze unwavering as it held his. Still, her jaw seemed tense as she spoke. "I thought if I did not admit the truth to myself, I would not feel its pain."

Staring into her face, Richard felt all tension leave his body. "Do you care for me?" he asked boldly, wondering at the woman who had made him so daring within so short a time.

"I do," she whispered as a slight shiver shook her frame.

"And how did it make you feel when I kissed you?" he pressed, unwilling to abandon the matter as every fibre in his body strove to know the truth.

To not merely suspect it.

Guess it.

But *know* it instead.

Evelyn swallowed, her fingers clenching around the band of her robe. Still, a soft smile played on her lips. "Partly, it frightened me," she said, and he held his breath, "because I feared it would force me to see the truth, that I do care for you without knowing whether or not you returned my affections."

Recognising her fear as one of his own, Richard asked, "And the other part?"

Her smile deepened, setting her dark eyes aglow. "It rejoiced in the feel of you."

"Truly?" Richard asked, staring at her as though she had just now risen from the ground.

Evelyn chuckled, "Do you doubt me? Do you doubt my word?"

"No." He shook his head, still feeling dazed. "I merely...At times, you seemed reluctant. That's all. A part of me cannot believe your words to be true."

She drew in a shuddering breath. "Perhaps that is because you, too, fear to not have your affections returned." Her jaw quivered as she spoke, and Richard wondered if she still doubted how he felt about her. Certainly, he had not spoken of his affections for her. Only she had. But could she not read how he felt about her on his face? Did other people not possess this ability? Or was there another reason why she seemed on edge?

Richard's eyes narrowed as they swept over her face, trying to read on her features what she did not say. "You seem nervous," he observed, trying to piece together the subtle details in her expression that might help him understand. However, although she had given him context to assist him in his understanding of her, Richard could not be certain. "Is it because I have not yet given you an answer?"

Her brows drew down, and he supposed that his question confused her.

"You asked to postpone our wedding night," he clarified, taking note of the slight widening of her eyes when understanding found her. "Are you concerned I would refuse your request?"

The ghost of a smile on her face, she shook her head. "I am not concerned."

Richard inhaled a deep breath, his gaze once more gliding over her face. A familiar frustration set in when his mind failed to interpret what he saw, unable to draw the conclusions others would have come to. "What then?" he asked, his voice harsh with beginning frustration. "I would ask you to speak plainly."

For a moment, Evelyn remained silent. However, from the way her gaze grew distant, Richard believed she sought to find the right words to express herself. Then her dark eyes came to rest on his once more. "Do you truly believe that you are the only one who has doubts about others' intentions, motives, affections? Do you truly believe that everyone else knows with certainty how others feel?" She shook her head. "Let me tell you that it is not so. While I admit that you may be at a greater disadvantage when it comes to reading others, you are not the only one who struggles with this."

Never had Richard discussed this with anyone. Never had he spoken of his own shortcoming. Never had he asked for advice or sought to share his doubts with another.

Therefore, no one had ever spoken to him of their own experience. Always had Richard assumed that the people around him simply knew.

Knew how others felt.

At least if they cared to know.

"My eyes see...affection when you look at me," Evelyn finally said, her voice trembling as she held his gaze, "and yet, I do not dare believe them for it would be foolish to believe something simply because one wishes to. Can I trust my eyes? Or are they deceiving me? Simply showing me what I wish to see?" Swallowing, she shrugged. "How can I know? I'm hindered, blinded by fear of rejection." She inhaled a slow breath. "Just like you."

Chapter Twenty-Two

NO ONE ELSE

Feeling her insides quiver, Evelyn stood her ground.

A part of her could see that her words had stunned him speechless. Still, another part of her was too preoccupied with her own fear of having her affections rejected that she could not be certain of her husband's deeper feelings.

The way he had lit up when she had shared her own feelings with him had given her hope. However, in this moment, when her emotions ran wild, she did not dare trust her own observations. Never had she felt so vulnerable.

Her husband blinked then, and the paralysis that had befallen him evaporated into thin air. A smile tickled the corners of his mouth, and Evelyn felt her own heart skip a beat when he suddenly reached for her.

His fingers gently grasped her chin as his grey eyes held hers without doubt, without hesitation. "I do care for you, Evelyn," he whispered, the words feeling like a caress against her skin as his other arm pulled her closer into his embrace.

A moment later, his mouth closed over hers and all thoughts fled her mind, leaving not a single doubt behind.

The gentleness with which he held her against him, with which his lips moved over hers spoke of more than mere passion. Indeed, if Evelyn dared trust her own instincts, she could not help but believe that he truly did care for her. Why else would he have shared so much of himself with her? Opened up about something that clearly pained him? Shamed him?

"Do you believe me?" he whispered when he lifted his head and gazed down into her eyes, his own suddenly calm.

Evelyn nodded. "I do." Relief and joy tugged on her lips, and she smiled up at him without restraint.

A rare smile flickered over her husband's face as well before he took a step back, his hands still gently holding hers. "And yet you wish for me to leave?" he asked, his voice, however, held a teasing note. "You wish to postpone our wedding night?"

"I never said I wanted you to leave," Evelyn pointed out as her body relaxed at the lightness in their conversation. "But I wish to get to know you better. I wish to speak to you and have you speak to me."

Her husband nodded. Still, there was a touch of confusion in the way his brows drew down, and his mouth opened as though he wished to ask a question but closed once more before he dared.

"What is it?" Evelyn dared him. "Honesty. Remember?"

He cleared his throat. "I do not mean to pressure you," he voiced carefully. "But can you tell me for how long you wish to postpone it?"

Evelyn's mouth opened, and she was about to repeat what she had said before when he stopped her. "I know what you said, until we know each other better." The space between his brows wrinkled. "But what does that mean? How will I know?"

Evelyn nodded, relieved that he dared reveal his insecurity to her. "Well, since I cannot give you a specific date, I would suggest that I let you know. Does that seem fair?"

Her husband nodded, a touch of relief on his face. "It does." For a moment, his gaze held hers, and he seemed indecisive before he stepped back. "I bid you a good night, my lady."

"Call me Evelyn."

Stopping in his tracks, his gaze remained on hers, searching. "Evelyn," he whispered as though to test what her name would feel like on his lips.

Watching him, Evelyn held her breath, knowing that his use of her given name was not something that came easily to him. It might seem like an insignificant detail, and yet, it was not. "If you don't object, my lord," she said, feeling her hands tremble with anticipation as well as a hint of fear to be rejected.

The right corner of his mouth curled up slightly, and his grey eyes darkened as he approached her. "Under one condition only, *my lady*."

Evelyn swallowed. "Name it."

"That you call me Richard."

Joy filled her heart. "I will," she agreed wholeheartedly, smiling up at him with utter delight. "I'd like that very much."

"Good." Returning her smile, he gently brushed the knuckles of his right hand along her jaw. "Good night then."

"Stay."

Confused, his brows drew down. "But...you said–?"

"I said I never asked you to leave," Evelyn pointed out, enjoying their way of communicating with one another very much. Although it did not yet come easy to either one of them, there was a gentle delight in the way they tried to understand each other. She could only hope they would always be able to speak so honestly. Perhaps his *deficiency* was a blessing in disguise. After all, without it, Evelyn doubted that they would have spoken to each other the way they were now.

"I admit I don't understand," Richard said, his shoulders tense. And yet, the look on his face was not nearly as pained as she had seen it before.

"Then I shall explain," Evelyn replied as she looked up into his darkened eyes. "I would like you to spend the night."

His brows rose, and he stared at her.

Evelyn smiled. "Sleep next to me."

The grey in his eyes darkened as he watched her carefully. "Sleep?"

Evelyn nodded. "Sleep."

When her husband nodded his head in agreement, Evelyn stepped away and slid into bed, gesturing for him to join her. Her pulse hammered in her neck, and she had to will her breath not to rush in and out as though she were on the run. *Calm*, she whispered to herself, glancing at her husband as he lay back, his eyes staring up at the ceiling above.

Would this awkwardness ever subside? Evelyn wondered. But then she reminded herself that they had already embarked on the one journey that could lead to a deeper understanding of each other. "It is your turn to answer a question," she whispered after extinguishing the last candle.

In the dark, she could hear him draw in a slow breath and felt rather than saw his renewed tension. She, too, felt apprehensive about asking him this. However, her heart needed to know and although doubts remained, Evelyn had hope. More than before. His words and actions had given her hope, allowed her to believe that theirs would not always remain a marriage of convenience.

"Why did you marry me?" Evelyn asked, her hands clenched around one another. "Only because of your father? Or...?" Closing her eyes, Evelyn's voice trailed off, hoping he would answer and fearing it all the same.

Taken aback, Richard stared up at the dark ceiling, his wife's shallow breaths reaching his ears more acutely now that he had been robbed of his sense of sight. He could almost picture her chest rising and falling, her face tense as she lay in the dark, waiting.

Waiting for his answer.

But what was he to say? How was he to explain without offending her? Without ruining the tender understanding that had begun to blossom between them so unexpectedly?

And yet, they had promised each other honesty. He could not break his word. He would not. Never had he lied for any reason whatsoever. Lying was deceitful, and he had never understood the many reasons people had for lying to someone they supposedly cared about.

Richard sighed. Even if it would hurt initially, there was no other choice than honesty. If not tonight, then perhaps one day she would be able to understand even if he chose his words poorly.

"When I first read my father's letter," Richard began, his ears straining to hear the rhythm of her breathing, to have any indication for how his words were received, "I was angry."

His wife inhaled a rapid breath through her nose, but otherwise remained quiet.

Swallowing, Richard knew that his words upset her, and yet, a part of him could not help but delight in the fact. She truly did care for him, did she not? Why else would his words upset her? Or was he misinterpreting her reaction? Had she already fallen asleep?

Glancing at her out of the corner of his eye, Richard thought to see the slight movement of her lashes rising and falling and breathed a sigh of relief. Then he inhaled a deep breath of his own and continued on. "I was angry because there seemed to be no good reason for us to marry." He sighed, "And I cannot deny that I...disliked that my father went over my head and did not even have the courage to inform me of his decision himself. I was never able to understand him, which ought to come as no surprise. However, I always thought that I had his respect," he scoffed. "And then my mother handed me his letter, and everything changed. His decision made me doubt how he truly saw me, and I could not help the anger that followed."

Glancing at his wife once more, Richard wished he could see her face. Even if he only read another's expression with more luck than knowledge, it would at least give him some indication.

"I'm not angry with you," her soft voice echoed to his ears, "if that's what you think. I asked for honesty. You did nothing wrong." Despite her words, Richard could not help but feel that he had disappointed her.

And it pained him more than he would have expected.

"It is true that I disliked my father's decision," Richard continued, knowing that although he had been honest, he had not yet answered her question fully. Inhaling a deep breath, he rolled onto his side, his eyes trailing the dim outline of her profile in the dark. "But it is also true that there is no one else I'd rather have beside me. Right here. Right now."

The moment the words had left his lips, Richard held his breath. Had he said too much?

A slight quivering in Evelyn's jaw was her first sign that she had heard him before she, too, rolled onto her side, her dark eyes almost glowing in the faint light drifting in through a gap in the curtains. A soft smile played on her darkened features, and Richard felt his heart beat wildly in his chest.

"I feel the same," she finally whispered. "The way this marriage came to be was not...the way I would have liked it, but I am glad that my father tied me to you and not another."

Watching her snuggle deeper into her pillow while her eyes remained on his, Richard suddenly felt the deep desire to stay in this bed forever. He felt at peace, understood and...even cared for.

"I thank you for speaking so openly," his wife said, her features gentle. "I know it's hard to speak without restraint. People rarely do so. They observe and deduce, and they're often wrong. Figuring out what goes on in another's heart and mind is not an exact science. Only because someone is smiling does not mean that he or she is happy. There is so much more to it."

Richard nodded. "I've come to the same conclusion, which makes life rather frustrating. Is nothing ever truly as it seems? Are there always hidden meanings, agendas, intentions?"

"Not always, and I promise I shall make an effort to always say what I mean."

"I thank you for that...Evelyn." Even in the dark, Richard could see her answering smile at his use of her given name and it made his heart soar. Perhaps he had not given his father enough credit. Perhaps he had been wiser than Richard had thought. Perhaps he had found his son the one woman who would come to understand him and help him understand the world.

Richard liked that thought very much.

Chapter Twenty-Three

FAMISHED

Upon awakening the next morning, Evelyn found her husband still in her bed. Deep down, she had expected him to be gone, to have sneaked out in the middle of the night or early that morning, knowing how new, unfamiliar situations made him uncomfortable.

And yet, he had not.

The thought warmed her heart despite the look of unease on his face as they looked at one another across the pillows.

Evelyn felt her cheeks warm and she had to fight the urge to drop her gaze. "It feels as though waking next to a stranger, does it not?" she asked boldly, hoping he would not misunderstand. Dimly, she wondered if she would spend the rest of her life hoping her husband would not misunderstand her meaning.

Brushing a hand over his face, Richard nodded, a quirk to his lips that spoke of relief rather than offence. "It is indeed," he agreed, his grey eyes slowly returning to hers. "As though the night washed away all familiarity."

Relieved, Evelyn sighed, "Then we shall recapture it," she suggested, sitting up, a teasing tone in her voice. "And then we shall endeavour to guard it well, for I assure you that it will try to sneak off again."

A soft chuckle escaped his lips, "We must be steadfast indeed."

Sitting side by side in bed, Evelyn smiled at him, but felt her breath catch in her throat when his knee brushed against hers as he shifted his position. Still, she willed herself not to react startled, to flinch, to allow this moment to slip away. After all, awkwardness still lurked on the horizon, and she knew she could not allow it to reclaim them.

"I shall see you at breakfast then," Richard said, a hint of a question in his tone of voice.

Evelyn nodded.

For a moment, his gaze lingered on hers, and she got the distinct feeling that he was reluctant to leave. The silver-grey of his eyes shone brightly in the early morning light as his gaze seemed to tie them together with an invisible bond.

Everything remained still before only his hand moved. Slowly, ever so slowly, it gently descended upon hers. His skin felt warm, comforting, and yet, the sensation of his touch sent shivers down Evelyn's back. Gently, the pad of his thumb brushed over the back of her hand, moving over the sensitive flesh where thumb met index finger.

Drawing in a rapid breath, Evelyn could not look away as his gaze still held her captive. All her senses were focused on him, the softness of his breath against her lips, the tenderness of his touch, the warmth of his body. Never would she have thought she could be that aware of another's presence. She felt him almost as much as she felt herself, her own limbs, her own heartbeat, her own breath.

"I believe it is my turn," he whispered, his face barely a hair's breadth from hers. "If you don't object."

Evelyn smiled. "I wouldn't dream of it."

His kiss was soft and tender as his body leaned into hers, not demanding, but merely touching, seeking contact. His hand left hers and rose to caress her cheek, his fingertips gently tracing a line over her cheekbones and down along the line of her jaw.

Goosebumps broke out all over Evelyn's body, and she reached out her own hands to feel him as well. His skin was rougher than hers, but her fingers delighted at the new sensation. She could have remained here with him forever...

...if her stomach had not had other plans, voicing its neglect with a rather loud and unmistakable protest.

Laughing, Evelyn broke their kiss, feeling her cheeks flame red-hot as she reluctantly met her husband's gaze. "I apologise, my lord. I suppose the morning is later than we thought."

He, too, had a smile on his face. "I suppose it must be." His gaze sobered, his eyes settling on hers once more. "And you are to call me Richard."

Evelyn nodded. "Well, then, Richard, if you would be so kind as to leave so that I may dress and head downstairs to breakfast."

The hint of a grin touched his face, and Evelyn wondered how she could ever have thought him cold and detached when in truth the man who was now her husband was full of warmth and tenderness, well-hidden, but there nonetheless. "And if I do not leave?" he teased, his brows rising into daring arches.

Evelyn crossed her arms, meeting his gaze with an insistent one of her own. "Then I'm afraid I shall take a bite out of you."

Instead of the expected laughter, Evelyn found her husband's face grow still and his eyes darken, not with anger or distance, but with intensity. Then he leaned towards her, and before she knew what was happening, his lips claimed hers once more.

This time, his kiss was demanding as he drew her into his arms, holding her tightly as though he feared she might slip from his grasp. His lips teased hers, and when she opened her mouth, she felt his teeth against her lower lip.

It was no more than a soft nip, and yet, it was enough to make her realise her earlier words and put them in perspective.

Drawing back, her husband grinned at her, his brows quirking in challenge.

Evelyn stared at him, her mouth falling open when she saw the teasing humour that clung to his face. "That is not what I meant!" she clarified. "All I meant to do was stress the fact that I'm famished."

"As am I." Again, his brows wiggled, and his gaze briefly drifted to her lips.

"For food!" Evelyn clarified once more, inwardly delighted with his playfulness. Who was this man? How had he managed to hide this side of himself so completely?

Richard laughed, his face relaxing and losing that somewhat annoying twinkle that had come to his eyes when he had been teasing her. "Then get dressed," he said gently, his hand once more squeezing hers. "And I shall see you downstairs in the breakfast parlour."

Still stunned, Evelyn watched him as he climbed out of bed and headed toward the door that led to his adjoining bedchamber. Before he managed to open the door, Evelyn rediscovered her wits and said, "You kissed me out of turn."

Her husband turned to look at her, the corner of his mouth curling up in delight. "I believe you're right."

"Now, you're in my debt," Evelyn announced, trying to force a stern expression on her face. "The next two kisses will be mine."

Once again, Richard laughed. Would she ever tire of this sound? "I cannot say that I mind," he replied. "But you should wipe that look off your face before you get a headache." Then he turned and vanished through the door, the mild echo of his laughter tickling her ears.

Sinking back into the covers, Evelyn stared at the ceiling, wondering about the man she had thought him to be and the man she had discovered him to be within the last few short hours.

"I was wrong," she whispered into the empty room. "So very wrong."

A delightful smile spread across her face as she scrambled out of bed and hastened to meet her husband downstairs for breakfast.

Richard barely noticed his valet's presence as the man assisted him into more appropriate attire for the day. His thoughts remained with his wife and the night they had shared. Never had Richard felt so connected to another person. Never had he felt so at ease. He barely recognised the man he had become in her presence.

And yet, it had felt natural...as though he had always been meant to be that man.

The hint of a smile tugged on the corners of his mouth when he remembered her widened eyes. She, too, had been surprised by the change in him. And yet, he liked to believe that it had been a positive surprise. She had been pleased, had she not?

Although Richard had worried that their wedding night would receive a similarly arranged quality as had their wedding, he had hoped that Evelyn would not solely consider her new role a duty. That she might actually come to care for him. At least a little.

However, what she had revealed to him the previous night had surpassed all his hopes and dreams. How had he not noticed her partiality toward him all those months ago? But then again, neither had she.

Richard's heart felt a thousand times lighter when he recalled their conversation, and realised that despite his lifelong belief to the contrary, he was not the only one who failed to interpret other people's emotions correctly. Although others might be more adept, they, too, could be wrong.

It was a comforting thought.

No longer did Richard feel as isolated as before. No longer did he feel as flawed. Certainly, the urge to hide his shortcoming was still there—had been all his life—but now for the first time, Richard had hope that he might be able to overcome it.

Now, that Evelyn was by his side.

As he strode downstairs toward the breakfast parlour, Richard felt his hands clench into fists in an effort to contain the energy that burnt in his limbs, urging him onward and back to his wife's side.

Cheerful chatter reached his ears, reminding Richard that they had indeed risen late. The rest of his family as well as their guests were already seated, enjoying a warm, hearty breakfast, safely tucked inside, away from the crisp winter's air.

As he stepped forward and the footmen opened the doors for him, Richard held his breath, wondering if his wife was already there or if she was still upstairs, taking her time to ensure that her appearance was flawless. Was that not a common concern among ladies?

Stepping over the threshold, Richard felt a jolt go through him when his gaze fell on his wife, seated not across the table from his place at the head but rather next to it. Had she done so purposefully? Or had it been an accident? But then again, the far side of the table was unoccupied. She could have chosen her rightful place if she had wanted to. Had she instead chosen to sit by his side?

The moment Evelyn lifted her head and her dark brown eyes met his, a dazzling smile drew up the corners of her mouth, and Richard felt as though she beckoned him forward. As though in a daze, eyes locked onto hers, he moved forward, almost mechanically greeting his family and friends before he sank into the seat beside his wife.

"I hope you don't mind," she whispered, leaning closer, her eyes sparkling as they looked into his, "but I'd rather not sit too far away from you."

Richard smiled, gently placing his hand on hers. "I do not mind at all."

Evelyn drew in a shuddering breath, and he could feel a slight tremble in her hand beneath his. Did she feel as unhinged as he did himself?

"I must say married life becomes you, old friend."

At the sound of Sebastian's voice, Richard's head all but snapped up.

Turning down the table, he found his childhood friend grinning at him, a smirk on his face that spoke louder than a thousand words. As Richard's gaze swept those seated along the breakfast table, he noticed that not only Sebastian had a rather pleased and somewhat teasing expression on his face. His mother, too, looked beyond herself with joy, and even Claudia looked at him with tenderness in her eyes. They were happy for him, were they not? Could they see that he had changed since the day before? That his wife had made him a different man? Was he so transparent?

Momentarily, Richard felt terrified by the thought that others could read him so easily. In answer, his features hardened as he met his friend's gaze. "I take that as a compliment."

Sebastian laughed, apparently not in the least put off by Richard's cold reply. "It is indeed. More so to the lady than to you." His brows rose in a brief challenge before his gaze drifted to Evelyn. "My lady, may I offer you my sincerest gratitude for giving my friend a reason to smile. I had almost feared he'd forgotten how to accomplish it."

Everyone laughed, their eyes bright and their faces smiling.

Still, Richard tensed.

Only when he felt his wife's hand gently squeezing his did he remember to breathe. His eyes found hers, and there in the warmth and peacefulness of her gaze, he found the reassurance he needed.

Inhaling a deep breath, Richard smiled at her before he turned his attention back to his family and friends. Indeed, they were not laughing *about* him. They were laughing and teasing because they were happy to see him happy, were they not? And why would they be happy to see him happy if not for the simple reason that they cared for him? Was it possible? Did they care so much for him despite his cold and detached demeanour?

Feeling his wife's warm hand beneath his, relaxed and without tension, Richard knew it to be true. As unlikely as it appeared to him to be so, it was nonetheless.

How had this happened? How had he not noticed? Would the world never cease to surprise him?

But then again, as he had only recently learnt, not all surprises were bad.

Chapter Twenty-Four
TO BE DEEMED WORTHY

The eagerness with which her husband reacted to her suggestion to take a stroll through the gardens delighted Evelyn. Bundled up against the cold, they walked through the snow-covered grounds, the fresh smell of fir and pine trees in the air as more flakes here and there drifted down to the earth.

At first, they walked side by side, their elbows brushing when the path got narrower. Occasionally, he would glance down at her as she would glance up at him. They would smile at each other, but quickly return their gaze to the path ahead.

It was a strange atmosphere that lingered around them. The past night they had shared so much, and yet, in the light of day, there were still things left unsaid.

When Evelyn was about to step on a patch of ice that reached farther onto the path, Richard grasped her arm and pulled her closer to his side...and to him. "Perhaps a stroll was not the best idea after all," he commented as they walked around the treacherous spot.

Feeling his arms holding her tightly to him, not releasing her even once they had passed the slippery corner, Evelyn smiled, enjoying the warmth of him wrapped around her. "Are you criticising my idea?" she teased, remembering how these easy words never failed to bring them closer. "Or me?"

Grinning, he looked down at her. "Is there an answer I can give that will not put me in harm's way?"

Evelyn laughed, relieved to feel that ease return. "I'm afraid not," she replied, stopping in the middle of the path. "I'm afraid you must suffer the consequences."

"Is that so?" he asked, his gaze expectant as it swept her face.

"Indeed, it is." Finally pulling her arm from his, Evelyn closed the remaining distance between them. Then she reached up to wrap her arms around his neck and kissed him soundly.

When she stepped back, Richard smiled. "If this is a punishment, I shall endeavour to upset you as much as I possibly can."

"I never spoke of a punishment," Evelyn corrected him cheerfully, "merely of consequences."

Standing in each other's embrace, they laughed, enjoying the peacefulness of the moment. Still, if they were to become even closer, know the other as they knew themselves, more needed to be said.

"Is something wrong?" Richard asked, a slight frown drawing down his brows. "You look...thoughtful."

Smiling at his efforts to try and decipher her expression, Evelyn nodded. "I am, and you're right. There is something I wish to speak to you about." Swallowing, she licked her lips, trying to think of the best way to make him understand.

Watching her, Richard waited patiently, his gaze intent, observant and perhaps a little tense.

"May I ask," Evelyn began, wrapping her gloved hands more tightly around his, "why you invited Lord Weston and his family to our wedding? From what you said earlier, you were and are concerned that your sister's condition becomes common knowledge. Then why risk inviting anyone?"

Clearly having expected anything but such a question, her husband remained still for a moment, his gaze moving from hers as he sorted his thoughts. "I understand your concern," he said as his grey eyes returned to meet hers, "however, with Sebastian, there is no risk. I've known him and his family my whole life and I...I trust him. He will guard this secret as much as I do. He would never allow Claudia to come to harm if it is within his power to prevent it."

Pleased by his answer, pleased to see that there were people in his life he trusted without restraint, Evelyn nodded, hoping that one day she might be one of them. "I understand," she said, inhaling a slow breath. "I had hoped you would say so because it will make it easier for you to understand what I need to tell you."

The hands wrapped around hers tensed, and she could feel him lean back as though bracing himself for a blow. Despite the tenderness in his heart—or perhaps because of it—he feared nothing more but to be vulnerable. To not see an attack coming. To not be prepared. To open himself to pain.

"After last night," Evelyn began, her hands once more tightening on his, unwilling to allow him to withdraw himself, "there is something I believe I need to share with you. Something I hope will allow you to understand me better. Will you listen?"

Holding her gaze, Richard nodded, his eyes intense as he focused all his attention on her.

"Thank you." Lifting her chin, Evelyn held her husband's gaze with the same honesty she saw in his. "This is not meant as an accusation or criticism, but only a way to deeper understanding."

Her husband nodded.

Evelyn drew in a deep breath. "I wish to tell you how it made me feel when you called on Mr. Bragg to tend to your mother." Again, her husband's hands tensed, but he did not make to turn away or object. "I know we've spoken of this before, and I told you that I am more qualified than Mr. Bragg and ought to be called on instead of him."

Her husband gave a brief nod of acknowledgement. Still, his eyes remained open and focused, and Evelyn hoped he truly wished to hear what she had to say.

"However, what I didn't say last time we spoke of this," Evelyn continued, "was how much your decision hurt me."

His jaw clenched, and a pained look came to his eyes, apologetic in the way he looked down at her. However, instead of fleeing this uncomfortable situation, his hands closed more tightly around hers, and he stood his ground.

"By calling on Mr. Bragg, you all but told me that you did not trust me to take care of those you love nor that you trust me to speak honestly and ask for help when a situation is beyond my abilities." Evelyn sighed, praying he would not misunderstand her. "It hurt me deeply, more than I can say, because this is the one thing I've always been passionate about. It is something that defines my character, defines who I am, and your doubt felt like...you were rejecting me." Her teeth sunk into her lower lip as she drew in a strengthening breath. "As though you deemed me not worthy." Her eyes began to mist, and Evelyn cursed herself for being so emotional, knowing it would make this all the harder on him. "It was all the more painful because it came from you."

Her husband swallowed, but then his eyes softened. He reached out a gentle hand and brushed away the lone tear that stole down her cheek.

Evelyn sniffled, her view blurred as she looked up at him. "I want you to look at me and see someone you trust. I want to be among those who have gained your respect. I want..." Her heart tightened in her chest, and her words broke off as fear overwhelmed her.

Fear of rejection.

What if she asked him to love her and he refused? Would she ever recover from this?

The tears that streamed down her cheeks puzzled him. Never had she seemed so vulnerable. Always had she stood tall, unafraid and unyielding. Always had he been impressed by her bravery. Had envied her even. Had wished to know her secret.

But now, Richard knew that he was not the only one afraid to be rejected. To be thought less of by those he cared for.

Pulling her into his arms, he lifted her chin, waiting until her eyes met his. "I did not know," he whispered, willing her to believe him. "I did not know, and I did not intend for you to feel—"

"I know." A brave smile curled up the corners of her lips. "I know you didn't, and I only said what I said to make you understand...who I am."

Richard nodded.

"Will you give me a chance to prove myself?" she asked unexpectedly. "To prove that you can trust me? That I would never allow any harm to befall you or yours?"

Watching her dark brown eyes look into his, so intent and honest, Richard could not remember what had ever made him doubt her. He certainly had to have been a fool to see her for anything less than the remarkable woman she was. "It is not you who needs to prove herself," he finally said, realising that he had been the one in the wrong. "It is I who needs to beg for another chance to prove myself. I hope that one day you will come to see that I'm not the unfeeling—"

"I know you're not," she interrupted, her voice once strong and full of conviction as she looked up at him. "I know I misjudged you as well, but I never thought of you as unfeeling." A smirk came to her lips. "Perhaps in a moment of anger. But even then I never truly believed it."

Relief flooded Richard's being as he found her smiling up at him, her fingers digging into his coat as she pulled herself closer. "I see another consequence approaching," he whispered against her lips as his arms tightened on her as well.

A soft giggle escaped her mouth. "Do you object?"

"Only a fool would," he whispered as her lips brushed against his, "and whatever other shortcomings I might have, I have never been a fool."

"I'm glad to hear it," was the last thing she said before her mouth claimed his. His mind whispered that now it was his turn once more. He smiled inwardly. Would they ever stop counting? Keeping track? Not that he minded. This was a delightful game, and he could not imagine that he would ever wish to stop playing.

Then a most inconvenient cough from down the path drew them apart.

Reluctantly, Richard stepped back to find his footman standing only a few steps away, his face rather pale as he looked at his feet before lifting his gaze. "I apologise, my lord," Maxwell said, his gaze drifting back toward the house. "But Lady Northfield's son is running a temperature, and the dowager lady bade me to fetch Lady Ashwood."

Turning to his wife, Richard wondered if another would note any signs of alarm on her face. He, however, did not. "Can you take care of the boy?" he asked, unable not to, but hoping that she would not see it as a sign of mistrust.

Her brown eyes found his, and she nodded. "I can."

"Good." A smile came to his face as he took her hand and they started back toward the house, following Maxwell's hastened footsteps.

Chapter Twenty-Five
MOTHER & CHILD

Even from a distance away, Evelyn could hear the infant's agitated cries, and her heart clenched as it always did when she was called to tend to one so small, so young. Still, her senses registered something else - the hint of panic that hung in the air.

Voices spoke, some louder than others, some barely audible. Footsteps carried across the floor only to return to their former spot. It was an atmosphere of restlessness, of dreadful helplessness when faced with the pain of another.

"There you are, my dear." Breathing a sigh of relief, Camilla strode forward and enfolded Evelyn in her arms for a brief moment. Then she stood back, and her eyes looked into Evelyn's. "Lady Northfield's son is unwell. Will you see to him?"

Evelyn nodded, glad to see such unfailing trust in her new mother-in-law's eyes. If only her husband would look at her thus. One day he might. Was this not the perfect opportunity to show him the extent of her abilities?

A hint of guilt crept into her heart at such a selfish thought. Certainly, she would never wish harm to come to anyone, merely so she could prove herself. Still, there was no way her thoughts could have brought this about. Never had Evelyn believed in the kind of superstition that often seemed to rule others' lives.

Giving Camilla's hand a gentle squeeze, she stepped past the waiting family and friends as they hovered around the open door to Lady Northfield's bedchamber, their worried gazes following her across the threshold.

Inside, she found Lady Northfield holding her crying son as well as the lady's mother. While the child's mother could barely keep herself from crying, her eyes red-rimmed and wide with fear, the boy's grandmother tried her best to calm her daughter...to no avail.

The moment Lady Northfield's gaze fell on Evelyn, she shot forward. "Please, help him! I don't know what to do. He is so feverish. His head is burning. What can I do? Please tell me what I can do."

A reassuring smile on her face, Evelyn placed a comforting hand on the young mother's shoulder before her eyes drifted down to the crying child. Her trained eyes took in his pinkish skin and forceful cries as he lay swaddled in his mother's arms, a thick blanket wrapped around him. As though to make his anger known, he waved his little fists about.

Touching a hand to his forehead, Evelyn found it burning hot. Still, the tension in her shoulders dissipated as she felt the strength of this young life under her fingertips.

Turning to the maid awaiting instructions, Evelyn said, "Please bring me a bowl of lukewarm water, not hot, not cold, lukewarm." The maid nodded. "As well as a sponge." The maid nodded again and disappeared out the door.

Then Evelyn turned back to Lady Northfield. "May I?" she asked, holding out her hands to take the infant.

Lady Northfield swallowed and for a second clutched her precious son tighter. In answer, the baby seemed to wail louder.

"I only wish to look at him," Evelyn reassured the young mother. "I will not take him from you."

Gazing down at her child's face, Lady Northfield nodded, then reluctantly handed over her son. "What is wrong with him?" she asked, brushing her hands over her reddened face. "What caused this?"

Feeling the child's soft weight in her arms, Evelyn instinctively began bouncing him up and down. Then her gaze travelled to the still open door, filled with concerned relatives peeking inside. Turning to the child's grandmother, Evelyn said, "Mother and child need a little time alone right now. Could you assure them that the boy is not gravely ill?"

The dowager Lady Weston held Evelyn's gaze for a moment as though trying to determine if the young woman spoke the truth. Then, however, she nodded resolutely and stepping around Evelyn headed toward the door. "Let us give them a little peace and quiet and wait downstairs in the drawing room. Lady Ashwood assures me the boy will be well."

As the door began to close behind the throng of people, Evelyn caught her husband's gaze, relieved to see a trusting smile touch his lips. She could not have hoped for more.

"Now," Evelyn said, turning back to the worried mother. "Let's see what ails him." Gently, she placed the screaming child on the bed and removed the blanket as well as most of his clothing. Although his skin felt feverish, Evelyn was encouraged by the strength of his movements as well as his cries.

"What is wrong?" Lady Northfield asked. "Did I do something wrong?"

"Not at all," Evelyn assured her, then once more picked up the child. Holding him tightly, she rocked him in her arms as she spoke to his mother. "Has anything changed recently? Has there been any difference in feeding or sleeping?"

Lady Northfield's brows drew together as she tried to focus despite her child's wails. "Everything was fine before our departure," she said, her gaze distant as she tried to recall everything that might be important. "But since we've arrived here, he refuses to sleep in his crib. He's always been a good sleeper, but now he only cries."

Checking the baby's throat, which was easy enough to do as it stood wide open as he wailed, Evelyn detected a tinge of redness. "His throat looks a bit sore," she said calmly so as not to scare the already frightened mother. "Do you nurse him yourself?"

Lady Northfield nodded. "After he was born, I couldn't seem to part with him," she said almost apologetically.

Evelyn gently squeezed the lady's hand. "I do believe that it is best for a child to be nursed by its mother. It strengthens their bond."

A soft smile came to Lady Northfield's lips, and her eyes misted. "I always felt so, too."

Then the door opened, and the maid returned, quickly depositing the bowl of water and sponge on the bedside table. "Is there anything else you require, my lady?"

"No, thank you, Agnes."

The maid nodded and left.

"Is he not getting cold?" Lady Northfield asked, worried eyes on her half-clad son. "People always stress how important it is to keep a baby warm."

Evelyn nodded. "It is, but he is already running a fever, and we must take care that he does not overheat. Here, feel his feet. Are they cold?"

The young mother gently wrapped her hands around her baby's little feet. Then she looked at Evelyn, a hint of surprise in her eyes. "They're not. They're warm."

Evelyn smiled at the young woman. "I think you should nurse him."

"Now? But his next feeding is not due for another hour."

Evelyn tried to keep her features relaxed as the baby's wails continued on. "When a child is ill, the normal routine no longer matters."

Lady Northfield nodded and with practised fingers unlaced her dress. Then she settled into the cushioned armchair by the window and held out her arms to receive her son.

The moment she put him to her breast, the wails stopped, and the child drank hungrily, his little fists finally stilling. "He's nursing," his mother exclaimed, joy clear on her face. "I never thought he would. He was so agitated."

Coming to stand next to mother and child, Evelyn smiled down on them. "He was agitated because you were, my lady. Children often feel their parents' unease and respond to it with their own. Try to calm down and relax as much as you can. Take deep breaths. In and out. Slowly."

Holding her child, Lady Northfield closed her eyes and then slowly inhaled and exhaled until her features seemed to relax. Then she opened her eyes once more, a grateful smile playing on her lips. "Thank you."

Evelyn nodded, then turned and collected the bowl and sponge from the bedside table. Kneeling down by Lady Northfield's feet, she sat the small basin beside her and dipped the sponge in. Then she gently ran the sponge along the child's heated arms and legs.

Not impressed in the least, the little boy kept nursing, his eyes closing as he relaxed.

"He is usually not so hungry," Lady Northfield said, her gaze focused on her son's calm face. "I wouldn't have thought that mere nursing would relax him so."

Evelyn smiled. "It is normal during a fever as his body tries to stay hydrated. From the looks of it, he might also have a sore throat, and I've often seen infants calm down when nursing. Perhaps it is the soothing contact or the fluids running down their throat, reducing the pain. I often wonder if there might be something in a mother's milk that soothes the throat."

Sighing, Lady Northfield nodded. "But what caused it? You said he is not gravely ill, didn't you?"

"I think he will be fine," Evelyn reassured the young woman. "He is already cooling down. Feel his forehead."

Placing her hand on her son's head, Lady Northfield exhaled a sigh of relief. "He is, isn't he?" She turned grateful eyes to Evelyn. "Thank you so much. I cannot say how…"

"There is no need," Evelyn assured her. "Neither is there reason to seek blame. You are a good mother to him. Never doubt that." Holding Lady Northfield's gaze, Evelyn nodded to her. "Children respond to all kinds of influences, especially this young. It might have been the excitement of your journey, the unfamiliar environment and people. It is very likely that he is simply overwhelmed. Some children handle change easily while others have a hard time. We're not all the same." Thinking of her husband, Evelyn smiled. "I suggest you keep him with you as much as you can. He feels safe with you and will learn that everything is all right."

"I will," Lady Northfield breathed, brushing a gentle hand over her son's sleeping face. "He looks so peaceful."

"He is," Evelyn replied. "He's in your arms. The safest place he knows. Why should he not be peaceful?"

Lady Northfield smiled at her, and for a moment, her eyes closed.

"You should lie down," Evelyn suggested gently. "You need sleep as well."

"What if he wakes up? What if he cries again? What if–?"

"Keep him with you," Evelyn said, urging the young mother slowly to her feet. "As long as he is near you, he will be fine."

As Lady Northfield settled onto the bed, lying on the side and embracing her child, her son stretched out a little arm as though waving his fist at the disruption of his sleep. A moment later, though, he settled back into her arms and was lost to the world.

"Close your eyes," Evelyn instructed as she placed some pillows on the far side of the bed in case the child rolled out of his mother's arms. "He will be fine, and you will need your strength."

Lady Northfield nodded and closed her eyes.

"If you need anything, call out," Evelyn said. "There will be someone waiting outside your door."

Already half-asleep, Lady Northfield mumbled her agreement before her breathing came to match that of her son's and she was fast asleep.

With a last smile, Evelyn stepped from the room to find her husband waiting outside the door.

Chapter Twenty-Six

OVERWHELMED

The moment his wife stepped over the threshold, Richard felt his heart thudding in his chest so strongly that it nearly knocked him off his feet. Not only had he missed her–actually missed her! – during the brief hour she had tended to Lady Northfield's son, but more than anything he had also wanted to see her tend to her patient. He wanted to know the woman she was when she used her abilities to take care of others. Had she not herself said that it was who she was? That she could never be herself if she could not treat those around her?

Now, they were married, and yet, Richard did not know that side of her.

"Why are you here?" Evelyn asked after closing the door quietly behind her. Her brows were pulled down a fraction of an inch, and Richard stopped.

How did she interpret his presence here? Did she think that...?

He frowned, wondering how to best address her when she spoke up first.

"I can see that you're confused," she sighed, "although I don't know about what. But I need to tell you honestly that I am...worried that you're here because you fear I may not be capable enough to –"

"No!" Now that he knew what she was thinking, Richard knew exactly what to say. "I never thought that. Not for a moment," he assured her, his gaze holding hers, willing her to believe him. When he thought to see a hint of doubt on her face, he reached for her hands. "I am here because I suddenly find myself...craving your company." He gritted his teeth as the words left his lips, as he felt the defences around his heart come down, making him vulnerable.

For a long moment, she looked up at him, her brown eyes searching his face before she slowly exhaled a breath and a radiant smile transformed her face. "You do?" she whispered, a touch of awe in her voice.

Closing his eyes briefly, Richard exhaled a rushed breath. "It would seem I do. I cannot help it."

"Neither can I." Squeezing his hands, she stepped closer, her gaze once more on his, once more inquisitive. "Does it bother you?"

Richard swallowed. "A little."

"Why?"

"Because I never wanted to be dependent on another." The words flew from Richard's mouth before he had any chance of thinking them through. Still, it might be for the best, for if he had allowed himself to consider all repercussions, he might not have found the courage to answer her honestly.

"It is a risk, is it not? To one's heart and happiness?" his wife said, her eyes full of compassion and understanding that Richard wondered about his ability to read her. How was it that he suddenly felt beyond the shadow of a doubt that she understood him? That she did not hold his words against him?

"I thank you for speaking so honestly," Evelyn said, gently placing her hand on his cheek. "I hope we will always be able to speak to each other thus."

Richard nodded.

"Come," Evelyn said, pulling him with her as she stepped down the corridor. "I need to speak to Lady Northfield's family. They'll be worried."

Again, Richard nodded. "Is the boy all right?"

"I think he will be." As she walked with her arm looped through his, Richard felt her hand close more tightly around his arm, and she exhaled a slow breath. "Infants are always very susceptible to infections. It seems people obtain their resilience over time. Still, the boy does not seem gravely ill. I've often seen infants who have a high temperature for a day or two and then the fever breaks and they are perfectly fine." Lifting her head, she smiled at him. "I'm not worried. He'll be fine."

Relief washed over Richard, knowing how precious that little boy was to his friend's family. "Thank you for what you did." He smiled at her. "I saw how calm you were when you spoke to the dowager and Lady Northfield. You reminded me of your father. You have the same calm and gentle authority he does. You seemed very competent."

Stopping in her tracks, she turned to him and he barely had a moment to notice that her eyes were brimming with tears before she flung herself into his arms, her body shuddering with silent sobs.

"What's wrong?" Richard asked, feeling his heart tightening in his chest. "Did I say something wrong?" What had he done? He had merely tried to pay her a compliment, an honest compliment. How had he ruined even this?

"Nothing," his wife sniffled before stepping back. Wiping at her eyes, she smiled at him. "You did nothing wrong. I was just...overwhelmed. I had no idea how much it would mean to me to hear you say that." Pushing herself up on the tips of her toes, she placed a gentle kiss on his lips. "Thank you."

As though in a daze, Richard nodded, his eyes fixed on her beautiful face, so vibrant and alive with emotions. Emotions she had for him. It had been his words that had put that smile on her face, that had touched her heart. His opinion that mattered to her.

He mattered to her.

It was a thought as overwhelming as no other he had encountered before.

Still musing about how on earth he had managed to win her heart, Richard followed her downstairs. Transfixed, he watched her speak to Maxwell and instruct him to tell Agnes to sit outside Lady Northfield's chamber in case she needed help. She spoke kindly but with authority, and Richard was pleased to see her words obeyed without hesitation.

When they finally stepped into the drawing room, his wife was instantly swarmed by worried mothers, brothers and sisters, all begging her to tell them that their precious little boy would be well again. Quickly relieving their fears, Evelyn also gave stern instructions not to disturb mother and child. "They're both sleeping now, which is good because they need their rest. As hard as it is to give them time alone, it is what they need."

Everyone nodded their agreement, and Richard's chest swelled with pride. In that moment, he could not remember why he had ever thought it a disadvantage that his wife was a doctor.

After all, she was magnificent.

And he was clearly not the only one who thought so.

Chapter Twenty-Seven

ANOTHER'S TURN

Inhaling a deep breath of the crisp morning air, Evelyn marvelled at the changes her life had undergone recently. Not only had she left behind her old home, but she had also become a wife, a daughter, a sister. She had found a new family. A family her father had wanted for her. A family her father had known would be a good fit for her.

As she walked deeper into the snow-covered garden, Evelyn smiled, realising that she no longer held a grudge when she thought of her father's agreement with the late Lord Ashwood. Although she still wished he had consulted her, she knew that she would not have listened. Her pride would not have allowed her, and so in the end, her father had known best after all.

Now, she was happy. Happier than she ever would have thought possible. Not only did her new husband care for her, which in itself was a dream come true, but he also seemed to warm to the thought of her being the doctor she knew herself to be. Could she ask for more?

Love, a small voice whispered. *Trust.*

The snow crunched under her feet as Evelyn strolled onward, her thoughts returning to the man she now called husband. Indeed, he had confessed that he cared for her, and yet, he had not spoken of love. Truth be told, neither had she.

And what of trust? Certainly, he had come to trust her to a certain degree, but Evelyn still felt as though his trust had limits. Would he trust her with his life? Or would he hesitate to put his well-being in her hands? Would he have doubts?

Evelyn sighed, brushing a lone snowflake off her cheek. "If only I knew."

"If only you knew what?"

Spinning around, Evelyn glimpsed her husband coming around an evergreen hedge, a gentle smile on his face as he beheld her. The grey in his eyes sparkled in the bright morning light, and Evelyn felt her heartbeat quicken at the mere sight of him.

Was this love? She wondered. Did he feel it as well?

"If only you knew what?" he repeated as he came to stand before her, his hands wrapping around hers as though they belonged there. His eyes lingered on her face as they always did, trying to understand what was going on in her heart and mind.

Evelyn drew in a deep breath. "I–"

"Is it the boy?" her husband interrupted, tension gripping his shoulders. "My mother said that he was fine, that the fever was gone."

Evelyn nodded. "He *is* fine. There is no reason for concern. Do not worry."

Her husband exhaled a relieved breath. "Then what brought you out here into the cold?"

For a moment, Evelyn considered answering honestly. However, then courage failed her when she realised that his latest question had given her a way out. "I was thinking about your sister," she said instead, noting with a hint of annoyance the way his eyes moved from hers as though he faulted her for bringing this subject to his attention once again.

"This is not what I came to speak to you about," he said, his tone a bit brusque as he spoke. Then he took a step back, his hands sliding from hers.

Evelyn felt her body tense. "Then what did you come to speak to me about?" she asked with the same hint of reproach she had heard from him.

His shoulders slumped, and when he raised his chin to look at her, his eyes held a mixture of longing and vulnerability, which instantly softened Evelyn's heart.

Swallowing her own irritation, she stepped toward him. "I'm sorry," she said softly, a gentle smile on her lips. "I did not mean to speak to you thus. Please tell me what you came to speak to me about."

Richard inhaled a long breath. "I am sorry as well," he said as his features relaxed. "I should not have lashed out at you. Of course, you are free to speak your mind."

"Thank you." Glad to hear these words, Evelyn placed a hand on his arm, her eyes seeking his. "But now it is your turn to speak your mind."

An amused smile curled up the corners of his mouth, and for a split second, his gaze drifted lower, touching her lips. "Will we forever take turns?" he asked chuckling.

Evelyn shrugged, feeling her heart grow lighter. "I do not know. Would it be so bad?"

He shook his head. "Not at all. However, I'm afraid I might not always remember whose turn it is, especially if we add to the things we take turns for."

Evelyn laughed, wondering if this truly bothered him or if it was simply an enjoyable way of teasing one another. "Fine. I admit I expressed myself poorly. It is not your *turn* to speak, but you are free to do so nonetheless. There, better?"

His gaze lingered on hers just like the soft smile lingered on his lips. It seemed as though he had all but forgotten the world around him, so still had he become. Only his dark grey eyes sparkling in the early morning sun betrayed the depth of the emotions that lived just below the surface of his calm exterior.

"Richard?" Evelyn whispered, her own brown eyes searching his as she gently put a hand on his chest. "Are you all right?"

In the next instant, his hands reached for her, sweeping her into his embrace. A small gasp escaped Evelyn before his mouth closed over hers, kissing her with a passion she had never known before. What had brought this on? She wondered. After all, neither one of them had confessed their love. Had they not simply spoken of trivial matters?

When he pulled back, his eyes shone even brighter as he looked down at her, a touch of awe on his face. "You truly understand me," he whispered.

Evelyn smiled when she finally understood the source of this passionate encounter. "I try," she whispered back, smiling up at him. "As do you."

Richard nodded, his gaze holding hers as though time stood still, and they could remain locked in each other's arms forever. "I came here," he finally said, "to share something with you. Something of myself. Just as you shared something with me the other day."

Evelyn inhaled a shuddering breath, feeling the weight of his words all the way to her soul. Had she truly gained his trust that he would open up to her? That he would tell her something he had never shared with another before?

Her husband swallowed, a hint of doubt on his face. "All my life," he began, his arms tightening on her as though she gave him the strength to speak, "I felt as though I did not belong. I don't know if you can understand what it feels like to see the world unlike those around you." He licked his lips. "It's...it's as though people speak of the sky as blue, and yet, you can see with your own eyes that it is green. You try to see what they see, but in the end, it is still green no matter how hard you try to will it to be blue." He scoffed, shaking his head in defeat. "At some point, I gave up and accepted that this was not a world made for me, that I was merely a guest, a curiosity to those who called it home."

"Have you ever spoken about this to anyone?" Evelyn asked, hearing the loneliness in his words. Deep down, she knew how it felt to be the only one of one's kind. For a woman to wish to be doctor had taught her early on that she would have to walk this path alone, misunderstood by those around her. At least, she had had her father.

Richard shook his head. "Not as I am speaking to you right now," he admitted, his gaze briefly dropping from hers as though he did not dare look at her. "Once or twice, I mentioned something to Sebastian, but I knew right away that he did not know of what I was speaking. He showed me no ill-will, but neither could he understand me."

"It feels lonely, does it not?" Evelyn asked, encouraged by the look of utter incredulity on his face. Had no one ever truly been able to understand him? To make him see that though different, he belonged as much as everyone else?

"It is," he whispered, his grey eyes searching her face as though he could still not believe that she understood him. "You've felt it, too. I have made you feel like that, haven't I?" His brows drew down in shame. "When I questioned you, your abilities, I made you feel as though you did not belong."

Feeling tears brimming in her eyes, Evelyn nodded. "As I have done to you. We've both misunderstood the other." She drew in a shuddering breath. "Let's not do so again."

Nodding, he pulled her back into his arms, almost crushing her to him as they held each other tight, feeling understood and at peace for the first time in their lives.

Chapter Twenty-Eight
IN THE SERVICE OF ANOTHER

With Christmas fast approaching, Richard watched as the house was transformed into a place of warmth and laughter. Not only did he notice the evergreens that took up residence over each window, but also those strung along each arched doorway and decorated with brightly coloured bows and ribbons. Neither was it the warmth of the fires or the delicious smell of biscuits and pastries mixing with the fresh scent of pine and fir. No, more than anything, it was the glowing eyes and bright smiles of the people under his roof.

Although Richard generally objected to having guests stay in his house as their presence represented a loss of control for him, he still could not wish them gone. Certainly, some routines were altered. Some rules bent. However, his wife's calm presence allowed him to manoeuvre the treacherous sea of the unknown. Always by his side, ready to assist him without making him feel less of a man, she guided his hand and helped him to see that not all chaos was bad.

His friends as well as his family seemed to be enjoying themselves, welcoming each other's company whether they spent their time indoors or outdoors. And now that Lady Northfield's little boy had recovered, everyone was in high spirits enjoying the holidays.

Sitting in his study and tending to a few last things before Christmas would be upon them, Richard looked up when a knock sounded on his door. Upon his call, his wife entered, and he could feel his heart speeding up. Strangely enough, his body felt as though it was no longer his own when she was near. She was like a light in the dark and he the moth that could not stay away.

"Do you have a moment?" she asked, closing the door behind her.

"For you, always." Rising from his chair, Richard felt his heart skip another beat as a radiant smile lit up her features. He took a deep breath so as not to act like a love-struck boy before gesturing to the set of armchairs arranged under the windows. "Have a seat," he said, his voice feeling hoarse as he tried to focus his thoughts. Why was it that she could unhinge him like this with her mere presence alone? "What is on your mind?"

Seating herself, his wife sighed, and the glow in her eyes dimmed. "I've come to speak to you about Claudia." Her eyes held his carefully, and he knew that she was aware that this subject was most displeasing to him.

"What is there left to say?" he asked, trying to keep his voice even as he sat down across from her. "The decision has been made."

Evelyn sighed as she wrung her hands, clearly looking for the right words to begin.

Dimly, Richard realised that he was becoming more and more familiar with his wife's tell-tale signs that spoke to her emotions and helped him understand what went on in her heart and mind.

Lifting her gaze, Evelyn looked into his eyes. "I just came from the drawing room where all the ladies are currently seated on the floor around the young Lord Northfield, entertaining the baby with songs and silly faces." A fleeting smile crossed her own face as she no doubt recalled one such silly face. "Only your sister is standing off to the side." She leaned forward, and the intensity in her eyes stole his breath. "Her eyes, however, are fixed on the child and heavy with sadness."

Richard sighed, feeling a stab of pain at his sister's unhappiness. Did this truly affect her that much? Never had she seemed like the maternal type. Never had she sought the company of young children. "I do not deny that this whole affair saddens her," Richard finally said, trying to tread carefully lest his wife might receive the idea that another solution could be found. He did not wish to give her false hope. "However, I do believe it is a sadness that will pass once she resumes her old life. Naturally, without anything to distract her, her thoughts linger on the child."

His wife leaned back in her seat, her gaze roaming his face. "What if she wishes to keep the child?"

Richard tensed. "Did she tell you so? Did you ask her? I beg you not to put ideas in her head."

Rolling her eyes, Evelyn scoffed, "These ideas are already in her head. How could they not be? This is her child we are talking about. By now, she is probably feeling it move inside her. How can she not think of keeping it? It's her child!"

At the agitation in his wife's bearing, Richard inhaled a slow breath, trying to stay calm. "I understand your frustration," he said, "Believe me, I feel it as well. However, there is no other solution to be found. She cannot keep the child. Her life would be ruined, and my sister is not the kind of woman content with living her life in the country, shut away from society. And besides, did you ever think what this would do to her child? It would be a bastard with no prospects. Do you truly want this?"

Evelyn's shoulders slumped, and he thought to read resignation in her brown eyes. "Of course not," she whispered, her voice subdued. "But this cannot be the end." Shaking her head, she sighed. "Lady Northfield is unmarried and a mother. Perhaps–"

"But she *was* married," Richard pointed out before his wife was swept away by an idea that would only lead to disaster or disappointment. "The boy has a father. He may be dead, but the child is legitimate. He is not a bastard, but the new Lord Northfield. These are two completely different situations."

"I know," Evelyn admitted, frustration balling her hands into fists. "I simply hate to see her so sad. I wish there was something we could do."

"As do I," Richard assured her, wondering if she doubted his affections for his sister. "Do you truly believe that her sadness does not affect me?"

For a long moment, his wife looked at him, and Richard could feel goose bumps crawling up his spine. She could not truly think him so heartless? Not now! Not after everything they had shared with each other!

"No, of course, not," she finally said, her face softening as she looked at him. "I know that you care for her. I just thought..." Trailing off, she shrugged. "Did you ever ask her if she wanted to keep her child?"

Richard swallowed. "I did not."

His wife's eyes narrowed, and he thought to see a hint of accusation in them. "Why not?"

For a long moment, Richard contemplated what to say. If anyone else had asked him this question, he would have said that he was the head of this family and he did what was best for his sister. After all, there was no other solution.

But this was his wife. This was Evelyn, and they had spoken to each other in a way he had never experienced before.

Honestly.

Without restraint.

"To protect her," Richard finally said, noting the way his wife's brows narrowed in confusion. Inhaling a deep breath, he leaned forward, resting his elbows on his legs, and met her gaze. "I know very well that she might come to regret giving up her child," he began, "and when that day comes, she will turn her anger toward me because I forced this decision on her." He swallowed. "Instead of toward herself."

Evelyn's jaw dropped open as she pushed to her feet. "You are willing to let her hate you for it?"

Rising to his feet as well, Richard nodded. "Better she hates me than herself. No one can live hating themselves. It would destroy her."

Evelyn blinked as tears clung to her lashes. "I didn't know," she whispered as she stepped closer, her hands coming to rest on his chest as her eyes gazed up at him. "You love her very much."

Blinking back tears of his own, Richard shrugged. "She's my sister."

His wife nodded, then stepped forward and wrapped him in her arms. "Thank you for telling me."

Relief relaxed Richard's body, and he held her tightly, welcoming the comfort she gave him. "I do not wish to keep anything from you," he finally said, "and I do not want you to think me...heartless and unfeeling."

Stepping back, Evelyn met his gaze. "I did not. I assure you. You must believe me when I tell you this. Never will we be of one mind about everything. There will be instances when we disagree; however, that does not mean we think less of each other, does it?"

"You're right," Richard said, nodding his agreement. "In this we disagree, but that does not mean I doubt your abilities to come to a reasonable solution in any way. Perhaps our focus is simply elsewhere."

"It would appear so." His wife sighed, her gaze narrowing as she looked at him. "I admit what I'm most concerned with are the consequences of her having to give up her child, and by consequences, I speak of her state of mind. I fear that she might not recover from such a loss."

"I understand," Richard said, relieved that they were able to speak so openly to each other. "I worry about that as well. However, I see the greater danger in the consequences that will arise should her condition become known. I do believe the solitude she would be forced into would destroy her. But if she can stay in society's good graces and make a suitable match, then she can have another child." Seeing his wife's brows tense and her mouth open in objection, Richard hastened on, "Of course, I do not believe that one child can be replaced with another. I am well aware that the loss of this child will always stay with her. However, she might still find happiness in being a mother one day. More than she might if she kept this child, accepting the consequences that come with doing so."

Closing her eyes, Evelyn rested her forehead against his shoulder. "You're not wrong," she whispered. "We don't know what will happen." Lifting her head, she met his gaze. "But what if Claudia were to tell you that she wanted to keep her child? What would you do? Would you allow her? Or would you force her to give it up?"

Richard tried to swallow the lump in his throat. Although he knew what he ought to do, what was rationally the right course of action, he was not at all certain he would be able to do so if pressed.

What if indeed.
If only he knew.

Chapter Twenty-Nine

A WINTER'S MORNING

With Christmas only a day away, the servants bustled about the house, rushing to set everything right for the big feast the next day, and so Evelyn, Claudia and Charlotte—as Lady Weston insisted they call her—went outside into the gardens for another refreshing stroll.

"When are you to depart?" Charlotte asked, her brown eyes clouded as they looked at Claudia.

"In a fortnight." Inhaling a deep breath, Evelyn's new sister-in-law placed a gentle hand on her belly.

Slipping her arm through hers, Evelyn squeezed it reassuringly. "But your mother will accompany you, will she not?"

Claudia nodded, and yet, the prospect did not lift her spirits.

Exchanging a glance with Charlotte, Evelyn wondered if she ought to ask about Claudia's wishes after the conversation she had with her husband. Would it do her good to be given a choice? Or would it ultimately lead to her utter desolation?

Since Lord Weston had shared what he knew of Claudia's situation with his wife, Charlotte had joined Evelyn in her attempts to raise Claudia's spirits. Both women could see only too clearly the sadness that more and more clung to Claudia with each passing day. And both were concerned about the outcome of this affair.

"And then you are to remain there until the child is born?" Evelyn asked, once more glancing at Charlotte, who momentarily closed her eyes as though to steady her nerves.

Claudia sighed. "Yes," was all she said.

"And what of the child?" Charlotte enquired, a hand pressed to her stomach as though the mere thought of giving up one's child made her feel ill.

Claudia's lower lip began to quiver as she looked up and met their eyes. Then, however, she clamped them shut until they were pressed into a thin line. "My brother assures me he will find a good...a good family for him." Gently, she brushed a hand over her growing belly. "He will be fine."

"And you?" Evelyn asked carefully, holding on to Claudia as the young woman made to walk ahead. "How will you be?"

Eyes drifting into the distance, Claudia heaved a long sigh. "How am I to know?" Her gaze focused and then shifted back to Evelyn. "In a strange way, none of this feels real, and then there are moments when it overwhelms me in a way that I can scarcely breathe."

Seeing her sister-in-law's pain, Evelyn reached for the young woman, offering the comfort of an embrace. Claudia, however, stepped away, her lashes blinking fiercely against the tears that collected in her downcast eyes.

Glancing at Charlotte, who looked almost as grief-stricken as Claudia herself, Evelyn allowed the young woman to put a little distance between herself and her friends. Although Claudia stood tall as she gazed toward the far horizon, there seemed to be a heavy weight resting on her shoulders, threatening to bring her to her knees. "All my life, I've felt trapped," she mumbled as though to herself that Evelyn had to strain her ears to make out what she was saying, "my actions limited to the most boring activities. And whenever I would cross a line, my father and brother were there to rein me back in." Shaking her head, she briefly closed her eyes and inhaled a shuddering breath.

Evelyn glanced at Charlotte as the lady's hand suddenly grabbed her own and squeezed it tightly. "Are you all right?" Evelyn whispered, taking note of the paleness on the woman's cheeks.

Gritting her teeth, Charlotte shook her head, her eyes brimming with tears.

"Always was I told that my choices were wrong," Claudia continued, unaware of the silent pain and sympathy that held her friends in their grip. "And yet, I could not help myself. I longed for adventure, and love is the greatest adventure there is." Turning on her heel, Claudia's blue eyes found theirs. "Is it not?"

Charlotte nodded without hesitation. "I do believe so. Now."

Then Claudia's gaze travelled to Evelyn. "Do you love my brother?"

Taken aback by this completely unexpected question, Evelyn felt put on the spot, afraid to do either, speak the truth or lie. After all, what was the truth? Had she truly come to love her husband? Certainly, she cared for him deeply, but was that—?

"You don't need to answer," Claudia said sweetly as she took a step back towards her confidants, "for it is written all over your face." Her gaze drifted to Charlotte. "As it is written on yours as well," she sighed. "This is exactly what I've always dreamed of, what I've always wanted. And then when it seemed as though it was within my grasp, I..." Her voice trailed off, and she shook her head in disbelief. "Was I so wrong to act on it?" Again, her gaze shifted from Evelyn to Charlotte. "You did, and you found true love."

Swallowing, Charlotte stared at Claudia as though there was something she wanted to say but did not dare speak.

Evelyn frowned, wondering if Claudia truly knew the whole story behind Charlotte's romanticised wedding in Gretna Green. Had hers not been a love match after all? Or at least not initially?

Reminding herself that there were more important things to discuss, Evelyn turned her attention back to Claudia. "I would never fault you for what you did," Evelyn said gently. "You followed your heart. But even our hearts can sometimes be led astray."

Claudia nodded. "I know that now. However, back then, my experiences were far too limited for me to see it. I knew very little of William, and I know now that I was not in love with him, but with the idea of being swept off my feet by true love." Shrugging her shoulders, she looked from one friend to the other as though begging for their understanding. "I wanted at least that one adventure if no other. And so, when William asked me to elope, I was so overcome that I mistook one adventure for another and thought it to be love."

"Are you certain it was not love?" Evelyn asked, still hoping that there could be another way to solve this dilemma. Perhaps if William and Claudia realised that they were in love, he could be persuaded to marry her after all. Perhaps...

"I am certain," Claudia said, shattering Evelyn's hopes. "He is a wonderful man, but I have come to realise that I do not care for him beyond the affections of a friend. I do not miss him or long to see him." A deep sigh left her lips, and a look of frustration came to her blue eyes. "I wish I knew who my child's father is." Her gaze returned to Evelyn. "I did try to remember more of what happened that day. I tried to hold on to my dreams as they slipped away with the morning sun."

"And?" Evelyn prompted, knowing from the look on the young woman's face that her answer would not restore hope for a happily-ever-after.

"Nothing," Claudia huffed in frustration. "Nothing tangible at least. Sometimes...sometimes, I wake up and it is as though I can feel him next to me. I reach out my arm, but he is gone. Then I wake up and remember."

"Do you remember what he looks like?" Charlotte asked, her hand once more reaching for Evelyn's as she slightly swayed on her feet.

Claudia shook her head. "I never see his face, or at least upon waking, I do not remember seeing it. And yet, I know that—" Swallowing, she wrapped her arms tightly around herself.

"That what?" Charlotte prompted, reaching out a hand and gently placing it on Claudia's shoulder.

Claudia scoffed, "That I care for him." Shaking her head, she briefly closed her eyes. "This is madness, is it not? I cannot even remember his face, and yet, I...I miss him. How is this possible?"

"Are you certain he did not force himself on you?" Charlotte asked all of a sudden, her cheeks pale as she swallowed.

Instantly, Claudia nodded. "I am. He wouldn't...I mean..." Inhaling a deep breath, her gaze turned inward. "When I woke up the next morning, I...I was happy. There was a smile on my face. Only I couldn't recall why." Her gaze focused. "Yes, I am certain. If he had harmed me, I would not have felt like that. It was like nothing I've ever experienced. Utter happiness." A fleeting smile crossed her lips. "There had to have been something there between us from the moment we met. A certain sense of recognition as though meeting a kindred soul. Otherwise, I would never have given myself to him. I'm certain of it."

Charlotte's hand on Evelyn's arm relaxed, and a small smile crossed her lips. "I'm glad," she whispered. "That is good."

"Is it?" Claudia exclaimed, throwing up her arms. "Is it? What I felt for William may not have been love after all, but this...this feels so real." Her lashes flew up and down as tears began to pool in her eyes. "Apart from having to give away *our* child, knowing and yet not knowing is the worst. I remember enough to know what I've lost, enough to want it, but not enough to go and claim it." Tears spilled over and ran down her cheeks. "What am I to do?"

Evelyn swallowed, knowing that her husband would disapprove, and yet, she could not stop herself. "What do you want to do?"

The forlorn expression on Claudia's face froze. "If only I could do what I wanted to do," she sniffed. "But this is not about what I want. This is about what's right for my child." Gently, her right hand settled on her belly once again. "For once in my life, I cannot follow my heart. For once, I need to be responsible. To do what's right for him, not for me. I am...I am his mother, and it is my duty to do what's best for my child."

The way Claudia spoke, Evelyn knew that she was afraid of succumbing to her own desire to keep the child, and so she spoke the words like a mantra. Perhaps she thought if she said them often enough, they would become true.

"I don't want him to be forced into the life of a bastard," Claudia sobbed. "I don't want him to be shunned, rejected by those who ought to love him. It's not fair, and yet, it is the way it is. No matter how much I wish for it to be different, I cannot change that." Burying her face in her hands, Claudia turned on her heel and hastened away.

Charlotte started after her, but Evelyn held her back. "Let her go," she whispered, feeling tears sting the back of her own eyes. "She needs some time alone."

Charlotte sighed, "It breaks my heart to see her like this."

"Mine, too," Evelyn replied, brushing a tear from her cheek. "But there is nothing we can do. My husband was right, there is no solution. None that would satisfy all. If this is truly what she has decided to do, then she will need to find a way to...to survive this. No one can take that pain from her."

Charlotte had gone quiet, her gaze distant and her right hand lying gently on her middle as she stared after Claudia.

"Have you told anyone?" Evelyn asked, a gentle smile on her face when the young woman turned to look at her with wide eyes.

"How do you know?" Charlotte asked, a hint of red coming to her cheeks as her gaze drifted down to her belly.

Placing a hand on Charlotte's shoulder, Evelyn said, "I'm a doctor. These things are not too difficult to spot if you know what to look for."

A small smile played on Charlotte's lips, and yet, there was a hint of regret in her brown eyes. "I'm not certain. I only began to suspect a little while ago." Once more, her gaze travelled to the corner of the house around which Claudia had vanished. "And I did not wish to say anything in front of her."

"That is very considerate of you," Evelyn replied, gently squeezing her hand. "But you have every right to be happy about this, to enjoy this."

"I know," Charlotte mumbled, unable to keep the smile from lifting the corners of her mouth. "I am happy. That is if indeed..."

"Do you want me to examine you?" Evelyn asked. "To be certain?"

The bright smile that lit up Charlotte's face was answer enough.

Chapter Thirty

WRITTEN ON ONE'S FACE

Christmas Eve passed in quite a jolly manner.

As though they were all still children, Richard's own mother as well as the dowager Lady Weston sat in front of a roaring fire in the drawing room and told them old stories. Stories they had all heard before as children, and although all pretended that Lady Northfield's little son was the sole beneficiary, everyone had a peaceful glow on their faces as memories overtook them. Richard, too, felt transported back to those days when he and Claudia had been young, when his parents had both been alive and in love with each other, when he had still felt part of his family. It had been a peaceful time.

After Lady Northfield handed her sleeping son to the nurse, who would see him safely to his bed, she sat down at the pianoforte and began to play. The music drifted through the air, continuing the peacefulness that had claimed that night. From the looks on their faces, Richard knew that most were tired, but still they all lingered, unwilling to lose the companionship that had developed over the past fortnight.

Seated on the settee, Richard looked up when Claudia came to stand in front of him. With a strange look on her face, she looked down at him before seating herself on his right side.

Taken aback, Richard did not know what to say. Never had they spoken much. Not since they were children, and especially lately, their relationship had been strained. Few friendly words had been spoken.

"You made a wise choice, Brother," his sister finally said, her eyes fixed on his face as though waiting for a specific reaction or perhaps to unearth his secrets—he could not be certain.

"A wise choice?"

"Your wife," Claudia clarified, glancing in Evelyn's direction where she stood speaking to Lady Weston. "I always thought you would choose a rather conceited miss with a large dowry and the family to match ours." A small smile played on her lips. "I must say I would not have liked such a woman for my sister."

Still staring at Claudia, Richard did not know what to make of this unusual behaviour.

"Don't worry, Brother," Claudia grinned. "I have not poisoned your tea if that is what you fear." She sighed, and the look on her face sobered. "I merely wanted to congratulate you and...wish you all the happiness in the world." She shrugged. "At least one of us should be happy...and in love."

Richard swallowed. *In love?*

His sister chuckled. "Don't look so shocked!" she chided. "It's written all over your face as it is written all over hers. Seriously, sometimes you do act like children."

Unable not to, Richard laughed. "Did you just call me a child?" he asked, delighted with the mischievous twinkle that came to his sister's eyes. "Is that not the pot calling the kettle black, dear Sister?"

Suppressing a grin, she shrugged. "I never said I was not also a child, mind you."

For a moment, brother and sister looked at one another, and Richard had the distinct feeling that their relationship had changed. Although they had just said otherwise, it was as though they had moved on from the confinements of their childhood relationship and become more than brother and sister.

Friends.

Reaching out, Richard placed a hand on hers. "It'll be all right," he whispered as he looked into her eyes; something he had not done in a long time. "I'll always take care of you."

Tears sprang up in her eyes, and she blinked fiercely to chase them away. "I know," she whispered back, her voice choked. "I know you will. You always have."

"I never wanted you to get hurt," Richard heard himself say. "I always wanted to protect you, and I hope that one day you'll be able to forgive me for failing you."

Shaking her head, Claudia grasped his hands. "There is nothing to forgive. You didn't do anything wrong. It was my choice, and now I have to live with the consequences." Sighing, she glanced over his shoulder. "You've made your choice, and it was a wise one."

"Thank you. It means a lot to me that you approve."

A soft smile came to her lips. "It truly does, doesn't it?" she whispered before she shook her head as though fighting off a daze. "Now, enough with the tears, go to your wife. She asked to speak to you, and I believe I have delayed you long enough."

"She did?" Glancing over his shoulder, Richard saw her standing in the doorway, back resting against the wall, a peaceful smile on her face. When their eyes met, it deepened, beckoning him over.

"Yes, go. Don't make her wait."

Squeezing his sister's hand one last time, Richard rose to his feet and quickly made his way across the room, his gaze fixed on his wife. "Claudia said you wished to speak to me," he said as he came to stand in front of her, transfixed with the way her eyes shone in the glowing light of the room.

"She did?" A frown came to her face.

Richard stopped. "I assure you I would not lie. I–"

"Of that I'm certain," his wife interrupted, the smile on her lips suggesting that she was far from offended. Glancing around him, she laughed. "Your sister, however, seems to have a bit of devious streak... but a good heart nonetheless."

Richard turned to see his sister grinning at them. Then she pointed upward, and as he and Evelyn turned to look, they found a familiar looking piece of greenery dangling above their heads. "She did this on purpose," Richard mumbled. "She believes we're in love, but unable to admit it to–"

"What?"

At his wife's voice, Richard spun around, belatedly realising that he had spoken aloud. Her face had lost all humour, and she stared up at him with wide eyes and a mouth slightly agape.

"I'm sorry," Richard apologised. "I did not mean to say this. I simply...I was only..." Gritting his teeth, he inhaled a deep breath. "Still, I cannot say she is wrong. At least, not where I am concerned."

From whence these words came, Richard did not know. All he knew was that they were true.

Still staring at him, Evelyn swallowed. "You love me?"

"I do," Richard replied, his voice hoarse.

"You love me?" she repeated as though unable to believe him.

Wishing they were not in a room filled with his friends and family, Richard nodded. "Listen, I'm sorry if I–"

In the next moment, his wife flung herself into his arms; she squeezed him so tightly that he feared she would break his ribs. And yet, he did not mind.

Pulling back, Evelyn smiled up at him. "I love you, too," she whispered, tears clinging to her lashes. "I do. I do love you."

Now, it was Richard's turn to stare at her for although he had hoped that she would come to care for him, deep down he had never thought it possible.

Taking his hand, Evelyn pulled him quietly out of the room and up the stairs. Neither one of them said a word as they walked down the corridor. Only when they came to stand in front of the door to her bedchamber did she turn to look at him. Her gaze was unsteady as though she was suddenly shy, but her hand still held his with the same determination he had seen in her eyes before. "I think we've both waited long enough, don't you agree?"

Remembering his words from the night of their wedding, Richard felt his heart skip a beat. Had she truly come to love him? To care for him and trust him so completely that she felt comfortable inviting him into her bed?

"Do you disagree?" his wife asked, her voice trembling. And only in that moment did Richard realise that he had not answered her, and that she could not read it on his face.

Stepping forward, he pulled her into his arms and kissed her with all the passion she had so unexpectedly awakened within him. Her hands travelled up his arms and then linked behind his neck as she pulled herself closer. Never did he wish to be parted from her again.

Despite all the uncertainties life possessed, Richard knew beyond the shadow of a doubt that this was the place where he belonged. Where he could be himself.

Right here, in her arms.

For all the days to come.

Chapter Thirty-One

IF OR WHEN

For Evelyn, Christmas Day was like a dream.

After their shared night, she awoke nestled in her husband's arms, felt his warm breath on her bare shoulder and his heartbeat matching hers. Over breakfast, they could not keep their eyes off each other, and Evelyn was certain that everyone knew what had happened between them the previous night after she accidentally spilled her second cup of tea.

However, no one commented. No one dared tease them beyond the occasional smirk. Even Lord Weston seemed pleased as his gaze swept over his childhood friend, and his hand tightened on his wife's. Everything was so peaceful. Evelyn felt as though she had finally come home.

Only the dark cloud that hungover Claudia's head reminded her that not everything was perfect. That not everyone was as happy as she.

Evelyn reminded herself to always remember how fortunate she was.

When the sun began to set that day, everyone retreated to their chambers and slipped into their most festive attire. Welcoming aromas wafted through the house, and Evelyn felt her stomach rumble at the prospect.

Descending the stairs, she caught sight of her husband in full evening attire pacing the hall. When he heard her footsteps, his gaze rose to meet hers. The dazzling smile that claimed his lips stole Evelyn's breath and try as she might, she could not recall ever having wondered what his smile might look like.

These days, it seemed she saw it from sunup to sundown. Had he always smiled this much? How was it possible that she had never noticed? Or was this truly a change? Did she have something to do with the smiles that now graced his face so often?

The thought sent delightful tingles down Evelyn's back, and she remembered only too well the moment he had confessed his love for her. A part of her still could not believe it was true. That such utter happiness could exist. And yet, she only needed to look into his eyes to know that it was indeed true.

"You look breath-taking, my dear," her husband whispered, his voice hoarse as his gaze travelled over her dress before once more focusing on her eyes. "I'm a most fortunate man." Holding out his hand to her, he helped her off the last step, and from the slight smirk that came to his face, Evelyn could tell the direction of his thoughts.

"You caught me here once," she whispered as his arm came around her middle. "Do you remember?"

A devilish smile came to his face as he pulled her closer. "And you kissed here once," he said, his breath brushing over her lips. "Do you remember that?"

Frowning at him, Evelyn wondered about his agenda. "I'm afraid you're mistaken, my lord," she corrected him, her voice teasing. "It was in fact you who kissed me."

He suppressed a grin. "Are you quite certain?"

Giving in to the game, Evelyn crinkled her forehead and put a thoughtful finger to her lips. "Well, now that you mention it. I kissed so many men that day that I might have gotten them mixed up. Remind me again, who are you?"

For a short moment, Richard stared at her, and yet, she could see the humour in his eyes. Still, this kind of teasing was new to him, and it would take a little while for him to accept it as a normal part of communication. As expected, the stillness fell from his face, and he laughed, sweeping her into his arms. "You better be jesting, my dear?" he whispered, his lips barely an inch from hers. "But just in case you truly are in doubt, I believe it wise to remind you of who I am." In the next instant, his lips claimed hers, and Evelyn felt her knees grow weak.

When the echo of voices drifting down from upstairs, her husband pulled away, a growl of displeasure rising from his lips as he took a step back. "These people have absolutely impeccable timing," he mumbled under his breath, and yet, it did not sound like a compliment.

Evelyn laughed, then slipped a hand around his arm. "These people are your family."

His silver-grey gaze found hers. "They are," he replied, a hint of incredulity in his voice.

"And they love you," Evelyn reminded him just in case there was any doubt. "As I do, too."

His hand rose to cup her cheek...the moment Wilton stepped into the main hall, followed not only by Evelyn's father but also Mr. Bragg.

Evelyn sucked in a sharp breath, feeling the hand on her cheek tense as she did so. Then her husband turned and upon seeing the man who had claimed to be her betrothed, his body became rigid and an angry scowl claimed his face.

"Do not act rashly," she counselled under her breath as her eyes flew over her father's kind face and then drifted to the hardened expression with which Mr. Bragg seemed to glower at her husband. Both men looked ready to tear each other's throats out. It was ludicrous!

Richard's jaw clenched, and his hands balled into fists. Never had Evelyn seen him like this, lose control like this. And yet, it only spoke to the depth of his feelings for her.

Pulling on his arm, she made him turn back to her, her eyes seeking his, holding him in place. "I'm yours," she whispered, aware that her father and Mr. Bragg were fast approaching. "I'm yours. Now and forever. He never had any claim on me, and I did not choose you because you were the lesser of two evils, but because I've always been yours. Can't you see that?"

The muscles she felt under her hands relaxed, and yet, her husband's face remained rigid. Only his eyes seemed to deepen with a new emotion. Something she had never seen in him before. And in the next moment, the man who had never broken a rule in his life kissed her right then and there in front of her father and Mr. Bragg.

Despite her words, he was staking his claim, and yet, Evelyn knew that it was much more than that. By acting against decorum and following his heart's desire, he had taken an important step toward balancing both. Toward having a choice and claiming it for himself. Although others might not approve, the choice was still his if only he dared to claim it.

And now, he had.

Evelyn felt her chest swell with pride.

"Good evening," came her father's cheerful voice from behind her husband's back, "and Merry Christmas."

Stepping back as though nothing out of the ordinary had happened, Richard greeted his father-in-law. "I'm glad you are well enough to spend this evening with us."

Kissing her father on the cheek, Evelyn smiled. "Yes, Father, I'm so happy to see you here."

"And I'm delighted to be here," her father beamed before gesturing to Mr. Bragg, who unlike her husband still bore the same angry scowl on his face as before. "I hope you don't mind that I've invited Mr. Bragg. As he has no family of his own, he already spent Christmas with us last year. Do you remember, my dear?"

"I do," Evelyn confirmed rather reluctant, slightly concerned by the momentary tension that seemed to grip her husband's jaw. Did it bother him that there had been a time—as innocent as it had been—that she had known Mr. Bragg better than him?

"That is quite all right," Richard replied, once more drawing her arm through his as he turned to look at Mr. Bragg, a polite mask on his face. "Welcome to our home. I hope you are well."

After a few more strained words were exchanged, the rest of their guests finally made their appearance, which in turn led to new introductions and well wishes. By the time they were finally all seated around the table to share a festive Christmas dinner, Evelyn began to feel dizzy with hunger.

The day had been quite extraordinary in so many ways, that she had all but forgotten to eat more than a few morsels here and there. After all, there were so many more important things in life than food. Especially today, when she had finally found her way to her husband's heart.

A perfect day if ever there had been one.

Although Richard seemed more and more at ease in the company of the people he had known all his life, Evelyn could tell that Mr. Bragg's presence made him feel uneasy on a deeper level than the simple notion of jealousy. Lord Weston, too, seemed to be aware of his friend's discomfort as his gaze lingered for a moment before he rose to his feet and said, "I know that this honour is due the master of the house," he declared with a smile on his face as he raised his glass in Richard's direction, "but I'm hoping as your old friend, I will get away with being so bold as to offer a toast for this wonderful Christmas celebration."

Chuckles echoed around the table as friends and family nodded to each other. Only Mr. Bragg continued to look greatly displeased. Evelyn wondered why he had even accepted her father's invitation.

"Please, champagne for everyone," Lord Weston said, gesturing for the footmen to come forward and fill their glasses.

Evelyn caught Mr. Adams' eye and quickly returned his warm smile before he hastened to fill her husband's glass and then proceeded further down the table.

"More than anything," Lord Weston began, "this year has proved that there is nothing more important than family." Smiling, he looked down at his wife and gently squeezed her hand before lifting his eyes to the assembled guests once more. "Family old and new is our strength and happiness, and I consider myself a lucky man to be part of such loving people. May we never lose sight of this."

Raising his glass, Lord Weston looked around the table. "To all of us."

"To all of us," echoed the rest of their family as they all wholeheartedly embraced his toast with smiling faces.

However, before they could take a sip, Lord Weston cleared his throat. "There is one more reason for joy tonight," he said, once more looking down at his wife tenderly.

Evelyn drew in a careful breath as she understood the meaning of his words, and her gaze travelled across the table where Claudia was seated next to Lady Northfield.

"In less than a year from now," Lord Weston said with the beaming pride of a father-to-be, "a new life will be joining our family."

Cheers and well wishes erupted around the table as everyone offered their congratulations to the happy couple, the future parents, whose faces shone with a happiness that seemed all the brighter when compared to the misery that overtook Claudia's face.

Evelyn tensed, wishing she could pull her new sister into her arms and offer what little comfort she might give her. However, that would only draw attention to the tears that stood in Claudia's eyes as well as the iron will that prevented them from falling. And yet, her face was still, almost ashen, as the corners of her mouth drew up in a grotesque imitation of a happy smile and she joined in the congratulations offered so cheerfully.

"I never knew how strong she was," Richard whispered next to her, and Evelyn turned to meet his eyes, his own filled with sadness as he looked across the table at his sister. "She always seemed so carefree, so unwilling to see anything but her own enjoyment. She never seemed to worry about anything, no matter the trouble she often got herself in. Not as a child and not as a grown woman."

Placing her hand on his, Evelyn smiled at him. "You envy her."

"I did," Richard confirmed. "The way she saw life, the way she approached it seemed so...uncomplicated, so easy." Swallowing, he shook his head. "But I was wrong to think that nothing affects her. No, she merely has the strength to bear it. Although for the life of me, I cannot fathom where she found it."

Evelyn nodded. "We all have parts of ourselves we hide away and do not show to those around us. As they say, there's always more than meets the eye."

Richard nodded solemnly before he inhaled a slow breath, squeezed her hand for comfort and then turned back to his friend's beaming face.

"To our son!" Lord Weston exclaimed, grinning at his wife. "Or daughter! We cannot wait to meet you!"

Everyone raised their glasses and as they drank to a new life cherished and welcomed into the family. Evelyn could not stop herself from thinking of the unfairness of the world. Why was Claudia's child any less precious? Why could it not be a part of their family? Because it did not have a father? Because its parents were not married?

More than anything, it seemed foolish to restrict happiness in such a way. It made no sense, was not reasonable in any way. Why should not everyone treasure happiness no matter where it was found? Or in what way it came to be?

Pushing these gloomy thoughts aside, Evelyn tried her best to join in the celebration; however, her heart was not in it. Turning to her husband, she found him frowning at the drink in his hand. He pinched his nose as though he disapproved of the smell. "Is everything all right? Is it not to your liking?"

Richard shrugged, clearing his throat. "No, I simply..." He swallowed, then cleared his throat once more.

In that moment—the moment before her world would come crashing down around her—Evelyn knew that something was wrong.

Very wrong.

There was something in his eyes. In the way he tried to swallow. In the way his hand reached to loosen his necktie.

Evelyn saw all this unfold slowly as though time had slowed down. A part of her knew what to make of these subtle signs, and yet, her heart refused to see the truth, for it would shatter her new-found happiness and leave her a mere shell of herself.

It could not be true!

It simply could not!

And then Richard's eyes were on hers, wide and full of panic as he clawed at his necktie, trying his best to draw breath.

Awakened from her stupor by the terror in his eyes and the soft wheezing of his laboured breaths, Evelyn swallowed, grasping his arms.

"You can't breathe?" she exclaimed, needing confirmation despite everything she knew to be true.

Shaking his head, her husband pushed to his feet, knocking over the chair as he threw away the necktie. And yet, it did no good. He continued to gasp for air as before.

"Is something wrong?"

"What's the matter?"

Her family's voices echoed around her, their tone merely curious at first and then full of panic, as they slowly came to realise what was happening.

Noise erupted around Evelyn as chairs scraped over the floor, their former occupants rushing to Richard's side, crowding helplessly around him. Lord Weston spoke to him, his face pale as he tried to make sense of the situation. Then, he drew back his arm and struck Richard between the shoulder blades.

Unfortunately, that only brought her husband to his knees but failed to facilitate his breathing.

"Wait!" Amidst the sea of faces, Evelyn met her father's eyes, a presence of calm on a stormy day. "Wait!" he ordered toward the assembled group once more before striding toward Evelyn. "Did he swallow anything?"

Evelyn shook her head, her eyes focused on her husband as he sank to the floor, his skin turning a pale blue.

"Evelyn!" her father called, gripping her by her upper arms. "Look at me!"

Evelyn blinked as her father's voice pierced the daze that had befallen her. Pain gripped her heart, and the only – admittedly absurd! – thought that entered her mind was that the day had come. This was her chance to prove herself!

Not that she wanted it.

Not like this.

Not where his life was concerned.

And yet, the choice was not hers.

Here she was, holding her husband's life in her hands...and she could not move. What if she failed him? What if he...?

"Evelyn!" her father called again. "Do I have to slap you? Focus! Your husband needs you right now!"

"From what I can tell," Mr. Bragg said, from where he knelt beside Richard, "he didn't swallow anything. For some reason, his throat is closing up. It won't be long before he won't be able to draw breath."

It was the finality of Mr. Bragg's words that finally brought Evelyn back to the here and now. Her mind began to focus, overruling her heart, her emotions, allowing her to think clearly. If she tried to help her husband, she might fail him. That was true. She might make a mistake. That was always possible. Or she might lose him because there was simply nothing anyone could do. All that was true, and yet, it was also true that if she only stood here and did nothing, he would die for certain.

Then there would be no *if*.

Merely a *when*.

Chapter Thirty-Two

A SILENT GOODBYE

Feeling his throat close up, Richard could not think straight.
Panic and terror claimed him whole, dulling his senses as he lay on the hard ground. Voices drifted to his ears, but they seemed distant and shrill. His vision blurred, became brighter, then darker as though day and night could not decide whose turn it was.

Deep down, Richard knew that this was the end. With devastating certainty, he knew he would die, and it broke his heart.

Everything in his being cried out against the cruelty of fate's timing. Not now, when he had only just found the woman he loved. Not now, when they were about to start a life together. Not now, when they had only had days with each other. This was not fair. This could not be the end!

It simply could not!

And yet, it was.

Blinking, Richard strained his eyes until he spotted his wife standing off to the side with her father. The doctor's hands were wrapped around her arms as he spoke to her, Mr. Bragg by his side.

Her face was pale and her eyes dull as she stared at her father. Always had she seemed so confident, but now in this moment, Richard could read the same fear in her eyes that he felt in his own heart.

She loved him, didn't she? She truly did.

Despite their confession of love the day before—had that only been a day ago? – the realisation of how deeply they cared for one another gripped him with a force so powerful, Richard felt certain it would crush his chest.

If only he did not have to die.

If only he could tell her once more how much she meant to him. How much she had changed his life. How much he had felt since she had become his wife.

As though his thoughts had conjured her, Evelyn suddenly appeared by his side. Her hands reached for his throat, and he could feel the touch of her fingers as they slid over his skin.

Her face was tense, her eyes focused as they travelled over his face without seeing him.

As much as Richard wished she would look at him with love in her eyes, he knew that the woman tending to him in that moment was not his wife. No, in that moment, she was Evelyn, a

Doctor focused on her patient.

If only she could save him, Richard thought as his body fought to draw air into its lungs...and failed to do so. His muscles convulsed and jerked uncontrollably. Panic claimed him once more, and he tried to stand, a survival instinct kicking in and urging him to try and run from this threat.

Although his distant mind knew it would do him no good, Richard could not help himself.

"Hold him down!" Evelyn ordered, and then hands seized him, pushing him to the ground as his lungs closed off completely.

There was no more air.

It was over.

Closing his eyes, Richard whispered a silent goodbye.

Chapter Thirty-Three

A DARING WOMAN

As her husband's eyes began to flutter closed, Evelyn had to will her emotions back down as they threatened to overwhelm her. If she lost control now, she would lose him for good.

Gritting her teeth, she looked up and found Mr. Adams standing by the side wall with the other footmen. "Mr. Adams, run and fetch me a sharp knife as well as a fresh quill," she called. "And hurry!"

Instantly, the man darted away.

"What will you do?" her father asked from behind her, and Evelyn lifted her head to look at him. For a moment, her eyes held his and then his widened as realisation dawned.

Evelyn swallowed. "I don't have a choice," she explained, her hands still on her husband's throat feeling his pulse growing fainter. "His airway is closed. I don't know why, but...he needs another way to breathe." Swallowing the lump in her throat, Evelyn realised that she was prattling, and yet, she could not stop. "I once heard of something that can be done in such a case." Again, she lifted her gaze to meet her father's. "I've never done it myself, but..." She inhaled a deep breath. "It's his only chance."

Her father nodded.

"Do you have another idea, Father?" Evelyn pleaded. "Please,

228

anything you know. Anything at all. Is there anything that can be done? Anything but...this?"

Slowly, her father shook his head. "Your idea is his best chance." He knelt down beside her. "Trust your instincts. They've never led you astray."

Glancing around, Evelyn searched for Mr. Adams but only looked into one terrified face after another as their family stood around them, staring down at her husband's still body. "Where is Mr. Adams?" Evelyn demanded, then cursed under her breath. "Camilla," she called, and the woman fairly jumped forward, her face pale and tear-streaked. "Go to your son's study and fetch a fresh quill. Hurry!"

Before Evelyn had finished talking, Richard's mother was already out the door.

Then Evelyn rose to her feet, her eyes gliding over the Christmas feast they had all sat down to enjoy not too long ago. Next to the roasted pheasant, she found what she was looking for: a carving knife.

"Lord Weston, the bottle of brandy," Evelyn said, gesturing behind the man.

Grabbing the bottle, he rushed toward her. "What will you do?" he asked, glancing at his friend. "What do you need that knife for?"

Evelyn swallowed. "To save him."

"How?" Mr. Bragg demanded, walking up to them. "There is nothing you can do."

Sobs echoed over, but Evelyn ignored them. "Don't you dare say that!" she snarled, then pushed him out of the way and knelt down beside her husband once more.

"You'll kill him!" Mr. Bragg continued to object. Hands stemmed at his sides, he glared down at her. "You have no idea what you're doing. If you cut his jugular, he'll bleed out in a matter of—"

"I won't!" Evelyn snapped, returning the man's disdainful glare with a fiery one of her own. "I know what I'm doing." *Oh, how she wished this were true!* "Besides, if I do nothing, he'll be lost for good."

Pouring the brandy over the tip of the carving knife as well as her hands, Evelyn then once more ran her fingers over her husband's throat, feeling for the small indentation between his Adam's apple and the cricoid cartilage roughly an inch below.

"You can't be serious!" Mr. Bragg snarled, starting toward her. "You–!"

"Keep him away from me!" Evelyn ordered, relieved to see that Lord Weston complied without hesitation and grabbed a hold of Mr. Bragg. Although her father's apprentice squirmed like a fish on a hook, he was no match for her husband's childhood friend.

Praying that Camilla would return within moments, Evelyn placed the knife in the small indentation. Her teeth gritted together, and she thanked the heavens that he had already lost consciousness. Then she closed her eyes for a brief moment and inhaled a deep, steadying breath.

A moment later, her eyes opened, focused on the task at hand. Her hand moved, and the knife dug into her husband's throat, making a small horizontal incision.

Blood well up, but Evelyn kept the pressure steady until she felt the tip of the knife go through the last barrier.

Around her, everything was deadly quiet. No one dared to move or say a word. Everyone stared silently as Evelyn fought for her husband's life.

"Here is the quill," Camilla called, rushing to her side. "Oh, my god!" she exclaimed when her eyes fell on the knife in her son's throat.

Ignoring her mother-in-law, Evelyn held the knife where it was and looked up at her father. "Cut off the ends and make certain it is clear. Then–"

"I know," her father replied, taking the quill out of Lady Ashwood's limp hands, then quickly proceeded to do as his daughter had said. "Here," he said, barely a few seconds later, holding out the quill to her.

Taking it, Evelyn willed her hands to still. Then she brought the quill to the incision and slid it downward along the blade of the knife, slowly pulling it out of the incision as the quill went in replacing it.

Releasing the knife, Evelyn heard it clatter to the floor before she wiped her hands on her dress. Her focus remained with her husband as she leaned forward and breathed into the quill. Two puffs of air went in, and hope surged into her heart when his chest rose and fell with each.

Around her, Evelyn dimly heard murmurs, but she could not make out what was said. Instead, she searched for her husband's pulse, relieved to feel it. Weak, but there.

He was still alive.

Evelyn had to make certain it stayed that way.

She repeatedly breathed into the quill, seeing his chest rise and fall with each breath.

Seconds ticked into minutes as Evelyn waited for him to recover, her pulse hammering in her veins as she fought the panic that threatened to extinguish the last shred of hope she had left.

Leaning forward once more to give him her breath, Evelyn suddenly felt his chest rise under her hands. Her head jerked up, and her eyes focused. Fearing that she had only imagined it, Evelyn stared down at him, willing him to breathe in again.

And then he did.

Evelyn almost slumped to the floor in relief.

"Richard," she whispered, dimly aware of the sighs of relief around her. "Richard, can you hear me?" Bending over him, she gently cupped his face with her hands, rejoicing at the sight of his eyelids beginning to flutter.

The moment they opened and their familiar silver-grey looked back at her, Evelyn could have wept with joy.

Blinking, Richard opened his eyes to find his wife's beautiful face hovering above him. Voices whispered in the background, but he only had eyes for her. Her warm brown eyes as they looked into his. A tear welled up and then spilled over, dropping down onto his cheek.

Licking his lips, Richard swallowed, feeling a strange pressure in his throat.

Then panic welled up as the memories returned in a sudden flash.

He could not breathe!

Instantly, his arms flew up, trying to reach for his throat, trying to remove the obstruction that squeezed the life from him.

But his wife interfered.

Lightning-quick, her hands grabbed his arms and pushed them

down onto the floor beside his head. For a moment, her eyes vanished from his sight as she looked up. "Help me hold him down!"

Instantly, Sebastian appeared by his side, his face taut and pale. His hands clamped mercilessly around Richard's arms, pressing them onto the wooden floor.

"Richard."

Hearing his wife call his name, Richard stopped struggling, his eyes finding hers once more.

"Listen to me," she pleaded, her voice soft but insistent as her hands gently settled on his face once more. "Listen. You need to stay calm. Everything will be all right, but you need to stay calm and breathe slowly. In and out. In and out."

Richard froze as he felt his chest rise and fall, and yet, no air passed his lips. Staring up at his wife, he opened his mouth.

But no sound would come out.

Once more panic gripped him mercilessly.

Instantly, her hands tightened on him. "Richard, look at me! Look at me!"

And he did.

"You need to trust me," she whispered, her brown eyes warm and reassuring. "Can you do that? Can you trust me? You will be fine. I promise you. But you need to trust me."

Swallowing, Richard once more felt a strange pressure on his throat when his instincts kicked in, urging him to remove it. However, his heart halted his movements.

Looking up at his wife, Richard nodded in confirmation. As much as he felt compelled to give in to panic, he knew he could not. His wife was here by his side, urging him to believe her that he would be fine. And whether or not it was reasonable to do so, he realised that he did believe her. Trust her.

Slowly, his heart calmed down. He unclenched his hands, feeling the strain of this ordeal on his muscles as they began to ache.

"Good," his wife whispered. "Good. Try to relax. You will be fine. You can breathe. Feel it. You can breathe."

Concentrating, Richard realised that she spoke the truth. His body filled with air, and yet, it felt different.

Strange.

"If you promise me to stay calm," Evelyn said, her thumbs tracing gentle circles over his cheekbones as her hands still held onto him, "I will tell you what happened. Agreed?"

Again, Richard opened his mouth, only to be disappointed when words refused him. Swallowing, he nodded instead.

"You couldn't breathe, remember?" Evelyn began. "Your throat closed up. Why, I cannot say." She swallowed, and her eyes moved, became distant for a second before they settled on his once again. "I had to make a small cut and insert a tube to allow you to breathe."

Panic once more licked at him and he felt his eyes widen, but Richard fought it back down, doing his best to keep his promise. To remain calm.

"That is why you cannot speak," his wife explained. "Until the swelling is down, the tube needs to remain in." Her gaze intensified as her thumbs stopped their movement. "If you pull it out, you will suffocate. Do you understand me?"

For a long moment, Richard held her gaze before he nodded, currently his only option.

Relieved, his wife smiled down at him before she sat back on her heels and closed her eyes. Her face held utter relief as well as exhaustion, and for a brief moment, Richard could feel her hands tremble as they brushed over his chest.

Mesmerized, he stared at her, realising how hard she had fought to bring him back. He had stood at Death's door, and yet, he had returned.

Because of her.

Because she would not let him go.

Because she loved him.

Richard's eyes misted with tears, and he wished he could tell her he loved her as well. But his time would come. He was not dying after all. There would still be a new chance to prove himself to her.

And she deserved nothing less.

Chapter Thirty-Four

A GLASS OF CHAMPAGNE

Entrusting her husband to Lord Weston's care and emphasising the necessity of the quill remaining where it was, Evelyn stood back as Richard was moved to his bedchamber. Her hands balled into fists as she inhaled a slow breath.

One.

Then two.

Then another.

Her hands still shook as her thoughts and emotions ran rampant, the adrenaline in her body urging her to act.

But what could she do?

"Thank you," Claudia spoke beside her, her eyes red-rimmed as she grasped Evelyn's hands. "Thank you for saving my brother."

Evelyn smiled at her, nodding her head, as her fists loosened, and she gripped her sister-in-law's hands tightly. More expressions of gratitude followed from the rest of their family before they all dispersed. Some to tend to Richard while others felt the need to be with those they loved the most, once more aware how precious life was and how quickly and unexpectedly it could be snatched away.

A warm hand descended on Evelyn's shoulder, and when she looked up, she met her father's eyes. Swallowing, she glanced around, ensuring that they were alone before she voiced the thoughts that had assaulted her the moment her husband had returned to her. "He did not swallow anything that could have blocked his windpipe," she whispered, feeling her father's gaze on hers as insistent as was her own. "I'm certain of it."

Her father nodded, and she saw understanding take root. "But how? We all ate the same food, drank the same champagne." He turned to gesture toward their glasses. "How did this happen?"

Evelyn shrugged, her gaze drifting over the festively decorated banquet. "I do not know." She walked toward the table. "But it started after Lord Weston's toast. I turned to Richard and saw him crinkle his nose as though he smelled something unpleasant." Evelyn inhaled a deep breath as she came to stand in front of her husband's glass. "It must have been in the champagne."

"But only in his," her father added, coming to stand next to her. "No one else has shown any symptoms."

Reaching for her husband's glass, Evelyn slowly brought it to her nose.

At first, she could not detect anything out of the ordinary. However, when she inhaled a few more times, a faint odour touched her nostrils. Something familiar, but unpleasant. Something that did not belong there.

"Here, smell it," she said, handing her husband's glass to her father before reaching for her own. Holding it to her nose, Evelyn knew instantly that hers was fine.

"It might be prussic acid," her father mumbled, slowly moving the glass back and forth under her nose. "However, I cannot be certain as the scent is fairly faint."

"Prussic acid," Evelyn echoed, closing her eyes and praying that the dose had indeed only been small. Extracted from the seeds of stone fruits, prussic acid was a lethal poison.

Only too well did she remember the day her father had come home from tending to a little boy who had ingested a handful of bitter almonds as a dare. His throat had closed up so quickly, he had died before his friends could alert their parents.

Her father had seemed like a broken man that day.

Defeated.

Helpless.

He had held her close, his eyes gliding over her as though to assure himself that it was not his child that had been lost. Evelyn had been no more than eight years old when it had happened, and yet, she still remembered the horror in her father's eyes.

"This was no accident," Evelyn said, finally finding the courage to voice her suspicions. "This was deliberate." Gritting her teeth, she looked at her father, wishing he would contradict her.

Instead, he nodded in agreement. "It seems that your husband has an enemy."

Releasing a puff of air, Evelyn sank into the chair she had vacated upon her husband's collapse. A cold shiver ran down her back, and her head spun. "Who would do such a thing?" she whispered, unable to believe that anyone would dare harm her husband. Certainly, he was not the most amiable of men and often appeared cold and detached to those who did not know him. However, that was far from a sufficient reason to wish him harm, let alone ensure it by one's own hand.

"We better find out," her father said, placing a gentle hand on her shoulder, "before whoever did this tries again."

Settled in his bed, Richard found himself the centre of attention as his mother and sister as well as Sebastian and Mr. Bragg stared at him. However, only the latter had a most unpleasant look in his eyes that bothered Richard more than he could say.

As though the man was shocked that Richard had dared to survive. Hateful man! There was definitely something wrong with the way he looked at him. Richard wished he could remove the man from his house personally.

However, at present, that was not an option.

Not only because of the quill sticking in his throat—which he could not even see, but perhaps that was for the better! —but mostly because of the sudden weakness that seemed to have claimed his limbs. They felt heavy as lead. His head pounded, and his stomach twisted and turned as nausea rolled over him.

Unable to lift even a finger, Richard tried to concentrate on breathing in and out. Slowly and steadily, as his wife had told him. Still, it felt beyond strange not to breathe through his mouth and nose, and the pressure on his throat constantly urged him to lift his hands and relieve it. Fortunately, his limbs would not comply.

As his head began to spin, Richard closed his eyes, dimly wondering what had happened. How had he ended up like this on Christmas Day? Everything had been perfect, and now this. How had this happened?

Then the door opened, and Richard's eyes snapped open the moment he heard his wife's voice.

"How is he?"

About to reply, Richard sighed...or wanted to, but that was not possible, either, as no air currently travelled through his mouth. All that could be heard was a faint rushing sound as the air moved in and out of the quill.

Holding his gaze, Evelyn smiled at him, and instantly, Richard's world righted itself at least a little.

However, instead of approaching the bed, she exchanged a glance with her father and then turned to Mr. Bragg, her eyes hard, calculating, before she leaned forward and spoke to him in hushed tones.

Instantly, the man's face grew hard, his lips clamped shut, before he stormed out of the room, banging the door loudly behind him.

Exhaustion once more closed Richard's eyes, and he could not bring his mind to focus. Perhaps all he needed was rest, and tomorrow, he would speak...or write to his wife and find out what had happened.

Dimly, he saw his mother turn to Evelyn and her father. "What is going on? Why is Mr. Bragg so upset?" Then she turned to look at him. "What happened to my son? Will he be all right?"

Once more, glances were exchanged that Richard could not make sense of, especially in his current state. However, he did notice his wife finally approach the bed and sit by his side, her warm hand finding his.

Forcing his eyes open, he looked at her, feeling peace wash over him at seeing the gentle smile on her face. "You must drink," she urged him, holding a cup to his lips. "At least a little."

Richard did as she asked although swallowing felt even stranger when water travelled down his throat. Dimly, he wondered why it did not run out the quill. After all, there was a hole in his throat, was there not?

Closing his eyes, Richard felt his head fall back. Tomorrow he would ask her about that.

"Claudia," he heard his wife say, "would you go and see to Lord Weston's family. Assure them that all is well."

For a moment, everything remained quiet as though for once his sister did not know what to say. Then he heard footsteps approach the bed, and before long she grasped his other hand, squeezing it gently. "Don't you dare leave me, big brother," she warned him, her voice choked, and Richard wished he had the strength to reassure her, to tell her that he had no immediate plans of leaving this world.

Not now.

Not when he had finally found his place in it.

The moment he heard the door close behind his sister, more footsteps shuffled across the floor as Sebastian, his mother and Evelyn's father drew closer.

"If I didn't dare suggest it," Sebastian all but whispered, his voice tense as he spoke the words rather reluctantly, "I would think he was poisoned."

Richard's mother drew in a sharp breath.

With his emotions dulled, Richard did not experience anything resembling shock. He merely thought that poison would explain why he felt so poorly.

Once more, he tried to open his eyes, tried to listen to what was being said, but his body would not comply. His breathing evened, and he felt himself slipping away as sleep claimed him for good.

Richard could not say that he minded much.

Chapter Thirty-Five

SUSPICIONS

A shriek escaped Camilla's lips, and her face went pale as her hands flew up to cover her face.

Spinning on her heel, Evelyn looked at her husband, panic quickening her heartbeat as she all but flung herself toward him.

His head had rolled back, and his eyes were closed. His skin looked still pale and was clammy to the touch. For all intents and purposes, he looked like someone who had been poisoned.

And yet, his chest rose and fell with the steady rhythm of sleep.

Closing her eyes, Evelyn allowed her fingers to linger a moment longer on the faint, but steady pulse that proved that he was still with them.

That he was not lost.

"He fell asleep," she said over her shoulder, meeting Camilla's eyes. "He's only sleeping."

Relief washed over her mother-in-law's face, and she seemed about to sag to the floor as her shoulders slumped forward. Once more, she buried her face in her hands as tears streamed down her cheeks and quiet sobs rose from her throat.

Giving her husband a gentle squeeze, Evelyn hastened to Camilla's side and wrapped her in a tight embrace. Over the woman's shoulder, she met her father's gaze.

"Will he be all right?" Lord Weston asked, his gaze going back and forth between her and her husband's still form. "If it was indeed poison, then..." At a loss, he held her gaze, unable to express the concern so clearly written on his face.

Once again, Evelyn met her father's eyes, hoping against hope that he would simply nod his head in confirmation, assure her that her husband would be fine.

But he did not.

He could not.

There was no way to know yet. They had to wait. They had to be patient.

Stepping back, Evelyn kept an arm around Camilla's shoulders as she met Lord Weston's gaze. She knew even before she opened her mouth to speak, he could read the truth on her face.

His shoulders slumped, and his lips grew taut as anger claimed his features.

"The poison still lingers in his body," Evelyn said quickly before her husband's childhood friend could lose his battle for control. "Also, we cannot be certain what kind it was and how much he ingested."

Lord Weston's teeth gritted together.

"I'm hopeful though," Evelyn added, feeling Camilla cling to her like a woman drowning. "His pulse is steady. His breathing is even." She met Lord Weston's gaze. "I am hopeful."

Nodding to her, Lord Weston squared his shoulders, determination coming to his features. "I thank you, my lady, for all you've done. I know very well that we would have lost him today if it hadn't been for you." Again, he inclined his head to her in respect.

Evelyn returned his gesture, and yet, she could not help but feel like a fraud. Had she not panicked when her husband had collapsed? Had she not been useless? Had it not been her father who had kept his wits about him?

"If someone indeed wishes to harm him," Lord Weston continued, his gaze wandering around their small group and locking with each of theirs, "then he is not out of danger yet." His brows rose for emphasis, and Camilla sucked in a sharp breath. "We need to find out who did this, who wishes to harm him," he swallowed hard, "before he tries again."

Evelyn briefly closed her eyes hearing Lord Weston's words echo in her head. The same as those her father had spoken to her not long ago. Then it was true, was it not? Someone wished to end her husband's life.

Eyes wide with shock, Camilla shook her head. "I cannot think of anyone who would wish to harm him, especially not in this house." Again, she shook her head, only this time more vehemently as though she could will her words to be true. "After all, there is no one in this house beyond family and trusted friends. Who could have done such a thing?"

"Perhaps a servant," Lord Weston suggested as he began to pace up and down the room. "Perhaps someone was approached and did so for a sum."

Evelyn felt her heart grow cold with dread. "But that would also mean that someone was willing to pay another to have my husband murdered." The moment the last word left her lips, Evelyn closed her eyes as the realisation of their current situation finally sank in. "I cannot believe that to be true. Certainly, Richard is not an amiable man—at least, if you don't know him well—but he is honourable. I am certain he has never done anything that would provoke another's hatred, another's revenge."

Lord Weston and Camilla nodded.

"Then let's look at this from a more practical side," Richard's childhood friend suggested. "If Richard dies," he all but spat the words, "who inherits the title? The estate?" His gaze drifted from Evelyn to Camilla. "Who would benefit? He does not have a son...yet."

Evelyn swallowed, understanding Lord Weston's meaning only too well. Had someone truly acted out of greed? Threatened even more now that Richard had taken a wife? Now that another heir had become a very real possibility?

Turning to look at her mother-in-law, Evelyn echoed. "Who would benefit, Camilla? Who would inherit?"

Camilla swallowed, her eyes closing briefly as though all this was suddenly too much. Staggering toward the armchair under the window, she sank into it with a pained sigh.

"As far as I know," Lord Weston continued, impatience in his voice, "there are no first cousins. Therefore—"

"There is one," Camilla interrupted, and Lord Weston's eyes opened wide. "But he is of no consequence."

"Why not?" Lord Weston demanded. "Why have I never heard of this?"

Camilla sighed, her gaze meeting Evelyn's. "My husband was the second son. He inherited the title from his elder brother because he and his wife were unable to have children."

"Then how?" Evelyn wondered aloud a moment before realisation dawned.

"He's illegitimate," Camilla said, a hint of embarrassment on her face. "My husband's brother fathered a child with his mistress."

Lord Weston shrugged. "Then he truly is of no consequence. A bastard cannot inherit." He crossed his arms, and Evelyn could see the tension in his shoulders. "Then who? Who would inherit?"

"A second cousin," Camilla said, "by the name of Steven Lambert. As far as I know, he is a barrister in London." She shrugged, her eyes apologetic. "I've never met him."

Evelyn felt a cold shiver grip her body. "Could he be here?" she whispered. "Could he have sneaked into the house?"

Camilla's eyes fell open in shock. "I do not believe so. Would not someone have noticed?"

Lord Weston scratched his chin, his eyes intent as he mulled this new information over. "Perhaps he is posing as a servant," he mumbled before his head snapped up. "Have you taken any new servants into your employ recently? Perhaps he's not even *posing* as a servant but was hired as one."

Camilla shook her head. "No, not recently. They've all been with us for at least a year."

Disappointment gripped Evelyn's heart as well as the fear to be left helpless once more. What would happen if they could not figure out who wanted to harm her husband? Would whoever had done this try again? Would she lose Richard, not today, but in a week, a month or even a year from now?

"Write to him," Lord Weston said through clenched teeth, his eyes urgent as he looked at Camilla. "Write to him and invite him here. It will give us a better idea of who he is and if he has a connection to any of the servants here."

Camilla hesitated, her gaze drifting from her son's childhood friend to Evelyn and her father.

"If we do nothing," Lord Weston said, his voice insistent, and yet, there was a hint of fear in it as well, "how will we prevent the same thing from happening again?"

Swallowing, Camilla nodded. "You're right. I'll write the letter immediately."

"Allow me to assist you," Lord Weston said, offering her his arm, which she accepted gratefully.

When the door closed behind them, Evelyn became aware of her father's inquisitive gaze. His pale eyes lingered on her face as though straining to read her thoughts. "You fear it might have been someone else; do you not?"

Evelyn swallowed, knowing that she did not wish anyone to be at fault while knowing very well that someone had to be. Still, thinking this possibility turned the world into a very dark place.

Stepping towards her, her father reached for her hands. "You fear it might have been Mr. Bragg."

Evelyn swallowed, knowing that her thoughts had strayed in that direction before Lord Weston had started to question Camilla about who would inherit Richard's title and estate. The thought weighed heavily on her heart because if it had indeed been Mr. Bragg, then had it not been her fault? Because for what other reason should the man have done so but her refusal of his hand? Had she not chosen Richard over him, would none of this have happened?

"I do not wish to think so," Evelyn finally said. "However, I cannot refute the thought to my satisfaction."

Her father nodded. "He was furious when you accepted Lord Ashwood's proposal."

"He was," Evelyn confirmed. "And yet, is this a good enough reason to try and end someone's life?"

"Everyone has his own reasons," her father said. "Whether or not they're motivation enough or not is not for us to say."

Evelyn gritted her teeth. "He did not want me to make the incision." Meeting her father's gaze, she felt tears run down her cheeks. "He did not want me to save him."

Gently squeezing her hands, her father looked at her, his eyes calm. "You might be right," he whispered softly. "Or he might simply have objected because of his mistrust in your abilities."

Gritting her teeth, Evelyn cursed under her breath. "Then who? Who did this?" she snapped as helplessness and panic mixed within her heart, sending a new cold throughout her body.

"We cannot know for certain," her father replied, his fingers tightening around hers as he began to sway on his feet. "But we must find –"

"You need rest, Father," Evelyn interrupted, urging him to take the seat Camilla had just vacated. "I'm sorry to put this on you. I –"

"Nonsense!" her father cut her off, resisting her attempts to push him onto the chair. "None of this is your fault," he said vehemently, his fingers gripping her chin and raising it so that she would look at him. "You saved his life today. Do not belittle that."

Evelyn sniffed. "I could not have done so without you. I fell apart." A sob tore from her throat. "I almost let him die. I asked him to trust me, and then I failed him."

An indulgent smile came to her father's lips. "You are a great doctor, my child. The best I've ever seen. But today, you were not only his doctor. You were also his wife, and it's not easy to stay focused when the life of someone we love hangs in the balance."

Swallowing, Evelyn nodded, feeling some of the weight lifting off her shoulders.

"I'll retire now," her father said, and she could see that he was exhausted, "but you must promise to call on me if the need arises."

Evelyn gave him a grateful smile. "I promise, Father. Thank you."

After watching her father leave the room, Evelyn returned to her husband's side. Quickly, she checked his pulse and breathing, reassuring herself that he was indeed fine.

At least for now.

Settling onto the mattress beside him, she drew his hand into hers, gently brushing a curl from his forehead. "I do love you," she whispered. "I don't know when it happened, but I do." A deep sigh rose from her chest. "No matter what happens, I can only hope you know that. That you know that I meant what I said."

Chapter Thirty-Six

COMFORT

Hours passed, and Evelyn continued to sit by her husband's side. Every few minutes, she would check his pulse as well as his breathing, ensuring that the quill was free of any obstruction.

Then when her eyelids grew heavy, she rose and paced the room, trying to chase away the exhaustion that threatened to claim her. Rubbing her hands over her face, she blinked her eyes vehemently, willing herself to stay awake.

Only when the pull of sleep receded did Evelyn sit by her husband's side once again. One hand curled around one of his as she watched him while the other gently brushed over his forehead, her thumb tracing the line of his brows. Even in sleep, her husband seemed tense, his muscles taut. Was he plagued by some nightmarish dream?

Occasionally, a groan would escape his lips, and the muscles in his hand clenched, squeezing hers almost painfully. Sweat stood on his forehead, and his skin turned frighteningly pale as though life was finally leaving him.

Again, Evelyn would check his pulse, terrified by what her eyes saw. Still, his heart beat at a steady rhythm, reassuring her that not all hope was lost.

Not yet.

The thought that her husband might not recover sent a jolt of pain through Evelyn's heart, and she bowed her head as tears rose in her eyes.

"How is he?" Lord Weston's voice asked from where he stood at the door, his face overshadowed with the same fear Evelyn felt in her heart.

Wiping away her tears, Evelyn cleared her throat. "I did not hear you enter, my lord," she replied, trying to regain control of her faculties. "He's sleeping," she finally said, raising her eyes to meet his as he came to stand on the other side of the bed. "His pulse is strong, but I'm afraid that he ingested too much of the poison." Unable to keep her fears to herself, Evelyn allowed them to pour forth. "There would be nothing I could do."

Lord Weston's face tensed at her open admission, and yet, his eyes were gentle as they met hers. "You already did more than anyone else could have," he said, a small nod of his head emphasizing his encouraging words. "You saved his life, and I will always be grateful to you for that." He inhaled a deep breath as his eyes narrowed, taking on a new intensity. "No matter how this ends, I am glad to know that he was loved."

Evelyn felt her eyes widen. "Did he...? What did he...?"

Lord Weston shook his head. "He said nothing. He wouldn't. He's not the kind of man to speak of his emotions."

"Then how...?" Evelyn sniffled, her gaze shifting to her husband. "I could see that deep down he always feared that he wasn't worthy of love. That there couldn't possibly be anyone who would ever feel about him that way."

Lord Weston chuckled, "He is a bit of a fool, I'm afraid to say." The humour vanished from his face as quickly as it had come. "I was never able to understand him, but that doesn't mean I don't care about him. He is like a brother to me, and although he never said anything to me about it, I do believe that deep down, he knows."

Evelyn nodded. "He did. He said that he would not hesitate to put his trust in you."

A gentle smile curved up Lord Weston's lips. "Thank you for telling me. I suspected as much, but it's always nice to hear the words, is it not?"

Again, Evelyn nodded.

"Has he told you that he loved you?" Lord Weston asked, his gaze travelling from his friend's still form back to Evelyn.

Although his question was of a very intimate nature, Evelyn did not feel uncomfortable discussing it with her husband's childhood friend. He was indeed family. One to be trusted. "He has."

"But you don't believe him?"

Evelyn's head snapped up. "I do. I do believe him." She sighed. "But I'm not certain he believed me, especially given how our marriage started."

Seating himself on the other side of the bed, Lord Weston inhaled a slow breath. "Marriage does not always start out as it ought to; however, it is never too late to lose one's heart to another." A soft smile came to his lips. "Still, I do not doubt that he knows. He might wonder how it happened or if he is in truth deserving of your love, but he knows. You only need to look at him to know that."

Evelyn's heart began to feel lighter, and she inhaled a steadying breath. "Do you truly believe so?"

Lord Weston nodded. "I know Richard is an odd fellow, but he has a good heart–a rather inexperienced one–but an honourable one none-theless. I've always thought that if he ever fell in love, it would be completely and ardently." Placing a gentle hand on top of hers, Lord Weston nodded to her encouragingly. "Do believe me, for it is the truth. You have nothing to fear, my lady. You conquered his heart a long time ago and judging from the look in his eyes when he looked at you tonight, he has finally come to realise that your heart beats for him as well."

Closing her eyes, Evelyn basked in his words, her hand closing more tightly around her husband's. She drew in a deep breath, and when she exhaled, her head started to spin and became heavy.

"You're exhausted," Lord Weston observed. "Go and sleep."

Forcing open her eyes, Evelyn shook her head. "I cannot. I cannot leave him. I need to make certain he can breathe. If he were to roll over–"

"I will stay with him," Lord Weston assured her. "In fact, I'm not asking you to leave. Stay, but lie down and close your eyes. I'll watch over him and wake you if I need your help."

His eyes held hers, a silent vow in them, and Evelyn felt her determination waver. "You'll promise to wake me?"

"I will." His brows rose, and his gaze focused on hers. "You are no good to Richard if you're exhausted. He will need you when he awakens."

Nodding her head, Evelyn gave in. Lying down next to her husband, her hand still linked with his, she felt sleep calling to her. Still, her mind would not abandon everything that had happened that day so easily. "How is everyone?" she asked, revelling in the feel of her lids closing.

"They are all right, but frightened and worried."

For a moment, silence fell over the room, but Evelyn thought to feel its weight, and her skin prickled with things unspoken.

"Do you suppose," Lord Weston finally spoke, "that Mr. Bragg could have done this?"

Immediately, Evelyn's eyes flew open.

An apologetic smile flashed over his face. "Richard mentioned how furious the man was when you accepted his proposal." He chuckled, "I've never seen him look so jealous than when he spoke to me of Mr. Bragg declaring you *his* fiancée. Never have I seen him express such strong emotions." He smiled at her. "You touched him deeply, and I'm glad you did. That you found each other."

Smiling, Evelyn felt her eyes close, and this time, they remained so. Her mind abandoned all thoughts, all doubts, all worries and joined her husband in sleep.

He couldn't breathe!

Panic spread through Richard's body, blind and all-consuming as he felt his lungs close off.

Looking about, he found himself surrounded by people. His family. His friends. However, they did not see his distress, did not notice him suffocating, but continued eating their Christmas dinner, smiling and chatting.

Ripping off his necktie, Richard felt his panic grow when he found his efforts in vain. His lungs burst with need for air, and yet, none made it down his throat.

His vision began to blur, and there was a piercing ring in his ears.

With his last strength, Richard tried to call out to them, to get their attention, but it was no use.

He was invisible to them.

Turning his head sideways, Richard froze when he found his wife staring at him, her eyes wide.

Relief spread through Richard before his body gave up, and he slumped to the floor.

Closing his eyes, he was about to surrender his life when gentle fingers touched his face. The shock of his wife's touch made his eyes jerk open, and he found her lovely face hovering above him, her lips whispering words of comfort.

Richard smiled as the world grew dimmer around him.

Chapter Thirty-Seven

A RETURN TO LIFE

Surging up, Richard found himself trapped in a darkened room, a dim light somewhere to his right. He opened his mouth to breathe, doing his best to shake off the nightmare, but no air made it into his lungs.

Panic seized him.

His hands flew up to his throat as his eyes blinked into the dark, his gaze flickering over a shadow fast approaching the bed.

"Richard, don't!"

Recognising his friend's voice, Richard paused, but only for a second. Again, his lungs strained to draw in air, but none would come.

As he began to claw at his throat, Richard felt his friend's strong hands wrap around his wrists, forcing them back until they were pushed into the mattress beside his head. "Evelyn!"

At the mention of his wife's name, Richard froze.

"Richard, look at me!" Out of nowhere, her face appeared before him, her fingers gently tracing the lines of his face. "Look at me!"

Looking up into her brown eyes, Richard felt his panic subside. She spoke to him, and yet, he could barely make out a word. Focusing his mind, Richard tried to listen.

"Richard, you need to calm down. I know this is terrifying, but you need to try and stay calm. You cannot breathe through your mouth, but you can breathe. Everything is all right. I'm right here." She kissed his forehead, her breath brushing gently over his skin. "I'm right here, Richard," she whispered in his ear. "I'll never leave you. Breathe."

Lost in the soothing sound of her voice, Richard found a familiar calm wash over him. He still felt no air travel past his lips, and yet, his chest moved up and down.

He was breathing!

Relief claimed him, and Richard opened his mouth to whisper her name, but no sound would emerge.

"You cannot speak at the moment," his wife whispered, her brown eyes holding his, "as no air travels by your vocal cords." Her gaze locked with his. "But you can breathe. In and out. In and out."

Slowly, Richard nodded, lifting a hand to touch her face. She smiled at him then, but her eyes grew moist with tears and the look on her face changed to one of utter relief. In the next moment, she all but flung herself into his arms and her lips found his in a desperate kiss.

Overwhelmed, Richard held her tight, enjoying the warmth of her body and the peace he felt in her embrace.

"I'm sorry," she whispered, pulling herself off him. "I'm just...I'm so relieved to see you awake. I was so afraid that..."

Her voice trailed off, and Richard could see the fear that had lived in her heart all through the night. In a strange way, it was the very proof he needed to truly allow himself to believe that she did love him.

If he did not feel so weak, he would have danced with joy.

"Do you feel any pain?"

Besides an odd pressure in his throat, there was none, and so he shook his head.

"Do you feel dizzy?"

Testing, Richard moved his head. Then he shook it no.

"Do you feel nauseous?"

Again, he answered in the negative, and her face relaxed, her eyes closing briefly and her lips dancing upward into a heart-warming smile.

Once more, Richard reached out to touch her face, but before he could, she clasped it with her own and pressed a kiss onto his knuckles. His breathing quickened, and his heart beat thudded loudly in his chest. He still felt weak, but Evelyn's presence and the thought of a future with her gave him strength, and he shook off the daze that still clung to his thoughts.

When Evelyn glanced over her shoulder, Richard's gaze fell on his friend, standing by the foot of the bed, a large grin on his face. "I see you're feeling better," Sebastian teased. His eyes, however, looked overshadowed as well.

Richard smiled at him and nodded, then waved him closer.

"Help me sit him up," Evelyn said to Sebastian as he drew near. Propping up his pillows, they helped him into a sitting position.

Although Richard's body ached everywhere, it felt good to not be lying down. He still felt helpless and vulnerable when he remembered the tube in his throat, but it was better to sit. It felt less as though he was at somebody else's mercy.

"Here, drink this," Evelyn said, handing him a glass of water. Seeing him eye it suspiciously, she nodded. "It'll be fine. Swallowing will feel strange, but it'll work."

Nodding—as that seemed to be all he could do these days—Richard put the glass to his lips. His wife was correct, it did feel strange, but it worked. It was another little piece of his life reclaimed.

"Is there anything you need?" his friend asked, his gaze glancing from Richard to his wife. "Is there anything I can do for you?"

Richard shook his head, then he paused. Holding his left palm out flat, he used his right to mimic holding a quill and writing.

Sebastian nodded. "I'll be right back." However, he stopped halfway to the door, his gaze meeting Evelyn's. "How is he?"

Richard's wife smiled. "I think he will be fine." For a moment, they simply looked at one another.

Watching them, Richard could see that a new bond had formed between them. Both had been by his side in this ordeal, and it had brought them closer.

When the door finally closed behind his friend, Richard pulled his wife into his arms, his gaze seeking hers. He swallowed, feeling the pressure of the tube in his throat. Then he lifted his hand, gently touching it to the quill as his lips formed the word, *What?*

His wife sighed, and he could see that she was reluctant to answer him. "We don't know," she began, her hands holding his tightly. "But at this point, it seems very likely that...that there was poison in your glass."

Richard's eyes went wide before he dimly recalled hearing her speak to her father as well as his mother and Sebastian about it. But then sleep had claimed him, and he had not heard what else had been said. Nodding to her, he urged her to continue.

Reluctantly, she told him of their suspicions toward his second cousin, Steven Lambert. Try as he might, Richard could not recall ever having met the man. So, indeed, it was possible that he had found a place in their home without being discovered. The thought that the man might still be here sent a new jolt of panic to Richard's heart. What if he tried again before they could find him? What if he tried to harm someone else?

The door opened, and Sebastian walked in, a small stack of parchments as well as ink and quill in his hands. He set everything down on Richard's bedside table before stepping back towards the door. "I'll let the others know that you're feeling better," he said before his gaze once more travelled to Evelyn. "Have you told him...?"

Evelyn nodded. "I'm in the middle of it."

"Good," Sebastian mumbled, glancing at Richard. "We'll talk later." Then he left, closing the door behind him.

Sighing, Richard noticed a few rays of bright light reaching in through a gap in the curtains. He turned to look at his wife. *How long?* He mouthed.

"A day, I think," she said, her forehead in a frown as she tried to remember what day it was. Her face looked fatigued, and Richard felt his heart swell with love, knowing that his wife and his friend had been here, watching over him all night. Lifting a hand, he cupped her cheek, brushing his thumb over the corner of her mouth.

Smiling, she looked up at him through red-rimmed eyes, fresh tears collecting. "I was so terrified to lose you," she whispered, her teeth sinking into her lower lip as she fought to contain the sobs that rose from her throat.

Pulling her into his arms, Richard rested his head against hers, feeling at peace despite the dangers and uncertainties that loomed outside this chamber. For right here, right now, he knew he was loved and that he loved in return.

It was truly a blessing. One he would cherish for the rest of his life.

Chapter Thirty-Eight

THE WRONG MAN

E velyn was relieved to see Richard recover a little more every day as his body worked to neutralise the poison. She and Lord Weston as well as Camilla and Claudia took turns watching over him, ensuring that he could breathe and had everything he might need.

Still, Evelyn knew that they also formed a wall of protection around him, lest someone try to harm him once more. And that thought never failed to send a cold shiver down her spine. How much longer could they do this? How much longer without raising suspicions among their other guests? And among their servants?

After all, it was only one who was at fault. However, if they could not find him, then the blame and suspicions would destroy the friendly atmosphere at Farnworth Manor.

Evelyn smiled as she saw her husband gruffly brush his mother's hand away as she tried to straighten his blanket. Although the love and devotion his family had bestowed on him had touched him deeply, Richard was starting to get annoyed with all the fuss that was made over him.

Whenever they were alone, she tried to remind him that they were only doing so out of love; the one reason that always silenced him on the matter. Never had he realised how much he meant to his family, always thinking himself unworthy. Never had he been able to deduce from the way they looked at him or spoke to him how they felt. Never had he been able to read between the lines.

Always had he had doubts.

But no more.

Evelyn spoke clear words, pointing out the way they cared for him, reminding him of the little things they did. And slowly, step by step, Richard seemed to believe her. His countenance grew more lively, optimistic, and he himself grew more restless.

"I'm afraid I cannot allow you out of bed just yet," she said sternly when he had flung back the blanket and all but swung one leg out the side of the bed. "Not as long as your throat is not healed. The swelling is receding, but it is not gone yet. You need to be patient for it would be too dangerous to walk about. What if you fall?" She shook her head vehemently as he scowled at her, arms crossed like a child.

Leaving her husband in Claudia's care, Evelyn stepped from the room to find Mr. Adams waiting outside.

Upon seeing her, he pushed away from the wall he had been leaning against. "How is his lordship?" he asked, concern in his voice.

"He is fine," Evelyn assured him, noting a purple bruise on the man's forehead. "He will recover."

His shoulders slumping, he shook his head. "I want to offer you my apologies for failing you, my lady."

Evelyn frowned. "What for?"

"You bade me fetch some implements the night his lordship collapsed," he explained, and Evelyn nodded, remembering that he had never returned. "In my haste, I tripped and hit my head." He pointed to the purple bump on his forehead. "When I came to, you had already saved his lordship's life." He wrung his hands. "I thank you for that, my lady, and I hope that one day you can forgive me."

"Do not worry, Mr. Adams," Evelyn said, seeing the man's contrition. "All ended well. His lordship is fine."

Mr. Adams breathed a sigh of relief. "He is, yes."

Smiling at the young man, Evelyn took her leave and headed downstairs. Before she had even reached the ground floor, childish laughter echoed to her ears. Quickening her steps, Evelyn headed to the entrance hall where she found Camilla as well as Lord Weston receiving a young couple and their two daughters, who were no older than six.

"My dear," Camilla said upon seeing Evelyn, holding out a hand to her. "May I introduce Mr. and Mrs. Lambert and their two daughters, Mildred and Theresa." Although a polite smile clung to her face, Evelyn could see the tension that rested on her features only too well. Was this the man who had tried to kill her husband?

If so, Evelyn was certain that he had not done so himself as she could not recall ever having seen him anywhere near the estate. Or was Lord Weston correct and Mr. Lambert had paid off one of Farnworth Manor's servants? If only they knew who!

"Good day, Lady Ashwood," Mr. Lambert greeted her kindly, his green eyes meeting hers without hesitation, open and honest. "May I offer my congratulations on your wedding? May you find it an equal blessing as I do." A devoted smile came to his face as he looked at his wife, a slender young woman with gentle eyes.

"Thank you, Mr. Lambert," Evelyn replied, her heart sinking as her instincts told her that this man could not possibly be the one they sought. Or could he? Was he deceiving her even now? Reminded of her husband's inability to read others, Evelyn could have cursed in frustration.

"In your letter, you said Lord Ashwood had fallen ill," Mr. Lambert enquired, his gaze shifting to Camilla. "I hope he has recovered."

Camilla nodded. "He is feeling much better. Thank you."

Watching Mr. Lambert carefully, Evelyn found that he appeared genuinely relieved to hear the news of Richard's recovery. "That is wonderful to hear," he beamed, turning smiling eyes to his wife. "You mentioned it was something he ate. I have heard that some people react unusually to certain foods. In fact, a friend of mine almost died after ingesting a certain nut. It is quite alarming!"

"It is indeed, Mr. Lambert," Evelyn replied, doing her best to tread carefully. "We are grateful you came so quickly. We didn't dare hope as there has been a bit of estrangement in the past."

Smiling, Mr. Lambert shook his head. "I assure you, my lady, that nothing would have prevented us from coming. After all, we're family, and near or far, that means a great deal to me. I have no doubt would it have been I calling on you, you would have come for me as well." His gentle green eyes looked from Evelyn to her mother-in-law. "Please tell me what I can do. Anything to assist his lordship's recovery."

Judging from the look on her face, Camilla was equally surprised to hear Mr. Lambert speak to them thus. "You are too kind," she said with a sidelong glance at Evelyn. "But at the moment, all he requires is rest. I'm certain he will be able to receive you soon." Then she invited their new guests into the drawing room, telling them that their rooms were being prepared.

Watching them leave, Evelyn turned to see Lord Weston beside her. "He does not seem like one who would have orchestrated this," her husband's friend observed, disappointment and relief mixing in his eyes.

"He does not," Evelyn agreed, wondering if her initial thought might have been right after all.

Lord Weston's gaze narrowed as he looked at her. "You have someone else in mind."

Evelyn swallowed, knowing she could not ignore her suspicions any longer. After all, her husband's life was at stake.

With each word she spoke, Lord Weston tensed more. "I should have thought of this myself," he cursed, his eyes sweeping the entrance hall. "Where is he?"

Evelyn shrugged. "I don't know."

"We need to find him. Fast!"

Chapter Thirty-Nine
NOT WHAT IT SEEMED

Richard lay in bed resting.

Still.

It seemed all he was permitted to do these days was rest, and it was starting to make him restless. Quite the irony, was it not?

Nevertheless, even when his limbs urged him to jump from the bed, Richard knew that he was not up to the task yet. The one time he tried to get up without help, his head began to spin right away while his legs felt like pudding, ready to give out at any moment. Rushing to his side, Evelyn had immediately urged him back to bed, snapping at him for endangering himself.

A smile came to Richard's face at the memory of her fiery eyes, and he had to admit he rather liked her worrying about him. After all, did concern for another not come from deep affection? Without love, could there ever be concern?

Blinking, Richard focused his gaze on his sister as she sat beside his bed, her gaze focused on the book in her hand. It had been at least an hour since Claudia had come to visit him, and she had spent most of that time sitting there, reading to him. This, too, made Richard wonder if he had not been misinterpreting his family's feelings for him.

When Claudia had spoken to him Christmas Eve, Richard had first realised that his sister actually cared for him. But now, with the diligence and devotion she showed in caring for him, he knew beyond the shadow of a doubt that his family knew him better than he would have thought.

Knew him and cared for him.

This rather new and all the more startling realisation still overwhelmed Richard, and he did not know what to do about it. Should he speak to his family? Assure them that he cared for them as well? Or did they know? Had he once again been the only one in the dark?

The other reason for Richard's restlessness was without a doubt the threat that currently hung over his life. Despite his wife's as well as his friend's reassurances, Richard understood very well what danger still lurked somewhere in Farnworth Manor. And being locked away, unable to move, did not help the situation or his state of mind.

After all, until they knew for certain the motive behind this poisoning, they could not be sure that no one else would fall prey to the man's schemes—whoever he was.

Richard wondered if his second cousin would answer his mother's letter and if the man's reply would shed any light on the situation. Most likely, it would not, leaving them in the dark about how to proceed. After all, who was to say that the culprit would not wait them out until he once more felt safe to attempt to take Richard's life? Years could pass without them finding out who had done this.

Richard closed his eyes. They would never feel safe again.

As a knock sounded on the door, Claudia stopped reading and smiled at him. "It would seem you are in high demand, dear Brother." Then she rose and went to open the door.

The one-person Richard would not have expected to call on him now stood outside his chamber.

"May I come in?" Mr. Bragg asked, a polite smile on his face as he looked at Claudia.

"Certainly," she replied, allowing the man inside.

"I came to check on his lordship's condition," Mr. Bragg said, his voice even, and yet, there seemed to be something odd about the way he glanced from Claudia to Richard.

Then he cleared his throat and once more focused his attention on

Richard's sister. "You should be resting as well considering your own condition. I promise I shall see to your brother."

Sighing, Claudia nodded, then walked over and placed the book on Richard's bedside table. "Be a good patient, and don't grumble at the man too much," she teased him, a gentle smile on her face.

Richard held her gaze and rolled his eyes. His lips, however, remained smiling, and he could see that she had understood him.

When Claudia had closed the door behind her, Richard turned his attention to Mr. Bragg. Although the man had been called on before to tend to the sick and ailing of Farnworth Manor, it seemed odd that he was here now. In the last few days, much had changed, and Richard could not deny that he had expected to never see that man again.

And yet, here he was.

Why?

"Are you in any pain, my lord?" Stepping toward the bed, Mr. Bragg allowed his gaze to sweep over him. "You seem to be recovering well."

Richard shook his head, his eyes fixed on the man's expression, wishing he had the ability to interpret it with more accuracy.

Once more clearing his throat, his eyes as restless as Richard's limbs, Mr. Bragg proceeded to check first Richard's pulse and then his breathing by holding a wooden tube to his chest and pressing his ear to the other end. "Normal," he muttered as though to himself. "You truly seem to be recovering well."

Squinting his eyes, Richard watched the other man, uncertain if he was displeased with the fact that Richard was recovering or rather awed by it.

Swallowing, Mr. Bragg straightened, his eyes meeting Richard's. "May I have a look?" he asked, pointing to the quill in Richard's throat.

Nodding, Richard watched the man as he bent closer, his eyes focused on the small incision. Mr. Bragg turned his head this way and that, looking at the quill from all angles.

Richard did not know what to make of his behaviour. Although he did not detect anything threatening in it, he could not help but wonder why Mr. Bragg had come to see to him. Would Evelyn not have insisted on doing so? Would she not have told Mr. Bragg so? In turn, that meant that the man was here without Evelyn's knowledge, and if that were the case, then there was no telling what had motivated him to come.

Unexpectedly, Richard's thoughts were drawn back to an afternoon a few weeks ago when Mr. Bragg had left Richard's study, referring to Evelyn as his fiancée. Indeed, the man had been furious upon learning that Evelyn had accepted Richard's proposal. Since that day, they had not seen him again until...

...Christmas Day dinner.

The night Richard had collapsed.

The night he had been poisoned.

Richard froze.

Apparently having taken note of the change in Richard's posture, Mr. Bragg lifted his head, the look on his face one of careful calculation—as far as Richard could tell.

Cursing inwardly, Richard wished he was more adapt at reading others. If so, he might have seen this coming, would he not? In the least, he would not have allowed himself to be trapped alone with Mr. Bragg? A man who in all likelihood had only recently tried to murder him?

Richard's eyes darted to the door. However, without the ability to speak, to call out, there was not even a slim chance for him to alert someone to his situation.

Mr. Bragg sighed, and his brows drew down. "You believe it was me," he said, his gaze holding Richard's. "You believe I am here to finish what I started."

Unable to answer, Richard arched his brows in question. Then he reached out a hand and took the small lap desk from his bedside table, placing it on his legs. As he gathered the ink and quill, Richard kept watching Mr. Bragg out of the corner of his eye. Had he been mistaken? All of a sudden, there seemed to be nothing threatening about the man any longer.

Dipping the tip of the quill into the ink, Richard wrote, then held up the parchment to Mr. Bragg. *Why are you here?*

Mr. Bragg sighed. "To learn," he mumbled, his head bowed as though in shame. "To see how she did it."

Richard frowned, not having expected that comment. Was he speaking about Evelyn? About how she had saved his life?

"If I had been the one to tend to you that night," Mr. Bragg finally said, his voice feeble as he sank onto the chair Claudia had vacated, "you would have died, my lord." He shook his head. "I've never even heard of this method, and even if I had, I would never have dared to perform it." He scoffed, "She's good. Very good. On some level, I've always known that she had a rare skill for healing others, but I refused to see it. She is capable in a way I probably never will be." Sadness clung to Mr. Bragg's eyes before he suddenly straightened, his gaze full of determination. "But I want to learn. That is why I came here today."

Absorbing everything the man had said, Richard once more put quill to parchment. *Why did you come here alone? Why did you not speak to my wife?*

Leaning forward, Mr. Bragg read, then sank back into his chair. His jaw looked tense as he seemed to grind his teeth together. "I know I ought to have, but I was not yet...ready to admit to my failings, my shortcomings."

For a moment, Richard could have laughed, had the situation not been so dire. Was Mr. Bragg's reason not the very same one that had kept Richard from confiding in another? Did the two of them truly have something in common?

The thought was ludicrous, and yet, it seemed to be true nonetheless.

Holding Richard's gaze, Mr. Bragg asked, "May I take another look? I promise it will not take long. and then I'll leave you in peace."

Unable to detect any sign of deception, Richard nodded.

"Thank you." Rising from the chair, Mr. Bragg stepped back toward the bed, his gaze locked on the quill. Slowly, he reached out a hand and carefully touched Richard's throat about an inch from the incision. "Does that hurt?"

Richard slowly shook his head.

"Marvellous," Mr. Bragg mumbled, bending down further as he attempted to look into the tube.

In that moment, the door flew open and Evelyn burst into the chamber, Sebastian following on her heel. His eyes darkened, and a growl rose from his throat as he pushed by her and grabbed Mr. Bragg by the jacket. Flinging the startled man around, Sebastian slammed him into the wall.

"Are you all right?" Evelyn asked breathlessly as she rushed to her husband 's side, her quick eyes examining the position of the quill. "Can you breathe?"

Richard nodded, placing a hand on her arm. Then he picked up the quill and wrote, *It wasn't him. He meant no harm.*

Frowning, Evelyn raised her eyes to meet his. "Are you certain?" she asked, doubt clear in her voice. However, when Richard nodded, she turned to Sebastian without hesitation. "Lord Weston, please release him."

"What?" Holding on to a struggling Mr. Bragg, Sebastian turned his head to stare at her with wide eyes. "Why?"

"We were wrong," she explained, putting a gentle hand on Sebastian's arm, urging him to release the other man. "It wasn't him. Richard is certain of it."

Cursing, Sebastian stepped back, his hands finally releasing Mr. Bragg, who slumped to the ground, coughing and wheezing. "Then why are you here?" Sebastian demanded.

Pushing himself to his feet, Mr. Bragg straightened his jacket, his gaze never quite meeting any of theirs. "I came to see...Lady Ashwood's work. I assure you I had no intention of harming her husband."

Once again, Sebastian cursed before turning to look at Richard. "Are you certain?" he asked once again.

Richard nodded, and he could see that his friend believed him—though reluctantly. The trust these two placed in him warmed Richard's heart, and he realised that his life was not as empty as he had always thought it to be.

"If it wasn't him," Sebastian growled, long strides carrying up and down the room, his hands gesturing wildly, "then who? Who did this?"

Unfortunately, all Richard could do was shrug.

Chapter Forty

AN UNFORESEEN DEVELOPMENT

All his life, Richard had loved being on his own as he had always had a hard time getting along with people, especially in larger crowds. A friend here and there was fine, but not a gathering. Not of any kind. Not even of people close to him.

Now, thanks to Evelyn, all that had changed as Richard had gained a deeper understanding of those around him.

And especially now, trapped in his chamber, Richard felt as though he was close to losing his mind. On the one hand, he understood Evelyn's concern and knew very well that he was too weak to walk even to the end of the corridor. However, on the other hand, he felt an almost desperate need to go outside and use his own legs. What annoyed him even more were his daily visitors!

Not that he did not treasure the knowledge that they cared for him—deeply even! It was rather the fact that they all treated him like an invalid. Certainly, he was somewhat incapacitated at present. However, the fact that they all felt like *reading* to him nearly drove him mad!

Every now and then, he wanted to scream at them, reminding them that he could not speak. His eyes, though, worked fine, and his hands were at the very least able to hold a book. Yet, he did not dare as he did not wish to insult them. After all, they did what they did out of kindness and affection. How could he fault them for this?

Thankfully, a few days after the man's arrival, Evelyn and his mother escorted Mr. Lambert into Richard's chamber so that he could meet the man himself. Although, of course, the man could be lying, Richard had to agree with his family's assessment that Mr. Lambert was an honest and genuine, young man who was devoted to his family.

The only fault Richard did find in Mr. Lambert was that he bore the same somewhat pitying look on his face as did most of his family, which, however, in turn only meant that the man fit right in. That conclusion once more left them with no idea who had tried to poison Richard on Christmas Day. It was a constant dark cloud over all their heads, dampening the generally joyful atmosphere of the holidays.

The only one who seemed to take a somewhat twisted delight in Richard's inability to speak was his childhood friend. Sebastian teased him endlessly as he always had when they had been children. However, Richard knew that his friend only tried to distract him, his own tense jaw attesting that he, too, was on edge about what to do.

Sighing, Richard leaned back in bed, trying his best to listen to his mother as she read to him from one book or another. Perhaps if he did pay attention, it would indeed distract him, and time would pass faster.

At present, it was the only hope Richard had.

Well, not the only. His greatest hope was that his wife would pay him a visit soon. At the thought, a smile curled up his lips. Evelyn was the only one who did not read to him.

When a knock sounded on the door, Richard pushed himself up, eager eyes turning to the entrance...only to be disappointed a moment later when instead of Evelyn, Maxwell stepped over the threshold.

"Yes, Maxwell," his mother asked, "what is it?"

"I apologise for the intrusion, my lady," his footman said, respect-fully inclining his head. "However, Miss Davenport is asking for you."

"Oh!" Closing the book, Richard's mother rose from the chair, her brows in a slight frown as her eyes grew momentarily distant. "I better see what the matter is. I hope she is not feeling unwell. If you'll excuse me, Richard." Smiling at him, she then turned to his footman. "Would you mind reading to him? It is the only distraction he has these days."

Richard could have groaned. He felt as though he was a child again, and he did not care for it in the least.

"Certainly, my lady," Maxwell agreed, taking the book and holding the door open for her. Once his footman had closed it once more, he stepped toward the bed. However, instead of seating himself and opening the book, he placed it on Richard's lap desk, sitting on his bedside table.

Grateful, Richard offered the young man a smile, but stopped when he took note of the odd expression on his face. Arms linked behind his back, Maxwell stood with his lips pressed into a thin line as though it was all he could do not to lash out at Richard. His eyes were fixed on him, dark and accusing, and the snarl on his face sent a shiver down Richard's back.

It was him!

His mind screamed the words, and yet, a part of Richard did not dare believe them. After all, what reason could Maxwell have to seek to harm him? Had Richard not given him a chance when he had come to Farnworth Manor seeking employment without anything to recommend him? At least nothing besides his honest countenance and assurance that he was hard-working and more than willing to prove himself if given the chance? And had Maxwell not done precisely as he had promised?

From the very first, he had seemed utterly devoted to serving Richard's family, often anticipating in advance when he would be needed. Richard had been proud of the young man, giving him more responsibilities as time wore on. And Maxwell had fulfilled them all to his greatest satisfaction.

What had changed?

Or had he been fooled? Had Maxwell sought to harm him even then and Richard had not seen it?

Looking at his footman, Richard found the man's usual good-natured and respectful look had vanished. Instead, dark fury rested in his eyes as he stepped closer. "It never occurred to you that it could have been me, did it?" He laughed, but it was a dark, twisted laugh. "I was hiding in plain sight, and yet, you never saw me."

Richard swallowed, his mind racing with what to do. Why had

Maxwell come to him now? Why was he revealing himself to be the culprit?

Gritting his teeth, Richard knew that the only reason Maxwell would dare to do so was that he had come once more to end Richard's life. No doubt, he planned to finish him off and then escape the estate before anyone knew what had happened.

"But I should have expected no less, should I?" Maxwell demanded, a sneer of disgust on his face. "Your kind never sees anyone beyond those of equal station. You never look at those you deem unworthy. This is your world, and all we are good for is to serve you. Never once do you stop to think about what we want, what we deserve!" With each word, Maxwell's voice grew darker, his feet slowly carrying him closer.

Richard knew that there was very little he could do once Maxwell chose to attack him. At present, his strength was no match for the man's who was currently advancing on him. Would he try to poison him again? Or had he brought a weapon? A knife perhaps?

As his mind contemplated all possibilities, Richard suddenly realised how Maxwell planned to kill him a moment before the young man shot forward.

Renewed panic claimed Richard's heart when Maxwell's hand grabbed a hold of the quill in his throat. Reflexively, his arms jerked upwards, his hands wrapping themselves around the young man's wrist. Momentarily, Richard thought he could prevent Maxwell from pulling back his arm and with it the quill. But it was a fool's hope.

Grinning devilishly, Maxwell tightened his grip…and then jerked back his arm, pulling the quill out of Richard's throat. "It is time someone pays!" he snarled, watching in delight as Richard's hands came to wrap around his throat.

Eyes wide, Richard stared at his footman as his lungs began to burn with lack of air.

Chapter Forty-One
THE FINAL CLUE

S itting in the drawing room, Evelyn tended to their guests as was expected of the new mistress of Farnworth Manor. Although Mr. and Mrs. Lambert were utterly wonderful people and their daughters Mildred and Theresa a joy to watch as they fawned over Lady Northfield's son Philip, Evelyn wished she could simply rise and leave to see to her husband.

Glancing around the room, she took note of Lord Weston and Mr. Lambert discussing who-knew-what over by the windows as well as Charlotte and Claudia as they sat with Lady Northfield, watching the delighted children. The look on Lady Northfield's face spoke of utter adoration as she looked at her precious son while the other two women looked rather wistful. Still, Charlotte's eyes held hope and promise of a future she longed for while Claudia could not quite hide the heartache Evelyn knew she had to feel. Especially now that she knew Charlotte would also be a mother soon.

Only Charlotte would be allowed to keep her child.

Evelyn sighed, certain that there was something wrong about a world that forced a mother to give up a child she wanted.

If only there was something that could be done! And yet, Evelyn had to admit that she could not think of a solution that would preserve both, love as well as reputation. Although she had berated her husband for being unwilling to look for a different solution, she knew now she had done him wrong. It had simply been easier to blame him instead of admitting that her hands were tied as well as his.

In the end, nothing could prevent Claudia from being ruined if she decided to keep her child in order to raise it herself. And her child, too, would not fare well. Never would it be received in fine society. Not as a bastard. Not in this world.

Still, giving away her child would break Claudia's heart. If not now, then somewhere down the line. It was inevitable.

Entering the drawing room at a quick pace, Camilla gave Evelyn a quick smile and then hastened to her daughter's side. Evelyn wondered if she could take her leave now that her mother-in-law had returned. Perhaps in a few minutes.

Excitement rushed through her at the thought of seeing her husband, and Evelyn shook her head at herself. When had his presence become the very air she breathed?

Seeing mother and daughter exchange a few words, Evelyn stopped when both their faces turned into frowns, confusion written in their eyes. Concerned, Evelyn excused herself to Mrs. Lambert and quickly hastened over to where mother and daughter stood by the pianoforte. "Is something wrong?" she asked. "Is Richard all right?"

Camilla turned to her, a gentle smile on her face. "He is fine, my dear. Do not worry." She glanced at Claudia. "No, this was merely a misunderstanding I suppose."

"What do you mean?" Evelyn asked, glancing from Camilla to Claudia and back.

"Maxwell came to fetch me from Richard's chamber," her mother-in-law explained, "saying that Claudia had asked for me."

"But I didn't," Claudia objected, an apologetic look in her eyes as she turned to her mother. "I'm sorry. I do not mean to offend you, but I did not ask him to fetch you. I'm perfectly fine."

Although Evelyn doubted Claudia's last statement, she could not help but wonder how such a misunderstanding had occurred. "Did you speak to him at all?"

Claudia shook her head.

Camilla shrugged. "Perhaps he simply misunderstood. After all, he has always been very devoted to this fa—"

"Where is he now?" Evelyn interrupted as goose bumps rose on her arms.

"With Richard," Camilla replied. "I asked him to read to him." A frown came to her eyes. "Child, are you all right? You seem pale."

Barely hearing her mother-in-law's words, Evelyn felt herself transported back in time to the evening her husband had collapsed. Once she had settled on what to do, she had looked around for a composed face. Someone reliable and not lost in hysterics. Her eyes had fallen on Mr. Adams, who had been the only one looking at her with anything resembling composure. And so, she had asked him to fetch her the instruments she needed to save her husband's life.

As expected, Mr. Adams had dashed away instantly. However, remembering the moment now, Evelyn recalled seeing him out of the corner of her eye as he slowed his steps once he had reached the door and strolled out as though he had all the time in the world.

And he had not returned.

In my haste, I tripped and hit my head. When I came to, you had already saved his lordship's life.

But it had been a lie!

"It was him!" Evelyn gasped when all the pieces suddenly fell into place. "It was him!" Staring at Camilla, she could see the very moment her mother-in-law understood her meaning. Camilla's eyes grew round with fear, and her face turned pale.

Spinning on her heel, Evelyn darted toward the open door. "Sebastian!" she called over her shoulder, not bothering to uphold etiquette. "It was Mr. Adams! He poisoned Richard!"

Evelyn barely had time to note the look of shock that came to his face before she was already out the door and started climbing the stairs two at a time. Dimly, exclamations of shock and disbelief from the others in the drawing room echoed to her ears. However, the only thing she did note with a conscious mind were Sebastian's approaching footsteps as he raced to catch up with her.

The corridor that led to her husband's chamber seemed endless as Evelyn urged her legs not to tire. Her sides hurt, and her lungs complained about the sudden exertion. But she pushed on until his door came in sight.

Hearing Sebastian's breath right behind her, she all but threw herself against the door, pressing the handle down and pushing it open.

Inside, Evelyn found her worst nightmare realised.

Mr. Adams stood by the bed, an evil sneer on his face, self-satisfied and superior, and in his hand, he held the quill that had served as Richard's lifeline.

Instantly, Evelyn's eyes sprang to her husband, and her heart twisted painfully as she found him trapped in his bed, unable to flee, his hands wrapped around his throat, panic widening his eyes.

And yet, she took note of the hint of relief that came to his face when his eyes found her.

"You bastard!" Sebastian growled, his gaze fixed on Mr. Adams as he pushed past Evelyn with quick strides, Mr. Lambert following on his heel. Together, they tackled Mr. Adams to the ground and Sebastian's fist landed on the man's chin for good measure.

Ignoring the commotion, Evelyn rushed to Richard's side, seeing the terror on his face. A terror she remembered only too well from the night of the poisoning.

Chapter Forty-Two
LOYAL & DEVOTED

Richard's chest tightened as panic swept through him. He gritted his teeth and held his breath, terrified to once more be denied the air he sought.

Then the door flew open, and all Richard could see were Evelyn's warm brown eyes, reassuring and gentle. Instantly, his body began to relax its tight grip on his soul, and he felt an overwhelming need to be near her.

As though she had read his mind, Evelyn flew to his side, her calm eyes holding his as she scrambled onto the bed beside him. Her hands cupped the sides of his face, and for a brief moment, Richard closed his eyes at the comforting feel of her touch.

"Look at me, Richard!" Evelyn ordered, her voice strong and commanding. "Yes, good! You need to breathe!"

Terrified, Richard shook his head.

"Yes, you can!" she insisted. "Believe me, you can. The swelling is down enough. I meant to remove the quill in a day or two in any case. Breathe!"

Terror still lived in his heart, but as the need for air became too overwhelming, Richard had no choice. Parting his lips, he took a careful breath, expecting the familiar refusal that had almost cost him his life not long ago.

"Yes, good," his wife whispered, a soft smile on her face as she looked at him, her thumbs gently brushing over his cheekbones.

Blinking, Richard realised that his chest was moving with each small breath he took. Slowly, his lungs filled with air and his body relaxed, pushing away the terror that had held him in its grip. Exhaustion washed over him, and closing his eyes, Richard slumped into his wife's arms. "Evelyn," he whispered, closing his eyes at the sound of his own voice, raspy and strangled, but there.

In the stillness of the room, footsteps echoed to Richard's ears as well as the wonderful, life-affirming sound of others drawing breath. Lifting his head, he found his chamber crowded with his family and friends, many eyes misted with tears as they looked at him.

"Welcome back!" Sebastian exclaimed, a relieved grin on his face as he held Maxwell shoved against the far wall, Mr. Lambert beside him. When his gaze darted to the former footman, Sebastian's face darkened. "We'll lock him up for now until you decide what to do with him." Then he nodded to Mr. Lambert, and the two of them removed the struggling man from the room.

After embracing him warmly, tears streaming down her face, his mother ushered everyone from the room. Before she joined them though, she turned to look at Evelyn, gently brushing a brown curl behind her ear. "Thank you," she whispered, her voice almost breaking. "Thank you."

Evelyn nodded, and Richard belatedly realised that his wife's face was streaked with tears as well. When the door finally closed, his wife fell into his arms and they sank back into the pillows, holding each other as the shock of the past minutes slowly wore off.

"How did you know?" Richard finally asked after a small eternity had passed, his voice still faint and scratchy.

Moving a little away, Evelyn lifted her head to look at him. "Your mother came back and said that Claudia had asked for her, but then your sister said that she hadn't." The words flew from her mouth in a near panic, and Richard got the distinct feeling that his wife had not quite recovered from the day's events, either. "We were all confused, and your mother said it might have been a misunderstanding, but how could it have been if Claudia had never even spoken to Mr. Adams?" Closing her eyes, tears welled up once more and she shook her head. "And then I knew. I remembered seeing his face the night you were poisoned, and suddenly I realised that there was something odd in the way he looked at you, the way he left to fetch the quill. I just knew." Sinking back into his arms, she snuggled closer. "I'm sorry it took me so long to realise it had been him. I'm sorry."

"Don't be," Richard whispered back, wishing his voice did not sound so hoarse. "None of this was your fault. You saved my life." He kissed the top of her head. "Twice. And I'll always be grateful for that, and for you." He swallowed. "I love you, Evelyn. I hope you know that."

Gazing down at him through tear-filled eyes, a sob mixed with laughter as she lifted her head to say, "I love you as well, and I, too, was afraid that you did not know, that you did not believe me when I told you." Smiling at him, she leaned down and kissed him gently.

Closing his arms more tightly around her, Richard wished they could stay here in this moment forever. Still, there were things to be done before their life together could finally begin.

"I cannot believe it was him," Evelyn whispered, her thoughts wandering in the same direction as his. "He always seemed so kind, so loyal and devoted." Again, she raised her head to look at him. "Why do you suppose he did this?"

Richard shrugged. "I cannot say. He spoke to me, lashed out at me, but I cannot say that I understand what his grievance with me is." He drew in a deep breath, relishing in the feeling. "I suppose there is only one way to find out. I need to speak to him."

And he would. Once he was recovered, Richard would find out what had almost cost him his life. And then he would move on, never to look back.

After a lively debate with her husband a few days into the new year, which Evelyn had enjoyed more than she ought to have under the circumstances, he finally agreed to allow her in the room when he questioned his former footman. Still, she had to promise him to stay in the back for her own safety.

Evelyn smiled. Although a part of her was annoyed with his refusal to allow her to participate as an equal, she knew it came from a place of deepest affection as well as utter fear to see her harmed. After the ordeal Richard had been through, that was not surprising, and Evelyn decided to be lenient with her husband...for now.

Following Sebastian to a remoter part of the house—she had not called him Lord Weston since the day they had apprehended Mr. Adams—Evelyn took a deep breath, her arm tightening around her husband's as they came to stand in front of the door behind which Mr. Adams sat waiting for them.

"Are you certain you wish to be here?" Sebastian asked, looking at her with doubt as he drew a key from his pocket and slid it into the lock.

Richard chuckled, "Save your breath, my friend. You will not change her mind."

Enjoying the warmth in her husband's tone, Evelyn straightened her shoulders as Sebastian swung open the door to reveal a dishevelled Mr. Adams tied to a chair, a purple bruise forming on his chin. The man's cold gaze raked over them, hatred burning in his eyes. "To hell with all of you!"

As they stepped into the room, Evelyn marvelled at the change this young man had undergone. How had this happened? Had he truly deceived them from the beginning? Or had something happened to change him so? And what had brought him to Farnworth Manor in the first place?

Meeting the man's gaze with an unflinching one of his own, Richard stepped forward, releasing Evelyn's arm as he did so. His eyes grew cold and detached, more strongly resembling the man Evelyn had first met...before he had become her husband. "Why?" he demanded, his gaze fixed on Mr. Adams. "Why did you seek to kill me?"

After staring at Richard for the better part of a minute, Mr. Adams then shook his head, laughing, "You did not even see me coming.

You're blind and self-obsessed. You see nothing outside your own sphere."

"Answer him!" Sebastian growled, his usually teasing grin and smiling eyes gone, replaced by a hardened man.

After spewing a few more hateful observations at Richard, Mr. Adams leaned back in his chair, arms still tied behind his back. "Do you truly not see it?" he asked, a hint of vulnerability suddenly in his voice. "There is a certain resemblance after all."

Richard frowned as Evelyn's mouth slowly fell open. Her eyes swept over the man's face, and she took note of his piercing blue eyes and dark brown hair, thick and with a slight wave to it. All of a sudden she saw the resemblance she had not noticed before, and Evelyn wondered if she had taken to Mr. Adams so quickly because on some level he had reminded her of Richard.

"We're cousins!" Mr. Adams all but spat the words at Richard's feet. "My father was Vincent Davenport, Viscount Ashwood, and your title should have been mine."

Richard's eyes narrowed. "You're the child he had with his mistress?"

Mr. Adams' gaze grew dark. "Naturally, that is the first thing for you to point out. That I'm an illegitimate son, and as such worth nothing. Not to my father. Not to the rest of his family. Not to anyone." Leaning forward, Mr. Adams strained against the rope that bound him to the chair, his eyes fixed on Richard alone. "My mother and I lived shunned by all those around us. She was no one, and neither was I. Certainly, my *father* provided for us, saw us fed and clothed, but that was as far as his care extended." His jaw clenched. "My mother died in loneliness, forgotten by the rest of the world."

"But why did you come here?" Richard asked, his voice even and detached, and yet, Evelyn could see the slight tension in his shoulders, revealing only too clearly that Mr. Adams' tale did not leave him unaffected. "Even if you had succeeded in taking my life, you would not have inherited the title. Why bother?"

At that question, all the tension and anger seemed to leave Mr. Adams' body as though evaporating into thin air. Slumping back in the chair, he closed his eyes briefly. "When I first came here," he mumbled, his voice suddenly weak, "I did not plan for this. All I wanted was to get to know...my family." His eyes opened and met Richard's, a silent plea in them that almost broke Evelyn's heart. If only he had simply come to them, spoken to them, shared his story. All of this could have been avoided!

Crossing his arms, Richard held his cousin's gaze.

Mr. Adams sighed before his eyes dropped to the floor. "I was curious...and still hopeful," he whispered, a hint of disillusionment in his voice, "and so I asked to be employed here as I did not wish to be sent away without a second glance." His gaze returned to meet Richard's. "That is what you would have done, isn't it? If I had told you the truth, you would have sent me away because I am nothing to you and yours. Only a shameful reminder of your uncle's indiscretion. You never would have acknowledged me as family, would you?"

Richard scoffed, "Family?" His lips pressed into a thin line. "Does family try to kill each other?" he demanded, his voice deathly quiet. "*You* have made it very clear that I'm not family to you, not the other way around."

Mr. Adams glowered at him, his lips moving, his mouth opening and closing as though he could not decide how to retort. "It would seem neither is Miss Davenport," he spat, his lips curling into a complacent smile.

Richard's eyes hardened as he took a menacing step closer, grabbing Mr. Adams by the shirt and hauling him toward him, chair and all. "What did you do to my sister?"

Chapter Forty-Three

WHAT FOLLOWS

As the blood boiled in his veins, Richard could barely breathe, and for a moment, an old panic grabbed a hold of him, squeezing his chest until he felt certain he would suffocate. Then he saw Evelyn take a step forward out of the corner of his eye, and that small glimpse freed him from the chains of his past.

Whispering a silent thank-you, he turned his attention back to Maxwell, his heart aching with concern for Claudia. "What did you do to her?" he demanded once more when his former footman remained silent, a self-satisfied smile on his face.

"Not I," Maxwell retorted, his lips curled into a snarl. "You!"

Confused, Richard stared at the man, then abruptly released him so he rocked back in his chair and almost toppled over backwards. "What on earth do you mean?"

"Like an inconvenience, you plan to rid yourself of her child," Maxwell spat, his face contorted into a sneer, "like my father rid himself of me!"

As though he had taken a blow to his chest, Richard stared at the man before him. "I would never," he forced out through clenched teeth. "I would never see my sister's child as an inconvenience."

"And yet, you cast it off because it threatens your well-structured life, because it's a threat to your family's reputation, to your standing in society," his new-found cousin snarled. "Because it would be a disgrace to your family, just like I was."

Gritting his teeth, Richard fought the feeling of nausea that washed over him as he could not help but wonder if Maxwell was right. Was he truly acting out of selfish motives? Did his sister believe he only wanted to rid the family of a disgrace? Did she think of him thus?

Movement caught his eye, and Richard found himself staring at his wife as she stepped forward, her jaw set and her eyes intense as she came to stand beside him, her gaze directed at the man before them. "I am truly sorry for what you have been through, for all you have suffered," she told Maxwell, her voice kind but strong. "I agree that society's rules are limiting and restricting in many ways and were not made to promote happiness. I know it to be true from personal experience. As a woman, I am often seen as less capable in many ways."

Maxwell swallowed, and his face softened as he nodded in agreement with her words.

"However," Evelyn stated, her tone now sharper than before, "my husband did not make these rules. He is merely trying to find the best way to live with them."

As Maxwell's face darkened once more, Richard found himself staring at his wife, utterly taken aback that she would defend him so. Had she not accused him of not taking his sister's feelings into account herself?

"I have tried again and again to think of a solution that would benefit all," she admitted, a hint of resignation in her voice, "and I'm afraid that I could not. The world is the way it is, and no matter how much we wish we could, we cannot change it. Not now. Not for us. Change takes time." Her face had a gentle note as she took a step toward his cousin. "Whether you are illegitimate or not should not matter, and yet, it does as do other things that should not. I agree that this ought to change, but you cannot blame my husband for the wrongs of the world. If you had truly wished to be a part of this family, then you should have offered trust and loyalty and come to us honestly and not with deceit. Lies never serve anyone as you now know."

Pulling Evelyn back into his arms, Richard smiled at her. "You're a wise woman," he whispered, "and I am proud to call you my wife."

Seated beside Claudia and her mother-in-law, Evelyn looked up at her husband, who stood with his friend Sebastian as well as Mr. Lambert, his brows drawn down in contemplation as they discussed what to do with Mr. Adams.

"Report him!" Claudia insisted, her voice full of anger as she looked up at her brother, the gaze in her eyes intense. "He tried to kill you. He deserves no mercy for he himself showed none."

Evelyn could see the soft smile that touched her husband's lips and knew how much his sister's devotion warmed his heart. It seemed he was only now slowly becoming aware of the fact that his family loved him.

Sebastian nodded. "I agree. His attack was devious like a knife to the back. He did not confront you."

Beside her, Camilla sighed. "I cannot help but feel sorry for him," she all but whispered, the look in her eyes somewhat apologetic. "He was wronged. I cannot deny that, and it makes me wonder if we should not consider showing mercy. After all, he is family."

"But, Mother, –"

Placing a hand on her daughter's, Camilla silenced her with one glance. Then her eyes came to settle on her son. "Of course, the decision is yours, Richard. You are the one who was wronged in this, the one who suffered. I will support whatever you decide."

Richard nodded, and Evelyn could see the indecision in his eyes. She knew now that despite his cold exterior, he had a caring heart. If he were to hand Mr. Adams over to the authorities, the man would most likely be executed. After all, he had tried to murder a peer. His fate would be sealed.

Could her husband live with his? Could he remain the kind-hearted man he was if he condemned another to death? It was far from an easy decision.

"If you let him go," Sebastian counselled, reading the doubt on his friend's face, "he might return to try again. You cannot know what he will do. You and yours would be forever in danger."

Richard swallowed hard, his jaw tensing as he looked up and met Evelyn's eyes. Yes, this was the other side of the medallion. If he allowed Mr. Adams to go free, would they ever feel safe again?

"I do not want his death on my conscience," Richard finally said, holding Evelyn's gaze as though he spoke only to her. Nodding her head in support, Evelyn found his shoulders relax slightly, and she revelled in the knowledge that he needed her thus. "Still, I cannot allow any of you to be put in danger." He glanced around their small circle. "Another solution must be found."

Silence fell over the room at his words.

Wracking her mind, Evelyn once more felt like a failure as she could not conjure a solution that would ensure both, her husband's peace of mind as well as their safety.

"There is no other solution!" Claudia exclaimed, and Sebastian nodded. "You must do what must be done. Not every decision is easy, but that does not mean we do not have to make it." Tears stood in her eyes as she spoke, but her chin remained raised as she held her brother's eyes.

For a long moment, brother and sister looked at one another, and Evelyn could see her husband begin to crumble under her imploring gaze.

"There is a way," Mr. Lambert spoke up, all heads turning toward him. He had remained so quiet throughout their discussion that they had all but forgotten about him.

Turning his gaze to his second cousin, Richard lifted his brows. "What is it?"

Mr. Lambert inhaled a slow breath. "I understand that you are reluctant to seal Mr. Adams' fate. However, if you ever wish to see yourself and yours safe again, he cannot be allowed to go free."

Her husband nodded in agreement.

Mr. Lambert's face tensed, and Evelyn could tell that what he was about to say, weighed heavily on his conscience. "Then accuse him of a

BREE WOLF

lesser crime," he finally suggested. "Something that would see him in prison, but not executed." He inhaled a slow breath. "If you wish, I could advise you."

Remembering that Mr. Lambert was a barrister, Evelyn nodded to her husband as their eyes met. It was indeed a good idea, and the only one they had. It would ensure their safety as well as her husband's peace of mind. And it would teach Mr. Adams that actions did have consequences while also showing him mercy. Still, Evelyn wondered if he would see it like that? Accused of a false crime, would he not feel betrayed even more?

Still, there was no choice.

"I will accept your generous offer," Richard said, nodding to his second cousin, a soft smile on his face. "Thank you. You have truly proven an invaluable friend, and I'm proud to call you family."

Returning Richard's smile, Mr. Lambert nodded. "I am glad to hear it," he replied, then lifted his hand as Richard was about to turn away. "I do have one question though."

"Anything," Richard said, nodding.

"Did you invite me here," he began, his gaze drifting around the room, from one of them to the next, "because you thought I had a hand in the poisoning? In order to inherit?"

Briefly bowing his head, Richard met the man's gaze. "It was the reason, yes," he admitted, stepping forward and placing a companionable hand on the man's shoulder. "I apologise for misjudging you. You are an honourable man, and I regret that we have not known each other all our lives."

Relief came to Mr. Lambert's eyes, and an honest smile showed on his face. "I do regret the same, dear cousin. What you say is true. You could not have known the kind of man I was, and you were right. Objectively speaking, I do have a motive." A small chuckle escaped the usually so serious man. "However, I do hope that this will not be cause for unease between us in the future." The expression on his face sobered. "I assure you I would never dare to harm you or yours."

"I have no doubt," Richard replied, and Evelyn could see joy in his face over connecting with another member of his family. "I'm certain

284

we can avoid such a misunderstanding in the future by being better acquainted in the present."

Smiling, Mr. Lambert nodded. "I would like that very much."

Chapter Forty-Four
FALSE ACCUSATIONS

Richard felt his shoulders tense as he stepped toward his former footman. Despite the safety that would come from his second cousin's offer to have Maxwell detained through a false accusation, Richard could not deny that it felt wrong to walk down that path. It felt dishonest. It *was* dishonest. And yet, he could not think of a better way.

Glancing at his wife standing beside him, Richard hardened his features before he met Maxwell's hateful glare. "For what you have done," he began, "I should see you executed. I would be well within my rights to do so, and it would ensure not only mine but also my family's safety."

Maxwell's glare turned darker, and heat crept up his face. Still, a hint of fear showed in his dark gaze. "I would have expected no less from someone like you."

"Still, I will show mercy," Richard continued, seeing the subtle change his words caused in Maxwell's face. A sense of relief as well as disbelief hung there, and for a moment, Richard wondered what relationship they would have had had life allowed them to walk side by side. "I will not condemn you to death, however, neither can I allow you to go free."

Maxwell's face darkened with renewed suspicion. "Will you keep me tied to this chair until the end of time?" he snarled as though Richard had been the one to wrong him.

Shaking his head, Richard crossed his arms. "No, I could not abide to have you in my house." Taking a step closer, he bent forward, his gaze fixed on Maxwell's. "Instead of accusing you of attempted murder, which would ensure your execution, I will accuse you of a lesser crime, which will see you spend the rest of your life in prison. I'll leave the details to a friend of mine."

Guessing wrong, Maxwell cast a hateful glance at Sebastian standing by the far wall before his eyes returned to Richard. "I am not surprised that once more you will cast me off, but know that—"

"Cast you off?" Richard demanded. "What do you expect? Do you truly believe any man would allow you to go free? Would welcome you into his family after what you have done?" Shaking his head, Richard snorted, "Only a fool would. No, *Mr. Adams*, you've crossed a line from which there is no coming back, especially not since you still do not see that you acted wrongly. You still believe yourself in the right, insistent in your wrong notion that this decision has anything to do with rank." Leaning forward, Richard brought his face closer to Maxwell's, his eyes trying to see a glimmer of understanding in the man's gaze. "You're wrong. This is about loyalty and trust, about doing the right thing even when it breaks your heart." Stepping back, Richard inhaled a deep breath, momentarily reminded of his sister's quivering lower lip as she had spoken to him so vehemently the day before in his study.

Eyes cast down, Maxwell gritted his teeth as the fight seemed to have left him. "What about your sister's child?" he asked, not looking up. "What will happen to it?"

Concern gripped Richard unexpectedly, and he wondered if he was making the right decision. "That is none of your concern," he snarled. "She and her child are mine to protect. Not yours."

Raising his eyes off the ground, Maxwell glowered at him. "Then I pity them."

Gritting his teeth, Richard fought the anger that rose in his veins. However, it was Sebastian who suddenly flew forward, gripping Maxwell by the front of his shirt and hauling him to his feet. "You know nothing of which you speak," he snarled before dropping the man back down with a loud thud. "Nothing but lies and false accusations come out of your mouth!"

Maxwell laughed, but it spoke of a man at the end of his rope, a man on the brink of madness. "Isn't that ironic?" he asked, still chuckling. "You are falsely accusing me? Shaking his head, Sebastian turned to him, his chest heaving with calming breaths. "You should leave," he said, glancing at Evelyn. "I will speak to Mr. Lambert and ensure that everything is done as discussed."

"Thank you," Richard replied, clasping Sebastian's arm. "You're a good friend."

A smirk came to Sebastian's face. "Don't I always tell you that?"

Smiling, Richard nodded before he turned around and pulled his wife's arm through his. Her eyes were gentle as they met his, and he sighed at the peacefulness on her lovely face. If anyone could calm the anger in his heart, it was her.

As they closed the door behind them, Evelyn stopped in her tracks after only a few steps and turned to him. "You're a good man," she whispered, a gentle smile on her lips as her eyes sought his. "I've always known that. Do not believe what he said. I can see that it gnaws on you. Do not let it."

Richard swallowed. "I would never..."

"I know." Her hands tightened on him. "It is always easy to speak when one is not the one responsible for the happiness of others. I know that now. I, too, was wrong. I misjudged you. I'm sorry."

"No, you were right," Richard objected, pulling her deeper into his embrace. "I do want what is best for my sister and her child, and you were right to say that I cannot exclude her from that decision. It is her life and her child, so it should be her decision as well."

Evelyn nodded, and her thumb brushed over the small indentation in his chin as she smiled up at him. "In every way, you're the man I always hoped I'd find," she whispered, "and call husband." Then she pulled his face down to hers and kissed him soundly.

And despite everything that had happened in the past few days, Richard knew that he had finally found his place in this world.

And it was right here.
In Evelyn's arms.

Chapter Forty-Five
A CHOICE GIVEN

Sitting on one of the armchairs in her husband's study, Evelyn watched as Richard paced up and down the length of the room, his hands linked behind his back and his brows drawn down. When a knock sounded on the door, he almost flinched before his long strides carried him across the room.

"Please come in," he said gently as he held open the door for his sister.

Stepping inside, Claudia eyed him curiously before her eyes drifted to Evelyn. "What is the matter?" she asked, taking the seat her brother offered her. "Is something wrong? Did that evil man–?"

"This has nothing to do with Mr. Adams," Richard interrupted, sinking into the chair opposite the two women. "This is about you... and your child."

Watching her sister-in-law carefully, Evelyn immediately noticed the tension that gripped her shoulders at the mention of her child. Her eyes widened, and she inhaled a calming breath. Still, her hands trembled as she tried to act unaffected. "What about...my child?"

Clasping his hands together, Richard met her eyes. "I asked you here because I do believe it right that you have a say when it comes to your own as well as your child's future."

Gritting her teeth, Claudia shook her head. "Why are you doing this?" she demanded as tears began to pool in her eyes. "It was already settled. There is no need to discuss it." She made to rise, but Evelyn held her back, putting a gentle hand on Claudia's trembling ones.

"Please listen," she whispered, drawing her sister-in-law's right hand into hers. "Please."

Richard swallowed, giving Evelyn a quick nod of gratitude before turning his attention back to his sister. "You've always said that this was your life and that you ought to have a say in it. You've always complained that we, Father and I, did not ask your opinion, not even when the decision concerned you." An apologetic look came to his eyes. "And you were right. We did not, but we should have, and I am sorry for failing you thus." Reaching out, he took Claudia's other hand in his. "This *is* your life, and from now on, you will have a say in it. I promise."

Clenching her jaw, Claudia fought the tremors that shook her as she stared at her brother, tears spilling silently down her cheeks. "Thank you, Richard," she mumbled, and Evelyn once more felt awed by the silent strength that lived in Claudia's heart. "But you know as well as I that there is no choice. Not truly. Yes, I wish things had gone differently, but wishful thinking will not change the fact that this child is a bastard." Her voice hitched as she spoke the last word, and she pulled her hand from Evelyn's grasp to gently place it on the soft swelling of her belly. "I'm not as naive as you think me, Brother. Not anymore. I know what life would await me and my child should I choose to keep it." Briefly closing her eyes, she shook her head. Then her gaze came to rest on her brother's once more, and Evelyn wondered where they would stand today if they had found a way to speak to each other sooner.

"I want my child to grow up safe and protected," Claudia continued, the sinews in her own hand beginning to stand out white as she clutched her brother's hand. "I don't want it to be shunned and looked down upon. I want it to have a good family. To be loved. To be cherished. To be respected." A sob escaped her lips, and she clamped her mouth shut. "If I were to keep it, it would only suffer."

Tears stung Evelyn's eyes as she watched Claudia's misery. Sadness clung to every word, and yet, her new sister fought like a lioness to protect her child, to be brave and stay strong. *To do the right thing even when it breaks one's heart.* Had those not been her husband's words?

Still, Evelyn could not silence the quiet hope that lived in her heart. "What if...?" she began, feeling like an intruder in this moment between brother and sister. And yet, she had to speak her mind before it was too late and the time for regrets had come. "What if you were to...marry? What if someone could be found who—?"

"No!" Shaking her head, Claudia turned to look at her. Her hand, though, stayed safely wrapped in her brother's. "I cannot. I am not the type to sit idly at home. I've proved that, have I not?" A heart-wrenching scoff escaped her. "Deep down, my heart still aches to find true love, and I will never have that if I marry now, marry someone simply to give my child a father."

Although Evelyn understood Claudia's reason, she could not help but think that there was more. Another reason, Claudia would not share. Did she still long for the man she only saw in her dreams? Had her heart still hope?

Claudia swallowed, wiping at the tears that wet her face. "I fear I might come to resent my child for it, as unjustified as it would be. After all, there are many ways to ruin a life, and I will not allow myself to cling to false hope." Clearing her throat, she blinked back the last tears and turned to look at her brother. "I would ask you to find a good home, a good family for my child and to never tell me anything about it." Abruptly, she rose to her feet, her hand slipping from her brother's grasp.

As Richard rose to his feet, his eyes full of sadness and regret as he looked at his sister, Evelyn joined him, slipping her hand into his and squeezing it gently. His skin felt warm, and she could feel him take comfort in her touch.

"I want to pretend it never happened," Claudia said, her hands balling into fists as she took a step back. "I must, or I will not be able to continue on." She swallowed, her teeth clenched. "Will you do that for me, Brother?"

Shoulders tense, Richard nodded. "Of course."

"Thank you." Then Claudia spun on her heel and hastened out the door. The look on her face had spoken volumes, and Evelyn suspected that she was headed somewhere quiet where she could be alone and weep for the loss of her child that approached with every passing day. Evelyn would go and find her later, but for now, there was nothing she could do but give Claudia space and time to mourn her impending loss.

Later, she would offer comfort, and she could only hope Claudia would take it.

"Perhaps we should not have asked her," Evelyn wondered, leaning on her husband's warmth. "It pained her greatly. Perhaps you were right."

Richard shook his head, then kissed the top of hers. "No, it was good to give her a choice. She needed to know that she matters, that I see her, that I love her."

Tilting up her head, Evelyn saw unshed tears clinging to his eyes.

"Thank you," he whispered, and his gaze found hers as a single tear ran down his cheek. "Without you, I would never have known how to speak to her. I would never have been able to get closer to my family. I wouldn't have known how." Closing his eyes, he shook his head. "All my life, I thought they resented or at least disliked me for my inability to show emotions and interpret theirs."

Reaching up, Evelyn cupped the side of his face. "You seem quite adept at it now," she teased gently, a soft smile on her lips.

Returning it, Richard pulled her tighter into his arms. "Only because of you," he whispered, kissing her tenderly. "I often reacted wrongly because I didn't know any better. Rules give me security because they tell me what to do. And yet, they're not all there is. For even if there is no other choice to be made," he said, his eyes shining as they held hers, "being asked sometimes makes all the difference."

Evelyn nodded, pulling him into her arms and holding him tightly. His hands brushed over her back as he whispered near her ear, "I hope she will be happy again one day."

"As do I." Enjoying the warmth of his embrace, Evelyn vowed to stand by Claudia through this trial and do whatever might be in her power to ensure that she, too, would find a place where she felt at home...and loved.

Epilogue

London, April 1809

Four Months Later

Over the past fortnight a new routine had developed between Evelyn and her husband. Unless the weather prevented it, they met outdoors in the early afternoon and then strolled arm in arm through the garden of their London townhouse. The slowly awakening plants and blossoms were a balm to their aching souls and raised their spirits at least a little.

After that, they would head inside for tea, seeking to extend the comfortable warmth of each other's company.

Only today, Richard failed to appear.

Making her way back to the house, Evelyn wondered what could have kept him. She knew it had to be something of great importance—and possibly great concern? —for him to have forgotten about her. After all, he had not even sent a servant to inform her of his absence.

Knowing that in all likelihood she would find her husband in his study, Evelyn lost no time and proceeded briskly down the corridor.

After a quick knock, she entered to find her husband slumped over his desk, face buried in his hands.

Instantly, Evelyn's heart clenched, and fear shot through her body. "Richard," she exclaimed, closing the door and hastening over. "What is the matter? Are you all right?"

Lifting his head, her husband looked at her, momentarily stunned as though he had forgotten where he was. Then he blinked, rubbing his hands over his face, as he sat back, and his eyes focused on her. "Evelyn," he mumbled, holding out a hand and pulling her onto his lap. "I'm sorry. I forgot. I should have sent someone. I..." Pulling her into his arms, he held her tightly as though to reassure himself that she was here...and not gone.

"What's wrong?" Evelyn pressed, unable to ignore the sinking feeling in her stomach. Leaning back, she looked at him, her right thumb and index finger grasping his chin. "Tell me what happened."

He smiled at the familiar gesture, and yet, his eyes remained troubled. "I received a letter."

Glancing at the document in question, Evelyn all but held her breath. "Whose letter?"

Swallowing, Richard closed his eyes as though he prayed for interference so that he would not have to answer her.

A cold shiver ran down Evelyn's back.

"Apparently," Richard began, and his arm around her middle tightened, "the carriage that was to take Claudia's child to its new family was...waylaid by highwaymen."

The blood in Evelyn's veins turned to ice, and her hand involuntarily went to cup the small bump under her dress. "The child?" she gasped, breathing heavily as fear engulfed her. "What of the child?"

Richard gritted his teeth, his pulse in his neck thudding rapidly. "Taken." Inhaling a held-up breath, he shook his head and reached for the letter. "Mr. Lambert writes that they came out of nowhere. They—"

"Is he all right?" Evelyn interrupted, her concern drifting from the child to her husband's second cousin and back.

Richard nodded. "A bump on the head, but other than that he seems to be fine." Again, her husband's eyes travelled to the parchment. "He writes that they wore masks, two or three—he is not certain—

and knocked him out right away. When he came to, the child and all their belongings were gone, and the nurse was cowering in the corner of the carriage. She seems to be in shock and still hasn't spoken a word."

Staring at the letter as though she could will it to change the truth, Evelyn felt tears well up in her eyes. Lately, she had become quite emotional, succumbing to tears at even the smallest reason. "But why take the child? Why would anyone...?" She turned to look at her husband. "Do you think anyone knows whose child it is? Do you think anyone will be demanding ransom?"

Richard shrugged. "At this point, we cannot be certain of anything. Mr. Lambert asks if he ought to hire men to help search for the child considering the situation is most delicate."

"Claudia does not know yet, does she?" Evelyn asked, slumping against her husband's shoulder as all strength left her.

Only a fortnight after giving birth, Claudia had left Crestwood House despite her mother's objections and returned to London for the remainder of the season, claiming she was bored out of her mind and needed the diversion. In truth, Evelyn knew it was a desperate attempt to keep herself from falling apart as the thought that she would never see her child again began to consume her.

That had been five days ago.

"Do you think we should tell her?" Richard asked, doubt clear and loud in his voice.

Evelyn nodded. "No matter what, she is the child's mother. She deserves to know."

Closing his eyes, Richard sighed, resting his head against the back of the chair. "It will break her heart all over again."

Snuggling closer, Evelyn knew that he was right. Still, Claudia deserved to know. There was no way to keep this from her. After all, they were family, and they would face this together.

Claudia was not alone.

That was what mattered.

Placing a gentle hand on her belly, Evelyn prayed that Claudia's child was all right and that they would find it.

Soon.

THE END

Thank you for reading *Oppressed & Empowered*!

Do you remember Henri & Juliet from *Condemned & Admired - The Earl's Cunning Wife?*

The charming French privateer and his delicate English lady get their own adventurous love story in *Scorned & Craved - The Frenchman's Lion-hearted Wife.*

Do you want to know how to capture the heart of a French privateer?

Get your copy now or read on for a sneak-peek!

Read a Sneak-Peek

Scorned & Craved

The Frenchman's Lionhearted Wife

(#6 Tales of Damsels & Knights)

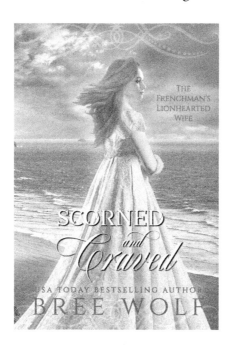

Prologue

London, 1808 (or a variation thereof)
Four Years Earlier

Lady Juliet, daughter to the late Earl of Goswick, did not dare believe her eyes. She tried not to stare but to keep her gaze averted and merely glance at the stranger through lowered lashes.

Yet...

Was it possible? A pirate! He had the look of a pirate, did he not? Not that Juliet had ever laid eyes on a pirate before. Considering the sheltered life she had lived, she knew next to nothing of the world.

Yet...

The man's dark green eyes seemed to spark with something almost devilish, matching that sinfully wicked smile that curled up his lips as he shifted his attention from Juliet's newly discovered stepsister Violet to her.

Juliet immediately dropped her gaze and retreated another step toward the window, dabbing a handkerchief to her eyes. If only there was a way to hide from the man's inquisitive gaze, for the way his eyes swept over her made her feel...

...vulnerable,

...lightheaded,

...and strangely out of breath.

"Lady Silcox, may I speak to you?" Violet addressed Juliet's mother, urging her as well as her husband Lord Cullingwood out of the drawing room...

...leaving Juliet alone with...

...the pirate!

Juliet knew she ought to protest. After all, the door had yet to close. Violet still stood upon its threshold, exchanging a few whispered words with her cousin.

Her cousin, the pirate!

Who pronounced her stepsister's name *Violette*!

Juliet shook her head as bright spots began to dance in front of her eyes. None of what had happened today made any sense, and a part of her wondered if perhaps she was still asleep, lost in a dream that felt... too real.

Again, Juliet dared a peek at the tall, dark-haired stranger with the roguish smile. He wore his hair unfashionably long and tied at the nape of his neck, his chin covered in a mild stubble that gave him a most dangerous allure. He stood tall with broad shoulders and large hands, and the way he moved made Juliet think of a feline she had once seen in a zoological garden.

Yes, he was no doubt a dangerous man, and she ought to object to being left alone with him.

Yet, she did not, for a traitorous part of her wanted to know more about this pirate—this Frenchman!—who had so unexpectedly found his way to London and into her life.

And then the door did close, and they were alone.

Juliet felt ready to faint on the spot, and she pinched her eyes shut against the bright spots that returned with full force, their light almost blinding. Was her new-found stepsister mad? Why would she leave her alone with a man like that, cousin or not?

For a long moment, silence lingered as she fought to regain her composure, her thoughts focused inward so that she did not even hear him approach.

"Will you not look at me, *Cherie?*" he asked in a deeply tantalizing voice.

Instantly, Juliet's eyes flew open.

Shocked to find him so close, no more than a few steps from where she stood, she stumbled backward until her back hit the window, her breath coming fast as she stared up into his face.

The corners of his mouth curled upward. "Do I frighten you?"

Juliet swallowed. "N-No, s-sir," she stammered before reminding herself that she *was* a lady and ought to hold her head high. "I...I am merely surprised that my sister—stepsister — deemed it right to leave us alone together." Her face felt as though it were on fire, and it was a considerable effort for her not to drop her gaze.

Instead of being offended as a true gentleman would be, the Frenchman chuckled. "Violette knows that I would never lay a hand on you...without your permission." The dark look in his eyes whispered of daring and temptation, and Juliet could not help but wonder what he would do if she were...to give her permission.

Not knowing how to reply, Juliet drew in an unsteady breath, her mouth opening and closing as she desperately searched for something to say.

A half-sided grin came to his face before he took yet another step closer. "I hear you're about to be married, *non?*" His brows rose in a challenging gesture.

Juliet felt her hands begin to tremble for the mere thought of her impending nuptials never failed to make her feel sick to her stomach.

"I hear you are to marry an old man," he continued, measured steps moving him ever closer, his dark gaze never once leaving her face.

Juliet bit her lower lip, aware that she simply ought to step around him and leave. Why then could she not bring herself to move?

Barely an arm's length in front of her, the French rogue lowered his head down to hers and whispered, "Do you think your future husband will honor your wishes and not lay a hand on you without your permission?"

Feeling the faint brush of his warm breath against her lips, Juliet felt herself begin to sway. Her knees threatened to buckle at any moment, and those dreaded bright spots once again hindered her vision. "You are...not to speak of such things," she managed to say, doing her utmost to hide her mortification, her temptation even, behind righteous indignation. "A gentleman would never address a lady thus, and we are not even acquainted in the least." She lifted her chin a fraction. "I do not even know your name."

The rogue grinned then dipped his head in a greeting gesture. "Henri Duret, *Mademoiselle*, at your service. You may call me Henri."

Juliet barely kept herself from curtseying. "You're French?"

Again, he grinned. "What gave me away?" he asked, his French accent now thicker than before.

Juliet tried her best to ignore his mocking tone. "And you're...a pirate?"

"A privateer," he corrected, a touch of pride in his voice that surprised her. "For God and country and above all my family."

His words pleased her; although, she knew they ought not. "You're Violet's cousin?"

He nodded. "Not by blood." Something warm and deeply affectionate came to his green eyes. "But she is like a sister to me, and I would give my life to see her safe."

Juliet swallowed; her throat dry as she tried her hardest not to allow his words to weaken her resolve. "Is that why you're here? To protect her?"

His eyes searched hers, and then he inched closer, and for a shocking moment, his gaze dropped to her lips. "Here in London? Or here in this room?"

Her breath lodged in Juliet's throat as she felt the tips of his fingers touch her arms, then trail lower, running along the fabric of her sleeves.

"*Ma chère cousine* asked me to speak to you," he whispered in that voice of his that never failed to send unfamiliar sensations dancing across Juliet's skin. "She asked me to give you a reason to choose differently." His gaze held hers, teasing, daring, challenging, as his hands moved from her arms and reached for her waist.

Juliet drew in a sharp breath. "I am betrothed," she defended herself. "My stepfather arranged this match for me and—"

"Though he did not ask your opinion, *n'est-ce pas?*" Henri whispered as his hands settled more firmly upon her waist.

"He did not," she managed to reply and then surprised herself by tilting up her head to meet his eyes more fully. All of a sudden, she could not seem to look away as though those green eyes of his were a beacon she did not dare let out of her sight.

"Do you wish to marry the man he chose for you?" Henri questioned her as his hands slid farther onto her back. "Perhaps as an innocent lady you're not aware of the intimacies shared between husband and wife." A dark chuckle rumbled deep in his throat as he urged her closer, urged her to bridge that last bit of distance between them. "Would you care for me to enlighten you, *Cherie?*"

Warning bells went off in Juliet's head. Innocent or not, she knew very well that this was her last chance to escape the drawing room unscathed.

To escape *Henri Duret* unscathed.

And then the moment passed, and instead of rushing out the door, Juliet found herself taking that last step...closer.

A wickedly triumphant smile curled up Henri's lips before he slowly lowered his head to hers. "You are a rare treasure, *Cherie.* Any man would enjoy kissing you." His lips brushed against hers in a feather-light touch, and Juliet felt herself respond in a way she would never have expected. Her eyes closed, and her hands came to rest upon his broad chest. "But would you enjoy every kiss bestowed upon you?"

Again, his lips returned to brush against hers. Only this time, they lingered, their touch no longer feather-light but with a tentative depth. "Be warned," he whispered against her mouth, "for an arranged match is rarely of a passionate nature." One hand grasped her chin before he nipped her lower lip.

Juliet gasped at the sensation, and heat shot into her cheeks.

"Be certain of what you want, *Cherie.* Be very certain," Henri whispered huskily before words became obsolete and his mouth claimed hers without consideration for her innocence or any measure of restraint.

Juliet completely lost herself in his kiss. It was wild and passionate and dangerous like the man himself. She knew next to nothing about him, and yet, she felt oddly complete and almost at peace in his arms.

For the first time in her recent memory, Juliet felt her heart beat not with dread or apprehension or a sense of foreboding, her impending nuptials to her stepfather's oldest friend a constant threat looming upon the horizon.

No, for the first time, the rapid thud against her ribcage made her feel strong and daring and...

...hopeful.

Henri's left hand moved into her hair, and she could feel pins come loose before they fell to the floor. He grasped a fistful of her tresses and gave a soft tug, tilting her head back.

Then he deepened his kiss, his other arm slung around her, holding her pressed to his body so she could feel his heartbeat as though it were her own.

Perhaps in this short, precious moment, it was.

It was also in this very moment that Juliet realized that she had to accept Violet's daring offer to escape the match her stepfather had arranged for her. There had to be more to life than duty and sacrifice, didn't there?

Juliet desperately hoped that it was so.

LOVE'S SECOND CHANCE: TALES OF LORDS & LADIES

LOVE'S SECOND CHANCE: TALES OF DAMSELS & KNIGHTS

LOVE'S SECOND CHANCE: HIGHLAND TALES

THE WHICKERTONS IN LOVE

FORBIDDEN LOVE SERIES

SERIES OVERVIEW

About Bree

USA Today bestselling and award-winning author, Bree Wolf has always been a language enthusiast (though not a grammarian!) and is rarely found without a book in her hand or her fingers glued to a keyboard. Trying to find her way, she has taught English as a second language, traveled abroad and worked at a translation agency as well as a law firm in Ireland. She also spent loooong years obtaining a BA in English and Education and an MA in Specialized Translation while wishing she could simply be a writer. Although there is nothing simple about being a writer, her dreams have finally come true.

"A big thanks to my fairy godmother!"

Currently, Bree has found her new home in the historical romance genre, writing Regency novels and novellas. Enjoying the mix of fact and fiction, she occasionally feels like a puppet master (or mistress? Although that sounds weird!), forcing her characters into ever-new situations that will put their strength, their beliefs, their love to the test, hoping that in the end they will triumph and get the happily-ever-after we are all looking for.

If you're an avid reader, sign up for Bree's newsletter on **www. breewolf.com** as she has the tendency to simply give books away. Find out about freebies, giveaways as well as occasional advance reader copies and read before the book is even on the shelves!

Connect with Bree and stay up-to-date on new releases:

facebook.com/breewolf.novels

twitter.com/breewolf_author

instagram.com/breewolf_author

bookbub.com/authors/bree-wolf

amazon.com/Bree-Wolf/e/B00FJX27Z4

Printed in Great Britain
by Amazon

10139256R00185